2 NOVELS

GREAT VALUE

HOME ON THE RANCH:

WYOMING LEGACY

REBECCA WINTERS

AND

NEW YORK TIMES BESTSELLING AUTHOR

RACHEL LEE

PREVIOUSLY PUBLISHED AS

HER WYOMING HERO AND *REUNITING WITH THE RANCHER*

HARLEQUIN®

SPECIAL EDITION

When you're with family, you're home!

The Harlequin® Special Edition series offers heartfelt tales of family, friendship and love. Romance is for life, and these stories show that every chapter in a relationship has its challenges and delights and that love can be renewed with each turn of the page!

Six new stories are available every month wherever you buy books.

ISBN-13: 978-1-335-50715-0

From passionate, suspenseful and dramatic love stories to inspirational or historical, Harlequin offers different lines to satisfy every romance reader.

HSEIFC2018

Praise for Rebecca Winters

"A delectable read that readers won't want to end!"
—*RT Book Reviews* on *Whisked Away by Her Sicilian Boss*

"Winters effortlessly produces beautiful sound throughout this love story, which teaches readers a valuable lesson about the significance of family. Memorable characters and an exquisite backdrop make this a standout."
—*RT Book Reviews* on *A Marriage Made in Italy*,
RT Top Pick, 4.5 stars

"A fully fleshed-out relationship history, sizzling chemistry and charming romance make this a one-sit read."
—*RT Book Reviews* on *The Bachelor Ranger*

Praise for *New York Times* bestselling author Rachel Lee

"Lee's tale is an emotional rollercoaster set in the wilds of Wyoming. While the relationship-building excels, it is the heroine's strength in the face of such personal adversities that is the real scene-stealer."
—*RT Book Reviews* on *A Conard County Baby*

"With a narrative that breathes life into the terrors of war and the hardship of re-acclimation to civilian life, [Lee] eloquently describes her couple's dreams, disappointments and torments while they tear up the sheets and fall in love."
—*RT Book Reviews* on *Thanksgiving Daddy*,
RT Top Pick, 4.5 stars

"Wonderful, heart-pounding tension combined with a serious look at responsibility and probably the best sensual love scene this reviewer has ever read."
—*RT Book Reviews* on *Her Hero in Hiding*,
RT Top Pick, 4.5 stars

HOME ON THE RANCH:

WYOMING LEGACY

REBECCA WINTERS

New York Times Bestselling Author

RACHEL LEE

Previously published as *Her Wyoming Hero* and *Reuniting with the Rancher*

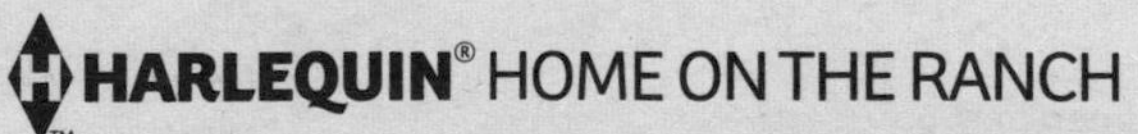

ISBN-13: 978-1-335-50715-0

Recycling programs for this product may not exist in your area.

First published as Her Wyoming Hero by Harlequin Books in 2013 and Reuniting with the Rancher by Harlequin Books in 2014.

This edition published by arrangement with Harlequin Books S.A.

For questions and comments about the quality of this book, please contact us at CustomerService@Harlequin.com.

Printed in U.S.A.

CONTENTS

Rebecca Winters, whose family of four children has now swelled to include five beautiful grandchildren, lives in Salt Lake City, Utah, in the land of the Rocky Mountains. Living near canyons and high alpine meadows full of wildflowers, she never runs out of places to explore. They, plus her favorite vacation spots in Europe, often end up as backgrounds for her romance novels, because writing is her passion, along with her family and church.

Rebecca loves to hear from readers. If you wish to email her, please visit her website, cleanromances.net.

Books by Rebecca Winters

Harlequin Western Romance

Wind River Cowboys

The Right Cowboy

Sapphire Mountain Cowboys

A Valentine for the Cowboy
Made for the Rancher
Cowboy Doctor
Roping Her Christmas Cowboy

Lone Star Lawmen

The Texas Ranger's Bride
The Texas Ranger's Nanny
The Texas Ranger's Family
Her Texas Ranger Hero

Visit the Author Profile page at Harlequin.com for more titles.

HER WYOMING HERO

REBECCA WINTERS

To all strong women everywhere with the
courage of their convictions to make a
difference in their lives despite the odds.

Chapter 1

July 10
Bar Harbor, Maine

Kit read the letter postmarked from Wyoming one more time, positive it had been sent to her by mistake. The honor to her deceased marine husband thrilled her, but didn't make sense.

Dear Mrs. Wentworth,
My name is Carson Lundgren. You don't know me from Adam. I served as a marine in Afghanistan before I got out of the service.

When we returned to the U.S., I, along with Buck Summerhays and Ross Livingston, fellow retired marines, went into business at the Teton Valley Dude Ranch. Our idea was to offer what we could to the families of the fallen soldiers from our various units.

Your courageous husband, Winston Pettigrew Wentworth, served our country with honor and distinction. Now we'd like to honor him by offering you and your son Andrew an expense free, one week vacation at the dude ranch anytime in August. We'll pay for your airfare and any other travel expenses.

You're welcome to contact your husband's division commander, Colonel Hodges, at the phone number below. His office helped us obtain your address. If you're interested and have questions, please call our office. We've also listed our web address, where you'll find a brochure with more details about the ranch. We'll also be happy to email you any additional information.

Please know how anxious we are to give something back to you after his great sacrifice.

With warmest regards,
Carson Lundgren.

His words touched Kit beyond measure, but she was the daughter-in-law of Charles Wentworth, an East Coast billionaire. Such an honor should go to a grief-stricken family whose loss of the husband and father from the home would have affected them financially.

Without hesitation she reached for the phone. In a few minutes she was able to speak to Colonel Hodges. When he came on the line she explained the reason for her call.

"I think this invitation is the most wonderful thing that has happened to me and Andy since the funeral.

But I fear it was sent by mistake. There are so many soldiers who've died in this ghastly war. They've left families who are now struggling to make a decent living without them. I'm not in that category and wouldn't dream of accepting this generous offer."

"Mrs. Wentworth, I don't think you understand. These retired marines out in Wyoming know who you are. I've talked with them at length. They admired your husband for serving when he could have stayed home and enjoyed all the privileges of his life, but this invitation is about something much more important. A rich man can suffer as much as a poor one, don't you agree?"

"Well, yes. Of course, but—"

"They want you and your son to know that your husband's heroism hasn't gone unnoticed. Perhaps you don't realize that these men are trying to deal with their own grief and the many losses they've seen.

"This isn't about money. It's about helping you find a way out of your grief any way they can. During your week there, they would like to get to know your son and talk to him about his father's great sacrifice. The truth is, they need healing, too. Does that help you to understand and accept their invitation?"

Kit was so humbled by his comments, she could hardly speak. "Yes," she whispered. "You've given me a new perspective about a lot of things. I appreciate your kindness more than you know. Thank you, Colonel."

After hanging up, she stared into space while she digested the full impact of Winn's commander's words. He could have no idea what this meant to her. For once she and Andy were being offered something that hadn't been prescribed and paid for by her father-in-law.

Little did the colonel know she and Andy had both been grieving in silence for years—long before Winn's death. Now the loss of his father had caused a change in her withdrawn and morose son. Lately he'd been acting out in negative ways, and Kit was so heartsick for him she didn't know where to turn.

This letter was one he needed to see. It would make him proud of his father, and a trip to a ranch out west would be something neither of them had ever experienced before. The idea of getting away from her grieving in-laws for a whole week where she could be fully in charge of her son filled her with guilty excitement.

While Andy was still at his piano lesson, she hurried through the house to her father-in-law's den. It was almost time for dinner. She needed to talk to him before she mentioned anything to Andy.

She found him at his desk, where he was studying some papers. "Charles?" Since the day Winn had brought her to the Wentworth mansion after their wedding ten years ago, her father-in-law had told her to call him that. "Can I talk to you for a minute?"

He lifted his graying head. "If this is about that notion of yours to move out on your own, we've had this conversation too many times before. It's out of the question."

Winn had wanted to live with his parents following their marriage, and he had dismissed Kit's questions about living away from the mansion. Now that her husband was gone, she intended to get a job and a place of her own for her and Andy. But she had to figure out all the details first before she told her son what they were going to do. Once she'd discussed it with Andy, then she'd find the right moment to tell her in-laws.

"No, I'm here about this letter I received." She placed it on the desk in front of him.

He put on his glasses. After reading it, he cleared his throat. Mr. Lundgren's words had gotten to her father-in-law, too. "I'm pleased they would like to honor Winston this way, but you can't think of accepting. This offer is for widows who have no money."

She told him about her conversation with Colonel Hodges. "He helped me understand that going to the ranch is for those retired marines, too, so I'd like to accept. I'll let Mr. Lundgren know we'll be coming for the last week of August."

"You can't go then. We have other plans."

Her cheeks grew warm battling him for every inch of ground. "But I'm in charge of the Cosgriff Memorial Library benefit. There's so much to do throughout the beginning of August, I won't be able to get away until it's over. When Andy realizes these men want to do something wonderful for him—because of his father's heroism—I'm hoping it will help him to feel a little happier before he starts school. Please. You and Florence take the rest of the family on that cruise of the fjords without us and enjoy yourselves."

"What do you mean, without us?" Florence spoke behind her.

Kit turned around to face her always stylish mother-in-law. "Andy and I are going to take a trip to Wyoming the last week of August. We're to be the special guests of some retired marines who want to honor Winn by inviting us to their dude ranch. It's all there in the letter." Her eyes darted to the desk.

"Have you forgotten we've had this trip planned for months?"

"No." *What to do...* "I could call Mr. Lundgren right now and find out if it will be all right if we come the first week of September. We could leave on a Friday and come back the next Saturday. Now if you'll excuse me, I'll go get Andy ready for dinner."

August 31
Teton Valley Dude Ranch

"You've got a faraway look in your eye, Ross." A cough had preceded the statement. "Is it possible there's a woman on your mind?"

On this beautiful Saturday morning, Ross Livingston and his partner Carson Lundgren had been inspecting the border of Carson's Teton Valley Dude Ranch, located fifteen minutes from Jackson, Wyoming. They could exercise the horses and talk business at the same time.

Buck Summerhayes, the other retired marine making up their triumvirate, had just married a woman who had come to the ranch in July as their invited guest. At the moment he was understandably detained, so he couldn't attend this meeting. Carson had married in June, leaving Ross the lone bachelor.

"I'm thinking a lot of things, but not about a woman." They'd ridden to the eastern section of the property away from the forest that provided spectacular blocks of color. It was the last day of August. Another week of temperatures in the lower seventies, and then it would be fall. Carson had told his friend from a more southern clime that the cold came a little earlier here, so enjoy the warm weather while they could.

Ross's dark brown eyes followed the flat, treeless sweep of sage with no sign of civilization in sight. He loved every square inch of this fabulous property watched over by the magnificent Grand Teton.

"If you're having reservations about our recent decision to keep the dude ranch running year round, I'm open to anything you have to say. This place hasn't operated in the black for years. It's nothing new."

That's what worried Ross. Though their regular dude ranch business was growing, he wanted Carson to be able to get out from under the constant worry of making ends meet, a problem Ross had never been forced to deal with.

"No reservations. Like you, I'm anxious to keep this going for a year to see how we do in our venture."

Turning the working ranch into a dude ranch had been Carson's idea when the three of them had been hospitalized together at Walter Reed in January. He'd inherited it from his deceased grandfather and wanted to make it into a profitable business.

The guys had gotten together and pooled their resources. Once they'd been discharged from the hospital, they'd started making their dream a reality. Besides building new cabins and making renovations to the ranch house and other structures, they'd created a website and done enough advertising to attract people from all over the country who wanted to experience life on a ranch. It had been a major endeavor that had included the hiring of staff.

Throughout all that process they'd also discussed how to manage their guilt for surviving the war and had come up with the idea to give a week's free vacation once a month to a son or a daughter of a fallen soldier. To be a substitute daddy for a week to the fatherless children had been a part of their goal, but there was much more to it.

The guys hoped that in helping the mothers and children explore the outdoors on horseback and take in the wonders of the rugged natural world, they'd let go of some of their grief and learn that there was joy in being alive despite their loss. The children needed to know their fathers were good men who'd made an invaluable contribution to their country and would always be remembered. Hopefully the activities the ranch provided would help restore their confidence.

So far the "daddy dude ranch" experiment, as they called it, had produced wonders far beyond anyone's expectations. Not only had the two women and children who'd come this summer found new joy here, his partners had lost their hearts to them and there'd been two marriages.

Ross found it uncanny what had happened, marveling over the happy coincidences. Now there was one more military widow with her son due to arrive this evening—Kathryn and Andrew Wentworth. Their husband and father happened to have been the son of Charles Cavanaugh Wentworth from Maine, an established and wealthy East Coast family.

According to Colonel Hodges, Mrs. Wentworth had been hesitant to accept the guys' invitation, feeling it should go to a family in financial need. That piece of information did her credit, but her husband's exceptional valor had decided them on giving him and his family the special recognition he deserved.

Ross had still to decide what it was going to be like taking care of two people who'd been given every luxury life had to offer. Having been born a Livingston of the billionaire oil barons of Texas, he knew firsthand the kind of society she and her son had come from. He would reserve judgment, however, until after he'd spent some time with them.

As for now, he was excited about an idea he wanted to explore with Carson. It had been percolating in his mind for a long time, but he hadn't wanted to bring it up until he could see how well their dude ranch business had been doing.

"So, what gives?" Carson prodded him.

Ross would have answered, but like Carson and Buck, he had a cough they'd picked up in Afghanistan that had ended their military careers. This morning there was a hint of smoke in the air from a forest fire in nearby Yellowstone. It had aggravated their coughs. He pulled out his inhaler prescribed by the doctor. Pretty soon he got some relief, but the medicine had a tendency to make him sleepy, something he had to fight while they were out on the range.

When he finally caught his breath, Ross began. "Correct me if I'm wrong, but didn't you once tell me your great great grandfather obtained the mineral rights to this place before the government could get their hands on them?"

Carson eyed him with curiosity. "I did."

"I've been giving it a lot of thought since Sublette and Fremont Counties bordering you have been seeing a boom in natural gas."

"That's right. You graduated in petroleum engineering. You think there's gas under my land?" he asked before letting go with a cough.

"With more and more energy companies springing up around Lander and Thermopolis, I think there's a pretty good possibility you're living on top of a big pocket of it here in Teton County. Wyoming has the second largest proven natural gas reserve in the U.S. behind Texas."

I ought to know, he thought with a grimace. His last name was synonymous with oil in the Lone Star State, where he'd been raised.

"The money you'd derive from a producing well could keep the ranch solvent for years to come. It's just a thought." One Ross would like to see happen for his friend.

"A few years ago my grandfather told me he'd been approached by a gas company, but he wouldn't hear of doing anything about it."

"I can understand that. Wyoming is a pristine environment that has been underexplored and underexploited. I'm sure he wanted to keep it that way."

"He feared the onslaught of progress."

"You can't blame him. But the ever-increasing demand for gas in the U.S. has led to a quadrupling of the price, causing companies in Russia and Venezuela, both big natural gas suppliers, to have shut off access to foreign companies. The same in the Gulf of Mexico where easy-to-drill reserves have been depleted. Progress has made its way to your door."

Carson pushed his cowboy hat back on his head. "You're talking about drilling for it right here?"

"This is the flattest uninhabited section of your land away from people and animals. Bringing in a road over this section would cause the least amount of disturbance to the environment and would be virtually invisible. Naturally I can't give you proof there's gas here without doing some preliminary drilling."

His friend was quiet for a minute. "Wouldn't that cost a ton of money I don't have?"

Ross nodded. "But I have some savings I can draw from. It would be my way of investing in your ranch to give you something back after what you've done for me. Then I'd feel a real part of it."

"You already are," Carson answered solemnly.

"I'd like to do more for you."

After a pause Carson asked, "What all would be involved?"

Ross was pleased his friend was at least listening to his proposal. "Wyoming's gas is unconventional. It doesn't sit in easy pools above oil, but thousands of feet beneath the earth in pockets of sandstone and coal formations. If the gas is there, the steel pipe will have to drive 11,000 feet into the ground to capture it.

"One good thing. Nowadays gas companies can put the derricks down on mats instead of the ground in order to preserve the top soil and roots. But there's no way around the fact that there are still a lot of negatives, and always will be."

"You've got me thinking," Carson said as Ross's phone rang, interrupting their conversation.

When he saw it was the ranch calling, he clicked on. "Hey, Willy. What's up?" The part-time mechanic helped run the front desk.

"There's been another change in the Wentworths' itinerary you need to know about."

He coughed. "What's that?" Earlier in the week their

latest invited guest had already indicated she wouldn't be able to make it on Friday and would come Saturday instead.

"The fax says she and her son will be flying into Jackson Hole at three p.m."

He frowned while Carson looked on. "I wonder why they aren't coming in on the flight we arranged." They weren't supposed to be due in until six-thirty this evening.

"I don't know. Since you're out touring the ranch, do you want me to go for them?"

Ross checked his watch. There was time to get back and shower if he and Carson left now. "No." This was his responsibility. "I'll do it. Thanks for the heads-up, Willy." He clicked off.

"What's going on?"

"Mrs. Wentworth will be here at three instead of six-thirty. I need to get going."

"I'll ride with you. I promised to spend part of the day showing Johnny how to ride bareback."

"That boy gets better every day."

"He's a natural."

"Just like his new dad." Ross smiled at his friend. "Carson? Give what we talked about some thought and let me know later."

"Why don't you get a few bids together and we'll go from there."

"I'm going to get on it pronto."

They took off at a gallop. Carson hadn't said no. Drilling a hole from start to finish would take a month. It would be better to do it before winter set in. Ross would arrange to meet an oil engineer out here on Monday. Then he could present it to Carson with more information to back up his idea.

But right now he had other things on his mind. For the next week he would have his hands full entertaining a nine-year-old boy who'd lost his father and was grieving.

Ross hoped he was as sweet as Johnny Lundgren, Carson's newly adopted seven-year-old son. The boy had charmed everyone on the ranch with his curiosity and good nature, and had walked right into his friend's heart. For that matter so had Buck's new stepdaughter, Jenny. Ross was crazy about both the kids.

Once they'd returned their horses to the barn, Carson took off for his new house, the one Buck had built for him, Tracy and Johnny on the property near the Snake River. Buck came from a family who owned a construction business. As for Ross, he drove the Jeep back to the main ranch house to get cleaned up.

Since Buck had moved downstairs with his wife, Alex, and her granddaughter, Jenny, Ross had the whole top floor of the place to himself. For the first time since his return from Afghanistan last January, he was aware of his "aloneness" and didn't like it.

With his mood becoming decidedly morose on that score, Ross was lucky he had guests to pick up.

Carson's earlier question about a possible woman on Ross's mind had hit a nerve. *One day, I'll have a family of my own.*

The jet from Denver taxied to a stop at the Jackson airport. Kit's heart hammered in her ears. She undid the seat belt and got to her feet, glancing at her desperately unhappy son who was still sleepy from the medicine she'd given him for air sickness.

This was it. The day she'd been praying for had come.

Freedom.

Joy of joys, she and Andy were the *only* ones in the Wentworth family invited to stay on the Wyoming ranch. They would have a whole week to themselves to get closer and make plans for the future. When they left, they would be going to a new place to live. She had it all arranged. If her in-laws wanted to remain in her life and Andy's, they would have to deal with her move and accept it.

The letter inviting them here had served as a stepping-stone to their new life. When these retired marines had shown such kindness and generosity, she'd been moved to tears, not only for Andy's sake, but her own. Not that her son hadn't had a different attitude than hers when she'd first told him.

"I'm *not* going." He'd sounded so much like his obstinate deceased father, with that same mulish tone of voice that often crept in these days. "I don't want to go anywhere."

"Honey, this is a great honor for all of us. Think of it—these military men are trying to show you how much they care what your dad did to save lives."

"I don't want to go." He'd kicked the end of his bed in anger.

"Andy—I never want to see you do that again!"

"But a dude ranch sounds stupid!" He'd turned away from her.

To her horror, he was becoming more and more unmanageable lately. He hadn't seemed to enjoy the cruise vacation at all. His grandparents were so cold and controlling. Winn's death only served to have brought a permanent winter into their lives. Though she'd been out of love with her husband for years, she ached for Andy and what he was going through, after losing his father.

"How could a vacation like this be stupid?"

"They're a bunch of lame marines. I *hate* them!"

Kit thought she understood. To Andy, a letter from the marines represented death and was a terrible reminder of the many months over the years his father had been away on deployment.

This trip would be the first time in years the two of them were completely on their own without the family there to run Andy's life. Though he'd finally stopped fighting her over the decision to bring him to Wyoming, she saw the deep misery in his eyes. Unfortunately, her darling son had no idea how much more misery was in store for him if they didn't make the break from his grandparents, who were swallowing them alive.

Winn and his parents had decided years ago that when Andy turned nine, he would be sent to a special elite boarding school located an hour away from Bar Harbor where discipline was strictly enforced. He'd be granted a weekend pass twice a month if he kept up his grades. He was due to start school there in mid-September.

Winn had been sent to the same school at his age and expected that for Andy. It was tradition among the Wentworths, one of the founding families of Maine. Her husband had paid the $50,000 deposit years earlier to reserve his place.

It didn't matter that he was no longer alive. Andy's grandfather would carry out his son's wishes and ignore hers. But Andy was *her* son and her *raison d'être.* When Kit had objected because she wanted Andy at home with her, he'd stated the matter was closed.

Since his death the tension at the Wentworth mansion had grown much worse. The out-of-the-blue letter from the ranch was a miracle, and had helped give her the jump start she needed to make some serious decisions. She knew that for her to move out and get a life of her own would be a huge change for both of them—not to mention traumatic for her in-laws.

That's why she needed this week in Wyoming first to prepare Andy. It would mean treading carefully to broach this plan with her son. If his anger grew any worse, he could possibly require professional help. What if in time Andy turned into his grandfather, outgrowing the sweetness of his nature he'd been born with?

"Honey?" she said quietly. "We've arrived."

His eyes blinked open. They were a lighter gray than Winn's. His cheek had a line indented into it from lying against the seat. When he slept he became her dear son again, instead of the impossible nine-year-old child she no longer knew.

"Do you need to go to the bathroom before we leave the plane?"

"No." His rude answer resonated in the jet's interior. He unfastened his seat belt and got up with a scowl on his face. "I told you I don't want to be here."

She was sick for him, knowing he was a volcano ready to explode from all of the pain and emotion he held inside. Kit had lost her influence over him years ago, but she was his mother and he needed her. Even if he wasn't aware of it.

Because the family had her trapped in an emotional vise of guilt, she'd been ineffectual in dealing with him. Now, that was going to change—she couldn't live under the same roof with her in-laws any longer. She had to leave, and when she did there'd be no going back.

With his shoulders slumped, Andy started down the aisle behind the other passengers without saying anything else. She grabbed her handbag and followed him to the exit. When they reached the inside of the terminal, Kit saw a cowboy in well-worn boots striding toward them with unconscious male authority. A brown Western shirt and jeans covered his tall, fit physique.

The striking male looked to be in his early thirties. He tipped back his sand-colored cowboy hat, revealing a widow's peak of raven-black hair. There were no rings on his fingers. "Mrs. Wentworth?"

As she moved closer his dark brown eyes sized her up. They were neither admiring or leering, one of the two looks she was used to receiving from men. For the first time since she could remember, she saw a guarded look coming from the stranger's eyes and wondered why.

"Are you Mr. Lundgren?"

"No. I'm Ross Livingston, his business partner." He possessed a deep voice, but his civil response didn't have the Western twang she'd expected.

"I remember your name from the letter. It's a great pleasure to meet you. This is my son, Andy. I'm sorry if you had trouble meeting this earlier plane. We've been in Norway and caught a flight out of New York to Denver that put us in here ahead of schedule."

"No problem at all. We're glad you arrived safely."

Still feeling unsettled by the way he'd been looking at her, she said, "We're very honored you would choose our family when there are so many others affected by the war. Andy's father would be incredibly proud."

"After your husband's sacrifice, we consider it our pleasure." He stepped forward to shake their hands but focused his attention on Andy. "Welcome to the Teton Valley Dude Ranch, son." After a cough he asked, "Have you ever been to Wyoming?"

"No." The peeved sound that came out of Andy was totally mortifying to her.

Kit glanced at their host. "I'm afraid he just woke up from a sound sleep."

"I understand. Long transatlantic flights do the same thing to me." He'd said it with urbane sophistication, acting as if nothing was wrong, but she knew *he* knew there was plenty wrong with her son. "Let's gather your luggage."

They walked over to the carousel. "We have three cases. They're the navy ones with the red-and-white trim."

He reached for them, and they followed him outside past the other passengers to a black, four-door Jeep. He stowed the suitcases in the rear with what looked like effortless ease. To her consternation, the play of hard muscle across his back and shoulders drew her attention without her volition.

Andy just stood there without helping, causing Kit more embarrassment. Their host spoke to him. "Do you prefer the front or backseat?"

"Back," he mumbled.

"I'll sit with you, honey." Kit opened the rear door and climbed in before Mr. Livingston had time to help.

Andy got in next to her and pulled the door shut. Their host slid his powerful body behind the wheel of the Jeep, coughing again before they took off.

She glanced out her window so she wouldn't be tempted to stare at the way his black hair curled in tendrils against the bronzed skin of his neck. Since seeing him walk toward her in the terminal, she'd felt breathless, assuming it was because of the six thousand feet or more altitude after coming from sea level. But upon closer examination, she realized it was the stunning-looking male driving the Jeep who'd caused her lungs to constrict.

The farther away they got from the airport, the freer she felt, despite the tension emanating from both her son and the enigmatic male in front.

Maybe not enigmatic. That wasn't the word she was looking for. Still, something wasn't right. The cowboy's attitude wasn't as warm as the tone of his partner's letter that had touched her heart. She would have to wait until tonight after Andy had fallen asleep before she'd be able to apologize to their host about her son.

Perhaps coming here for the first week of September rather than anytime in August had put them out, though they hadn't seemed to mind when she'd asked if she could change the dates. After the generosity of these marines, changing the dates to please her in-laws had embarrassed her terribly. When she got the opportunity, she would explain what had happened.

Still troubled by her thoughts, she saw a jet climb into one of the bluest skies she'd ever seen. With the Grand Teton in the background, the sight was magnificent beyond words. She watched until the plane was a mere speck before she sighed with relief. They were really here, delivered to the small town of seven thousand people. It wasn't just a dream.

She'd been living for this moment. From now on their future plans rested solely with her.

Suddenly she felt their host's piercing glance on her through the rearview mirror. She could almost believe he was reading her mind. "If you're hungry, say the word and we can stop for a bite to eat in Jackson. Otherwise dinner is served from five to eight in the dining room of the main ranch house."

Anyone watching or listening would think he was being perfectly polite. He was, but behind his benign suggestion she still sensed he had reservations about her.

"I don't want to eat," Andy muttered to her before he turned and hunched against the door.

Kit didn't know if their host had heard him or not. Her son had completely forgotten his manners. "Thank you for asking, but we had a meal before we landed so we're fine until later."

"You don't even want something to drink?"

"No, thank you."

He turned onto the main highway. "We'll be at the ranch in fifteen minutes. There'll be drinks and snacks in your cabin."

"That sounds wonderful." In order to shut his compelling image from her vision, she closed her eyes, but another cough from him reminded her he was still there. He must be getting over a cold.

The first stage in her plan had been accomplished. She and Andy were far away from Maine and her in-laws. Unfortunately she hadn't expected a complication like Mr. Livingston. Despite the fact that he seemed to have reservations about her, she'd already become aware of him as a man, a disturbing one. This *awareness* hadn't happened to her since before her marriage to Winn. She didn't like it.

Chemistry had been responsible for their ill-advised union. Of course she could never regret Andy, who was the joy of her existence, but she was ten years older now and knew better than to get carried away a second time.

Kit's one purpose in life was to make a new life for her and Andy. Beyond that she couldn't think.

Chapter 2

Ross hadn't known what to expect while he'd been waiting for the Wentworths inside the terminal. He'd spotted a nice-looking dark blond boy of about nine or ten, dressed in shorts and a collared shirt, emerge from the doors. When Ross saw the mother directly behind him with her dark hair styled in tousled waves, he let out a low whistle.

She might be close to thirty at this point, but he did have to admit that in her recent widowhood, she could have passed as a top model for a fashion magazine. He liked her pleated white pants and the chic, short-sleeved khaki blouse that tucked in at the waist. She looked polished and sophisticated. Her sex appeal stood out a mile, catching the eye of most of the males in her sight, including his.

Damn if Charles Wentworth's daughter-in-law

wasn't a knockout. Because of his own privileged background, he had a tendency to cast a jaded eye on women who thrived in a culture he'd found too shallow to tolerate.

The affluent society he'd grown up in was what had finally caused Ross to join the marines. A complete break from the life plan his father had mapped out for him was his only way out. He'd needed to get out, or his life wouldn't have been worth living. But his desire for a lifetime career in the military had come to an early end when he'd been discharged after six years of service because of his chronic cough.

Except to visit his parents after being released from Walter Reed Hospital in March, plus the monthly phone call home, he hadn't been near that world until today. By some strange quirk in the universe, it had fallen to him to be the personal host of this woman and her son.

Ross saw himself in Andy at that age and was haunted by it. The boy had grown up in the same kind of environment as Ross. Better than anyone else, he recognized a kid who could be corrupted by that kind of money and lifestyle. A child who was born to walk one path with no room for deviation.

But before he allowed past bitterness to overwhelm him, Ross needed to remember this mother and son had lost their husband and father. They'd come to the ranch at the guys' invitation and were his responsibility for the next week. Death came to every class of society, and they were still dealing with their grief.

Ross knew the usual tactics to win over a child the way Carson and Buck had done wouldn't work with Andy. It had been ingrained in this boy from infancy that he was superior to everyone else.

He came from an establishment fueled by money and power beyond most people's ability to imagine. Already he could see in the boy's eyes what an insufferable week he would have to spend in this back-of-beyond place. Ross would have to rely on his gut instinct to make any headway.

Once he turned onto the road leading into the ranch, he pointed out the ranch managers' complex with homes and bunkhouses, the machinery and hay shed, the calving barn, the horse barn and corrals. Maybe the boy was listening, maybe not.

"Oh, Andy. Look how beautiful it is here with the river and the pines, honey. I'm reminded of a Disney cartoon where everything in nature is so perfect. Don't you think it looks like a peaceful little city immaculately laid out with the forest on one side and the Tetons standing guard on the other?"

To Ross's surprise her words echoed his own thoughts the first time he'd laid eyes on Carson's ranch.

Still no response from Andy, who looked and acted miserable.

"That's the main ranch house on the right. The cabins are farther on." Ross coughed again and kept driving until he came to the one reserved for them. As he pulled up to the front steps, she opened the door and got out to look around.

"We're surrounded with sage!" she exclaimed. "It's a heavenly smell."

"I agree," Ross muttered, confused by her reactions. Instead of a blasé view of everything topped off with a patronizing nod, she reminded him of a child who took delight in what she saw. If she was pretending to be something she wasn't, he'd be hard-pressed to prove it.

Andy climbed out his side of the Jeep. For the first time he looked at Ross. "How come you cough so much?"

"Andy!" she cried in embarrassment.

Contact at last. "It's all right, Mrs. Wentworth, a perfectly normal question. I'm not sick in the way you might think, Andy. My partners and I picked up a cough in Afghanistan from breathing bad air, the contaminants of war. You can't get it from being around me. Today it's a little worse because there's some smoke in the air from a forest fire. Smoke is our enemy. We always keep oxygen around to breathe in case it gets bad."

Andy studied him for a minute without saying anything. Mrs. Wentworth's exquisite sea-green eyes fringed with black lashes sought his. "Will you get better?" She sounded as if she really wanted to know.

"Maybe."

"In other words, you might never recover completely. I'm so sorry."

Ross shook his head, taken back by her seeming sincerity. "We're fine."

He transferred his gaze to Andy who was still eyeing him. "If anyone's sorry, we are for what happened to your father. He was a very brave marine who made himself a decoy under heavy fire and saved eight lives. I'm sure you've already been told the circumstances, but it bears repeating.

"Hold that knowledge to you, Andy. Not every person born on this earth has a dad like yours, who was willing to give his life for his friends and country. What he did was remarkable. None of us will ever forget. It's an honor to meet his son. If you'll let us, we'd love to show you a good time while you're here. Tomorrow I'll take you riding if you want."

If Ross didn't miss his guess, the boy's light gray eyes grew suspiciously bright before he looked down. Illness and death seemed to be the only two areas that had reached him so far. "You must be tired. I'll take in your luggage so you can get settled." He opened the back of the Jeep to get their bags.

"Come on, Andy. Let's help." She grabbed a case and handed it to him, then reached for one for herself. She kept surprising Ross. He took the other one and went up the steps first to open the cabin door.

"I love it!" she announced once they were inside. "Yellow and white are my favorite colors. This place is charming, Mr. Livingston. We're going to be so happy here, aren't we, Andy?"

Ross didn't expect him to answer, and the boy didn't disappoint him.

"There are two bedrooms." They followed him past the front room to the hallway. "The bathroom is behind that door. Which room would you like, Andy?" One room had a queen-size bed, the other contained twin beds.

"I guess that one." He meant the one on the right with the two beds.

"Good." Ross set down the case.

His mother joined them and lowered her case to the floor. "This cozy room will be perfect for both of us. We'll figure everything out later. Let's go check out the snacks."

Andy put the other suitcase down and gave his mother a startled glance before they all moved to the other room. "We're going to sleep in the same room?"

"Why not? We don't ever get to do it at home. I think it will be fun. We'll read stories to each other." She walked over to the table near the minifridge. "What's in these little pouches?"

"Pine nuts gathered on the ranch."

She smiled at Ross before putting a couple in her mouth. "Umm…nummy. Here, honey. Try some. Put out your hand." When Andy did her bidding, she poured a few in his palm, then she turned to Ross. "What about you?"

How could he say no? He didn't like admitting it, but she had a disarming way about her. "Thank you." He tossed back a few. "Just so you know, the maids come in daily to do housekeeping. If you need wash done, put it in the laundry bag hanging on the bathroom door and they'll return your clothes before evening."

"Talk about being pampered," she murmured. Just as he was thinking what a statement for her to make when you considered her background, her cell phone rang. She pulled it out of her pocket to check the caller ID. It wiped the smile from her face.

"Excuse me. I need to answer this." She clicked on and said hello. After a minute she said, "I planned to call you, but we just walked in our cabin with Mr. Livingston."

Another pause, then, "Yes. He's right here." She called to Andy, who was looking in the minifridge. "Your grandfather wants to talk to you."

"Do I have to?" he grumbled.

"I think you better."

Andy didn't look happy about it, but he walked over and reached for the phone. "Hello?" There was more silence before he said, "It's a nice ranch. I guess we'll be going riding. Mr. Livingston's going to take us." Whether that explanation was meant to satisfy his grandfather on some level or whether the idea of it actually sounded interesting to Andy, Ross didn't know yet.

"I'll be careful, but I've got to go now." Another pause. "I will." He hung up and whispered something to his mom.

Mother and son needed to be alone. Ross eyed them. "If you'll forgive me, I have an errand to run before dinner." Because of the smoke in the air he needed to take his medicine. "The dining room will be open in an hour. Shall I come by for you in the Jeep, or would you like to walk and meet me there? We'll discuss an itinerary for you while we eat."

"Oh, walk! Definitely." She escorted him to the door where he stepped out on the porch. "Thank you for everything, Mr. Livingston."

He detected a catch in her voice. His little talk to Andy would have affected her, too. She'd lost her husband, yet was trying to remain upbeat for her son. Ross admired that. Somehow her emotion had gotten under his skin. Facing her he said, "You're welcome, Mrs. Wentworth. Call me Ross."

"I'm Kit."

His brows lifted. "Is that your given name?"

"No. I was named Kathryn, but the grandmother who raised me after my parents died called me Kit and it stuck."

Ross liked it. She was the antithesis of the woman he'd been expecting once he'd known her background. Despite his initial misgivings, there were a dozen questions he wanted to ask, but this wasn't the time.

"I'm sorry about Andy," she said in a quiet voice.

"What do you mean?"

"He's been going through a bad time and knows better than to whisper in front of company. My father-in-law wants me to call him before I go to bed, that's all."

She hadn't owed him an explanation. "Don't worry about it. I'll see you later then." He climbed in the Jeep and took off without looking back.

After parking at the rear of the main ranch house, he entered the back door and strode swiftly down the hall to the stairs. He kept his medicine in his bathroom on the second floor.

"Hey, Ross?" At the sound of Willy's voice he swung around. "I saw you drive up when I was outside. You had a phone call that sounded important, if you know what I mean." He handed him a piece of paper with a phone number on it with a wink.

Ross was afraid he did. "Thanks." He took the stairs two at a time. When he reached the bedroom, he medicated himself and then lay down on the bed to find out who'd called him. It was Cindy. He needed to put an end to her hopes. She answered on the second ring.

"Hey, cowboy. Am I going to see you tonight?"

Cindy Lawrence had been a lot of fun, but the hungry kiss she'd given Ross last night had offered too much. He should have enjoyed it. The beautiful moonlit night, unusually warm, should have worked its magic. But if Ross hadn't known on the bar's dance floor that it would be the one and only hour he spent with her, he knew it now.

He'd made the mistake of asking the flirtatious waitress to do some line dancing with him because he hadn't wanted to go back to the ranch house last night until he was ready to crash. The upstairs of the house was too empty.

"Much as I'd like to drop in tonight, I won't be able to," he said, trying to let her down gently. "A new family of a fallen marine just arrived in Jackson this afternoon. They're our guests on the dude ranch for a while and I'm in charge. Thanks for the dancing. It was fun."

The eagerness faded from her voice. "In other words you're not coming back anytime soon."

No. The attraction simply wasn't there. He'd been with a lot of women since coming to Wyoming, but so far all his relationships had been fleeting. "You never know. It's a busy time on the ranch. See you around, Cindy."

Without wasting any more time, Ross phoned the oil company he'd been researching and arranged for a meeting on Monday out at the site. Then he hung up and set his watch alarm. The medicine was working on him, making him drowsy. He closed his eyes, realizing that when he was awakened in an hour, he'd be seeing Kit Wentworth again. The thought shouldn't matter to him, but somehow it did.

Kit watched her son go through the DVDs in the entertainment center. "Have you seen a movie you'd like to watch?" She got up from the kitchen table with a granola bar in her hand to look through the stack with him. The luxury of them being free like this had already gone to her head.

"How about *Up?* I know you haven't seen that one." The grandparents had his life so regimented, he rarely found time to watch TV or films.

"No. That's a dumb kid's movie."

"Dumb" had made up most of his vocabulary since he'd found out they were coming to the ranch. Kit had hoped a new adventure might put him in a little happier mood. But it was possible the few friends his grandparents allowed him to play with had said something negative about going to a dude ranch and he was only echoing their comments.

Kit's eyes took in the attractive surroundings. All the comforts of home were included in this small rectangular log cabin: a table and minifridge, a couch and upholstered chairs in front of the fireplace. After living in the Wentworth mausoleum, she loved its rustic simplicity and the lightness of the decor.

Everything a person needed was right here, reminding her of the tiny home she'd once lived in with her grandmother in Point Judith, Rhode Island, where she'd been happy. It was there she'd met Winn.

The Blue Attic Book Shop where she'd worked had an outdoor display of discounted books. She'd been busy taking them all inside when Winn had walked by and begun chatting her up. He'd taken out one of the family yachts from Bar Harbor and had sailed down the coast with his friends. They'd pulled in at Point Judith to eat dinner. But he hadn't told her that information at the time and had only explained he and some buddies had been out sailing.

Kit had fallen hard for him and they'd married soon after. He'd taken his nineteen-year-old bride home to meet his family in Maine. They'd ended up living there in a controlling world of wealth and privilege she grew to detest.

It devastated her that the twenty-two-year-old man with the sun-kissed blond hair, smiling eyes and dark tan she'd fallen in love with had changed so much after they'd exchanged vows. Once under his parents' thumb, nothing she'd done had been right. The way she'd looked and behaved hadn't satisfied him.

In an effort to please him, she'd transformed herself into the woman he'd seemed to want, a style maven like his mother Florence, or his two older married sisters, Corinne and Sybil, who considered themselves the original aristocrats of Bar Harbor. Still, Kit had never fit in.

After Andy had been born, Winn hadn't shown as much interest in her except when they'd gone to the family's various exclusive clubs where they'd been seen in public. Then it had all been show. They'd grown so far apart, she'd begged for them to get a home of their own. His sisters and their husbands had their own homes. But Winn had told her there was no reason for them to move when they were living in the mansion and offered every luxury.

The years had gone by—empty years for her. Winn's long deployments in the military had driven them further apart. When she'd found the courage to tell him she wanted a divorce, he'd told her the Wentworths didn't divorce. If she filed, she'd lose Andy because he wouldn't let her take him anywhere.

As a member of the family now, she had the responsibility of carrying on as his wife and widow. The man she'd married had disappeared, never to return. The best part of him, the part she preferred to remember, lived in Andy.

But her son's life had been strung out with long periods of waiting for his father to come home on leave. Even when he came, they hadn't spent enough quality time together because his parents had had other plans for him. For the long months in between visits, Andy had been expected to mind his grandparents who ruled his life.

She'd cried herself to sleep at night for years worrying about her darling son. Though he would be good-looking like Winn when he was grown, it wouldn't be long before he turned into a clone of his rigid grandfather.

Kit had kept her demons hidden from Andy the best she could, but now that they were here, she would have the conversation with him she'd been waiting for since Winn's death. Maybe tomorrow or the next day when he'd had a good sleep and was more relaxed.

She went in the bedroom to open one of the suitcases. After gathering up some items, she put them on the bedside table in their room. Besides a pocket radio, there was a photograph of Winn and another of her grandmother. She carried some treasured books to the living room. Kit planned to read aloud to Andy if he'd let her.

Once that was done, she went to the bathroom to brush her hair. When she came out she said, "I don't know about you, but I'm starving. Let's walk to the ranch house." He mumbled something and went out the door. She followed with the cabin card key Mr. Livingston had left on the table and made sure the place was locked before starting off.

The magnificent Tetons were right there in her vision, stunning her with their beauty. They headed for the fabulous ranch house in the distance. She was reminded of one like it on the cover of one of her favorite Louis L'Amour Western novels. That was among the books she'd packed for this trip.

Kit had loved books in her early teens and had grown into a voracious reader. Her grandmother had gotten her hooked on all kinds of fiction, especially Westerns. One of the rooms in the house she'd rented had been turned into a virtual library.

After her grandmother died, Kit had kept a few favorites and donated the rest to the bookshop where she'd worked. The owner had allowed her to establish a lending library with the understanding that Kit would take the collection back when she had her own place. Winn didn't want them at the mansion. It almost killed her when last year she'd found out the shop had been sold and turned into a restaurant. All those precious books were gone....

Just seeing the ranch house with the pines clustered around the side brought back fond memories for the girl who'd grown up on the cape of Point Judith with her sweet grandmother and her books. But besides horses, this Western scene included the Jeep and all sorts of modern vehicles that must have belonged to the staff.

They followed some other guests inside and entered a large foyer. The mid-twenties guy behind the front desk flashed her a friendly smile loaded with a lot of male interest, the flattering kind. "Hi! Can I help you?"

"Yes. I'm Kit Wentworth, and this is my son, Andy. Mr. Livingston told us to meet him here for dinner."

His eyes widened. "You're our special guests from Maine?"

She smiled. "That's right."

"Welcome to the ranch. Here's another card key so you can both have access to your cabin."

"Thank you." She handed it to Andy, who looked surprised before putting it in the pocket of his shorts. "We're very grateful to have been invited."

"I guess you haven't had the grand tour."

"Not yet."

"The dining room's right through the great room across the foyer. There's a games room at the other end, and beyond the doors you'll come to a swimming pool with a lifeguard on duty. Go ahead and look around. I'm sure he'll be along shortly."

"Thanks so much."

They walked through the next room past the massive fireplace and into the dining room filled with the regular dude ranch guests, many in Western gear. One of the first things on her list was to buy them some fun cowboy stuff so they'd fit in around here.

Andy looked up. "They've got wagon wheels for lights!"

Her gaze went to the vaulted ceiling. "These are the kind of chandeliers I prefer any day. Pretty cool, don't you think?" Red-and-white checkered cloths covered the tables. She liked the yellow-and-white daisy centerpieces that reminded her of their cabin's colors.

"I guess." Though he played it down, the fact that he'd noticed gave her hope he was starting to thaw a little at having to be here.

She found them an empty table over on one side of the room. They each took a menu and studied it. "What do you think you want, honey?"

"A hamburger?" Hamburgers weren't on the menu at the Wentworth mansion. She had come to dread their five-course meals where the inevitable question-and-answer period lasted at least an hour. She knew Andy hated the length of time they had to stay at the table.

"That sounds good to me, too, with lots of French fries. Shall we splurge and get chocolate malts for dessert?"

"Can we?"

Why not? This was a night of celebration. "We can have anything we want here." She eyed him with concern. "This dude ranch isn't turning out to be such a bad place. Right?"

He looked away without answering, but when the friendly waitress came over, he gave her his order instead of just sitting there silently. This was the Andy she needed to see come back.

"How are you feeling by now? I know that medicine made you feel kind of strange."

"I hate the way it makes me so sleepy."

"I know, but at least it kept you from throwing up."

Before long the waitress returned with their food. He swallowed his in no time. It was surprising to her, considering he hadn't shown much appetite on the cruise. She was only halfway through her meal but could tell he was already restless. Who wouldn't be after their long flights?

"While I finish eating, why don't you go have a look around? The man at the desk mentioned a games room and swimming pool."

"You mean you'll let me?"

His grandparents had kept him on a short leash. "Sure."

He eyed her in surprise. "Thanks." Kit hadn't heard that word from her son in a long, long time.

Kit watched him dart away with more energy than

she'd noticed in ages. Relieved to see him behave like a normal boy for a few minutes, she ate some more French fries and kept an eye out for her host. Just when she decided something must have detained him, she saw him walk through the door from the kitchen.

His dark brown gaze panned the room. The male charisma oozing from him took her breath. Judging by the female guests in the room, they had the same reaction. Though there were quite a few men seated around, none of them affected her like Ross Livingston. Marine or cowboy, he seemed a breed apart.

He still hadn't seen her and started walking through the tables. As he drew closer, she called to him. His head turned in her direction. The second their eyes met, it grew into one of those moments when the world stood still for her. It was happening again. That awareness...

Ross moved toward her. Without his cowboy hat, his head of wavy black hair and arresting male features pretty well dazed her. She wondered who the lucky woman was who'd captured this attractive man's attention. There had to a woman, maybe a wife, even if he didn't wear a ring, and she would be exceptional.

"I'm sorry I was too late to eat with you. Business detained me." He sounded disappointed.

"Please don't apologize for anything." The pulse in her throat was throbbing so hard, she couldn't finish the last bites of her meal.

"Where's Andy?"

"When he was through eating, he went out exploring. I'm almost done and was about to look for him."

"Then let's go together."

"What about your dinner?"

"I had a snack already and will eat later."

Ross walked her out into the warm air. The sun wouldn't be going down for a while. There were half a dozen people in the pool. He nodded to the lifeguard.

"Hey, Uncle Ross—over here!"

A dripping wet Johnny Lundgren stood by the diving board talking nonstop to none other than their latest guest. Johnny was a little short for his age. Andy seemed to be tall for a nine-year-old. But the difference in height and age didn't mean a thing to Johnny. He was the friendliest kid on the planet. Ross smiled at the scene.

"That's Carson Lundgren's adopted son talking Andy's ear off," he said in an aside to Kit. "He's already adopted me and Buck as his uncles."

"How sweet," she murmured with genuine tenderness. She'd just described Carson's son. They walked to the end of the pool.

"Johnny? This is Andy's mom, Kit. They're from Maine."

"Hi, Johnny," she said with warmth.

"Hi! I just asked Andy if he wants to come riding with me and Jenny in the morning. He's never ridden on a pony before."

"I think that sounds fun, but we don't know what Ross has planned for us yet."

Johnny turned to Andy. "He'll probably take you fishing, but I think riding is more fun. Do you want to get in the pool and swim with me?"

If anyone could make a dent in Andy's armor, it was Johnny, who'd just given Ross an opening he'd take.

"Why don't we all swim? I'll go inside and put on my suit. It's the perfect temperature out here."

"Hooray!" Johnny cried in excitement.

Andy turned to his mother. In a quiet voice he said, "I don't want to."

"Then you don't have to, but after sitting on a plane for hours, I feel like a swim. I'm going to run to our cabin for my suit."

"Mom—"

"I'll be right back, honey."

Ross could see and feel Andy's frustration as she disappeared. The fact that she'd taken Ross up on the idea meant she wasn't about to coddle her son. Again he gave her marks for expecting Andy to deal with this new situation despite his unhappiness.

"Don't you guys have fun without me!" he said to the two of them.

Johnny laughed. "You're funny, Uncle Ross."

No sound came out of Andy. He just looked at him in bewilderment before Ross took off. At least that was a change from the scowl he'd worn during the drive from the airport.

Ross reached his room and changed into his black trunks. After grabbing a towel, he hurried back down and belly flopped next to Johnny on purpose, causing him to laugh. Ross noticed Andy sitting in a deck chair by himself.

"Come on, Johnny. Let's go talk to him." As he hoisted him on his shoulders, he saw Kit come out on the patio carrying a rolled-up towel.

"Hi, everybody!" In seconds she removed her wrap. Ross's breath caught to see her shapely body clad in a light blue bikini dive into the deep end of the pool from the side. When she surfaced, she swam over to her son. "I brought your suit in the towel. If you change your mind, use the cabana."

When he didn't respond, Ross said, "We're going to play sharks and minnows."

Johnny's head jerked around. "Hey—I haven't played that game before."

"It's a new one I've been waiting to teach you. I'm the shark and you guys are the minnows. I'll be at the end of the pool. You and Kit get up on the side of the deck. I'll call out, sharks and minnows, one two three, fishies, fishies swim to me. That's when you'll dive in and swim to the other side. If I don't catch you, then you'll be the shark for the next round. If I do, then you'll stay a minnow."

Johnny giggled. "That sounds silly."

He grinned. "You think? Just wait until I come after you." His gaze swerved to Kit who'd climbed up on the deck ready to play. Ross had a devil of a time concentrating when he couldn't take his eyes off her.

"Come on, Johnny. Let's see if we can beat this big shark at his own game." The way she'd said it heightened Ross's anticipation.

"Yeah!" Johnny got out of the water and walked over by her.

"Sharks and minnows—" Ross called out after coughing. The game was on. They must have played six rounds, but Ross beat them every time. Both she and Johnny came up laughing and spurting.

"How come you guys can't catch me?" Ross baited them. "I thought you said this was a silly game, Johnny."

Out of the corner of his eye he saw Andy, who'd come out of the cabana in his suit and was watching.

Well, what do you know. Nothing like a little healthy competition.

"Come on, Andy," Johnny shouted when he saw him. "Help us win!"

Once again they lined up along the side, but this time Andy had joined them. "Sharks and minnows—" Ross called out. There was plenty of splashing as everyone dived into the pool. Ross went after the other two first so he would barely miss tagging Andy.

"Hey—now Andy's a shark!"

"He sure is, Johnny." Ross smiled at Kit's son. "How did you learn to swim so fast?"

"I don't know."

"You're good!" Ross climbed up next to Johnny and Kit. She thanked him with her eyes. While he was still staring into them Andy shouted, "Sharks and minnows—" The boy was a quick study.

By Ross losing his concentration, Andy tagged him and Kit with no problem. That made Johnny the winner.

"Bravo!" another voice called out.

"Mom!" Johnny cried. Tracy had just come out to the pool. "Uncle Ross taught us a new game and I won this time! Put your suit on and get in."

"Honey, it's late. The pool is closed now. Time to get out."

"Oh, heck."

"Your mom's right, Johnny. But there's always tomorrow."

He scrambled out of the pool to his mother who wrapped him in a towel. After kissing him, she said, "It looks like we have some new guests."

"Yup. That's Andy and his mom, Kit. They're from Maine."

Ross took over. "Kit Wentworth? Meet Carson's wife, Tracy."

"It's so nice to meet you, Mrs. Lundgren. Andy and I are thrilled to be here."

"We've all been looking forward to your arrival, haven't we, Johnny."

"Yeah. Please, will you come riding with us in the morning?"

Andy shrugged. "I guess."

"Goody! We'll let you pick out one of the ponies to ride, but I think you'll like Raindrop. She's a dappled gray. You're older than we are and she's a little bigger than the others. She likes apple nuggets for a treat."

Ross chuckled. "She does love those."

Kit smiled. "I can't wait to see her. With that settled, we'd better get out of the pool and change. After our long flight we're about ready for bed and will see all of you tomorrow. Come on, Andy."

"Bye, Andy. See ya later." Johnny walked away with his mother.

"Bye."

Ross turned to his guests. "I'll meet you in the foyer in five minutes to drive you back to the cabin."

"We'll hurry," she assured him.

Before long the three of them met by the front desk where there were a few guests checking in. Ross was pleased to see their normal dude ranch business was continuing to grow.

Willy looked up. "Hey, Ross—I see they found you." But his eyes were so focused on Kit, Ross would have laughed if the situation weren't so precarious. Her dark hair still had natural curl when it was damp. She looked good. Too good. He had to remember they were honoring her husband's memory.

"We did," Kit spoke up. She appeared oblivious to Willy's gawking. "Thank you."

Ross walked them through the front door to the parking area on the side of the ranch house. "We'll go in the truck." He opened the rear passenger door for them, and they climbed inside.

Once on their way, he heard Andy talking to his mother in the back. "That Johnny's funny."

"He's very cute. I think it will be fun to go riding with him."

"Ponies are for babies."

"Johnny didn't look like a baby to me."

Good for Kit.

When they reached the cabin, Ross shut off the engine and turned in the seat to expand on her comment. "When you're seven, a pony is a lot easier to handle. Johnny's adoptive father, Carson, is a champion rodeo rider who owns this ranch. He got him started on Goldie in June. You should see how he rides already."

Ross could hear the boy mulling everything over in his mind. "What happened to his real father?"

Andy didn't miss much. "He was a brave marine like your dad who died in the war. Like you, we invited him and his mom to come to the ranch for a week. They ended up staying, and now they're married."

"How wonderful for them," Kit murmured.

Ross agreed, but the boy had gone quiet. Figuring he'd said enough for now, he climbed down from the truck and opened the rear door for Kit. They both got out the same side. Kit pulled the key card from her pocket to unlock the cabin door, drawing his gaze to the shape of womanly hips below her waist. As for the curves above…it was no wonder Willy couldn't keep his eyes to himself.

She turned to him. "Good night. Thank you for everything."

To his surprise he didn't want to leave. "I'll come by for you at eight in the morning, and we'll have breakfast together before planning our day. Good night, you two."

Ross got in the truck and took off for the ranch house. Before heading upstairs he made a detour to the kitchen for a sandwich and bumped into Buck stealing a donut on his way to bed.

These days his friend wore a continual smile. That's what being deeply in love did for you.

"Hey—" He nudged Ross, then coughed. "Willy just told me about Mrs. Wentworth and her son. Apparently she's one gorgeous babe. His words, I swear."

"If you like brunettes."

"You don't?"

"I never said that." The last word came out on a cough.

He studied him. "What's she like? Don't tell me she's *nice.*"

Ross bit into his ham sandwich. "What if she is?"

Buck chuckled. "And her son?"

"He's got problems."

"But nothing you can't handle."

"I don't know. It's early days yet." The conversation Andy had had with his grandfather earlier still puzzled him. Until the phone call, the boy hadn't said two words. Then he'd switched to talking mode, but only after he'd been urged by his mother to come to the phone. Ross didn't know what to make of the tension.

"Are you all right?"

"Ask me in a week." Ross couldn't take more of the interrogation. He finished off his sandwich, knowing sleep wouldn't come for a while. "Good night."

The guys had warned Ross that lightning could strike three times in the same place, and they had the documented video to prove it. He'd laughed off their teasing, but for some reason he wasn't laughing now.

Chapter 3

After washing and blow drying her hair, Kit got ready for bed. When she peeked in their bedroom, she discovered that Andy had fallen asleep. Considering their long day, it didn't surprise her. Without waiting another minute, she went into the living room to phone her in-laws.

"Hello, Florence? Andy told me you wanted me to call before we went to bed."

"We expected to hear from you before now."

"I'm sorry, but we swam until late with the owner's son, Johnny Lundgren. He's two years younger than Andy, but a real joy and a lot of fun."

Ross's suggestion that they all swim had turned out to be inspirational. By dreaming up that little competition, Ross had nudged Andy out of his mood. Andy hadn't been able to resist joining in and had won a round. The praise their host had given him had made a subtle difference in her son, increasing his confidence. Kit could have hugged Ross for it.

"Where's Andy?" Charles spoke up from another extension.

"In bed, sound asleep."

"What are your plans for tomorrow?"

She frowned. "I don't know yet. Probably riding. Why?"

"I'm concerned about Andy. The weather can change on a dime out there. I don't want to hear you took my grandson up on the Grand Teton with all those lightning strikes. You shouldn't have gone to Wyoming."

He's my *son, Charles,* she wanted to shout at him. But she understood that after losing Winn, her in-laws were fearful of other losses. Instead she said, "There are too many other activities planned right here on the ranch for you to worry about that. It's supposed to be warm weather the whole time while we're here. We're going to concentrate on riding horses and fly-fishing on the Snake. This is a glorious place." Like a piece of heaven.

"I was there years ago. The Snake River can be dangerous."

She took a deep breath. "Charles? I promise our hosts aren't going to allow us to do any activity where we can get hurt. They're trying to make this an exciting adventure for Andy." Kit had already been given proof of that at the pool with Ross.

"But you're there without Winn."

"Andy and I have each other, Florence. Now if you'll forgive me, I'm exhausted and need to get to bed. It's late for you, too."

"We'll talk tomorrow," Charles announced in his imperious voice.

Oh, she knew that. Twice a day and every night like clockwork. "I'll have Andy call you after our ride tomorrow. He'll have lots to tell you, I'm sure. Good night."

She hung up and hurried to bed. Moonlight kept the cabin room from being totally dark. Sleeping in the same room with her son was a brand-new experience. When Winn had been home, he'd never allowed Andy to get in bed with them, even when he was a small child.

And when he'd been away, he'd insisted Andy stay in his own bedroom on the next floor, and his parents had enforced his rule. She'd slept by him a few times over the years when he'd been sick and needed comfort, but this was different. While they were on vacation, she relished this time alone with him so they could really talk.

Kit turned on her side to face him. As she drifted off, her mind relived those moments in the swimming pool with Ross. She wished she didn't find him so appealing. She hadn't come here with the idea of meeting a man. Anything but.

Unfortunately, Ross was the first person on her mind when she woke up the next morning. The knowledge that he'd be coming for them in a few minutes gave her stomach flutters.

Andy had already gotten out of bed and was watching TV. She called to him to come and get ready.

"How did you sleep?"

"Good."

"Are you hungry?"

"Yeah."

She mulled over his answers while they put on their shoes. "Good" and "yeah" were signs his mood had improved. If only he would stay this way…

"Mom? Did you call Grandfather last night?"

He'd been her little worrier for years. "I did, but let me ask you something. What would you think if I hadn't phoned him?"

Andy swung his head toward her. She saw that nervous look he often got. "You know," he muttered.

She'd finished doing her hair and put the brush down. "You mean he'd get mad. You can say it, honey."

His eyes slid away.

"It's not much fun to be around someone grumpy, is it?"

He didn't respond.

"He and your grandmother get mad at me, too." She applied some lipstick.

"I know."

Her son understood a lot, but she still had to probe to get at the truth of how he truly felt about his life.

"That's why it's nice you and I can be on vacation by ourselves. We all need a break, don't you think?"

His faint nod gave her the sign she'd been hoping for, but they both heard a horn honk out front. She would have to continue this conversation with him later.

"Let's go." She put the card key in her pocket. With a happier heart, she followed him out the door into another day filled with sunshine, sage and Ross Livingston as she lived and breathed. He'd dressed in a brown-and-white plaid Western shirt and a pair of jeans that molded powerful thighs.

She felt his eyes on her as they filed out to the truck. Then they flicked to her son.

"Hey, Andy—how's it going?"

"Good."

"If you want, hop up in the back of the truck. You can ride on one of those bales of hay."

"Sure." Kit watched him heave himself up without Ross trying to help. Their host was the opposite of Charles who micromanaged him every second of his life.

"One of these days Johnny will be able to do that," he confided to Andy.

Thank you, Ross. His way with Andy, combined with his goodness, wrapped itself around Kit's insides, warming her through to the empty spaces in her heart.

"On the way to breakfast we'll pick up Johnny. Between him and Buck's new stepdaughter, Jenny, you'll be among friends. I know they're two years younger than you, but they'll like being with you. You've lived in Maine and know a lot of neat stuff they don't. And one more thing. They're fun."

"Johnny makes me laugh."

"He makes me laugh, too."

Keep this up, Ross. You're a genius.

His grin was infectious. Kit felt it radiate until her toenails curled. When Ross turned around, she was caught staring at him. "What about you? You want the joy of sitting on a hay bale, as well?"

She chuckled. He could have no idea what she was feeling at the moment, but now wasn't the time to try and put it into words. "I think I'll ride in the cab." In a minute she climbed in the passenger side of the truck and shut the door. Once settled, she turned to him, trying not to be distracted by his male charisma.

While they drove, she said, “When I accepted the invitation to come to the ranch, I didn’t expect to receive such personalized service. Since you mentioned your partners’ children, I assume you’re married, too. I don’t want any of you to feel you have to give us your attention round the clock.”

“This is my job. But to clear up any misunderstanding, I’m still single.”

Her heart fluttered in her chest. “Even so, you must have other calls on your time.”

“That’s true.”

He might not be married, but he’d just let her know he had his own love life. While she was immersed in contemplating that fact, she barely noticed they’d driven up in front of a fabulous glass and wood house beyond some pines. It overlooked the Snake River, and behind it she saw the majesty of the Grant Teton. The sight never ceased to thrill her.

He pulled to a stop. “I’ll see if Johnny wants to come and have breakfast with us.” Ross levered himself from the driver’s seat with that swift male grace particular to him. He called to Andy who jumped down from the back of the truck, and the two of them walked through the grass to the front porch.

Tracy, dressed in a robe, opened the door. A cute black-and-white Boston terrier ran circles around Ross and Andy, causing laughter before Tracy invited them in.

Several minutes later they came back out with Johnny, who was talking a blue streak. He’d dressed in a black cowboy hat and cowboy boots. Kit thought she'd never seen a cuter sight in her life. The dog followed him to the truck and then hurried into the house again.

While Andy climbed in the back, Ross helped Johnny, then he joined her in the cab, pinning her with his dark brown gaze. "Tracy wanted to say hi but it will have to be later, after she's dressed. Carson has already left to do chores." He backed the truck around, and they headed for the ranch house.

"That little boy is adorable."

"You have a great son, too, but it's clear he's passed the adorable stage."

She couldn't hold back a chuckle. "You can say that again. But I heard him laugh a second ago. Yesterday I feared that sound had become extinct."

"After losing his father, I'm not surprised. We'll see what we can do to get him to do it more often."

Kit decided that if anyone could perform that miracle, Ross could. She marveled over his dedication. There wasn't anything about him she didn't like…and the thought made her increasingly worried.

In a few minutes they reached the side parking of the ranch house. She got out so he wouldn't walk around to help her. Andy jumped down. Johnny tried to copy him, but Ross, ever alert, was there to make sure he didn't hurt himself. "Come on, everybody. Let's find a table and chow down."

Buck waved to their group from one of the tables. The dining room was full of guests, great news for business. "Over here. Jenny and I have been waiting for you guys."

Ross could always count on his partners and introduced Andy to the two of them before they sat down. "Buck Summerhayes? Jenny Forrester? Meet Andy and his mother, Kit Wentworth. They've come all the way from Bar Harbor, Maine, to be our guests."

"Andy and I are very pleased to meet all of you. Thank you for making us feel so welcome. We're the luckiest people in the world to have been invited here." When she smiled like that, she lit up the place.

Jenny looked up. She was a charming seven-year-old blonde girl who'd grow up to be as beautiful as her grandmother, Alex, one day. This morning she was wearing her white cowboy hat, ready to ride.

She looked at Andy with curiosity. "Did you fly here?"

"Yes."

"Did you like it?"

"No. I got airsick and had to take medicine."

"I got sick when I flew here, too. There was a big storm."

"I didn't get sick," Johnny piped up, "but it was sure scary. I thought we were going to crash."

Ross handed Andy a menu. "What do you like for breakfast?"

"I don't like breakfast that much."

"What do you eat?" Johnny asked. Now that they were seated, Ross could count on Carson's son to carry the conversation from here on out. "I like Froot Loops."

"I've never had those."

"How come?"

"We always have to eat poached eggs and toast. My grandmother makes me eat grapefruit so I won't get fat."

"Ew!" the two children said in a collective voice.

Jenny looked at Andy. “Does your grandmother live with you?”

“We live with both my grandparents.”

Andy had just dropped a bombshell on Ross. Until this second he didn’t know Kit and her son lived in the famous Wentworth mansion, too. Had this been since her husband’s death? He remembered Andy’s surprise when Kit had told him they would sleep in the same bedroom at the cabin.

“After my mommy died, I lived with my nana, but she lets me eat what I want.”

Johnny made a face. “If my mom gave me grapefruit, I’d feed it to Blackie.”

Ross’s chuckle brought on a cough. “I don’t think your dog would like it either.”

Jenny’s blue eyes had widened. “You’ve never had cereal?”

“We had oatmeal sometimes,” Kit explained, “but not many choices for uncooked cereal.”

“That’s *mean.*”

“That’s really mean,” Johnny concurred.

Ross thought he was going to crack up with laughter and noticed Kit was trying hard not to laugh, too.

“Do you want to try Boo Berry?” Jenny asked. “It’s my favorite.”

“Okay.”

“It makes your teeth blue,” Johnny informed him. “Will your mom get mad if you eat it?”

“Of course I won’t,” Kit supplied with spirit. “When I lived with my grandmother, we ate a lot of cereal.”

Andy stared at his mother in surprise. “You did?”

“Yes. Lucky Charms were my favorite, along with

eggs and fruit. Maybe Boo Berry will turn out to be yours."

As Buck flashed Ross a private glance that sent a message of masculine approval, the waitress came over to take their orders. He heard Kit tell Andy that since they were on vacation, he could get whatever he wanted. After listening to the other kids, her son asked for Boo Berry and hot chocolate. Pure sugar. What else?

"When does your school start?"

The question caught Kit's attention. "Since we're here on this wonderful trip, we're not worrying about that yet, Johnny."

"You're lucky. We have Back To School Night on Wednesday."

Jenny nodded. "Our classes start on Thursday. I hope our teacher isn't mean."

Buck grinned. "What's all this *mean* business, Red?" It was his nickname for her because she loved the color red so much. "When I was in school, I liked my teachers."

"All of them?"

"Well, maybe one or two of them weren't exactly my favorite people."

Johnny giggled.

"My grandparents are sending me away to a private school," Andy interjected.

Both children stared at him in shock. "Away from your mom?" Jenny asked.

He nodded.

Johnny put his spoon down. "How come?"

Kit wiped her mouth with the napkin. "Over the years all boys in the Wentworth family are sent to a special private boarding school when they turn nine. They can only come home twice a month if they've been good students."

"Boy, am I glad I'm not you!"

"Me, too," Jenny exclaimed. "My father and mother died. If I had to go to a school away from my nana, I'd run away."

Ross groaned inside, remembering his own painful years when he'd been sent away to the same kind of school.

At this point the waitress brought their food, and they tucked in. Ross looked at Kit, who'd gone quiet and was busy eating. When he got her alone he'd find out what was bothering her. In the meantime he had an idea to change the direction of the conversation.

"Before we saddle up, we need to drive into town and get some cowboy hats and boots for Kit and Andy."

"Goody!" Johnny enthused. "I need some more caps for my mustang. I've been saving up my allowance."

"I'm going to buy some more caps, too," Jenny chimed in.

"Let's get Andy a mustang, Uncle Ross."

"Only if he wants one."

Kit's son looked at Ross. "What's a mustang?"

"A cap gun."

"Yeah. Uncle Ross will be the bad guy and we'll go hunting for him." Johnny was one in a million. "Do you like cap guns?"

"I've never had one."

"Neither did I until my dad got me one at the Boot Corral. They don't have them in Cleveland. That's where my grandparents live."

Ross noticed a shadowed expression on Andy's face and wondered what had put it there.

"I have my nana right here."

"We sure do, sweetheart." Buck hugged Jenny.

To Ross, the children's conversation had been like a cacophony of enjoyable music until he'd looked at Kit's son; then the music had stopped.

He pushed himself away from the table and got to his feet. "If everyone's finished eating, let's leave for town. The sooner we get the shopping done, the sooner we can go riding. We'll take the van." Ross shot Buck a glance. "I'll look after Jenny."

His friend nodded. "I'll tell Alex. She's going to be at the front desk this morning. That'll give me time to finish installing that new cabinet in the office."

The kids ran out of the ranch house to the parking area and piled in the dark green van with the Teton Valley Dude Ranch Logo. Andy followed with his mother, who climbed in the front seat. He got in back with Johnny and Jenny.

"Everybody buckle up."

"You always say that."

He eyed Johnny through the rearview mirror. "And I always will."

"There's sure a lot of cars," Jenny observed as they turned onto the highway.

"That's because it's the Labor Day weekend."

"I completely forgot about that," Kit exclaimed. "No wonder the plane was full."

Ross coughed. "A lot of families want to come and have fun before school starts. All our cabins are full." So were the shops in town. Normally the Boot Corral wasn't crowded this early in the day.

The kids looked at all the cowboy hats. "What color do you want, Andy?"

"I don't know."

While the kids tried to talk him into hats like theirs, Ross walked over to him. "My partners and I have seen pictures of your dad. You look a lot like him and should have a distinctive hat that suits your coloring. See anything that appeals to you?"

After a minute of looking he said, "Maybe that one."

"You mean this brown Stetson?" He nodded. Ross picked it up. "This is a Seminole Gus Buffalo felt cowboy hat."

His gray eyes rounded. "Buffalo?"

"Genuine buffalo felt. Nice, huh? I like the sloped pinch-front crown. Want to try it on for size?"

"I guess." Andy put it on his head and looked in the mirror.

Ross lowered the brim a little for him. "With those gray eyes you have that make-my-day kind of look. I'd say you look like a real cowboy." He glanced at Kit. "What do you say, Mom?" His question ended with a cough.

She studied her son with pride. "It transforms you, honey."

The kids walked over. Jenny eyed him. "It makes you look taller and different."

"That's the whole idea," Ross told her.

"Thanks." Andy glanced at his mother. "You should get a hat, too."

"You think?"

Johnny hurried over to her. "Get a black one like mine and Hoppy's."

Her gaze met Ross's before she smiled. "You mean Hopalong Cassidy?"

"Yeah. I love him! So does my dad!"

"What a great idea! I happen to love him, too."

"How come?"

"Because I've read a lot of cowboy books in my life and I have a collection of all the books about Hopalong."

Kit didn't know it yet, but she'd just made Johnny's day and had given Ross a heart attack with that smile. Hopalong had been a fictitious cowboy of the Old West depicted in film whom Carson had loved. It had captured Johnny's imagination.

"Why don't you pick it out for me, Johnny?"

"Okay." He walked back and forth inspecting all of them. "I like this one."

Jenny smiled at her. "Put it on!"

"Go on, Mom."

Ross watched as another transformation occurred. A good-looking woman in a cowboy hat had an allure you couldn't beat. "You and Andy will have to get boots that match your hats."

Once they were fitted, they decided to wear their cowboy boots and hats out of the store and carry their regular shoes in a bag to take home.

After the kids bought more ammo with their allowance money, Ross insisted on paying for everything else and threw in a couple of cap guns and ammo for him and Andy. Johnny had designated him the bad guy, so why not play the part all the way?

"Compliments of the ranch," he told Kit when she protested.

Beneath the rim of her black hat, her eyes went a

darker green, if that was at all possible. "Thank you for everything." He knew what she was really saying. In his grief Andy might think a lot of things were dumb, but he hadn't fought getting himself a hat. Progress, inch by inch.

"We aim to please." He had trouble dragging his gaze away before turning to the kids. "I think we're ready to leave."

"Hooray! Daddy will be waiting for us at the stable." Johnny was the first one out the door to the van. Ross drove them back to Carson's house so he could get his cap gun, then they continued on to the ranch house. Jenny ran inside to get her gun while everyone got out of the van.

"Everyone in the truck for the ride over!"

Andy gave Johnny a nudge into the back before getting in himself. Good for him. Ross put the sack of shoes in back with the kids. Once he'd lifted Jenny inside, he shoved his hat on and they headed for the stable. Their little group was starting to mesh.

Kit watched them through the back window. "They're loading up like they're preparing to go to war, and Andy's doing it right along with them. When we flew in yesterday, I couldn't have imagined it. They all look so cute in their hats and boots. Can you see them?"

He could, but he preferred focusing on her. "Your son looks great in that Stetson."

She flicked him a glance. "You keep saying and doing the right things. You and your partners had to have been inspired to carry out this program."

"We needed to do something to justify our existence."

"I'm glad it's working out so well for you," she said

in a husky voice. “Too bad there’s no magic wand to take away your cough. It isn’t fair.”

“Is anything?”

Kit bowed her head. “No, but you handle it without complaint. You men are role models for the rest of us.”

“Don’t we wish.”

The sound of the childrens’ laughter accompanied them all the way to the stable.

Chapter 4

Kit drank in the beauty of the surroundings, needing to pinch herself as a reminder that this pine-studded paradise was real. They'd only been here since yesterday, yet already she needed to tamp down her euphoria or she might jump out of her skin.

Some of the other dude ranch guests were already saddled and had started out on a trail leading away from the corral. Her host pulled to a stop near the barn and helped Jenny down from the back. The boys got out, and the children disappeared inside with him.

Kit followed. She watched with sheer feminine pleasure as he strode toward the barn on those long powerful legs. In cowboy boots he was probably six foot four of lean, hard muscle. The usual adjectives didn't begin to describe Ross's effect on her senses or her psyche.

Once inside he flashed her a comprehensive glance.

"Kit Wentworth, this is Bert Rawlins, who's been running the stable for years. He takes care of everything around here."

She put out her hand to shake the seasoned cowboy's hand. "It's a pleasure to meet you."

"Welcome to the ranch. Have you done any riding?"

"Some."

"Then let's get you up on Daisy. She's a gentle mare, but she has spirit." He brought out a tan horse from one of the stalls and saddled her.

Ross took over and walked her outside to the corral to help Kit mount. "Are you all right up there?"

If he only knew. She gripped the reins. "I'm fine, thank you."

"I'll go help Carson with the kids. He has a way with them and will make sure your son is perfectly safe on Raindrop."

"I know that." His letter had conveyed an almost spiritual essence that was very touching. If the owner of the ranch and former rodeo champion had half of Ross's heroic qualities, she could believe anything about these remarkable retired marines.

In another minute all three children on ponies rode out of the barn in their riding gear. The ponies were as beautiful and unique as their riders. Kit reached for her cell phone to take a picture, but realized she must have forgotten to bring it with her.

"Mom—" Andy had finally noticed her on Daisy near the corral fencing.

"Hi, honey! Just look at you guys! I bet it's fun to be on a pony."

"It is!" His words came out on a laugh. "Ross was right. Riding one is a lot easier than a horse."

Another small miracle.

After flashing Ross a grateful glance, she lifted her gaze to the rugged, fit cowboy trailing behind them. He looked as if he'd been born in the saddle. Even from the distance separating them, his eyes burned a brilliant blue. He tipped his black hat with a smile. "Mrs. Wentworth!"

She smiled. "It's Kit. I'm so happy to meet you at last, Mr. Lundgren."

"Call me Carson. Your son's a fine horseman," he said on a cough.

Kit liked the owner already. "That's so nice to hear. As his mother, I'm afraid I'm biased."

He grinned. "Of course. For our first time I thought we'd ride to the south pasture. It's not far and the kids will enjoy seeing part of the herd."

"Sounds terrific."

With Carson in the lead, they left the corral taking a different trail from the riders she'd seen earlier. He kept up a running conversation with the kids. Ross dropped back to her side. They followed the others, meandering in and out of the forested area of the ranch. The underbrush was full of small animal life, delighting her. Ross looked over at her. "You've got a mysterious smile on your face. What's that all about?"

"You'll think I'm silly if I tell you."

"Try me."

Ross was so easy to talk to. "When I was a young teen, I think I read every Louis L'Amour book ever published. As you know, that included his novels about Hopalong. Riding through this forest is like reliving some of them. I've got gooseflesh. Look!"

His eyes roved over her arms, taking all of her in at

the same time without being obvious about it. "Carson's going to have fun talking to you. He has a library full of them at his house."

"You're kidding!"

"Nope. I still have a backache from carrying the collection into his new house." She chuckled. "It'll be interesting to hear the two of you compare notes on your favorite books."

"Because we were coming to a ranch, I brought several Louis L'Amours and a Jack London to read to Andy if he'll let me."

"*Call of the Wild* is one I'd love to be reading for the first time."

"I feel the same way. Jack London is another American author I particularly like. Andy has always wanted a dog, but his grandparents haven't allowed one. I think he'll like that book. The trouble is, he struggles a little in reading. Now that we're here, I hope to help him get more interested in books. My grandmother read to me and it got me turned on to it."

"How old were you when your parents were killed?"

"Eight."

"That's a tough age to lose your parents."

"Just a year younger than Andy."

"He's lucky to have you."

She was starting to feel emotional again and turned her head away. How was she ever going to repay these men for what they were doing for her and Andy?

Before long they came to an open meadow dotted with cattle. The sight of the herd combined with lowing sounds communicated a feeling of peace she relished.

Ross sidled next to her. "Another part of the herd is up on the mountain. We'll ride up there another day."

While she took it all in, her son rode over to her. The kids followed him. "See that border collie with the stockman, Mom?"

"Yes. He really keeps that herd in line."

"That's Buster," Johnny explained.

"I wish I had a dog."

"I know you do, honey." He would never know the losing arguments she'd had with the in-laws about letting Andy have a pet. Florence had no need for animals that she didn't deem "useful".

At that point the children got into a discussion about dogs while they watched Buster do his job. Carson gave out snacks and bottled water from his saddlebag. After another half hour had passed, he suggested they head back to the ranch.

While Ross rode next to Kit, Carson closed in on her other side, and the kids rode in front of them. "You're a good rider, too."

"Thanks. It's the horse beneath me. But it's also this ranch and everything that goes with it. You live in cowboy heaven." The men laughed. "I think I died and went there. With the Tetons looming over us, this is Bendigo Shafter country."

Carson's eyes lit up. "Aha! I can see you and I have a lot to talk about."

"Told you." Ross's aside made her smile.

Johnny turned in the saddle looking confused. "Who's that Bingo guy?" That kid had ears in the back of his head.

The men roared with laughter. Kit tried to suppress hers. Johnny was so cute. "He's a person in a book I love."

"Is he a cowboy like my dad?"

"Come to think of it, he *is*." Bigger than life, like these men.

"My mom loves to read," Andy piped up. His comment shocked Kit because he had been so withdrawn and rarely interjected into conversation.

"So do I!" Jenny exclaimed.

"What's one of your favorite books, honey?"

"The Goose Girl."

"Goose Girl!" Johnny started laughing.

"I've read it. That author won an award," Kit said.

"It's really good. Nana helps me with the hard words."

"Andy and I will have to read it."

"You can borrow it. I have it in my room."

"Thank you. And maybe one evening you guys would like me to read a chapter of *Call of the Wild* to you. It's great, too."

"What's it about?" Jenny wanted to know.

"A very special dog."

"Is he a terrier like mine?"

She shook her head at Johnny. "No. He's a cross between a collie and a Saint Bernard with the name Buck, the same as your daddy, Jenny. He gets stolen and sold to a trainer of sled dogs in Alaska. The man is kind, but then he dies. I won't tell you the rest."

"Let's do it tonight in the games room while we eat popcorn and drink sodas." Ross's suggestion excited the children.

Andy's gaze sought hers. "Can we, Mom?"

What? Was this her glum son from a day ago? "We're here to have fun. Right?"

He nodded.

Johnny and Jenny shouted hooray.

Carson made an unexpected announcement. "After we get back we'll go for a swim and have a water fight before dinner."

"You're on," Kit heard Ross say.

No doubt they did this sort of thing all the time. They lived on an exciting plane she'd forgotten existed.

The six of them headed for the barn in the distance. Johnny rode next to Andy. "Tonight's the barbecue. Do you like ribs?"

"What are those?"

"Beef you eat off the bone," Kit explained. "I'm afraid Andy's grandparents don't eat barbecued ribs."

"Oh. They're really nummy."

"And messy," Jenny piped up. Both she and Johnny giggled.

Kit smiled at them. "Even so, my mouth is watering for some already. You're going to love them, Andy."

By the time they returned the horses to the barn, it was decided they'd all get their swimming gear and meet at the pool. Carson and Johnny left the barn in the Jeep.

Ross dropped off Jenny at the ranch house before driving Kit and Andy back to the cabin.

"I'll be by for you in half an hour, unless you need more time."

"We don't need more time, do we, Mom?"

Again her son's question took her by surprise. He actually sounded eager. Johnny and Jenny were a lot of fun. Not for the first time did she wish she'd had another baby so Andy wouldn't be an only child. It was a different world growing up without siblings. Kit ought to know. She would have loved a brother or sister to confide in.

"No. We'll be ready. In fact there's no need for you to come and get us. We'll meet you at the pool."

He tipped his hat. "See you soon, then."

After he drove off they went inside. She spotted her phone lying on the table. With a sense of dread she reached for it and discovered four messages, three from her in-laws and one from Nila Thornton in Texas. Kit checked her watch. It was ten after four.

She would call her friend tonight but decided she'd better phone her in-laws now. There wouldn't be time later. First she freshened up and put on her bikini beneath a change of jeans and a crew neck sweater. While Andy was changing, she phoned them without listening to the messages.

"Hello, Charles? How are you?"

"Never mind me. Why haven't you answered any of our calls?"

"We've been out riding most of the day. Now we're going to take a swim before dinner."

"I want to speak to Andy."

"Just a minute." Her son had just walked in the living room. She handed him the phone.

"Hello?"

It took a long time before Andy could get a word in. "But we just barely got here, Grandfather."

His comment gave Kit a jolt.

This was the first time she'd ever heard her son argue with Charles. She was incredulous. A subtle change had come over Andy. For him not to fall in line with his grandfather's wishes meant he was really enjoying this vacation.

"But Ross has all this fun stuff planned." *Ross.* After another minute Andy handed her the phone. "He wants to talk to you," he whispered. "I don't want to go home yet."

Kit's adrenaline kicked in. "We're not leaving," she whispered back before saying hello to Charles once more. "I'm sorry, but we have to hang up now so we won't be late for dinner. We'll call you tomorrow. Good night."

Once she'd hung up, Andy stared at her in apprehension. "He's mad at me."

"No, honey, I'm the one he's upset with." Thank heaven. She put an arm around his shoulders. "Let's not let it spoil our trip. You know what he's like, but he'll get over it." *If only that were true.* "Shall we go?" Remembering the plans for after dinner, she wrapped up the Jack London book in some towels and they left.

Ross ran into Buck's wife, Alex, in the downstairs hallway. She smiled when she saw him. "Thanks for looking after Jenny. She had a wonderful time today. Apparently our newest young guest is a good rider."

"He's a good swimmer, too."

"So I hear." She handed him a folded note. "I took a message for you at the front desk. See you at the pool in a few minutes." Alex covered the counter when they needed help.

"Thanks." He took the stairs two at a time to his room. After a quick shower he'd change into his swimsuit. But first he looked at the message. The name Charles Wentworth caused him to pause in his tracks.

Why would he be calling the ranch? Surely he had his daughter-in-law's cell phone number. He pressed the digits and waited.

"This is Charles Wentworth."

Ross blinked. The man sounded like Ross's father

who, without preamble, assumed everyone knew who he was and expected to be catered to.

"Ross Livingston here." He could be just as peremptory. He'd learned from a master who'd happened to be his own father. "I understand you wished to talk to one of us in charge at the dude ranch. How can I help you?"

"You're the one I want to speak to about Andrew."

"He's a fine boy."

"Andrew's the reason I'm calling. Can you guarantee his safety for the rest of the time he's with you?"

Ross frowned. Could anyone? It was an odd question. What about *Kit's* safety? "We're doing our best. Being retired marines, we've never had a problem protecting our guests."

"I'm afraid that's not going to be good enough in an environment like yours. After our trip to Norway, I shouldn't have allowed Kathryn to take him."

Allowed? He held the phone tighter. "Why not?"

"Let's just say she shouldn't be there on her own and needs watching. I told her I want my grandson home by midweek and I expect you to make it happen. Do I make myself clear? Otherwise I'll hold you personally responsible."

For what?

Ross could feel hackles rising on the back of his neck. Nothing caused his blood to boil faster than a bullying tactic. Ross's father had tried that once too often until he'd gone into the military out of his parent's reach. As far as he was concerned, Charles Wentworth was of the same ilk as his father and could go to hell.

"Surely that will be up to your daughter-in-law to decide."

"Do you know who you're talking to?"

Ross had had enough. "You'll have to take this up with her. Now I'm afraid duty calls. Goodbye."

He was full of adrenaline after getting off the phone. *She needs watching.* What in the hell did that mean? Was there something wrong with her? With Andy? The man had sounded positively feudal. As he thought about their conversation, Ross grimaced, not liking some of the thoughts he was having.

By the time he got ready and went down to the pool, his good mood had been altered. He was riddled with questions that needed answering, but that couldn't happen until tonight after Andy went to bed.

The patio was filled with guests taking advantage of the late afternoon sun. The weather was perfect for the barbecue they held every weekend for all their dude ranch guests. He didn't see Andy or Kit. Maybe they hadn't arrived yet or were still in the cabana.

A few guests were swimming in the pool. His gaze traveled the length of it until he spotted a dark-haired woman with a heavenly body treading water in the deep end. The top half of the light blue bikini she filled out was barely visible. *Kit.*

Two males, probably in their twenties, had closed in to talk to her. Whether they were there on their own or with girlfriends, Ross had no idea. All he could see was that they were enjoying themselves and eating her alive with their eyes.

No sin had been committed, but an unfamiliar sensation attacked Ross in the gut. Driven by another gush of pure adrenaline, he dropped his towel on a chair and dived deep to reach those beautiful legs keeping her afloat.

"Ross!" She half laughed in surprise when he rose

out of the water next to her. In that first instant, he saw pleasure flash in those deep green orbs. Enough to satisfy him she wasn't indifferent to him.

"How are you this evening, Mrs. Wentworth?" He'd stressed the "Mrs." so the two guys surrounding her would get the point. That brought another laugh from her.

"I'm fine, Mr. Livingston." She gave as good as she got. He liked that.

"Where's Andy?"

"He went with Buck to find Jenny."

Good ol' Buck. "So, who are your friends?" he asked without taking his eyes off her. Wet and *sans* makeup, she was a lovely sight.

"I don't know who you mean." But a slow smile spread over the classic features of her face. "I guess you frightened off some of your guests when you surfaced like a submarine in enemy waters."

"They shouldn't have let their guard down." His pulse had taken off with dizzying speed. "Did I ruin anything important?"

"Well…if they had any plans, you successfully sabotaged them. Something you learned in the marines?"

It was his turn to laugh, which provoked a cough.

Her smile was replaced by a look of anxiety. "Does the water make your condition worse?"

"That depends on who's in it with me."

She was quiet for a minute before she said, "Aren't you ever serious?"

Where she was concerned, he was becoming serious way too fast. Now this phone call from her father-in-law was raising questions that wouldn't leave him alone.

"How about a race to the other end of the pool?"

Fire lit her eyes. "You're on!"

The battle had begun. They had to swim out and around a couple of guests to reach the shallow end. She was an excellent swimmer, a skill no doubt developed by spending many hours at the Wentworth mansion swimming pool. He had to pour it on to save face and came up coughing.

"Way to go, Mom! You beat Ross!" Andy had reappeared with Jenny.

"That's because he let me." Out of breath, she hugged the edge of the pool. Kit's gaze switched to her son. "You know what? The sun has gone down, and they're setting up for the barbecue. Let's change back into our clothes."

"Can't Andy swim with us a little longer?" Jenny stared at her expectantly.

"Sure. Do you want to, honey?"

He nodded. "Let's do dives off the board."

Johnny jumped up and down. "We'll play follow the leader."

The children took off for the deep end, leaving Ross alone with Kit. Everyone else was getting out of the pool. "You're a great swimmer."

A tantalizing half smile broke the corner of her mouth. "You want to know what's really great? The way you handled Andy today *without* handling him, if you know what I mean."

He cocked his head. "I'm afraid he's like me. I don't respond well to authority." The phone call with Charles Wentworth was a case in point.

"That's because you're your own person with the strength of your convictions. I'd like to see my son grow up like that. Now if you'll excuse me, I'm going to get changed."

* * *

The air had grown a little cooler, but that wasn't the reason Kit had the shivers as she showered and washed her hair. What she'd just said to Ross had sounded too personal, but she couldn't seem to control her thoughts or feelings. There'd been times in the pool when the way Ross had looked at her had sent a weakness through her limbs.

During their swim their bodies had brushed against each other. Every time there'd been contact, it had felt as if she'd been branded with liquid fire. If she wasn't mistaken, she noticed Andy starting to form an attachment to him. But Kit had a different problem because attached wasn't a strong enough word for what was happening inside of her whenever he came near.

She wanted him to kiss her, hold her.

You want him, Kit.

It was true, and there was no point in denying it. But she was mortified. These retired marines had honored Winn's memory by inviting her and Andy to the ranch for a week of fun-filled activities. Yet here she was, behaving as anything but her husband's grieving widow.

When she'd first met Winn, there'd been a strong physical attraction, but within a few years of their marriage it had died. To experience desire this powerful after years of feeling dead inside was so painful in its intensity, she was alarmed by it.

Over the years of charity work she'd done, there'd been a lot of attractive men she'd worked with. She could say the same for many of the waiters and staff at the various country clubs the family frequented. Several of the golf pros who'd given her lessons were exceptionally charming. The captain and crew of

Charles's favorite yacht were big flirts and a subject of conversation with the women of her in-laws' social circle invited on board.

Most of the men coming and going or passing through Kit's life under those circumstances were open to a flirtation and gave off signals. If she'd ever been inclined and hadn't clung to a strong set of morals, she could have had affairs with any number of them. That included some of Charles's own male friends who stayed over on weekends and had grown bored with their own wives.

Yet it was the tall, striking Wyoming cowboy communicating his seeming disdain of her the minute she'd met him in the terminal yesterday who'd set off hormones she didn't know she had. For an aloof stranger to have that kind of power over her—to care what he thought—meant something monumental had happened to her.

She had to do something to fight these feelings for him, starting right now! He was the kind of real man a woman dreamed about—a man so far out of her reach it was ludicrous.

"Mom?"

She wheeled around with her hair brush in hand. "Hey—had enough swimming?"

"Yeah. Ross sent me in here to get dressed. He wants us to hurry before all the food is gone."

"They won't run out of food. He was just teasing."

"I know."

Her pulse raced at the thought of being with Ross. Unfortunately she couldn't stop her nervous system from reacting over anything to do with him. In two days of being on the Teton Valley Ranch with him, she'd run a gamut of emotions that now included her own brand of hero worship coupled with an ache for him that was building inside her.

"Why don't you take a quick shower while I finish doing my hair?"

"Okay."

In a minute they were ready. She left the cabana with her book under her arm. Lots of suntanned, happy guests seated around enjoying the candlelit barbecue nodded at them as they made their way to the banquet table.

Kit noticed Ross over at one of the larger tables with his partners and their families. Her heart skipped a beat as he waved to her. She smiled back before remembering she wasn't going to pay him any undue attention.

The smorgasbord featured everything from barbecued ribs to steaks and all the trimmings. Kit found she was hungry. "Let's take a little of everything, Andy. What you don't want, I'll eat."

With their plates full, they walked over to Ross's table. He introduced Kit to Alex, Buck's wife, a lovely chestnut-blonde woman, then he helped her and Andy to be seated. When she felt his hand graze her shoulders, it almost melted her on the spot.

The fun dinner conversation helped her to relax. Out of the corner of her eye she noticed that her son seemed to be enjoying himself. During the delicious dessert of fresh huckleberry pie, Tracy brought up the plans for the next day.

"Alex and I thought it would be fun to take the children into Jackson for lunch and a movie. After tomorrow there won't be any more matinees. We thought we'd make an afternoon of it to celebrate the end of summer before they have to go back to school. If you and Andy would like to come, you'd be welcome."

She waited for her son to whisper he didn't want to go, but he didn't say anything.

"Thank you, Tracy. Will it be all right if we tell you in the morning?"

"Of course. We'll be leaving around eleven-thirty in the van."

"Sounds fun," Carson said, kissing Tracy's cheek. Kit could tell they had that rare kind of love. Her glance fell on Buck who'd brought his wife another helping of food. The tender way they looked at each other was truly something to witness. As for Ross and everything he was doing for Kit and Andy, there were no words.

She thought back to her marriage with Winn. It had failed before it ever got off the ground, but she shouldn't be comparing him to these men. Her husband had been raised under such difficult emotional circumstances it was amazing he'd survived to adulthood.

Now had come the time for her and Andy to make their own escape to survive. That's what she wanted for her son whom she hadn't seen this animated since he was a much younger boy. Her gaze lit on Ross who was making it all possible. Right now he was using his phone so Andy could look at the list of movies playing in Jackson.

There was no finer man anywhere. It would take an exceptional woman to win his heart. Whoever she was, she'd be the luckiest person on earth. Kit knew deep down in her soul she could never be that woman. She was Winn's widow, and she already had a growing child.

Apparently the rare woman he needed to meet

hadn't come along yet. He deserved one who'd never been married. Ross could start his own family with her. Someone who didn't have all Kit's baggage. Being Charles Wentworth's daughter-in-law presented problems no man would want to deal with. She lowered her eyes and drank the rest of her coffee.

Carson was the first one to get up. "It's time for a bedtime story from Kit. Let's go to the games room."

Kit watched Andy walk with the kids instead of holding back and telling her he didn't want to do anything. The change in him was too remarkable to be an aberration. She knew the reason why....

While the others took their places on the two leather couches, Andy sat on the love seat next to Ross. That left Kit, who sat in the big leather chair. She opened the book and laid the groundwork for the story about the dog named Buck. Kit had been afraid she'd lose the kids' attention, but they sat there intrigued by the animal's thoughts of his wonderful life with Judge Miller.

Halfway through the first chapter she shut the book, knowing it was better to quit while the children were still enjoying the story. They protested of course.

Jenny was totally caught up in it. "Something bad is going to happen to him, huh, Kit?"

"We'll have to keep reading to find out."

"Will you read to us tomorrow night?" Johnny asked.

"I'd love to. I'd rather read than just about anything."

Everyone got up. Carson thanked her. "That'll give us something to look forward to tomorrow night. Say good-night, kids."

Ross nodded to her. "If you're ready, let's go."

She turned to Andy. "Would you run to the cabana

and get our suits and towels, please? We'll meet you at the truck."

"Sure." He took off.

As Ross walked her outside and helped her into the cab, his hand gripped her upper arm. "Kit? We need to talk." All of a sudden his voice sounded an octave lower than usual.

She turned her head to look at him. Obviously something was wrong. How could anything be wrong on this beautiful night? "What is it?"

Long black lashes half shuttered the enigmatic look coming from his dark eyes. "After the phone call I received earlier from the timber king Charles Cavanaugh Wentworth, maybe it's just as well his grandson isn't around to hear this."

Oh, no.

The long reaching arm of her father-in-law didn't miss anything or anyone.

Chapter 5

Ross's news caused her to lose color. That as much as anything verified his suspicion that something ugly was going on.

Beneath her fetching brunette hair, still damp from a shampooing, he found himself staring into a pair of the same sea-green eyes that had beguiled him from the beginning, but right now they looked haunted.

"You know about him."

"I know his ancestor amassed a fortune in timber in the mid-1800s and his legacy grew from there."

"What did he say to you?" she asked quietly.

Though he'd managed to frighten the hell out of her, he had to admire her for maintaining her dignity. *Nothing but the truth, Livingston.* This was no time for games. "He wanted to make sure nothing happens to his grandson and ordered me to make sure you fly home midweek, or else…."

"Oh, no—" He felt the shudder that passed through her body. "W-What did you tell him?" she stammered.

"I told him we know how to keep our guests safe. Before I rang off, I explained that the decision for you to leave was up to you."

Her dark head reared back. *"You hung up on him?"*

The fear in her voice hit him in the gut. "In a manner of speaking."

A small cry escaped her lips before she turned away. Slipping into marine mode, Ross grasped her other arm, forcing her to look at him.

She presented a pinched white face to him. "Please, let me go before someone sees us."

"Not yet," he ground out. "I understand you're in some kind of trouble."

Panic filled her eyes. "I wish to heaven he hadn't called the ranch, but now that he has, this mustn't become your problem. I couldn't bear it."

"I'm afraid it already is." After witnessing her shock, he saw all the signs of someone planning to cut and run. He'd done it himself years ago and could relate.

"Please, don't say that." Her voice shook.

"I *have* to. After Andy's in bed asleep and we're alone, you're going to tell me what's going on. For the moment you need to present a calm front so he doesn't get alarmed. When we get back to the cabin, ask me to come in and watch TV with you. Hopefully he'll get tired and go to bed."

Another shudder wracked her lovely body before the fight went out of her, and she nodded. Reasonably confident she could see the wisdom in his plan, he let go of her arm and walked around to get in the truck. Andy was back in a flash and they were off.

When they drew up to the cabin, it was her son who asked him if he'd come in and watch the movie *Shrek* with them.

"I haven't seen that one."

"There's a donkey in it that's pretty funny."

"A donkey? That I have to see."

Andy preceded them into the cabin carrying the plastic bag with their swimsuits.

"Why don't you get ready for bed first, honey?"

"Okay."

For the next hour and a half Ross watched the entertaining film and laughed in the same parts with Andy. Kit pretended to be involved, but Ross knew she wasn't seeing anything. When it was over, she got up and turned it off.

"Time for bed, honey."

"I know."

Ross stood. "See you in the morning at breakfast, Andy. If you want to go fishing, Buck will take you."

He nodded. "Thanks."

"Good night."

Kit gave her son a hug. After he disappeared into the other part of the cabin and shut the door, she walked back and sat down on the couch with a wooden expression.

With his voice lowered, he said, "Before I ask you anything else, I need to know something. Has your father-in-law ever laid a hand on you or Andy?"

She smoothed the hair out of her eyes. "No," she answered in a quiet tone. "He's not like that and doesn't need to use physical force. He can merely guilt you into doing what he wants."

Those were the same tactics Ross's father had used on him. Though it shouldn't mean anything of a personal nature to him, he felt a sense of relief hearing it. "I may not know all the facts, but it's clear you're in a tense situation."

She got up from the couch again, hugging her arms to her waist. "We are, and I'm sorry you're involved in any way after inviting us here out of the kindness of your hearts. It isn't fair to you."

"Why don't you let me be the judge of that."

"When your letter came, I was deeply touched to think you soldiers would do such a wonderful thing for Andy. It meant so much to me, even if he doesn't truly understand the great honor you've shown us. I wanted to come more than you know and prayed my father-in-law wouldn't try to stand in the way."

Ross shook his head. "He's *that* controlling?"

"He's always been controlling, but since Winn's death he's been much worse. They have two married daughters, but Winn was their only son. They've been so grief-stricken, they've started to think of Andy as their own son.

"When I received your letter, I told him we were going to accept. He told me I couldn't because they had that cruise in Norway planned. It was just an excuse, of course. He didn't want us going anywhere. That's why I called the ranch and asked if Andy and I could come for the first week of September. Mr. Lundgren was wonderful about it.

"While we were in Norway, my in-laws tried to get me to cancel my plans. They worked on Andy, knowing he didn't want to come to Wyoming. It's my opinion that for him to think of being around some retired marines who'd survived the war was simply too painful for him. At that juncture I took matters into my own hands.

"After we returned to the hotel in Oslo, I left a note for them at the front desk telling them Andy and I had flown back to the States and would be in Wyoming for the next week. Because it was an earlier flight, that's why we arrived in Jackson at three instead of six-thirty.

"Andy was unhappy about it, but I gave him no choice. Since our arrival, all that has changed and he's becoming a different child."

Ross rubbed his lower lip with his thumb. "I'm glad to hear it. Go on."

"What do you mean?"

"What else aren't you telling me?" he questioned. "You've already let me know that Mr. Wentworth isn't physically violent with you, so what's really happening here?"

"I'd rather not get into it. I'm ashamed enough as it is. Already I'm sure you're sorry that you ever invited us."

Ross grimaced. "Forget about that. Since genes don't lie, you two are definitely mother and son. Now I need the answer to another question." He hated asking it, but he had to know before he made another move.

"Do your in-laws have custody of Andy? Remember that lying to me at this stage won't do you any good. Is that why he was warning me about you?"

"Warning? In what way?"

"He said you needed watching and he shouldn't have let you come."

She drew in her breath, as if she was holding herself in check. “Charles will stoop to any level to achieve want he wants.”

“What *does* he want?” Ross prodded her.

“He wants Andy to be the son he lost!”

“There’s more to it than that for him to phone the ranch asking for one of us in charge.”

A tortured moan escaped her. “No—I mean there *is* a reason, but it’s not what you think.”

“Then explain it to me.”

“I—I don’t know where to start,” she stammered. “It’s complicated.”

“Nightmares usually are. I’ve got all night, and you’re my responsibility while you’re here.”

“I don’t want you mixed up in this.”

His temper flared. “I already am. Does he have a case against you for being an unfit mother?”

He heard her sharp intake of breath. “In his mind he does.”

Ross felt like he’d been kicked in the gut. “On what grounds?”

“Grounds?” she cried out. “Winn married me without his parents’ approval. I was beneath their social class and not the woman they’d picked out for him. Because of guilt, he insisted we live with them at the mansion to make up for it.

“They wanted the marriage annulled, but by then I was pregnant. I thought our living situation was temporary, but it turned out to be permanent. I was a nineteen-year-old without an education from Wellesley or Vassar. I didn’t have the right stuff. I didn’t come from a family with money or connections.”

Ross was listening. In the lofty circles of the Wentworths and the Livingstons, the right background was of vital importance. He closed his eyes tightly for a moment. He got it. Because of his own highly privileged background, Ross got it with a vengeance.

"*That* made me an unfit mother for a Wentworth, but they adored Andy and took over the parenting, especially when Winn was away. Since his death, everything has been so much worse. I told them I planned to get Andy and me a place of our own because we need to be independent.

"The thought of it has upset them so much, they've refused to discuss it. He has warned me that if I leave the mansion, he'll cut me off without a penny. That wouldn't bother me, but I have to think of Andy's future. I argued with Charles and Florence about it before the trip to Norway. He called tonight because he's afraid I might actually move out."

"And are you?"

"Yes. I have it all planned. But I haven't told Andy."

Ross shook his head. "You mean he knows nothing?"

"Not yet. Since Carson's letter inviting us here, I've been making preparations. But nothing can happen until I have a talk with my son. I believe I know how he feels deep inside, but I've got to find the right time to get the truth out of him."

"If he's amenable, what's your plan?"

"When we leave the ranch, we'll fly to Galveston, Texas."

Galveston? Ross's mind reeled. That's where he had his own beach pad, but he hadn't used it in years. He paid a company to keep it cleaned and allowed needy college students to live there. It was an hour and a half away from his family's home in Houston.

"Why Galveston?"

"My hairdresser's daughter Nila lives there and has her own shop. When she visits her mother, who married an easterner, she comes to work with her and gives me a special manicure and pedicure. Over the years we've become good friends. She has a daughter Andy's age and they're friends, too.

"She's put me in touch with the owner of a small bookstore who's retiring and isn't going through a Realtor. I've always wanted to own one. Books are my fetish. I'm hoping to find an investor to go into business with me. I have some savings to keep Andy and me going for a while."

A while? Good grief!

"I've done my research and have written up a business plan that includes running a coffee bar with it."

"That's very enterprising of you. A coffee bar is an excellent idea." But she would need an investor with a hefty sum, or she'd never get the loan in the first place. A lot of small bookstores were going out of business.

"There's a suitable apartment complex nearby that Nila has checked out for me. I'm planning to fly there and look everything over. There's only one problem. It *is* just an idea, and if it doesn't work out, we'll do something else. But the truth is, Andy and I can't live with his grandparents any longer. They're swallowing us alive. I don't intend to cut them out of our lives. I'd never do that, but we need our own space now."

"And Andy feels the same?"

"Maybe I'm wrong, but I believe he wants his freedom as much as I do. Though I can't imagine it, if Andy can't bring himself to leave his grandparents, even if it means he has to go away to that school, then we'll fly back to Maine when our trip is over."

Ross was so amazed by what he was hearing, he could hardly think. "Of course. It's not my place to offer an opinion."

"You have every right after the way my father-in-law spoke to you."

Kit was embarrassed because she was about to lose it in front of this incredible man. "Since Winn's death ten months ago, they've exerted total power over my son. With systematic precision, they've been taking him away from me piece by piece."

"How could they do that?"

"Because my husband and I married in a private ceremony in Rhode Island without his family while he was on leave from the military. He'd said it was the way he wanted it. My grandmother had died with only $3,000 in the bank. I was alone, too naive for words. Once we'd gone on a short honeymoon, he took me to his parents' mansion to meet them.

"They would have gotten a judge to annul our marriage, but by then I was pregnant. Since I was carrying a Wentworth, that changed everything. Tragically, our marriage disintegrated. We ended up living with them against my wishes. I've never been able to leave since."

Ross studied her with enigmatic dark eyes, not saying anything.

"They've run my life and Andy's day after day for years, turning him into a Wentworth robot. With Winn gone so much on deployments, the grandparents took over raising him as if I scarcely existed. I wanted to leave years ago, but I was married with no means of support. Winn forbade me to get a job. Andy has no idea my love for his father died early in our marriage."

Good grief. "I'm sorry to hear that."

"It was a very unhappy time. They never forgave Winn for marrying me. That's why he insisted we live with them as his way of making it up to them. As for me, *I'm* the one they despised for luring their son into a marriage they found intolerable.

"The more Winn bent over backwards to make amends and placate his parents, the more the gulf between the two of us widened. I'm sure he had other women, but I can't prove it. And though I grieve over his death and grieve for Andy's sake, that world nearly destroyed me. It'll destroy Andy if I don't get us away from them."

He rubbed the back of his neck in a seemingly unconscious gesture. "What about Winn's siblings? Is Andy close to them?"

"Not really. Andy's male cousins are older and have little to do with him. Unfortunately, Charles and Florence dote on him to the point that I feel there's something intrinsically wrong with them. They're sick to cling to Andy as they do.

"I love my son so much, I can't say our marriage was a mistake, but divorce was out of the question because Winn would have gone to court to win custody of Andy if I'd left him, and he would have won. I couldn't let that happen."

"Do you have no one you can turn to closer to home?"

"Except for Nila and her husband, there's no one else I trust. You heard about that school they're sending him to. I told Winn how I felt about him being sent away from home, but he couldn't stand up to Charles about that or moving us out of the mansion. Only one man in a million could do it. Winn didn't have what it took.

"But what no one counted on was his getting killed in Afghanistan. His parents expect me to go on being his faithful, grieving widow who devotes her life to charitable causes. But it's no life, not for me or Andy." There was a finality in her tone. Ross believed her.

He shifted his weight. "My reply to your father-in-law didn't reassure him. What's to stop him from flying here to check up on you?"

"Absolutely nothing." She ground her teeth together. "So that means I'm going to have that talk with Andy when he wakes up in the morning. He's the key to everything. If he wants to continue living with his grandparents, then I'll phone them and tell them we'll be flying back to Maine after our trip.

"But if my son wants a new life with me, then we'll fly to Texas at the end of the week. After we get there, I'll let my in-laws know where we are. In either case, this cabin will be available for more of your regular guests and you won't have to be involved." Her voice held a tremor.

Ross sucked in his breath. "But I *am* involved!"

"I'm so sorry he threatened you. It isn't fair, not when you've done everything for us. Be assured I'll take care of the situation from here on out." She walked to the door and opened it.

His legs felt like lead as he moved toward her. "Are you going to be all right tonight?"

"Of course. I'm glad you told me about the phone call. Talking to you has helped more than you know.

Thank you for putting up with me and Andy. You've been a saint. God bless you and your partners for your goodness. Good night, Ross."

"Good luck with Andy."

Once back in the truck, he took off for the ranch house. After hearing about her plans, he felt so chewed up inside, he didn't know where to go with all his emotions.

Carson was just pulling away from the parking area in the Jeep, but when he saw Ross he braked and waited for him to catch up. "Hey, buddy—you look like a bull stomped on you."

"You could say that. I went a few rounds on the phone with Charles Wentworth earlier this evening."

Carson squinted at him. "What's going on?"

"You don't want to know."

"The hell I don't."

"Let's just say Kit's a widow with a big problem. I'll know a lot more tomorrow, then I'll fill you in." He coughed. "I'm not fit company right now. Go home to your family."

"You're sure? If you need to talk, Tracy would understand."

"I know she would. You're a lucky man. See you in the morning."

After her phone call to Nila, who was behind Kit a hundred percent and waiting for her and Andy to come to Texas, she went to bed. But she slept poorly, and her eyes popped open at six-thirty, anxious for Andy to wake up.

She lay on her side in the twin bed and watched him while he slept. He moved around a lot. One of his pillows had fallen on the floor, and part of his leg poked out from beneath the quilt.

His cowboy boots and socks lay on the carpet at the side of his bed where he'd taken everything off before collapsing under the covers. Yesterday had been a big day. Her dear, dear son. This morning would be their moment of truth.

She'd been rehearsing what she would say to him, but her stomach was in knots and nothing sounded right. Kit was about to ask him if he would like to leave the only home he'd ever known and trust her to make a new one for them. It terrified her to think what his answer might be.

Was it asking too much? Had she waited too long? Could he handle moving away from his grandparents and the home where his father had lived? Last night Ross had wished her good luck before he'd driven away. His comment had caused her a lot of tossing and turning because he knew she would need it.

Nila had encouraged her to open up her heart to Andy and hold nothing back, then wait for him to respond. Kit's grandmother would have given her the same counsel.

She heard his sheets rustle. Then, finally, she heard, "Mom?"

This was it. "Good morning, honey."

He raised himself up on one elbow. "How come you're still in bed?"

She'd always been an early riser, so she could understand his surprise. "I was waiting for you to wake up so we could talk."

Andy sat all the way up, leaning back against the headboard. "What about?" As usual, he sounded worried.

Kit's heart beat so fast it clogged up her throat. "About us."

"What do you mean?"

It was difficult to swallow. "Every day of your life I've told you how much I love you, that you're the most precious thing to me in my life. Now I'm going to ask you a question, and it's vitally important you tell me the truth. Do you love me? I mean *really* love me?" She couldn't remember the last time she'd heard him say it to her.

There was a long drawn-out silence. She had to wait ages before he said yes, without looking at her. He'd been closed up for so long, she feared he'd lost the capacity to share. Thank heaven for that admission, even if he couldn't say the words.

"I'm so happy you said that. Now I need you to be honest with me about another question I have. You know how I feel about you going away to boarding school. It will mean you and I won't get to see each other more than twice a month, if that. But the point is, how do *you* really feel about it?"

His gaze shot to hers. Those gray eyes went dark with emotion.

"Forget that your father wanted you to go there, honey. Forget that your grandmother and grandfather are insisting you go. Forget that your cousins Thomas and Jeremy went there. I want to know what *you* want. Whatever you tell me, I promise it will be our secret."

At first she wondered if he'd even heard her because he sat there so still. Then slowly he got out of bed in his camouflage pajamas and crept over to the window. She watched him looking at the Grand Teton for a long time before his shoulders started to shake.

"I…don't want to leave you, but Grandfather says I *have* to."

Thank heaven!

"No, you don't!"

Andy spun around with a shocked look on his tear-stained face. "I don't?"

"Come here, darling."

He ran over to her. She pulled him into her arms, and they lay on the bed, hugging so hard it almost knocked the breath out of her. Kit rocked him for a long time while he sobbed. Her heart broke to think he'd been carrying around this pain for so long.

"H-how can you stop him from making me go?" His voice faltered.

Her son understood too much. His question answered a lot of hers and gave her the backbone she needed. "Because you're *my* son. Now that your dad is gone, I don't want to live with your grandparents any longer. I love them, but I want us to find a place of our own and make our own decisions from now on."

He sat up. "Where?"

Her heart thumped so hard, she was certain he could hear it. "A place where I believe we could be happy."

For a minute there'd been a light in those wet eyes, but it suddenly dimmed. "He won't let us go." Just then he sounded so adult. Five little words. They told her Andy understood the kind of power his controlling grandfather wielded, and that he hated it. That was all she needed to know.

"He *has* to, honey. You're not his son. Your father was wrong to make us live with your grandparents. It was never what I wanted. We should have had our own home, but he insisted."

"Why?"

Oh, Andy. What to tell you without ruining your image of him.

"I think because he was the only son, he felt he had to stay with them. It's a shame they didn't encourage him to get out on his own the way your aunts did with their husbands. Instead your grandparents clung to him. But now that he's gone, you and I need to have our own home and live the way we want to live. Don't you agree?"

"Yes," he said in a solemn tone. "I love them, but I don't want to live with them all the time."

That was all she needed to know. "Then we won't. I've been planning this for a long time."

"You have?"

She nodded. "After you were born, I told your father I wanted to move out of the mansion and get our own place, but he said he couldn't do that to your grandparents."

"He was afraid of Grandfather."

Kit moaned inwardly. "Yes, honey. Charles can be a scary person when he wants his own way. But *you're* not afraid of him. I heard you on the phone with him yesterday. You told him you didn't want to leave the ranch yet. It's not his decision to make for us.

"Your grandparents have been wonderful. They've done everything for us, but now it's time for me to take care of us. I've saved some money."

"Really?" He sounded so happy, she couldn't believe it.

"It's not a lot, but it's enough to give us a start while I find us a place to live and get a job."

"What kind?"

"You know how much I love books. I'm hoping to buy a small bookstore and run it. There's one for sale in Galveston, Texas, where Nila lives. She has become a very good friend to me and I know how much you like her and Kim. There's an apartment close by where we could live."

"You mean we'll move to Texas?" He didn't sound thrilled about that.

"When we leave the ranch, we'll fly down and take a look. I already have our airline tickets. If we don't like the situation, then we'll put our heads together and decide where we want to go and what we want to do. If we like it, then your grandparents can come and visit when they want. I want you to be happy with this decision, otherwise we won't do it."

"But we won't go back to Grandfather's—"

"No, darling. That's over."

"Promise?"

That said it all. "Promise. But there's just one problem."

"What?"

"Your grandfather phoned Ross yesterday."

"He did?"

"Yes. He said he didn't like us being gone for so long and told Ross to send us home right away."

Andy gave a carefree laugh. "Ross wouldn't do that. He's not afraid of anything."

Nope. Andy had already sized up their host and knew exactly how amazing he was. "No. He told Charles that the decision to stay or leave was entirely up to you and me."

"I bet Grandfather's mad at him."

"I'm sure he is. It means your grandfather might fly here on his private jet before our vacation is over."

"Ross will protect us. He's nice, Mom."

"I agree." Andy had never applied that adjective to anyone he knew, especially not his stuffed shirt uncles who were too caught up in their own self-importance by marrying into the Wentworth family to show much attention to Andy. They jumped when Charles said jump. Poor Andy. After living with his iron-willed grandfather, Andy could see Ross was like the difference between night and day. The three of them had been together 24/7 since they'd arrived here.

"He's so cool. I wish he weren't sick."

"It's not the kind of sick that has put him and his partners to bed. It's more of a condition, honey. But you have to admire them for not letting it get in the way of living their lives. Now, let's get dressed and hurry to the ranch house for breakfast. I'm starving."

"Me, too." He jumped off the bed. "I'm glad Ross will be here if Grandfather comes."

"Honey—" she said in exasperation, "Ross has nothing to do with this. I'll deal with your grandfather and tell him you and I have other plans. He can't make us do anything. I'll tell him that when we're settled, we'll let them know. Hopefully when he and Florence see that we mean it, they'll understand and we'll all get along better."

"Does Ross know we're going to Texas?"

Ross again. She remembered Andy's reaction to Carson's letter they'd received in July. *They're a bunch of lame marines. I hate them.* There'd been an enormous change in her son's attitude since then.

"Yes. Just remember this is our business. Please, don't talk about this to him or the other kids."

"I won't. But what if Grandfather finds out we went to Texas?"

"He won't know where to look for us."

"How come?" he asked.

"Close your eyes. When I'm ready, I'll tell you to open them. Go on and do it for me. It's a surprise. Please?"

"Okay."

When they were closed, she ran in the bedroom and pulled a wig and a hat out of her suitcase. After she returned, she put the wig on.

"You can open them now."

He did her bidding, then blinked several times in sheer disbelief. Finally came the outburst. *"Mom—"*

"How do you like me with blond hair?" While he stood there speechless, she plopped the green sojourner hat with the wide rim on his head. "That covers your hair. People may think you're a cancer patient. Run in the bathroom and take a look."

He acted stunned before darting off. Andy used to like games when he was too young to understand what was going on. "Hey—it's cool!" he shouted from the other room. She hardly recognized such enthusiasm.

"I think so, too. When we leave here, we'll be different. See, honey? No one's going to be looking for a mother with blond hair and her son wearing that kind of hat. We'll wear these disguises until we get to our destination." He looked at her, and she looked at him before they burst into laughter and hugged like two crazy people.

On her way out of the room for a shower, her cell

phone rang. Andy was closest to the bedside table and reached for it. "It's Grandfather."

"I'll get it." With everything out in the open, Kit was no longer afraid to talk in front of Andy. She walked back and took it from him. "Good morning, Charles."

"I'm glad you answered. I'm calling early because there's a flight leaving Jackson at eleven o'clock this morning for Denver. Your connecting flight will have you home by evening. I've already made the changes to your tickets."

Kit sank down on the side of her bed. "Is Florence on the line?"

"Why?"

"Because I want both of you to hear what I have to say at the same time."

"Just a minute."

She waited until her mother-in-law got on the phone. "What do you want to talk to us about?"

"I have something to tell you. If you decide to hang up on me before I'm finished, then I'm sorry for that. When Winn brought me into your home ten years ago, I thought we would only be staying with you for a few weeks until we got our own home. But that never happened. Now that he's gone, I need to make a home for Andy and me."

Her son stood by her, watching and listening.

"You have a home!" Florence cried.

"Yes, but it's not mine, as I've reminded you many times. Andy and I love you. We're grateful for everything you've done for us, but it's time for me to build a new life with my son."

"I've heard enough from you!" Charles blurted before she heard a click. That was no surprise.

"Florence, are you still there?"

"Yes," came the brittle response.

"Andy and I are going to finish out this week of our vacation. When we leave the ranch, we won't be coming home."

A heart-wrenching cry escaped. This was as hard as anything she'd ever done.

"As soon as I've found us a place to live and get a job, I'll phone you and let you know. Once we're settled, I'll send for our things. There's no reason why we can't visit each other often for the rest of our lives. Andy loves you and the family, but we need our space. Can you understand that?"

"No, I can't. We've given you everything!"

"I know and I'm indebted to you, but now it's time for me to give my son everything the way you did for Winn."

"But you have no skills, no resources. Nothing. How can you possibly care for our grandson?"

Well it wasn't for want of trying. After all these years, that comment still hurt.

"I love my son and have the brains and the will to take care of him. The rest will come. I'm promising you now that we'll talk often and see each other whenever we can. Is there anything else you want to say to me before we hang up?"

Her question got lost because she heard Charles in the background. Florence was sobbing to him.

Kit clicked off and felt Andy's arms go around her. His love was all that was sustaining her right now.

Chapter 6

Ross had slept poorly and awakened at five, too restless to lie in bed. It was almost impossible to believe how much life had changed since Saturday. Thirty odd hours had passed, and already he was caught up in someone else's trial of fire.

After showering and dressing in a polo shirt and jeans, he'd gone down to the office to put out the payroll. A couple of faxes had arrived in response to his queries about the natural gas drilling project. He planned to meet one of the men from the oil company at the site on Carson's property later in the morning. While he was sending a fax back verifying their arrangement, the guys joined him.

He coughed as his partners filed in the room. They usually assembled in the ranch office early. This morning they sat on the chairs with their legs extended, hands behind their heads, staring at him expectantly. Carson said, "Let's talk about the widow with the big problem."

Ross found a spot on the end of the desk and gripped the edge with his hands. "Guys? When I joined up with you in this venture, you knew all about me and my background. Now let me tell you Kit's story." For the next ten minutes he held his audience captive, leaving nothing out. When he'd finished with another cough, he stood up.

"There are only two differences between her story and mine. My father isn't a sick tyrant, just misguided. She wasn't born a Wentworth, but she'll always be in hell because she gave birth to one, and her father-in-law doesn't know when to give up. I think he or one of his bodyguard types is going to fly into Jackson and make a scene here soon.

"I made the mistake of ticking him off when he phoned yesterday. Kit hasn't exaggerated a thing. He's dangerous because he's abusive and won't stop hammering her until he gets what he wants. In that regard he's exactly like my father. Without backup, she doesn't have a prayer."

Carson leaned forward. "How can we help?"

Ross took a fortifying breath. "Just keep an eye out. Warn Willy about strangers who aren't the typical tourists asking questions about the ranch. I'd like to see her and Andy enjoy the rest of their vacation."

"And when she leaves here, then what?"

Buck always dug deeper and had just asked the sixty-four million dollar question. It was the one Ross had been asking himself all night.

"I don't know yet." The thought of Kit leaving didn't

sit well with him. The only thing to do right now was drive to her cabin and talk to her. He couldn't force her to do anything such as forget her plan to go to Texas. Otherwise he'd be guilty of her father-in-law's sin. All he could do was let her know he was there to help.

The guys exchanged glances. Carson said, "Why don't you tell her we all want to pitch in by lightening her load. We turned this place into the daddy dude ranch for that very reason. Andy has lost his father and needs his mother. Those two should be allowed to live their lives as they see fit. That's what our letter to her was all about, right?"

Buck coughed before he stared at Carson. "You just took the words out of my mouth and said them more eloquently than I ever could." He turned to Ross. "No matter who might be coming to look for her, she and Andy should have no worries about staying on the ranch. You tell her that for us. If she's still hesitant, we'll talk to her in person. Between the three of us, we'll keep Andy guarded and entertained."

Ross swallowed hard as he eyed his friends. "You're the best of the best. I knew it in the hospital and know it even more now." He checked his watch. It was seven-thirty in the morning. "Got to run. I'll tell you how the meeting goes with Mac Dawson. He's the oil engineer who'll be meeting me later."

"Sounds good," Carson said.

Buck stood up. "Tell Andy I'll take him and his mom fishing with the Randall and Smoot families as soon as they eat. I'll have them back before Alex and Tracy leave."

"Will do. Thanks."

He left the office, grabbed a couple of donuts from

the kitchen and raced out to the truck. Much as he wanted to phone Kit, he couldn't. Ross didn't know her cell phone number. With her and Andy sleeping in the same room, he didn't want to use the house phone or it could awaken them if they were still asleep. The only thing to do was go to the cabin and wait for her.

At seven-forty on the nose he pulled up in front. Instead of sitting in the truck, he climbed out and walked up to the porch, hoping to hear voices through the door. If they were up, then he'd knock. To his surprise, it opened before he had to do anything.

"Hey, Ross—" Andy was wearing his boots and hat. He looked happy. That was good.

"Hey, yourself." They high-fived each other. Kit stood right behind her son. Their eyes met.

"Good morning, Kit. I came to drive you two to breakfast."

"We were just about to walk over." Kit knew she sounded a little breathless. But for Ross to be standing there in his cowboy hat, bigger than life and smelling wonderful, her heart thudded so loud she was sure he could hear it.

She could sense from his demeanor he had a special reason for showing up unannounced. Maybe he'd heard from her father-in-law again. Her stomach clenched because it was too soon after her own conversation with Charles. It would probably take years before Kit stopped reacting like that when she thought of him.

"I'd say this was perfect timing," he murmured. "After you eat, Buck is going to take you fly fishing while the trout are biting. He'll have you back in time to go to town with everyone if that's what you want to do."

"What are you going to do this morning?" Andy wanted to know.

"I have a business meeting scheduled out on the property."

"Oh."

Kit shut the door of the cabin, concerned that her son would become a nuisance if he kept this up. But she had to admit she was curious, too. Everything about Ross fascinated her.

She watched Andy run to the truck and climb over the tailgate as if he'd been doing it all his life. Ross helped her into the cab. Every accidental touch sent delicious sensations through her body. She was pathetic.

"We need to talk," he said after he got behind the wheel.

Kit was bursting with her own news about her talk with Andy. "He can start breakfast without me. Hopefully one of the kids will be there. Have you had another phone call from Charles?" She thought it best to get straight to the point.

His dark brown gaze searched her eyes intently. "No. I came to find out if you had that talk with your son."

Her eyelids smarted. "Yes. He doesn't want to live with them anymore. Andy getting that off his chest was liberating for both of us."

"Thank God for that." He started the engine and they took off.

"You'll never know how happy it has made me. Andy was so sweet. He's carried a terrible burden. The fear of going away to that school must have been torturing him all year. I should have done something about this sooner."

"The important thing is that you're doing it now."

"I know. But right after our talk, my in-laws phoned."

"And?"

"I—I had it out with them." Her voice caught. "It wasn't pretty, but I told them we wouldn't be flying back to Maine after we left the ranch. I didn't tell them where we'd be going, but I promised them I'd keep in touch. And after we were settled, I explained we could all visit each other the way other families do who live apart."

"What happened?"

"Charles hung up on me and Florence broke down sobbing, too incoherent to keep talking."

Ross reached out and grasped her hand. His warmth traveled up her arm to fill her body. "That took a lot of courage, Kit. I want you to know my partners and I are here to support you every way we can."

By now they'd reached the parking area, and Ross pulled into a free space, forcing him to relinquish her hand.

He didn't do it any too soon because Andy had jumped down and come around to her side. The window was already open.

"Honey? I need to talk to Ross. Do you mind going in first? I think you'll find Jenny in there with her dad. We'll join you in a few minutes."

"Okay."

Once he'd disappeared around the corner of the ranch house, she turned to Ross. "I was about to say that your offer of support is very generous, but as I told you last night, my problems aren't your concern."

"They are if your father-in-law decides to fly here and confront you."

"He probably will come, but I'll handle him. I've been doing it for years."

He grimaced. "Except that you've never threatened to move away before. I happen to know Charles Wentworth can be a formidable man when provoked."

She frowned. "How do you know so much about him?"

His sudden smile turned him into the most attractive male she'd ever met in her life. "Allow me to introduce myself fully, *ma'am.*" Suddenly he was speaking with a heavy Texas accent.

"My legal name is Rutherford Livingston V, son of Chauncey Livingston IV, son of Ramsey Livingston III, son of Homer Livingston II, son of Eli Livingston, of Livingston Oil of Texas."

Kit blinked in disbelief. Ross was *that* Livingston? The fabulously wealthy U.S. senator she'd heard her husband and father-in-law talk about with envy was Ross's father?

"I can tell by the look on your face you've heard of us," Ross said quietly, leaving off the accent. "The East Coast might have its blue bloods, but so does Houston, the province of the billionaire Livingston oil barons dating from 1900 with their mansions built in River Oaks and Galveston's Historic District. It would seem the divine right of kings is still alive and doing well in both Maine and Texas."

Shocked by the revelation, she was trying to take it all in. "But you're a rancher!"

"I'm working on it. After I was discharged from the service, I couldn't get away from that old life fast enough."

"Ross..."

"Through my mother, who does her share of philanthropy, I've heard of the Wentworth charities run by the women in that family. But I had no idea Kathryn Wentworth was such a beautiful woman until we met at the airport."

"That explains your behavior when I asked you your name. You expected to meet a spoiled, filthy rich society snob without a brain in my head."

His eyes traveled over her. "But we know you're not anything like that!"

"I'm relieved you've revised your opinion of me."

"Forgive me if you sensed any reaction from me. Whatever you assumed I was thinking, I promise it wasn't aimed at you personally. Just so you know, I approve wholeheartedly of giving to charity. If it were up to me, I'd give it all away. But I'm afraid I grew up in the same lifestyle as your husband, and the pall it leaves on the family still sickens me to think about."

Ross was such an extraordinary man, Kit could scarcely comprehend it. She took a deep breath. "Does that mean this ranch is one of your investments?"

"On the contrary," he drawled. "This is Lundgren land since Carson's great great grandfather purchased it in 1908. I'm just lucky enough to be working here."

Kit stared out the window, waiting for the world she'd been living in a minute ago to orbit back to its normal place in the universe. "But you don't have to be here."

"No. I *want* to live and work here. If all goes well, we hope to bring more war widows with their children out here next summer and the summer after that."

"You and your partners have been doing a wonderful thing for three children I know of, Andy in particular."

"I'm glad he's enjoying it, since I'm the one person who probably understands better than anyone else what your life has been like living with Charles Wentworth. Let me tell you a story about the time I ran away from my family dynasty for good and never looked back."

"*You* ran away?" she blurted. "But your family is worth billions. Wouldn't they have prevented you from leaving?"

"If my father could have done it, he would have, but there was someone even richer and more powerful to stop him."

"I can't imagine who that would be."

"Uncle Sam."

Kit gasped in surprise. With anyone else, she would have thought this was a huge joke, but that wasn't the case with this unbelievable man. "You joined the marines to get away?"

He shot her a dark sideward glance. "Yup. Can you think of a better place to be where my father was powerless to order me back to the Livingston empire? Where his minions couldn't lay a finger on me?"

She let out a sigh. "As a plan, I have to concede it was brilliant." She was beginning to wonder if Winn might have done the same thing to get away from his autocratic father for long periods of time. Andy's comment that his father was afraid of Charles could account for Winn's decision to join the military. Marrying her had been out of character for Winn, yet he'd done it. And they'd all paid a huge price for it.

To her despair, that choice had deprived Andy of a father's love for those same barren periods when Charles had ruled her and his grandson with an iron hand.

"One day during my second year at Harvard Law School, I was sitting in a lecture when I realized I had no idea who I was or what I wanted from life. Like Andy, I'd been told what, where, when and how to live from the day I was born. I was a robot."

"That's exactly what Charles is turning my son into," she whispered.

"No one can relate better than I can. I had to go to one of those elite, astronomically expensive, pre-adolescent prep schools in Houston when I was nine years old, too. It was called St. Luke's."

Kit sat spellbound as she listened to him tell her the story of his life. The parallel between his and Andy's experiences was uncannily similar.

"Before the end of the lecture one day in class, I had an epiphany. The professor had been discussing a law case that involved a military man. That word military lit up my brain like a neon sign.

"I figured out how to turn my back on my birthright for a nobler cause than helping my family get richer and richer. I would join the marines, not as officer Rutherford Livingston V with all the accompanying perks, but as Ross Livingston, an enlisted man, the same as every other enlisted guy. I wanted no perks.

"That very day I left class and went to the recruiting station to sign up. Once I put my signature on the dotted line, I was untouchable."

She shook her head. "What a shock that must have been to your parents."

"I'm sure it was. Probably no more of a shock than the one you delivered to your in-laws this morning. But when they received my letter, I wasn't there to see it. For the first time in twenty-three years I was free to find out who I was, and my father couldn't do a damn thing about it.

"Being a politician and one of Houston's leading oil tycoons, my father couldn't say anything negative about my choice. Otherwise it would get leaked to the press and possibly ruin his career with all the military voters in his constituency."

"I'm imagining he wanted you to go into politics, too."

"Oh, yes. His aspirations were for me to become President of the United States. He had an agenda all mapped out for me, but of course those were all *his* dreams, and mother was right there with him."

"How awful, Ross. Were you an only child?"

"No. Like your husband, I have two siblings, an elder brother and a younger sister who march to my father's drum and breathe when he breathes. The only real difference between me and Andy is that he's a grandson, not a son. Charles Wentworth got his chance to run your husband's life. That ought to be enough for any man."

She gripped the side of the seat. "I agree."

"Since I made my choice to go into the military, I've been able to love my family much better from a distance." He flashed her a piercing regard. "I applaud you for helping Andy get away before it's too late."

"The thought of my son being sent to a school like yours tears me apart." She bit her lip. "How many years did you have to go to St. Luke's?"

"Four. I hated being away from home. Then I was shipped off to the poshest prep school in the state. By the time I was sixteen, I'd learned to despise the name of Rutherford Livingston V. It was so pretentious I told everyone my name was Ross, after my grandmother Ross."

"Was she a favorite of yours?"

"Yes. When she died, I lost a real friend."

"I know how that feels. I lost mine. It took me years to get over it."

"Some things you don't get over. It didn't take long for me to understand we were one of the wealthiest oil families in Texas. After the Spindletop oil discovery in Beaumont, our great great grandfather joined with other men to form Texas Oil and everything took off. Just belonging to our family made me different from all the other guys I wanted to be my friends.

"I was sent to the best schools, associated with the best people, had the best education in mining engineering at Stanford, vacationed at the best places around the world. All of that to ensure I'd graduate from Harvard Law School before I worked for the family ensuring we amassed more oil. But after two years in, I couldn't do it anymore.

"Like you, I did a lot of reading on my own. By then I'd developed a social conscience.

"Though I'd done everything the folks had wanted for me, it wasn't what *I* wanted. Because I didn't earn any of it, I felt ashamed of all the money we have when millions of people around the world are starving.

"Money opens doors that are closed to people with ordinary incomes or no incomes at all. It made me doubt if the friends and girlfriends I did make were sincere or did they just want something from me. There was a woman my father wanted me to marry named

Amanda Hopkins. I liked her, but at the age of twenty-three, I had no clue who I really was.

"Don't get me wrong. I can see the pained look on your face. I'm not attacking my parents or my lineage that made us who we are. I love them and my brother and sister and always will, but I don't like the trappings."

"Trappings don't bring happiness," she whispered.

"No, just as Andy has found out." He coughed. "By law school I wanted to find out who I really was. I yearned to be an ordinary guy. I wanted to fall in love with an ordinary girl who would fall in love with me. That's why I left school and joined the marines. They call it the great equalizer."

She couldn't take her eyes off him. "Have you found out who you are yet?"

He rubbed the back of his neck. "I'm getting there. Buck and Carson are my *real* friends. There's nothing fake about them. They've never tried to use me and never would. As I've told you, my father is a political animal.

"Naturally I want Dad to win re-election in November because he's a decent man with a lot of great plans, but I don't want to be a part of them. For me to feel good about myself, I've got to make it on my own.

"When I left school, I told him I wanted to serve our country, and nothing could persuade me otherwise. He couldn't argue with that because it was for a good cause." He coughed again.

"But the truth is, I've found my life's work here on the ranch. One day I'll invite the folks here. Seeing how I live will say everything better than words ever could.

"After telling you all this, perhaps now you'll understand why the guys and I want to help you get on with your life. We talked over your problem this morning and are here for you should you run into any real trouble with your father-in-law."

She tried to breathe normally but couldn't. Kit couldn't stand for these wonderful men to be involved in her troubles. She shouldn't have come to the ranch. But if she hadn't, she might never have found the resolve to make the break.

"I feel honored that you would confide in me this way. Thank you for helping me find the strength to do this. And, please, thank your partners for their concern, but I'm sure it won't come to that."

"For yours and Andy's sake, I hope not."

His comment haunted her as she got out of the cab and hurried inside the ranch house dining room to join her son. When she couldn't find him she went into the games room and discovered him playing Ping-Pong with a boy who looked about twelve.

"Hi, Mom. This is Jayce."

"Hello, Jayce."

"Hi."

"He's staying in one of the cabins with his parents."

"That's great. Have you eaten, honey?"

"Yeah."

"Ross and I took a little longer than I thought we would. I'm sorry."

"That's okay."

"I'll be in the dining room when you're through playing."

"Okay."

She retraced her steps and found Ross waiting for her at one of the empty tables.

"Everything all right?"

"Yes. He's already eaten and found a new friend named Jayce. There were quite a few kids on the cruise in Norway, but Andy never played with them. He's so different here, I hardly recognize him."

The waitress brought coffee and took their orders. After she went off Ross said, "That's because the source of his tension is gone. Now that he knows he doesn't have to go back to the mansion to live, you're going to see a new boy.

"I used to be like him until I got completely away from my parents. That's when everything changed. Given his freedom, Andy's going to grow up a happy man."

Their eyes met. "That's what I want for him."

"With a mother like you, he's on his way."

Ross hadn't heard what Florence had said to her earlier. *But you have no skills, no resources. Nothing. How can you possibly care for our grandson?* Those words had pierced her, but the sting was gone. That was because of Ross's faith in her.

How was it that this marvelous man had been here all this time waiting like some guardian angel assigned to watch over them the second they arrived? But she had to remember that an angel was a mortal's friend, not a potential lover.

Kit might want him the way a woman wanted the man she was crazy about, but she was a fool to be thinking of him that way. Not only was he out of her league on every level, she didn't want a man in her life. Winn and Charles had been enough.

Before long their food arrived, and Andy joined them. Ross offered him a piece of bacon, which he ate.

Their behavior was so natural with each other. "Your mom told me you met one of our guests?"

"Yeah. Jayce is from Minnesota. He likes my cowboy hat and said he's going to get his mom to buy him one like it."

Ross smiled at him. "I told you it suited you." Andy beamed. Her son was coming to life being around Ross. "Buck ought to be here by now to take you fishing. Maybe he'll take Jayce with you."

"No. He and his family are going on a float trip with Carson. Do you have to leave for your meeting now?"

Kit blinked in surprise at his question.

"That's right."

"In the truck?"

"Andy—"

"Yes. Why do you want to know?" he asked, ignoring Kit's exclamation.

"I just wondered if I could ride in the back. I won't bother you. I'd rather do that than go fishing."

"You would? Well, I can tell you now I'd like the company." Ross's brown eyes found hers. There was a glint in them that made her feel feverish. "Do you want to come with us? I'm driving to the eastern part of the ranch. There's beautiful scenery along the way."

"But you're going there on business."

"If it's possible, I always mix business with pleasure."

Pleasure. That's what it was like being with Ross. "Andy and I would love to ride out with you." She shouldn't have said it, but this morning she was so happy and felt so free, there was nothing she'd rather do than be with him.

"There's only one problem, Andy. We might not get back in time for you to go into town with the kids."

"I'd rather go with you."

Andy had taken the words right out of Kit's mouth. "Then I'll ring Alex and let her know there's been a change in plans. She'll tell Buck. Do you two need to get anything before we leave?"

"No, but maybe we ought to take a trip to the restroom. Come on, Andy."

"While you do that, I'll get one of the cooks to pack us a lunch. We'll meet at the truck in ten minutes."

After refreshing themselves, Kit and Andy started walking out to the truck. Her son was the one who jumped when her cell phone rang. "It's probably Grandfather."

Kit pulled it out of her pocket and discovered it was her sister-in-law calling. That meant the whole family knew everything. "It's your aunt Corinne."

"I bet he's right there and is making her call you. He always makes her do stuff."

Andy was nobody's fool. "I'm sure you're right." Charles had guilted the whole family to death for years.

"Don't answer it."

"I won't."

He gave her a hug before climbing in the back of the truck. Kit got in the front seat and shut the door. Pretty soon another call came through from Sybil. She let it ring. When everything went silent she checked the message from Corinne.

I can't believe you've done this to my parents after they took you in. Winston did everything conceivable so you could live the enchanted life, and this is how you've repaid him?

Can't you understand the family is worried for Andrew? If you really love him, you'll come home.

Kit stared into space. As far as Corinne was capable of understanding, given the family she'd been born into, she meant well. Neither she nor Sybil could comprehend leaving the gilded nest to go out in the world with their children. But Kit hadn't been born a Wentworth. She was anxious for Andy to have a taste of freedom so he could grow into whatever person he wanted to be.

Her thoughts wandered to Ross who'd said he'd left home in order to find out who he was. As far as she was concerned, it had been the making of a fabulous man who had his feet firmly planted on this ranch. She could only hope the same thing happened to Andy, that he'd find himself and fulfill his potential.

Kit looked through the rear window. He was in the back of the truck shooting off his cap gun like any happy kid. No matter how much guilt the family heaped on her, she wouldn't trade this child for the sullen shadow of himself her boy had been since Winn's death.

Chapter 7

While he waited for one of the cooks to fill the picnic hamper, Ross took the time to inform the guys he was taking Kit and Andy with him for the day. He also told them to be on the alert now that Kit had let her in-laws know she and Andy were moving out of the mansion.

After stopping in the office for his notebook and a map, he headed for the truck in better spirits than he'd felt in months. His life suddenly seemed filled with new purpose. As he reached the parking area, Andy waved to him from the back.

He walked up and put the hamper in next to one of the hay bales. "You know what, sport? I'm going to swing by your cabin so you can get a sweater or jacket. If you're going to ride back here, it might get a little cool in the forest."

"I'm okay. The sun's really warm right now. If it gets cooler, I'll get in the cab with Mom."

That made sense. "Good enough." On impulse Ross handed him the map. "Have you ever seen a U.S. geological survey map before?"

"No."

He opened it up. "As you can see, it's different from a road map. We're here." He used his index finger to show him the exact location. "We're going to drive over here. This tells you the names and elevations of the land. If you follow it, you'll find it pretty interesting."

"Thanks."

"You're welcome. Holler if you need anything."

"Okay."

"You're sure you don't mind us coming with you?" Kit asked as he got behind the wheel and put his notebook on the backseat. "I'm sorry Andy didn't want to go fishing. I guess you realize it's because you had something else to do. He has a slight case of hero worship at the moment."

He darted her a glance once they'd driven away. "The whole idea of our project is for kids like Andy to open up and express what they want to do. I'm pleased to think he's starting to warm up and feel comfortable."

"You've given him so much attention, I think he's too comfortable. I was watching out the back window. What did you give him to look at?"

"A map so he can see where we're going."

"You're very thoughtful," she said. "What kind of business meeting is it, if you don't mind my asking?"

"Not at all." He had to cough. He hadn't shared his interests with a woman like this in years and loved it. "It's my opinion Carson's ranch is sitting on top of a pocket of natural gas, but we won't know until we drill. I've been doing the research and have received bids from several oil companies. Today I'm meeting one of the engineers from a local firm at the site where I think we should put in a well. If we're lucky, it'll pay big dividends."

He felt her studying him. "We?"

"I graduated as a petroleum engineer before I went to Harvard. Family business, what else?"

She flashed him a brief smile.

"Ranching with Carson has taught me it's a very tough business and money is always tight. I'm hoping a well like this will produce enough natural gas to help him and his family financially for years to come."

"Won't that require a good amount of capital just to get started?"

Kit wasn't just a beautiful face. "Yes. I invested the money I made in the military. It'll be my contribution to our partnership. Carson has already provided the land, and Buck takes care of any construction. Now it's my turn to see what I can do to carry my weight around here."

"But what if the well doesn't produce anything?" she asked. "You'll have lost the investment you took all those years in the military to build up."

"It's a risk I'm willing to take for a friend."

Her eyes darkened with emotion. "The world could use more friends like you. I'm in awe of you, Ross."

"No more than I am of you."

"What do I have to do with anything?"

"For the sake of your son's happiness, you're planning to head out into the unknown on faith and no backing."

"Be serious. My situation isn't the same thing."

They'd been weaving in and out of the forest area and were almost to the flat section of land where he'd ridden with Carson on Saturday morning.

"You're right. I at least have a job as a rancher if my plan fails."

She shook her head. "If my plan to open a bookshop doesn't materialize, I'll get a job right away doing any number of things. But you'll be out hard-earned money."

"I'll live. My concern is how *you're* going to live."

"We'll be fine. That is, if Andy can handle it. If not, we'll go someplace else."

While he pondered her brave words, he heard her cell phone ring. She pulled it out of her pocket and looked at the caller ID, but she didn't answer it. No doubt Charles was harassing her again. The second time it started ringing he heard a muffled sound come out of her. "I'm sorry. I'll turn the ringer off."

"Your father-in-law?"

"No. Now it's my sister-in-law Sybil. Corinne called earlier and left a message. They're both upset with me."

Kit had said she didn't have anyone in her family she could turn to. "Do you want to talk about it?"

"Thanks, but there's really nothing to say. When Charles gets angry, it affects all of them. They just want me to bring Andy home, so the trouble will go away. They know how he and Florence dote on him."

"Have you ever talked to them about the reason why you want to get a place of your own?"

She took a deep breath. "If I ever brought it up before Winn's death, they told me I was crazy. They have lovely homes, but they'd both rather live at the mansion with their children and be pampered. I would have traded places with them in an instant, but they brushed me off.

"I know they think me ungrateful and undeserving, but they've never stopped to consider Andy. Long ago I decided they were jealous that Winn and I could live there. In fact, I know they were jealous of him. It's been very sad, but there was nothing to be done about Charles always showing his preference for Winn."

"Tell me about it," Ross groaned. "My father doted on me. It didn't bother my sister, but my brother has always had a hard time with it. What do you say we change the subject and enjoy the day?" He was getting to the point where he needed to take her in his arms and satisfy this longing for her.

"I'd love to."

Past the trees now, they drove into full sunshine. In the distance Ross could see the oil company truck coming toward them from the road in the opposite direction. "Good. He's right on time."

"I'll keep Andy in the truck."

"You're welcome to get out and join me. This won't take long."

He pulled to a stop. After grabbing his notebook, he climbed out to help her, needing any excuse to touch her. Andy jumped down, and the three of them approached the man getting out of his truck. "Mr. Dawson?"

"You must be Mr. Livingston." They shook hands. His admiring gaze swept over Kit. "Mrs. Livingston? Nice to meet you, too."

"This is Mrs. Wentworth and her son, Andy," Ross corrected him. But the comment wasn't far from Ross's true thoughts. "They're guests on the ranch and wanted to come on the ride to see the property."

The man looked embarrassed. "Sorry about that. My wife tells me I should keep my thoughts to myself. I guess I assumed because you were riding in the truck that—"

"It's a natural mistake, Mr. Dawson," Kit cut in with a smile. "We don't mind, do we?" She hugged Andy, who shook his head. "I just found out Ross is an oil engineer and is thinking of having a well drilled here."

"You are?" Andy looked up at Ross with renewed interest. "How soon are you going to do it?"

"Hopefully soon, depending on my partners."

Mr. Dawson nodded. "With all the natural gas in Wyoming, my instincts tell me it's a pretty sure thing."

"I hope you start before we leave the ranch. I want to watch."

Ross chuckled. For a minute there, Andy reminded him of Johnny who was always curious about everything.

"Come on, honey. Let's take a walk so the men can talk business. Nice to meet you, Mr. Dawson."

"The pleasure's all mine."

Her eyes swerved to Ross a brief moment before she walked away. He watched her, mesmerized by the mold of her body. He enjoyed everything about her. Somehow in the past three days he felt she and her son had become a part of him.

Andy ran ahead of her to get the map out of the back. Before they climbed in the truck, he opened it for her. "Look, Mom. We're right here. This is a lot cooler than a regular map."

"I agree. It's like a picture of the earth itself."

"Ross knows so much neat stuff. I wish we didn't have to go to Texas."

It was his first admission that told her he was nervous about their plans and preferred to stay here. "You don't even know what Galveston is like, honey. It'll be exciting. Nila likes you so much, and you and Kim are friends. You can go to school with her. It'll be a place for us to get a new start."

"But what if we don't like it?"

She understood his fears and couldn't afford to ignore them. "Then we'll find another place to work and live."

"Maybe we could come back here."

"No, honey. This is a dude ranch. Once our trip is over, we have to leave."

"I know. I didn't mean the ranch. I meant Jackson."

Jackson? Kit hadn't realized her son had done this much thinking. "We could live there and you could find a job. I could go to school with Johnny and Jenny."

She needed to keep her wits about her. "You're only saying that because these retired marines have become your friends and have shown you such a wonderful time. But they have their own busy lives. We'll make new friends. You'll see."

"But I like Jackson."

"You've only been there twice."

He liked Ross. The man exuded confidence and made both of them feel protected. Already she could tell he felt a bond with the vet who instilled an intangible sense of safety. Kit felt it, too, which was one of the reasons it was equally hard for her to think of leaving.

She could feel Andy getting upset. "Tell you what.

Let's enjoy our vacation and then fly to Galveston. If we really don't think it's going to work there, then we'll talk about other possibilities."

"Promise?"

"Promise. Now, not a word to Ross. It looks like the men have finished their meeting. Let's get in the truck."

She quickly climbed in the front while Andy hopped in the backseat. Ross strode toward them on his long, hard-muscled legs. The sight of him never failed to thrill her.

"What do you two say we find ourselves a pretty spot and eat our picnic?" He levered himself in the truck, and they drove back into the forest. At a bifurcation, he took the upper road and they climbed into an area of tall, dark pines that grew close together.

"This is incredible, almost like we're in a green cathedral."

"It'll get even more beautiful in a minute."

Soon they came out in a small clearing of a lush meadow of wild flowers where she could see layers of pines beyond, each layer a different hue of green that went on and on. "What are those flowers?"

"Gentians and Indian paintbrush."

If she looked in the opposite direction, there were the majestic Tetons in all their glory. "The beauty of this defies description," she whispered in awe.

"I think so, too. That's why I thought you'd like to eat here."

"I'd like to live here," her son piped up, echoing her own sentiments.

"I'll let you in on a secret, Andy. This is the spot where I'm going to have Buck build my house. But don't tell anyone yet."

"How come?"

"Because he's still building a house for his new family. When it's done, then I'll talk to him about it."

"Okay. I won't say anything. You sure are lucky. What's it going to be like?"

"An alpine cabin, small and cozy."

Kit could picture it. When she and Andy were in Texas, she'd remember this day and this man....

Ross got out and handed him a thermal blanket from the back of the truck. "Put it anywhere you want."

"Okay." Her son found a spot and she helped him spread it out. Ross brought the hamper. Soon they were munching on sandwiches and salad. He handed them a soda and they sprawled on the blanket, basking in the sun.

Andy reached for more potato chips. "You know that flat place where you're going to drill?"

"Yes?" Ross had just finished off a second sandwich before coughing.

"It's not very far from here, but you can't even see it."

"Nope. That's the beauty of its location. It's out of the way. If the well is a producer, it'll be great news for Carson."

"How do you drill?"

"It's quite a process. A lot of different trucks come. One with pipes, another carries a cable, three others are pump trucks. There's a detergent truck—"

Kit stopped chewing. "Detergent?"

His dark brown gaze fell on her. "That's the material fed into the piping made up of water and sand and other chemicals. Once an open hole is made, you drive deep into the earth, hoping to find the gas."

"How deep?" Andy questioned.

"In my estimation, 11,000 feet."

"Are you teasing?"

Ross flashed them a white smile. "Nope. That's where it's lurking if it's there. Hopefully we'll get lucky. Then there'll be gas 24/7, and clients will come to buy it."

"I had no idea how much is involved." Kit was as fascinated as her son.

"Will it make a lot of noise?"

"Not after it's finished, Andy, but you'll hear its continual flow."

"I wish I could see you drill down. Are you going to let Johnny and Jenny watch?"

Amusement lit his eyes. "If I know those two, they'll be over here a lot."

"But what if there isn't any gas?"

"Then we'll close it back up."

"And drill in another place?"

He raised up on one elbow. "No. This ranch shouldn't be spoiled like that. I'll just have to pray this one works."

"I'll pray, too."

"Yeah?" Ross reached over and tousled Andy's hair.

Kit felt a swelling in her throat. "We'll all pray. You and your partners have given so much for so many, both in the war and here. It's time you got something back in return."

For a while they lay on their backs and rested in silence while Andy got up and walked around. In a minute she felt Ross's hand grasp hers. She turned on her side and saw a longing in his eyes that couldn't be mistaken for anything else.

"This is nice, Kit. You have no idea how nice."

"But I do," she said in a tremulous voice.

He rubbed his thumb over the inside of her wrist. "I want to kiss you more than you can imagine. If Andy weren't with us..."

She sat up and reluctantly removed her arm. "It's a good thing he's where I can see him because kissing you wouldn't be a good idea."

"Why not?"

"We both know why. We're ships passing in the night. Nothing else."

His lids narrowed. "Would it surprise you to know I haven't felt this strong an attraction to a woman in years?"

Her heart leaped. "Actually it would. Surrounded by women on the staff and in the Jackson area, let alone all the female guests who come to your ranch, an attractive man like you has ample, nonending opportunities."

"Opportunities, yes. But not the accompanying desire I need to feel to act on them. You want me, too, so don't deny it. I felt your pulse just now. It runs away with you whenever we're together. I see the throbbing in the hollow of your throat, and I want to put my lips to it."

She started putting things away in the hamper. "You're a bachelor and will feel the same way about another woman before long. But I'm not in a position to give into an impulse, especially not with our gracious host. I'm in the most precarious circumstances of my life. One wrong step could jeopardize everything. Andy is so vulnerable right now, it terrifies me."

Ross got to his feet. "I understand that, but the day

is coming before you leave when I'm going to give in to my own impulse, so watch out."

No. That day wouldn't be coming. By the end of the week, she and Andy would be flying to Galveston. Much as she hated the idea of leaving here, she needed to be out on her own.

Having been confined at the mansion for too many years by her broken marriage and Charles's domination, she needed freedom from any strings. Getting to know Ross any better would not be in her best interests. Intimacy blurred the lines, making it difficult to focus.

She closed the hamper for him to put in the truck. "Andy?" She waved to her son. "We're leaving. Come on!"

Kit folded the blanket. As she started walking toward Ross, her cell phone rang again. Her gaze automatically flew to his. He stood there with a distinct frown marring his handsome features. It was as if the sound punctuated better than words the instability of her situation. No words passed between them as he put the blanket away.

Andy joined them. "I wish we didn't have to go. I want to hike up higher and see everything."

"There's a lake up above those trees shaped like a sea horse."

"A sea horse?"

Ross chuckled. "Cross my heart. Carson has a picture of it from the air. It's got fish, but you have to work for them. What do you say we plan to come back here tomorrow? We'll hike around and have an overnight campout. Whatever we catch, we'll eat."

"That would be great!"

As far as Kit was concerned, Ross's plans had just

made Andy's whole trip for him. He was starving for attention, but the three of them alone for overnight probably wasn't the smartest plan. Better to add to the group.

She put an arm around his shoulders, warm from the sun. "I think it's a terrific idea." Without looking at their host, she said, "If it's all right with Ross, maybe Jenny and Johnny can come."

"The more the merrier," he said at once. "We'll ask them at dinner."

To her relief Andy didn't complain about the other kids coming and got in the backseat. That was another relief. As long as he rode inside the truck with them, she wouldn't be getting into another personal conversation with Ross she couldn't handle.

She hadn't stopped trembling since he'd told her he wanted her. *You want me, too.* The fact that what he'd said was true had really shaken her.

Thankfully Ross and Andy chatted on the way home about fishing and hunting. To her surprise it was already three-thirty when they arrived back. When she was with Ross, the time went by too fast.

Before her son asked Ross what he'd be doing later, Kit asked if he would drop them off at the ranch house. She announced that she wanted to get one of the puzzles from the game room. They'd walk back to the cabin and work on it until dinner. Without looking at him she thanked him for the outing, and they parted company.

"See you at dinner," Andy called to him.

"I'll be there."

Ross watched them round the corner of the ranch house. His ache for Kit had grown. Knowing she wanted him too helped him keep his sanity. Tonight after Andy went to bed, he'd get her alone and end this insufferable hunger.

After returning the hamper to the kitchen, he walked down the hall to the office with his notebook in hand. Now that Ross had met with Mac Dawson, Carson needed to see the recent figures and calculations for the project and give his okay. Ross was crossing his fingers because, like Mac, he had a hunch the natural gas was there waiting.

He entered his notes into the computer, excited for the drilling to get started. Andy's comment that he'd pray the well would produce had touched Ross's heart. He was a sweet boy like Johnny with a depth and intelligence Ross found exceptionally appealing. Andy was Kit's son. That accounted for a big part of it. No one could have a better mother. Naturally he'd inherited some of his father's good qualities, too.

Who would have thought all this had been hidden inside the unhappy boy who'd first arrived here? When Ross thought of his reservations at meeting her and Andy, he was ashamed.

A tap on the door caused his head to lift, bringing him back to the present. "Come on in."

"Boss?" Willy closed the door behind him. "I'm glad you're back. The Teton County Sheriff, Leo Barton, is out in the foyer wanting to speak to you personally about a missing person."

Personally?

Well, well, well. The sheriff, no less. After all those phone calls Kit hadn't answered this morning, Charles Wentworth had wasted no time.

"Do you want me to show him in here?"

"Please." The less drama in front of their guests coming in and out of the ranch house, the better. "Thank you, Willy."

The younger man paused at the door. "What's going on?"

"When I know, you will, too."

His brows lifted. "Okay."

A minute later he heard another knock on the door. Ross got up to open it. "Sheriff Barton? Come in and sit down."

"Thank you, Mr. Livingston."

"How can I help you?"

"Do you have guests staying here by the name of Kathryn Wentworth? She's with a nine-year-old boy named Andrew?"

"Yes, that's her son. They arrived on Saturday. What's wrong?"

"Her in-laws, Mr. and Mrs. Charles Wentworth, have reason to suspect they might have gone missing since then. I have a warrant issued by Judge Otis Marcroft in Knox County, Maine, to look for them."

Good grief.

Ross pretended to be surprised. "You mean the Wentworths think she's been kidnapped while she's been here on the ranch?"

"I can't answer that question. My job is to search the premises for them."

"You don't need to search. I'll take you to them in my truck. I was with them all day until about a half hour ago when I dropped them off. They're in their cabin."

The sheriff scratched his head. "You say you were with them all day?"

"That's right. I've been with them 24/7 since they came to the ranch. Today we were out at the eastern end of the property. I had a meeting with Mac Dawson from the Dawson Gas Company in Jackson. He can vouch for them since I introduced them to him."

"I'd be obliged if you'd show me to their cabin."

"My truck's around the side."

They walked out past a bewildered-looking Willy. Once the sheriff got in beside him, Ross headed for the cabin. He wished he could have prepared Kit and Andy, but his hands were tied. This could be a frightening experience for a young boy whose only fault was to be the grandson of Genghis Khan.

There was something mentally wrong with Charles Wentworth to be willing to scare his grandson like this in order to make Kit cave to his demands.

Over Ross's dead body.

He pulled up and followed the sheriff to the porch. The older man gave a loud knock.

Soon Kit opened the door. Andy was right behind her. He could see the puzzle they'd been working on set up on the table.

The sheriff examined them from head to toe. "Good afternoon, ma'am. I'm Sheriff Barton from the Teton County Sheriff's Office in Jackson. You're Kathryn Wentworth?"

Ross could read Kit's mind. She knew exactly what was going on and lifted her proud chin. He admired her more than anyone he knew for her sheer guts in handling a bad situation.

"I am, and this is my son Andrew Wentworth. How can I help you?"

"I'd like to see your identification, please."

"Just a moment." She went over to the table for her purse and pulled out a wallet. She came back to the door and showed him her driver's license. While he was at it, he looked through her pictures.

Andy had lost a little color, but he stood there at his mother's side like a man. A feeling of love for the boy swept through Ross.

"I was issued a warrant to locate you." He handed her back the wallet.

"By whom?"

"Your father-in-law has been looking for you and was ready to file a missing person's report."

"Be he *knows* I'm here. I don't understand. Andy and I have been on this ranch since the moment we flew in from Bar Harbor on Saturday. We've been in constant telephone contact with Andy's grandparents until today when Mr. Livingston took us sightseeing on the property.

"Check his telephone records and mine. They'll verify we've had several phone calls, sometimes twice a day, proving we've been in contact. Unless someone told him we'd been kidnapped today, Charles has no reason to think anything. At the invitation of the owners of this ranch who made this trip possible for us, Andy and I have been having a marvelous time!"

"Is that true, son?"

"Yup. Ross has shown me the best time ever."

Oh, Andy. The boy's genuineness and innocence stuck out a mile.

Ross had it in his heart to almost feel sorry for the sheriff who'd been sent on a fool's errand. By the ruddy color that crept into his face, the man knew it.

"How long will you be on the ranch?"

"We leave Saturday."

"And your plans after that?"

"Does that warrant include finding out my future plans? Because if it does, I'm not sure of them yet."

Kit knew what she was doing. She wasn't about to disclose her destination once she left here.

"No, ma'am."

"Then is that all, Sheriff?"

"Yes, ma'am. Sorry to disturb you."

"That's all right." She shut the door, but not before her eyes flicked to Ross with a glimmer of mirth. Kit Wentworth was a prize, packaged with the stuff men's dreams were made of.

He got back in the truck and drove the sheriff to his decked-out police van parked in front where everyone walking around could see it. Their guests had to wonder what was happening. After learning that Charles Wentworth was at the bottom of this warrant, Ross bet he'd driven in here all bells and whistles. He probably hadn't had a mission this exciting in years!

Carson stepped outside from the foyer. No doubt Willy had already told him about the visit. He walked over and tipped his hat. "Sheriff Barton?"

"Carson." They shook hands.

"Haven't seen you in a while. Did you find the people you were looking for?"

"Yup. They were at their cabin."

"Anything else we can do for you?"

"Nope. I have a hell of lot of things more important to do than come chasing out here for someone who's not missing."

"Oh, well. It's all in a day's work, right?"

He nodded and climbed in his van. "Looks like

you're doing a right fine business. Your granddad would be proud of you."

Carson smiled at Ross. "Thanks to my partners here, it's growing. That's for sure. Take care now."

They both watched until the van was out of sight before bursting into laughter. Ross turned to him. "You should have seen Kit after she opened the door. She handled him like a pro. So did Andy."

"To do this in front of Andy, that father-in-law of hers is a real nasty piece of work, Ross."

"You can say that again. I'm going back to the cabin to make sure they're all right."

"Go ahead."

"I take it the kids aren't back yet."

"Tracy called. They just got out of the movie and will be home soon."

"Good. Tomorrow I'm planning to take Andy and Kit on an overnight campout to Bluebell Lake. If the kids could join us, Andy would like it."

"I think we'd all love it! I'll talk to the girls and Buck about it."

"Good."

"Just so you know, I was reading over your notes on the meeting with Dawson when Willy came in the office and told me what was going on. We'll get together later with Buck and talk about it."

"I've got a feeling about this well, Carson."

"Yeah?" His friend's blue eyes darkened with emotion. Ross was glad Carson wasn't going to let his grandfather's reservations prevent them from trying this experiment. If it was successful, he'd be perpetuating the Lundgren legacy far into the future. One day Johnny and any other children they might have would be in charge and it would go on from there. "Your hunch means a hell of a lot."

On that happy note, Ross took off for the cabin. Instead of knocking, he called through the door so they'd know who was on the other side.

Andy flung it open. The concern on his face was too much. Without thinking, Ross pulled him into his arms and gave him a hug. The boy clung to him. "I was proud of the way you handled yourself in front of the sheriff. That took real courage."

"That's what I told him."

Ross saw Kit standing in the background and let go of Andy. "Neither of you should have been forced to go through that experience. If there'd been any other way..." His voice grated. "But since he had a warrant, I couldn't stop him or warn you. He had to come out here and see for himself."

"I know, and believe it or not, I'm not sorry. I've had a lifetime learning experience within the last half hour. Not only did I discover new things about myself, I learned a lot about my son who's much stronger than I'd ever imagined he could be, thanks to your example. And there's something else."

"What's that?"

"Andy, honey? Would you mind going outside for just a minute? I need to talk to Ross in private."

"Okay." He grabbed his cap gun and went out the door.

She shut it and backed up against it. "Andy doesn't know that this morning I listened to Corinne's phone message, and I have to admit it shook me up a little. But no longer. After this experience, I know I'm doing the right thing to move out. There's a cruel streak in

Charles. I'm positive Florence is disturbed by it, but long ago she made the choice to stay and support him.

"By sending that sheriff out here, he's committed the ultimate crime against Andy, in my opinion. No child should have to endure what happened today because Charles is upset with me."

"Amen."

Kit took a second breath. "He's done an unconscionable act."

Ross knew he was talking to the most extraordinary woman he'd ever met. For years she'd undergone a form of emotional abuse within the walls of the Wentworth mansion. He couldn't find the words to tell her how pained he was for her ordeal. But she was standing up to Charles. That told Ross what this woman was really made of.

In the next breath his hands shot out on either side of her, trapping her. The heat generated by their bodies worked like an aphrodisiac on Ross. His body moved closer until they were molded to each other.

"*Ross*—no—we mustn't." Her voice came out on a strangled whisper.

"A man can only take so much. I warned you."

He lowered his head and covered her mouth with his own, parting her lips because his hunger was so great. At first she held back, but with each kiss he drove deeper and deeper; she began to succumb until they were giving kiss for kiss.

Her response released an explosion of feeling he could hardly contain. While he was immersed in sensual ecstasy, she wound her arms around his waist, creating greater intimacy. Driven by this mindless passion for her, time ceased to exist.

"You have no idea how beautiful you are to me, Kit. I'm talking inside and out." Their kisses grew more prolonged. Somehow he'd moved so his back was against the door and his legs were cradling hers. Each kiss felt natural. Her soft, sweet body melted into his. He couldn't get enough of her as their mouths clung.

"I want you," he cried, "but you already know that." The feel and taste of her transcended any of his dreams. She was all warmth and beauty. Slowly their kisses grew more urgent. He pressed her closer, running his hands through her hair and over her back.

"I've been so afraid for you to touch me," came her feverish response.

"There's nothing to be afraid of. How could there be?" Growing along with his desire was this powerful need to protect her. Ross wanted to make up to her for the years she'd suffered at the hands of the Wentworth men.

Charles had been so blessed to have a daughter-in-law as sweet as Kit. Since his son's passing, he'd figuratively trampled her beneath his feet and had lost a lot of the love of his grandson in the process. Ross couldn't comprehend it or the sorrow she'd suffered, having lost a spouse who hadn't been there for her. If Kit would let him love her in all the ways she needed to be loved…

"You don't understand. This can't go on—" She tore her lips from his on a moan.

"Why are you pulling away from me?" he asked.

"Because I feel…cheap."

Ross was incredulous. "Do *I* make you feel that way?"

She eyed him with a frazzled look. "Of course not. It's not you."

"Then explain what you mean. You owe me that much."

"I owe you *everything!*" she cried. "That's the problem. I only arrived here last Saturday. Set free from my prison, I've already taken your protection, your good will. I've involved your partners in the ugliness of my life. Andy and I have taken up all your time."

"We invited you here, remember?"

"Yes I remember, but my husband only died ten months ago, and yet I'm here in this cabin making out with you like a high school girl looking for a good time with the first guy to look my way."

"By your own admission you fell out of love years ago. It's a wonder you've taken this long to feel alive again. I'm only thankful it's happened with me because you've made me feel alive again, too."

"But this is wrong."

He needed to understand. "Surely you realize that's your fear talking."

"Yes. I know it is and I'm sorry, Ross. Forgive me for venting," she begged. "I must seem like the most mixed-up, ungrateful wretch who ever lived. Can we just start over again and forget what has happened?"

Ross studied her features. "No. At least *I* can't. To try to forget would be pointless when I'd be fighting against nature. Would it surprise you to know I wanted to kiss you before I left the cabin the first day?"

Kit smoothed the hair away from her temples. "You didn't even like me."

"You're wrong. I didn't want to like you for the reasons we've already talked about, but I couldn't help myself."

"Now you're simply trying to make me feel better like you always do."

He let out a bark of harsh laughter. "I'm glad to hear that. Don't you know I'm trying to be as honest with you as I can? Here this grieving woman comes to the ranch with her grieving son at our invitation and I find myself desiring you. What does that say about me? So much for my being a saint."

She shook her head. "Don't you see? We shouldn't be spending this much time together alone."

"But we haven't actually been alone until now."

"And look what's happened!"

"Didn't you enjoy it?"

"Yes, but it was a guilty enjoyment I'm not proud of."

"Guilty?" he whispered.

"Yes. Don't ask me to explain."

"Then after I've figured it out, how about we try it again and see if you haven't changed your mind."

She pressed her hands against his chest. "Ross?"

"Yes?" He coughed.

"Please, be serious."

"In other words, try to pretend that you're not a beautiful woman I'd like to get to know better?"

Kit swallowed hard. "You don't want to know me."

"What in the hell does that mean?"

"You deserve a woman who can be your counterpart in every way. If we'd met under ordinary circumstances, you would have gotten your full measure of me in about two minutes and passed on by."

"Two minutes? You don't give yourself any credit, or me for having discernment."

"You're just being a gentleman. That's the trouble

with you. I'll never get to know the Ross Livingston who lives inside his own skin. You're saving that for the special woman who'll come along one day. That's one of the reasons why it would be wrong for us to get physical because of chemistry alone."

"What's the other reason?"

"Andy and I will be gone soon. I don't want to leave with regrets."

"Do you regret kissing me?"

"Yes."

"I think you actually meant that."

"I do. The fact is, I need a clear head."

"So any intimate involvement with me would muddy the waters?"

"After my past with the Wentworth men, I don't need more complications that will lead nowhere."

She'd pressed on a nerve. "You think having a relationship with me will lead nowhere?"

"I didn't mean that the way it sounded. All I'm saying is, it would be better if we don't start up anything. In a few days I'll be gone. My whole focus needs to be on making a home for Andy and getting on with a career."

On a groan of protest he buried his face in her dark, luxuriant hair. "A fire's been lit. There's no way we can let each other go. Not now, not ever."

Somewhere in the periphery he heard children's voices and caps firing. "*Mom?* The kids are here. Can we come in?"

"Ross—we have to stop!" Kit sounded frantic.

He pressed another hot kiss to her mouth before finally releasing her and taking a step away. "Only for now," he vowed and staggered his way over to the fridge. He opened a can of pop while he tried to get himself under some semblance of control.

One look at Kit and he saw she was having the same problem. She rushed into the bathroom and shut the door.

"Come on in, guys!" he called to the children and opened the front door.

Johnny was the first inside. "Daddy told us we're going on a campout tomorrow."

Ross stood there with his hands on his hips, still shaken by the desire he felt for her. "What's this? No hello first?"

Jenny came inside with Andy. "Hi, Uncle Ross."

"That's more like it. Hi, yourself! Did you guys have fun at the movie?"

"Yes. Are we going to Secret Lake?"

His laugh brought on a cough. That was the kids' favorite place on the ranch so far and the first thing on their minds. "Nope. We're going to one you've never seen before."

"Huh?" Johnny looked shocked. "Another lake?"

"It looks like a sea horse," Andy spoke up.

"Andy's right," he said when he saw the other children's surprised expressions. "Carson calls it Bluebell Lake because of the wild bluebells that grow near the tail. Since we're going to be doing some hiking, we won't be taking the ponies this time. We'll go up in the truck and set up camp."

"Goody!"

Kit came into the living room. Except for her glazed eyes, she looked composed for someone who'd just been kissed senseless. "I'm so glad to see all of you. You're just in time for us to go to dinner."

Jenny stared up at her. "After we eat, will you read some more to us about Buck?"

"Absolutely. I'm glad you reminded me." She reached for the book on the coffee table.

"Let's go."

"Everybody, pile in the truck!" Ross helped Jenny before he started the engine. Kit put on a good front, but he knew she was quaking inside over what had happened and would never be the same again. *Neither would he.*

Chapter 8

"Nila? Is this a bad time to call you?" It was nine o'clock at night. Kit and Andy had just gotten back from the ranch house.

"It's a great time. What's going on?"

After Kit had finished the first chapter of the Jack London book for the children, she and Andy had said good-night to everyone and come straight home. While he was in the living room watching TV in his pajamas, she paced the bedroom floor.

"For one thing, the local sheriff paid a visit to my cabin earlier today. Guess who got a court order to make sure I hadn't left Wyoming yet?" She kept no secrets from Nila.

"I'm not surprised. The sooner you get here, the better I'm going to feel."

She gripped the phone tighter. "That's why I'm calling. Ross has arranged an overnight camping trip for tomorrow with the children and—"

"Ross?" Nila broke in.

"Mr. Livingston, one of the partners here on the dude ranch. He's been the one in charge of us."

"Hmm. A retired marine. How old is he?"

"Early thirties I think."

"Tall, dark and handsome?"

"You got it in one."

"You're kidding."

"No. The cliché fits him down to his well-worn cowboy boots."

"Oh, boy."

"Oh, boy is right, but I don't dare talk about him at the moment. Because of this overnight outing, we'll be away from the ranch where Charles won't be able to find us *if* that's on his agenda. That's a good thing. We'll get back sometime Wednesday.

"Since my father-in-law knows my original flight arrangements, which have us flying back to Maine on Saturday, I'm thinking of leaving the ranch on Friday just to throw him off. That is if Andy can handle it. The children he's gotten to know here start school on Thursday and will be in class on Friday, as well. Knowing that, Andy might not mind leaving a day early." Kit knew she was avoiding how Andy would feel about leaving Ross. Never mind her own feelings.

"I've looked at the airline schedules and have booked a flight out to Salt Lake. From there we'll get a connection and be in Galveston at 5:30. I know it's a day earlier than we planned, but I think it's for the best." It was best for Kit. Ross had her so bewitched, she couldn't think clearly. "Don't worry about picking us up. We'll take a taxi to your house."

Andy wouldn't like it, but seeing the writing on the wall with Ross, she realized she needed to get away from him before she broke down and made a mistake she'd never recover from. While they were on the campout, the children would be her buffer. After that she would make certain they did safe activities with Ross until it was time to leave.

"I'm going to pick you up, Kit. Just let me know the time."

"All right. You're the best friend in the world."

"Ditto. How's Andy?"

"As you know, he didn't want to come out here at first, but now he's loving it."

"Something tells me Ross Livingston has a lot to do with his turnaround."

He had everything to do with it.

"Ross and his partners. They and their families have shown Andy such a great time already. He's never had this kind of attention and doesn't want to leave. But he doesn't want to live with his grandparents anymore, so he's willing to see what Galveston is like."

"He's a little trooper. We'll do everything we can here to make him happy. Kim's looking forward to it."

"I am, too. It'll be great seeing you again. Until Friday night, then."

Kit hung up and went back to the living room. Andy was munching on a granola bar. "Aren't you too full from dinner to eat that?"

"No. I just felt like one. They're really good. Do you want a bite?"

"Thank you, but I don't dare eat any more snacks

or I'm going to gain weight." Needing to do something with her nervous energy, she sat down at the table to keep working on the puzzle.

With each day Kit noticed more changes in him. A new confidence had taken hold, one she was grateful to see. The shadows and furtive looks seemed to be disappearing. She wanted him to stay like this and dreaded telling him they were leaving Friday. But that could wait until Wednesday evening after they'd returned from their overnight trip.

"Mom? Do you like Ross?"

His question didn't exactly surprise her. She'd known it would come up at some point, just not this soon. "Who wouldn't like him?"

He wandered over to the table to watch her. "Do you think you'll ever get married again?"

She felt a sudden burst of adrenaline. "Where did that question come from?"

"Johnny and Jenny were talking about it while we were playing Ping-Pong after dinner."

"I see." Kit had to force herself not to overreact. "That's because their mothers both got married recently."

"They wish you would marry Ross."

She couldn't help smiling. "They do?"

"Yes. They love Ross and think you are really nice."

"Well, that's nice to hear." Kit believed what her son was telling her, but she also believed Andy was projecting some of his own feelings where Ross was concerned. "You like him a lot, don't you?"

"Will you get mad at me if I tell you the truth?"

She reached out to hug him. "I could never get mad at you for being honest. Not ever."

"Now that my dad is gone, I wish Ross could be my new dad."

Oh, no, Andy.

Kit got up from the table and walked over to the minifridge for a can of cola.

"See? You *are* mad."

"No, honey."

"Yes, you are. You don't want me to like him because of Dad."

She spun around, almost spilling her drink. "That's not true. I know how much you loved your father and always will, but now that he's gone, it doesn't mean you can't learn to love someone else. Ross is a wonderful man, and any boy would be blessed to have him for a father. But in order for that to happen—"

"I know," he broke in before she could finish. "He'd have to love me the way Carson loves Johnny." Sometimes Andy sounded wise beyond his years. Just now the wistfulness in his tone crept into her heart. His gray eyes squinted up at her. "If he asked you, would you marry him? Johnny says Ross really, really likes you."

"Andy—" She shouldn't have taken that second swallow and choked on it. "We hardly know each other!" Insecurity was driving her son to say these things. "It's too soon for me to think about getting married. I want to work and take care of you. That Johnny—he does way too much talking."

"He's funny, Mom."

"I agree, but he sometimes says things he shouldn't."

"That's what Ross says. Did you know his parents got married five weeks after they came to the ranch? Jenny said her parents got married in private after ten days."

Kit put the can on the table. "I know their marriages happened fast." Incredibly fast. It was hard to believe, and yet these retired marines were exceptional men. It was no wonder Alex and Tracy had fallen in love with them.

But for those four people to marry so soon and be sure… Kit had been so sure when she'd married Winn, never realizing the nightmare that awaited her. The thought of going into another marriage where she could be dominated was frightening.

When the house phone rang, she jumped.

"I bet that's Ross!" Andy ran in the bedroom.

"Wait—" She followed, but he was too quick for her and picked up. "Hello?" After a pause, "Hi! Yeah! I'm in my pajamas. Hey, Mom? Can Ross come over and help us with the puzzle? He says he's not tired yet and I'm not either."

Ross had a definite reason for wanting to come over, but she didn't know what it was. As usual he knew how to handle Andy so he wouldn't get alarmed. In fact, her son was thrilled. "If he'd really like to."

Andy repeated her message before he hung up. "He says he's driving over now."

Right or wrong or unwise, he was coming and Kit couldn't do anything about it. With her heart thudding in her chest, she hurried in the bathroom to brush her hair and put on some lipstick.

Before long they heard the knock on the door, and Andy opened it. Ross's gaze darted to her. "Thanks for letting me come. I have the whole top floor of the ranch house to myself. Sometimes it gets lonely."

"My grandparents' mansion felt the same way to me when I had to go to bed."

Andy's comment squeezed her heart. "Well, tonight nobody's lonely."

Ross coughed. "Mind if I help with the puzzle?"

"Be our guest."

The three of them sat down at the table.

"I'm glad I don't have to go away to that school."

"I didn't like the boarding school I went to," Ross interjected. He'd already found some puzzle pieces that fit. "I only got to go home once a month."

"Johnny and Jenny are lucky they get to go to school in Jackson."

"I agree, except they're kind of scared."

"Why?"

"Well, Johnny went to school in Ohio before he came here, and Jenny was in school in California. They don't have any friends yet except each other. It's going to take them a little time to adjust at Snake River Elementary, but they're tough."

Kit suspected Ross was trying to prepare Andy for when they went to Texas.

"That's a funny name for a school."

Ross chuckled. "Speaking of snakes, has Johnny told you about the pet snake he keeps in his room? His name is Fred."

"Fred?" Both of them broke into laughter.

"No one knows why he picked that name. Last month Jenny gave him a T-shirt for his birthday that has a snake on the front. The writing above says 'Fred's Dad.'"

Kit smiled. "That's one shirt I've got to see. He's such a character."

"So's Jenny. She's the one who thought it up and designed it."

"They're both precious."

Andy looked at Ross. "Do you want to see a picture of my dad?"

Kit was stunned. More and more he was opening up around Ross. Already she knew Andy wouldn't want to leave here when the time came.

"I was hoping you'd show one to me."

"I'll get it." He was back in a flash. "Here he is."

Ross took the five-by-seven framed photo from him. "I've seen other pictures of him, but this one is special. He's one fine-looking marine you can be proud of. When you're a man, you're going to look a lot like him."

"Thanks. Did you like being a marine?"

"I learned to like it a lot."

"I don't want to be one. They get killed."

"You're right. Some of them do." His black brows lifted as he looked at Andy. "You know what? That's the great thing about being your own person. You get to do what you want with your own life. What do you think you'd like to be?"

"I've been thinking about that, but I don't know yet."

Kit couldn't believe what she'd just heard. Andy was talking like a grown-up.

"Well, you've got years to find out."

"Do you like being a rancher?"

"I love it, but I didn't know I wanted to be one until Carson invited me to his ranch last March."

"What happened?"

"Well, we got on horses, and he showed me the whole property. I felt like I was seeing country no other man had ever seen or walked on. Each time we came to a different spot, I marveled at the wild beauty of the land and the mountains. I felt like it was calling to me and I had to be a part of it."

Kit got gooseflesh while he described his feelings.

"As we rode, he told me the stories about his ancestors and how they came to settle here. It was such a different world from the one I'd come from, it was like I'd been living on a different planet. I kept thinking a man could live here, put down roots and be happy.

"The truth is, Andy, I'd never truly been happy because I had a dad who expected me to be a certain way all the time."

"Did he die?"

"No. He and my mom live in Houston, Texas, the home of the big oil wells. I have a married brother Scott and a married sister Georgianna, but I call her Georgie Porgie. She doesn't like that." Andy laughed. "I love them a lot, but I have to do my own thing."

"My dad had to do what my grandfather said."

He cocked his head. "But from now on, you and your mom get to do what *you* want. Right?"

"Yeah. Thanks for talking to me."

"Anytime."

Afraid she'd break down bawling if she heard any more, Kit said, "With that settled, it's getting late, honey. We've had a huge day. You need to brush your teeth and get to bed."

"Okay. Good night, Ross."

He handed the picture back to him. "Thanks for showing this to me. Get a good sleep. I'll see you in the morning. We'll pack up and head for Bluebell Lake."

"Yeah!"

Andy gave Kit a hug and left the room. No sooner

had he shut the door to the hall than Kit's cell phone rang. Ross shot her a glance.

She reached for it, but for the first time she didn't get that sick feeling inside. "It's Charles. He never gives up. I'm going to turn off the ringer so I won't be bothered for the rest of the night."

"That sounds like a good idea."

After fixing it, she said, "What's the real reason you came over tonight?"

He lounged back in the chair and extended his long legs. "I'm going to ask you a question, but you don't have to answer it. In fact you can tell me to take a hike."

She chuckled. "I'd never do that."

"I guess we're going to find out if that's true. As I recall, you told me that when you get to Texas, your savings will only keep you for a while. That could mean any number of things. How much money do you really have on hand?"

Kit clasped her hands beneath the table. "It's enough."

"That's what I thought." He got to his feet.

"Where are you going?" she asked jerkily.

"To take that hike."

"I didn't mean to be rude to you."

"I know that. I've asked you something that's none of my business and took the risk because I care what happens to you and Andy. Get a good sleep." He started for the door.

"Don't go yet. Please—"

He stood there rubbing the back of his neck. "I only asked because after ten years of marriage, I would have assumed you had enough money saved to keep you going a lot longer than that."

She let out a small moan. “Nothing about my marriage was conventional. I wasn’t allowed to work. That was unheard of for a Wentworth. Since I earned no money, I was dependent on Winn and his father for everything.”

Incredulous, he moved closer to her. “So what you’re saying is, you had no discretionary income if you wanted to buy something for you or Andy without their approval?”

“That’s what I’m saying.”

The silence that followed was deafening.

Ross stared down at her, appalled by the revelation. “Where’s the money your husband made while he was in the service?”

“Winn’s military pay was always funneled into a special investment I couldn’t touch.”

His dark brown eyes searched hers. “So, how do you have any money at all?”

“At my grandmother’s death, she willed me her books and the $3,000 she had in her savings account. I had it invested in a CD money account that grew interest before I met Winn. He didn’t know about it. Four days ago I drew out $10,000.”

He hooked the leg of the chair and sat down. “Throughout your entire marriage, you had no money that you could actually handle yourself?”

“That’s right.”

“So without that CD, you’d have nothing?” She felt his quiet anger.

“I know it sounds incredible. Winn and his father did it to prevent me from leaving with Andy. They never knew about my grandmother’s money. I never touched it because I knew that one day I’d need it.

When your invitation from the ranch came, I decided it was our passport to a new life."

"How did you get access to the money? Wouldn't they know if you went to Point Judith to get it?"

"Yes. When Nila knew about my plans, she came to Bar Harbor on the pretext of visiting her mother and gave me some money to help me. After Andy and I flew from Norway, we landed in Providence, Rhode Island. I rented a car and we drove to the bank in Point Judith where I withdrew my money.

"I asked the bank to write me a cashier's check, then we returned to Providence for the rest of our flight out here. That's one of the reasons Andy was extra tired. The poor guy had to endure too many plane trips in one day."

Her story was so unbelievable, she couldn't have made it up. "You still have that check on you?"

"Yes. I plan to deposit it in a bank in Galveston and pay Nila back."

Lines darkened his features so she hardly recognized him. "I'm still trying to get my head around the fact that you lived ten years at the mercy of your husband's family. How did it work?"

"Between Winn and Charles, they paid for everything I needed."

"And they decided *what* you needed, *when* you needed it?"

At this point Kit stood up. "Yes." She couldn't look at him.

"And you're going to Galveston to start a new life with only $10,000?"

"Minus the $1500 I have to repay Nila for taxi money and our airline tickets. I also have the diamond ring Winn gave me. It's the only piece of jewelry I possess. It was appraised at $18,000. I plan to sell it when I get there."

His mouth had thinned to a white line. "I'm afraid you won't get half of what it's worth if you try to sell it. There are other benefits that should be coming to you because of his years in the military."

"I know, but I haven't seen them. Charles goes through all the incoming mail first."

Kit heard him suck in his breath. "You need an attorney to bring a lawsuit in order to claim the investments your husband made throughout your marriage. That money, maybe all or a portion of it, is legally yours. Whatever the amount, you need it to help you get established in Texas or anywhere else."

"I can't count on it," she said. "I imagine Winn made an airtight will with his father's help. Any of that money will go to Andy when he comes of age. But Charles has never discussed it with me, nor would he."

By now Ross was on his feet once more. "Were you married in Rhode Island?"

"Yes, in a civil ceremony at the courthouse."

"That might have some bearing on your case. An attorney will know the probate laws for Maine and Rhode Island. Through discovery you'll find out the facts and go from there."

"I can't afford one."

His eyes studied her with an intensity that shook her. "I know an attorney who will take your case. It's the only way for you and Andy to receive what's rightfully yours."

"I appreciate your concern, Ross." She loved him for it. "He must be some kind of lawyer to take on my father-in-law's empire. But when you sent that letter inviting us to the ranch, I know for a fact your good will didn't extend to engaging legal counsel worth thousands of dollars to help out a stranger." Kit wished her voice wouldn't tremble. "You and I both know what it would take."

"For a fallen veteran's wife and child, this attorney would work out a plan that will be feasible and mutually beneficial. All I have to do is give him a call."

"Is there no end to your goodness?" She leaned forward to kiss his cheek. "The truth is, after Winn died I made up my mind that Andy and I would leave with the clothes on our backs, my paltry savings and never look back. I've witnessed the way Charles treats people when they oppose him. I want no part of it."

"Kit—" he whispered with urgency.

The pathos she felt from him was too much to handle. "Have you forgotten what *you* did? You left for the military with the clothes on your back and nothing else. Look at you now! You've made a whole new life for yourself and have become a rancher. Buck left his father's business to do the same thing. You and your partners are making it on hard work and faith despite your chronic health concerns. That's what I intend to do."

His hands formed fists at his side. "But I didn't have a child dependent on me."

"Millions of other people do, and they still make their own way no matter how hard and unfair. When my parents were killed, they'd been living paycheck to paycheck and only left a small insurance policy.

"My grandmother had to take over my support when she was already living in a rented house on a meager fixed income. My grandfather's pension barely covered the necessities. But she did it, and I was given a wonderful life!

"Now it's my turn to do the same thing for Andy, and *I'm* going to do it. After I told Florence I was leaving she said, and I quote, 'You have no skills, no resources. Nothing. How can you possibly care for our grandson?'

"Well, I'm going to show her how. I'm actually quite excited about it. I never want to be beholden to anyone again for my welfare. Thank you for your willingness to find me an attorney, but it isn't needed."

"What they've done to you is morally wrong."

"I know you can't comprehend it because you're such an honorable man, but please don't be outraged for my sake. It's all water under the bridge and has been for years." Putting on her best face, she said, "Andy and I are looking forward to the campout. When do you plan to leave?"

"Midmorning after I've assembled all our gear."

"We'll be packed and ready." She walked him to the door and opened it. There would be no repeat of what had happened earlier when he'd kissed her until she thought she might faint. "Good night, Ross."

Ross drove to the rear entrance of the ranch house to park, troubled by so many things, but most of all for one statement she'd made. *I never want to be beholden to anyone again for my welfare.*

How far had she thought it through? Did that mean she was ruling out ever getting married again? *Could you blame her, Livingston?*

Once inside, he headed for his bedroom. It was ten-thirty, but he had a vital phone call to make to Sam

Donovan in Houston. He disliked bothering anyone this late, but it was an emergency.

After the speech she obviously hadn't planned to make until he'd forced it, Ross felt gutted. Talk about ten years of being in a velvet-lined prison. It pained him what she'd had to live through.

Pleased that he'd reached Sam, Ross didn't waste any time explaining the reason for his call.

"What an astonishing story. I think Charles Wentworth has been off his rocker for a long time. Don't worry about this. I'll do some preliminary groundwork first thing in the morning and see what I come up with. Without looking into the matter of a will and funds due the spouse, here's what I can tell you up front.

"The death gratuity payment is $100,000 for those who died of hostile actions and occurred in a designated combat operation or combat zone or while training for combat or performing hazardous duty. Their lawful surviving spouse is the first in order to receive payment by the CAR assigned to the reporting or assistance base within twenty-four hours of the member's death."

Ross bit down so hard, he almost cracked a tooth. "Kit never saw one dime of that payment. Charles has defrauded her in that area alone."

"She's definitely got a case, even without looking into the existence of a will. If you can talk her into filing a suit, I believe she'll recover a great deal more money. Unfortunately, this is Charles Wentworth we're talking about. He won't play by the rules."

Ross coughed. "I know. My father never did, either."

"That's a fact."

"It's why I'm appealing to you."

"I appreciate that. As soon as I know anything, I'll get back to you. It's an honor for me to do something really important for a retired marine who served our country with distinction. I've always been very proud of you. In my opinion, you're the finest Livingston of them all."

Ross hardly knew what to say. "Those words mean the world to me. Thank you."

"You're welcome. We'll stay in close touch."

With that accomplished, he hung up and took a shower. Anything to help relax him after the horrific revelations Kit had unfolded to him earlier. Otherwise sleep wouldn't come for a while.

Before getting under the covers, he checked his phone messages. One was left by Millie Sands, a forest ranger he'd taken to dinner last month. She wanted to know if he'd like to go to a party with him on Saturday night. He left her a message telling her he had another commitment, but thanked her and told her he'd talk to her soon.

The other message was from his sister Georgianna. She told him to call her back no matter how late, but that it wasn't an emergency. Wondering what it was all about, he phoned her now, knowing he'd be too busy in the morning getting ready for the campout.

"Hey, Georgie Porgie—" He hadn't talked to her in several weeks.

"*Ross*— At last! I've been waiting hours!"

She hadn't phoned more than a half hour ago, but he didn't take issue with his dramatic sister. He hadn't seen her since March when he'd flown home from Walter Reed before coming here. "How's Doug?"

"He's fine. We both are."

"Where is he?"

"Busy flying all over Texas with Scott and Mom and the staff to help Dad on the campaign trail. I'm with them, too, but broke away long enough to phone you. Ross—you've got to come back home. The election's in November. Dad needs you. You promised him that when the summer was over, you'd give up this ranching idea."

Ross coughed and shook his head. "I never promised him."

"But you told him you'd think about it."

"No. That was simply wishful thinking on his part and you know it. He'll never change."

"I know," she admitted.

At twenty-two she'd been crowned Miss Bluebonnet of Texas. That was three years ago. With glistening black hair and blue eyes the color of the famous Texas flower, she was a real beauty like their society mother.

"Did you know Amanda is still waiting for you to come home and marry her?"

"Is *that* what this call is all about?"

"Don't get mad. She's gorgeous and you're already thirty-one. Dad says it's time you were married."

If his sister ever got a look at Kit, then she'd know what gorgeous was.

"Dad was saying that to me eight years ago," he teased. "If I'd been in love with her, I wouldn't have gone into the marines."

"Why *did* you go? Don't you think it's time you leveled with me?"

He closed his eyes. "If I told you the truth, you'd be offended and hurt. I don't want to do that to you."

"It's because Dad's a politician and you aren't. Right?"

"He thrives on that rat race all right, but that's not the reason I went into the military." Ross took a deep breath. "I wonder if you're capable of handling the truth."

"Thank you very much, brother dear."

"I didn't mean that the way it sounded."

"I know you think I'm some empty headed has-been beauty queen who has no substance."

Kit had accused him of thinking the same thing about her. Meeting Kit had given him new insights.

"You know better than that." The hurt in Georgianna's voice decided him to be honest. He confided the secrets of his life to her, leaving little out. When he'd finished, he heard her crying.

"I had no idea, Ross. No idea at all. I love you that much more for being strong enough to be your own person. I just wish you didn't live so far away from Houston. I missed you so terribly when you left home."

She was a sweetie. Always had been.

"I've missed you, too. Those words mean everything to me, Georgie. Naturally I want Dad to be successful, but that life isn't for me."

"I get that now." She sniffed. "Have you ever told our parents what you've told me?"

"No. After I made the decision to leave Harvard, I simply explained that I wanted to serve our country and nothing could persuade me otherwise. They couldn't argue with that because it was for a good cause."

"But you came back with that awful coughing disease. It almost killed all of us."

"Just remember that I'm alive and doing so much better than I was back in March. They know that because I talk to them once a month."

"Ross? Do you mind if I talk to them and try to help them understand?"

"You can if you want, but it won't do any good. I've got big plans for this ranch, honey."

That well had to be a producer! If he hadn't joined up with Carson and Buck, he would never have met Kit. "When they've come to fruition, I'll invite all of you here. Maybe when they see my life, they'll begin to understand."

"I hope so. Before we hang up, just tell me one thing. Is there a special woman in your life yet?"

He'd been honest with his sister about his past. Why not go all the way? "There could be."

"Only could?"

Ross gripped the phone tighter. "It's early days yet." He had his work cut out to convince her they belonged together.

"Can you tell me anything about her? I'll keep it a secret. I just want to know because I love you so much and can't bear for you not to have someone wonderful in your life."

Maybe he'd changed, or maybe she'd just grown more empathetic. Maybe it was a combination of both. Whatever the reason, he felt like confiding in her. "She's a widow with a nine-year-old boy."

A slight gasp escaped. "She has to be one of the mothers you invited to the dude ranch."

"That's right. You'd like her and Andy a lot."

Quiet reigned on her end for a full minute. "Then I'm going to hope it works out. I'd love to meet her."

"Maybe one day I'll bring her and Andy to Houston to meet my family."

"You deserve a great love, Ross. Call me if you ever need to talk. I love you."

"I love you, too. We'll keep in closer touch from now on. I promise."

"I'd like that more than anything. Bye for now."

He rang off and buried his head in the pillow. By the time they got back from the campout, he needed to have convinced Kit not to leave for Texas because there was something much more important waiting for her right here.

She had her heart set on owning a bookstore. He understood that. He also understood that her best friend lived in Galveston. But why not choose a town closer to the ranch where they could see each other, like Jackson or Afton?

Ignited by that idea, he got out of bed and went over to the desk for his laptop. After carrying it back to the bed, he lay down on his stomach and started checking some real estate websites for the sale of commercial businesses. For a half hour he pored over the information and found several possibilities that could be converted. He also noted twelve small bookstores existing in the two towns. Someone might want to sell, or at least hire her.

In the morning he'd go downstairs and print off what he'd found. At the right moment he'd show the results to Kit and ask her to think about it. The possibility that she'd be leaving Jackson for good was insupportable to him.

Ever since she'd mentioned Galveston, it had been in the back of his mind that the beach pad would be the perfect safe house for them in a protected environment.

Her son needed normalcy with friends and school and all that went to make up his child's world.

The problem was, she would never accept charity from him, and he wouldn't let her live there without him. His life was here.

The next best thing would be for him to fly down there twice a month and stay at his beach pad so he could see them. A long-distance relationship was the last thing he wanted, but he'd do it if he had to. She was that important to him.

But are you that important to her, Livingston? That was the big question, the one that haunted him until he knew no more.

Chapter 9

"Everybody ready to roll?" Kit and the children had assembled at the rear of the ranch house with Ross.

"Yes!" the kids cried in unison. Their excitement was contagious.

"Have you got your cameras? Sunscreen? Candy?"

"Yes!"

"Is Fred with us?"

"No!" Johnny blurted before breaking into laughter.

"That's a relief."

Ross grinned at Kit. He'd just packed up the truck with all the camping equipment they'd need. She decided to sit in the truck bed with the children while they drove through the forest, but she couldn't help sneaking glances at his hard-muscled frame as he moved around checking everything. His gaze caught her looking at him several times, causing her pulse to race.

His partners and their wives would drive up to sleep over and bring dinner. For now, Kit and Ross were in charge. She felt the heavy responsibility, but she had Ross with her to share it. He was amazing.

"Remember, guys. There's going to be a summer storm in the early afternoon, but it will pass. If anyone wants to stay home, let me know now."

Kit saw the children look at each other, but no one spoke up.

He walked over to Jenny. "How about you? Are you nervous, honey?"

No one was more caring than Ross. Kit's admiration for him just kept growing.

"A little," she answered honestly, "but I still want to come."

"I get a little scared, too," Kit confided. "We'll sit and watch it together until it's over. How does that sound?"

"Good." Jenny smiled.

"Isn't anyone worried about me? I'm going to get lonely in the cab all by myself."

"Mom—why don't you sit with Ross?"

Warmth crept into her cheeks. Andy had a little imp in him. He was learning it from Johnny. The two of them had been doing more talking. No doubt plotting.

"I promised to sit back here and make sure you children are all right."

"I guess that's that, then!" Ross sent her a look that warned her there'd be a penalty. A curl of excitement ran through her. "So we're off with a Hi-yo, Silver!"

With that comment they all laughed. It sparked a conversation about the Lone Ranger and Hopalong Cassidy.

He drove away from the ranch house and took the road they'd traveled yesterday. There were more clouds in the sky, but it was still a beautiful day. It wasn't hard to pretend they were a family out for an adventure. Kit didn't want any of it to end. For today she'd simply enjoy the delights of being with Ross in this little part of heaven.

Along the way he stopped the truck at an overlook. Here they got out to take pictures and enjoy a sweeping view of Jackson Hole and the panorama of the spectacular Tetons. With the fast-moving clouds gathering, it took her breath.

They eventually drove on and started climbing through the pines. The higher they drove, the darker it became because of the towering trees and the approaching storm. A change in the weather added a mysterious element to the landscape the children could feel as they gazed about in wonder. She heard thunder rumble in the distance. Before she could say anything, Ross stopped the truck and got out.

"This storm's going to be exciting. Let's get you inside the cab while I throw the tarp over the back." He reached for Jenny. "Down you go, honey." The boys climbed out.

Ross's eyes lifted to hers. "You last," he said as the children scrambled inside the truck. With effortless strength he lifted her out, crushing her against his hard body. Before he let her feet touch the ground he kissed her on the mouth.

"That wasn't fair," she whispered shakily.

"I don't always play fair. You're going to find out all sorts of things about me this trip."

On legs weak as water, she walked to the back door.

"Andy? If you'll ride in front with Ross, I'll sit back here between Jenny and Johnny."

"Okay." He sounded happy about it.

In a minute Ross joined them, and they started on their way again. Around another curve and they came out of the trees just as the sky lit up.

"Whoa!" Johnny cried. "That lightning was close."

"It's really far away," Ross said over his shoulder, "but it's so bright it's like daylight."

Kit put her arms around both children. "This is exciting being together like this." More lightning flashes lit their way up the mountain as they wound in and out of the trees. The thunder cracked and shook the ground.

"Pretty spectacular, huh?" He reached over to rub Andy's head. "This makes the Fourth of July fireworks look like a couple of candles on a birthday cake."

His comment made everyone laugh. "We need some heat if we're going to enjoy the show." He turned it on and they kept going. Under normal weather conditions, it wouldn't be dark till nightfall, but the thunderheads were moving in fast, blocking out the light. "We're almost to the meadow. This is better than going to an outdoor movie."

Andy turned to Ross. "I've never been to one. Is it fun?"

"Yup. Especially when I could drive and take a girlfriend."

What would it have been like to be his girlfriend? Kit would never know and needed to put him out of her mind, but the kiss he'd given her was still on her lips, making that impossible.

"I would have loved to take you to one, honey, but we know why I didn't."

"Yeah. I know."

"When my grandmother was alive, she drove us to the drive-in between Providence and Woonsocket. That was one of our favorite things to do. We'd buy treats, and she'd let me sit on the hood of the car with a blanket and pillow to watch the movie."

"I want to do that."

"We will," Ross declared. "One of these days we'll take a balloon ride to Cody and go to the outdoor movie there in a rental car."

Kit wished he wouldn't say things like that to Andy when he knew her plans.

"Can we?" Andy cried.

"Can we go, too?" the other kids asked.

"I don't see why not." When Ross looked at Kit through the rearview mirror, it was like one of those lightning bolts spiking the atmosphere had just gone through her.

Suddenly there was another flash that illuminated the forest. In that instant they caught sight of an enormous elk with an even more enormous rack of antlers crossing the road.

"Ross!" Johnny cried. "Did you see that?"

"It's the same one I took a picture of last month. That's the granddaddy you've been dying to see. He must be nine feet from nose to rump and sure gets around. Wait till you tell your dad you finally saw him."

Johnny bounced up and down on the seat in reaction. Just then another giant thunderclap shook the ground. Andy let out a yelp that caused Ross to laugh. "We're perfectly safe."

Ross brought the truck to the edge of the clearing

but still under the dense shelter of the trees. For the next little while they huddled together to watch nature's show. Ross passed out licorice for everyone. When the hail came down the size of marbles, it filled up the windshield and covered the ground. Soon it was followed by a downpour of rain that drowned out every other sound.

"Now you know how people felt who got in the ark with Noah."

"Would *you* have gone in it, Ross?"

"I'd like to think so, Andy."

"Me, too."

"Me, too," Kit echoed with the other children. "Can you believe that at this time yesterday there wasn't a cloud in the sky? The quick changes in weather are a constant source of wonder to me. I can see why you love it here so much. It's like the earth has been baptized. There's no place like it."

Ross turned in the seat so he could look back at her. "Certainly not in Texas."

"Not in Maine either," Andy piped up, sounding very grown up just then.

Both comments disturbed her in more ways than one.

In a few minutes the rain turned to drizzle. "The storm has passed over us. Pretty soon the sun will be peeking out of the clouds again. Keep watching for the elk."

They all kept their eyes peeled. "I can't see him," Johnny complained.

"He's probably sought shelter under a big pine by now where it's dry and he can eat."

"What does he eat?" Andy wanted to know.

Ross let out a cough. "Grass and low-growing plants, about twelve pounds a day."

"Twelve?"

"Yup, and ten gallons of water."

"My daddy says an elk has four stomachs," Jenny informed them.

"Whoa!"

"Can we get out now, Uncle Ross?" Johnny was getting restless. "The rain has stopped."

"You can as soon as I drive out into the clearing. After I remove the tarp, we'll eat sandwiches and go for a hike."

It had been a day to remember. That evening Ross's partners arrived in the Jeep with hot food because they'd dispensed with the idea of building a bonfire. Ross couldn't recall ever having this much fun. Everyone pitched in before going to bed. All food had been put away in the bear locker in Carson's Jeep parked away from them.

While Kit talked with the girls, it was Andy who worked right alongside him like a buddy as they erected the last of the three-man tents.

"Here. Have some more licorice on me."

"Thanks. I wish—" Suddenly he stopped talking.

"What do you wish, Andy?" he prodded.

"Oh, nothing."

"That didn't sound like nothing to me. Tell me what's on your mind."

The boy averted his eyes. "I wish Mom would buy a bookstore in Jackson. Then we wouldn't have to move to Texas."

Ross had to fight his sudden rush of adrenaline. The

papers he'd printed out early that morning were burning a hole in his back pocket. "Texas isn't a bad place. I grew up there."

"Yeah, but I don't know anybody there."

"I thought your mom said you were friends with Nila and her daughter."

"I am, kind of, but I really like Johnny and Jenny."

No one could help liking those two children. "I'm sure the idea of moving to a brand-new place makes you feel nervous. But just remember your mom loves you, and she's going to do everything she can to make you happy."

"I know." Andy helped him lay out the three sleeping bags. "Were you nervous when you came out here after the hospital?"

"Very nervous, but in a different way." He coughed.

"How do you mean?"

"I'd already made friends with Carson and Buck, but I was afraid I might not be good at ranching. There was so much to learn."

"You can do everything!"

"You know how to make a guy feel good, but you should have seen me in the beginning. Carson told me it was like he was teaching a kindergartner."

Andy grinned. "He was just teasing."

Kit's boy just kept growing on him. "I guess what I'm trying to say is, what if I didn't like it after I got here and then had to let the guys down because I didn't want to stay? It upset me so much that I might disappoint them, I didn't feel very good for a while."

"But you love it now, right?"

Ross nodded. "More than anything in my whole

life. Maybe that's how you'll feel about Galveston after you've been there a while."

Andy didn't respond to that. "Do you miss Texas?"

"Let me put it this way. It's where I was born, and my family lives there, so it will always have a place in my heart. But as I told you before, I wasn't happy there. Do you think you're going to miss Bar Harbor?"

"Not now that my dad's gone."

"I can understand that."

"Mom says she's glad we're moving. I am, too, but I'd rather move here. I like it a lot. Johnny and Jenny told me they love it here more than anything and wouldn't ever want to leave."

This ranch had a stranglehold on all of them.

"Have you told her how you really feel about all this, Andy?"

"I'm afraid to."

"Why? She's not scary." He turned on the Coleman lantern to make sure it worked. "You're her son, right? You always talk everything over, so why don't you tell her what's on your mind? All she can say is no."

"But I don't want her to say no."

He chuckled. "Maybe she'll surprise you. Today she kept saying how much she loved it here."

"I know, but she's already made plans with Nila."

"Plans can be changed. She hasn't bought a bookstore yet or paid money for an apartment." Her money problems made him break out in a cold sweat. Maybe because of talking to Andy like this, Ross would be struck by one of those lightning bolts that had lit up the forest hours earlier, but he didn't care.

"I guess I could talk to her."

"You've got time. You haven't even finished your

whole vacation here yet. Maybe tomorrow night or the next when you're back at the cabin. I know she'll listen to you. She loves you to death."

"I love her, too. You're going to sleep in here with us tonight, aren't you?"

Ross had been waiting for that invitation. He coughed. "I was planning on it, provided it's okay with your mom. Otherwise I'll sleep in the back of the truck. Have you ever camped out overnight before?"

"No. Once my dad took me sailing and we stayed out overnight."

"Just the two of you?"

"No. Grandfather came, too, but he got seasick."

"That's one memory I bet you'll never forget."

They were both laughing when they heard, *"Knock, Knock."* Kit lifted the tent flap and came in. "You were both in here so long, I wondered if you'd fallen asleep."

"No," Andy murmured.

Ross smiled. "We were just talking and time got away from us."

"Everybody has gone to bed."

"Then I'll leave the tent while you and Andy get ready."

He stepped outside and looked up at the sky. A few clouds partially hid the moon, shrouding parts of the Grand Teton. One day his house would sit on this spot where their three tents had been pitched. When Ross had been flown home from Kandahar to Walter Reed half dead, he could never have dreamed up a night like this, in a place like this, with a woman like Kit Wentworth.

"Ross?" Andy called to him from the tent door. "Mom says you can come in anytime."

More progress. She hadn't relegated him to the truck. Though she'd done it for Andy's sake, he'd like to think she wanted him inside with them, too. "Thanks. I'll be right there."

After a trip into the forest, he was ready for bed and found Andy in the middle sleeping bag. Kit was over on the other side, leaving him guardian of the tent door.

He removed his Levi jacket and boots, then turned off the lantern and climbed in his bag.

"Good night, you two."

"Good night," she said.

"Thanks for bringing us up here, Ross."

"You're welcome, sport."

Andy turned a couple of times in his bag. Pretty soon Ross could hear the kind of breathing that meant he'd fallen asleep.

Before long he heard sounds of movement coming from the other bag. "Ross?" Kit whispered.

"Yes?"

"Thank for being so good to Andy."

"He's a wonderful boy."

"I can see changes in him. All the worries he's had bottled up are coming out. He's talking more than he has in years. It's because of you."

"I can't take the credit. When you told him he didn't have to live with his grandparents anymore, you're the one who changed history for him."

"But you have to know you're the one representing security right now. Andy lost what little he had when his father died."

"You're not giving yourself any credit. You're his mother. Don't you know you're his whole world?"

"He's my whole world, too," Kit said quietly. "But

until that letter from the ranch came, I didn't know where to turn. I'm afraid you've become his hero."

"Why afraid? I've never been anyone's hero and kind of like the idea."

"Joke all you want, but it's true. In fact, it has me worried."

He sat up. "For what reason?"

"Last night he told me that now Winn was gone, he wished you could be his dad." The words sank deep in Ross's soul, causing his heart rate to triple. "Apparently he and the other children have been doing a lot of talking about the recent changes in their lives. I'm afraid Andy's going to talk to you about it, and I want you to be prepared."

Ross needed to maneuver his way carefully through this minefield. "Do you know when I was in the hospital, I got pretty down and worried I might never have a family of my own. Since you came, I've been thinking how great it would be to have a son like Andy."

"But if you were to tell him that to make him happy, he'd hang on to it."

"I'd only tell him that because it's true. Would that be such a bad thing?"

"You know it would."

"Because you'll be in Texas."

"Yes."

"Wherever you go there's nothing wrong with Andy knowing he's got a friend who loves him here in the Tetons. Yesterday when you were talking to the sheriff, that son of yours climbed right into my heart. You couldn't see what I saw. Andy stood next to you without flinching. For a moment I felt like I was back in Afghanistan.

"We occasionally came across a broken-down car in the road with a mother asking for help, her son at her side willing to protect her, a fearless expression on his face. I never knew if they were the enemy lying in wait. I always held my breath as I approached, anticipating fireworks.

"Andy dealt with the fireworks like a man. The truth is, I couldn't love that boy more if he were my own son. Considering he and I were raised the same way in terms of the emotional and financial environment, plus the domination factor, it's not so strange that we've bonded this fast."

"You're right," she admitted in a croaky voice.

"His vulnerability makes him that much more lovable. I don't need to tell you how terrific he is. Don't worry that he might talk to me about his feelings. He already has."

"What has he said?" She sounded alarmed.

"He's told me he doesn't want to live in Texas. He likes Nila and her daughter well enough, but he really likes Johnny and Jenny and wishes you would buy a bookstore in Jackson so you can live there. I told him that, given time, he might learn to love Texas the way I love the ranch. That's the way we left our conversation. The point is, we're buddies whatever happens in the future. I'll always be his friend."

Silence filled the interior of the tent.

He lay back down. Having delivered his salvos, he hoped they kept her tossing and turning until morning. For the first time since she'd come to the ranch, he knew he was going to get a good night's sleep for a change.

* * *

Kit got down with Jenny to examine the bluebells that grew in profusion around the end of the lake. "Aren't they beautiful?"

"I want to pick some, but daddy told me I couldn't."

"I know. The problem is, they're wildflowers and they'll die too fast to enjoy them."

She could hear Johnny talking to Ross in the background. "Are you sure there are fish in here?"

"I know there are, but they're not feeding today. Maybe the storm yesterday has caused them to feed on the bottom of the lake. We'll have lots of chances in the future to hike up here again."

"I won't," Andy muttered.

"'Cos you have to go to Texas, huh."

"Yes."

"Hey, guys—I'm afraid it's time for us to hike down to the truck and drive back to the ranch. You have Back To School Night and I promised your folks I'd bring you home in time for baths and dinner first."

"I don't want school to start. I want to stay up here."

Ross chuckled. "When you see all the cute girls in your class, Johnny, you'll change your mind."

"Girls?"

"Yeah. That's why I didn't like my boarding school. There weren't any."

Kit smiled in spite of the dejection she'd heard in Andy's voice seconds ago.

"I like school," Jenny piped up.

Kit put an arm around her. "I liked it, too. That's because you're a reader like me."

"Okay, everybody. Hand me your rods and we'll get going."

They followed Ross down the mountain. Since the conversation with him in the tent last night when he'd left Kit speechless with his admissions, they hadn't discussed anything. He'd been up before she'd awakened. After breakfast the parents had helped them pack everything before they'd left and Ross had led her and the children up to the lake.

The kids did all the conversing, for which she was grateful. She'd lain awake most of the night with a heavy heart. Kit realized she'd sprung the idea of moving to Texas on Andy without any preparation. It was a lot to ask of him, but these were desperate circumstances.

Naturally he'd rather stay in Jackson near people who'd shown him the time of his life. For Andy to want her to buy a business here and live probably shouldn't have surprised her. But after her talks with Nila, she'd been so focused on Texas, it never occurred to her that Andy would even think about her earning her living somewhere else.

Kit was grateful to Ross for being on her side and not trying to influence Andy. He continued to handle her son in a way that left her awed by his depth of understanding.

Her thoughts drifted back to the day she'd received the letter from Carson. She'd thought it had been a mistake, and she'd called Colonel Hodges. But he'd convinced her it was no mistake. Whether she had money or not wasn't the point. These men needed healing, too.

After listening to Ross last night, she understood what the Colonel had meant. Caring for these children who'd lost their fathers had brought fulfillment to the lives of these retired marines. She saw what it had done for three men who'd been discharged for health reasons and had come home low in body and spirit. What they'd done and were doing was a marvel.

As she watched Ross helping the children down the mountain, a feeling of intense love for him swept through her. Though it was too soon, there was no doubt in her mind she'd fallen terribly in love with him.

Terribly, because as much as she wanted to acknowledge her love to him, it meant handing over a part of herself. It meant being at the mercy of a man again. She didn't know if she could ever do that.

When they reached the truck, Kit got in back with the kids, but this time Andy quietly climbed in front with Ross. She understood. The sand was emptying from the top of the hourglass. The few days left to be with him were precious.

Later, after they'd dropped Johnny off at his house, they pulled into the parking area outside the ranch house. Andy came around as Kit and Jenny got down from the tailgate. She waved goodbye and ran around the corner to find her nana.

"Mom? After dinner Ross is going to take us for a horseback ride down by the river while the kids go over to school with their parents."

Her body quivered at the mere thought. "That's really nice of him, but aren't you tired after all the hiking we've done?"

"Heck, no. He says the horses need the exercise."

"Let's hurry to the cabin then and take a shower first."

"Why? We'll just get grubby again."

Kit couldn't fault his logic. "Maybe the horses would like it if we smelled better."

"Mom!" He ran over to tell Ross what she'd said.

Deep rich laughter poured out of him. Their eyes met for a moment in pure amusement before a look crept into his that made her legs tremble. "Let's freshen up inside and eat."

She nodded and hurried around to the entrance with Andy. It hadn't taken but one hour of arriving at the ranch on Saturday with Ross to get into the habit of eating, sleeping and having the time of their lives in between. But the fun was going to stop. The more she thought about it, the more she couldn't bear it.

Darkness had settled over the ranch by the time Ross drove them back to their cabin from the stable. After he pulled to a stop, he turned to them. "I'm going to give you an hour, then I'm coming by to drive you to my home where you'll stay with me until you leave the ranch."

Andy's eyes rounded. "But Buck hasn't built it yet!"

"That's true. I'm talking about the home I live in right now. The whole upstairs of the ranch house is mine. I have my own apartment. The other one across the hall used to be the one for Buck. Since I've lived in Wyoming, I've never invited anyone upstairs before. You'll be the first ones."

"Can we, Mom?"

He captured her gaze. "After sleeping with you in the tent last night, the thought of sleeping alone doesn't sound like much fun."

She knew what he was really telling her. He'd had his share of women, but no woman had passed over his threshold while he'd been living here. But he also had another more compelling agenda. For some reason he wanted her and Andy under the ranch house roof from here on out.

This had to do with Charles, otherwise Ross wouldn't be making such an unprecedented decision. As usual, he was handling it in a way that wouldn't alarm Andy.

Kit knew what she ought to reply to protect her heart, but her son's shining eyes defeated her. "Well, since we'll be your first guests, we can hardly turn down your gracious invitation. Maybe we should find a tree outside in the morning and carve your initials. 'AW slept here.'"

"Make it AW and K and we'll do it," Ross murmured.

"Cool!"

"Why don't you hurry and shower first, honey."

"You can wear your pajamas over, sport."

"Okay." After he'd gone inside the cabin she turned to Ross. "What's happened?"

"Your father-in-law left a message at the front desk. You're to expect a visitor sometime between now and tomorrow morning. I know you can handle him, but I'd rather you had some warning than simply answering your cabin door to him."

"So would I. Thank you, Ross."

He nodded. "I'll be back."

Kit hurried inside. Andy had already gotten in the shower. She started packing as fast as she could. They hadn't brought much with them, so it was no huge chore. Andy came out again in his camouflage pajamas so she could shower.

As she hurried in the bathroom, he said, "I just love him, Mom."

I know you do. So do I.

When they were ready, Kit did a once-over of the cabin to make sure they hadn't left anything before she went outside to the truck. Ross helped her inside next to Andy, and they took off.

He parked at the rear of the ranch house. Together they carried their things down a hallway that led to the staircase.

"This is fun. I've never seen this part of the ranch house before."

"It's about time you did," he said on a cough.

Buck was just coming out of the office and saw them. His eyes widened. "Hey—what's going on?"

"Ross is moving us into your old apartment!"

A half smile broke out on his face. "Is that right?"

"Yeah. He says he's been lonely."

"That's a fact. Jenny and Alex are going to be thrilled to have friends around this place."

Kit smiled. "We're happy about it, too, believe me."

Buck's gaze drifted to Ross. "What can I do to help?"

"Thanks, but Andy and I have it covered. How did Back To School Night go?"

"Pretty well, but they've put the kids in two separate classes. That kind of upset them. Alex is going to go over there in the morning and see what she can do to keep them together. We're hoping that when the administration understands the uniqueness of their situation, they'll cooperate."

"I'm sure they will," Kit said to assure him.

"See you guys in the morning."

As Buck waved them off, the three of them went up the stairs. Ross opened the door to the empty apartment and set down the suitcases. "This has a living/dining area and kitchenette, a bedroom with a queen and a twin bed, a bathroom and a small study. Housekeeping made this place ready for occupancy after Buck moved downstairs, so you should be perfectly comfortable."

"Hey, Mom." Andy put down the case he was holding and ran through the apartment to the study. "This is great!" He came hurrying back. "Where's your apartment?"

"Right across the hall. It looks exactly like yours. While we were building the cabins, Buck did some remodeling up here in the spring to update everything."

"It's lovely," Kit murmured, looking around. She lowered her case to the carpeted floor. "How lucky can Andy and I be?"

He flashed them a smile. "I'm glad you like it."

"Thanks for letting us stay up here."

"You're welcome." Ross couldn't resist giving Andy a hug. "Now it's cozy."

"I always felt lonely at my grandfather's. My bedroom was on another floor from my mom's, and he wouldn't let me keep a light on."

"Oh, honey." Kit threw her arms around her son. "I felt lonely, too, more than you'll ever know."

"But those days are over, right?" Ross high-fived him.

"Right."

He glanced at Kit. "Let's program each other's phone numbers right now."

"Good idea."

Once that was done, he said, "I know you're tired, so I'll say good-night. Sleep well."

"Thanks to you, we will."

After he left, Kit put on her pajamas and opened

the case with their toiletries so Andy could brush his teeth. "Could I sleep with you tonight?"

"You mean in the big bed?"

"Yes."

"I'd love it." Unlike other children, he had never been allowed to creep in their bedroom. For the first year after her parents had died, many was the night Kit had slept with her grandmother. "Come on. We'll read the second chapter of *Call of the Wild.*"

After he said his prayers and dived under the covers, she opened another suitcase to retrieve the book. The lamp at the bedside table shed enough light for her to read. A few pages into it, he said in a sleepy voice, "Judge Miller was kind to Buck…just like Ross is to me." A lone tear trickled out of his eye before he fell sound asleep.

Moved beyond words, she got out of bed. After putting on her terry cloth robe, she tiptoed out of the bedroom and shut the door. Without conscious thought she opened the door to the apartment and slipped across the hall. She could see light under his door and heard coughing before she knocked. In a second it opened to reveal the dark-haired cowboy who'd walked into her life last week and refused to go away.

In the semidark he stood there wearing only the bottom half of a pair of navy sweats. The dusting of black hair on his well-defined chest added to his male potency. She tried to smother the quiet gasp that escaped at the sight of him.

Lost for words she studied the cleft in his chin. Gazing at the lines of his hard mouth and handsome features, she couldn't quite catch her breath.

"Forgive me. I shouldn't have bothered you this late,

but when I was reading to Andy just now, he said something before he fell asleep I felt you should hear."

"Come in," he urged.

"I can't. He might wake up and wonder where I am. I was reading to him from Jack London's book. As his eyes fluttered closed, he said something so sweet and dear, I wanted you to know. You'll appreciate it because you read that book, too."

When she told him, Ross lifted his right hand and traced her features with his fingers. At his touch, little trickles of delight flowed through her body. "He's an easy boy to love."

"He's never known real kindness like yours, the kind that transforms lives. If it weren't for you, he wouldn't understand how great it is to be a good man, to *want* to be a good man like you. He's in awe of you, Ross. So am I. That's what I came to say."

"Kit..."

Suddenly she was in his arms. His head descended until his mouth covered hers.

She moaned for the sheer ecstasy his hands and lips created. Never in her life had she known hunger like this. At nineteen she'd been in love with love and flattered by Winn's attention, but it hadn't felt anything like this. Not even close.

Ross crushed her against him until there was no space between them. The fire he was whipping up inside her was so hot and intense, she was losing control.

Kit had started this by knocking on his apartment door. Now she had to be the one to end it *before she couldn't.* She slid her hands up his chest to ease herself away, but his reaction was to deepen their kiss. Much as she wanted to go on enjoying this mindless ecstasy, she didn't dare. Somehow she found the strength to tear her mouth from his and pull away.

"Don't leave me," he begged. "I'm in love for the first time in my life. There's no mistaking it for anything else. I want you, Kit. You have no idea how much." His dark brown eyes were glazed over.

"Forgive me for starting this tonight."

He ran his hands up and down her arms. "It's because you want me just as badly."

"You're right." Her voice shook. "But this isn't the time or the place, not when there's so much at stake. I'm afraid to get involved again."

"I understand that, so we'll take this slowly."

"No. That's unfair to you because I can't make any promises. I just can't!" she cried from her soul before wrenching herself from his grasp.

Kit heard him call her name, but she'd already shut and locked her apartment door. Unfortunately it wouldn't keep her in. She would have to exercise the greatest self-control of her life to go to bed and stay there.

While she stood there clutching the back of one of the chairs, her cell phone rang. She reached for it. "Ross?"

"Willy just phoned me. Charles is downstairs in the foyer demanding to talk to you. What would you like to do?"

She took a deep breath. "I'm going to have to talk to him, but we need to be private."

"I'll go down and bring him to your room. Is Andy still asleep?"

"Yes. The door's shut to the bedroom."

"Then there shouldn't be a problem if Charles doesn't raise his voice. Are you ready?"

A calm had settled over her. This confrontation had been coming on for years. "More than ready."

"Good girl."

After she hung up, she walked across the apartment and turned on the overhead light. Then she opened the front door and waited in the hall for him. She heard a cough.

Pretty soon she saw two figures coming toward her. Charles was almost as tall as Ross. But where the black-haired retired marine was hard and lean dressed in a sport shirt and jeans, her father-in-law with his thinning ash-colored hair looked soft and overfed in his suit, despite Florence's regimen.

The only surprise was the suffering she saw on his face when the light fell across him. His gray eyes stared at her for the longest time. "Where's Andrew?"

"Asleep in the bedroom."

Ross eyed her over the older man's shoulder. "I'll be across the hall."

"Call off your bodyguard, Kit. You don't need him."

"If you haven't understood by now, Charles, let me explain I have no use for another man in my life. After living with you and Winn, I don't need any man. Come in and say what you have to say. I'm exhausted and want to go to bed."

Chapter 10

Ross stared at the closed door.

I don't need any man. I have no use for another man.

Was that said for her father-in-law's sake? Or had she just sent Ross a message? If so, it had chilled his blood because it had sounded so final. Irrevocable.

His mind replayed what had gone on in here before Charles had arrived. When he'd told Kit he was in love for the first time in his life, she'd said nothing back. Though she'd admitted she wanted him, she couldn't make any promises.

Fragmented, he went back inside his apartment, but he left the door ajar so he'd be aware when the other man left. In an agony of thought, he went into his kitchen and made himself a cup of coffee. After draining it, he heard a sound coming from the corridor. When he reached his door, Ross saw the back of Charles as he stormed down the hall toward the stairs.

His first impulse was to rush over there, but her words had left their sting. While he waited for her to come to him, he phoned the front desk. Willy told him Mr. Wentworth just left in a car with another man. Willy had locked the front door behind him.

Ross thanked him and hung up. In another hour of waiting she still hadn't come. There was no phone call.

She's afraid of involvement, Livingston.

He couldn't blame her for that. Not after ten years of being trapped by two men.

Ross got it.

The papers he'd printed off to give her stared up at him from the coffee table. No way would he be giving them to her now. She'd see them as another man attempting to run her life, telling her what she ought to do, as if she didn't have the brains to figure out life for herself.

Before he did anything else, he left a message for Sam Donovan. "Mrs. Wentworth won't be filing a suit. Stop all work on her case and send me the bill." She'd told Ross she didn't want to sue for the money, but he hadn't listened to her. He'd gone ahead and phoned Sam.

Two more days to get through before she left for Texas. What a hell of a time for the kids to be back in school!

If it was all right with Kit tomorrow, he'd take Andy with him to repair some fencing and do a few chores. Let him see what it was like doing regular work on the ranch. They'd pack a lunch. Kit could take a well-earned rest and enjoy the day by herself or with Alex or Tracy.

On Friday they could do a float trip or take a balloon ride. Whatever sounded fun to Andy. Beyond that he wouldn't allow himself to think.

He got ready for bed once more. There was too much silence and too many hours left to try to kill it without help. TV had its uses.

When he went down to breakfast early the next morning, there were still a few empty tables. He spotted Kit immediately. She was wearing a new blouse with jeans he hadn't seen before. Andy sat with her and Jenny while they ate. Everything seemed so normal with Kit, last night's nocturnal activities with Charles Wentworth might never have happened.

If it killed him, Ross would pretend normalcy, too. He gazed at them. "Good morning."

Andy smiled at him. "Hey, Ross."

"How did you sleep?"

"Great!"

Ross had no idea if Andy knew his grandfather had come to the ranch house last night or not.

"Hi, Uncle Ross."

He sat down between the two kids. The waitress came over and poured him a cup of coffee, but he didn't order. The thought of food made him nauseous. "I like your new outfit for school. Are you excited?"

She nodded. "Nana's taking me and Johnny. Andy and Kit are going to drive into Jackson with us."

That took care of part of the morning.

He drank some of the steaming liquid to fill the growing pit in his stomach before he flicked a glance to Kit. She was just finishing the last of her omelet. "When you get back, I'll be at the south pasture. Give me a ring, and I'll take you on an afternoon float trip."

"Could we, Mom?"

"I'd love it."

"Then I'll see all of you later."

"See ya," Andy responded.

He couldn't deal with this any longer and got to his feet. On his way out of the dining room he ran into Alex in the foyer. "Big day for Jenny."

"For me, too. I brought the van around to the front. Oh, Ross, I want her to like her new school."

"Of course she will. I understand Kit and Andy are driving in with you."

"Yes. I'm going to do a little shopping, and she said she'd like to do some, too."

"Have fun then and stop worrying. We all got through our first day of school, right?"

She laughed. "I needed to hear you say that. Tell that to Buck. He's more of a nervous wreck than I am."

Alex didn't know the half of it. Seeing black, Ross bolted off down the back hallway for the rear door.

Eight hours later Ross was in the office on the phone with Mac Dawson when another call came in. His adrenaline surged when he saw who it was. After getting off fast with the oil man, he clicked on.

"Kit?" It was late. Tracy had already brought the kids home from school over an hour ago.

"Hi. Sorry that the day got away from us and ruined the plans for that float trip. I hope it didn't put you out too much."

How about my shattered dreams? "Not at all."

"Would it be possible for you to pick up me and Andy in town? If not, we can take a taxi back to the ranch."

He let out the breath he'd been holding. "Where are you?"

"At Pinky G's Pizzeria on Broadway Street having an early dinner."

Somehow he had to go on playing the cordial host until he drove her to the airport on Saturday morning. "I'll be there within a half hour."

"Thank you. We'll be outside watching for you."

Totally gutted, he strode swiftly out of the ranch house and started up the truck. He accelerated faster than he should have, passing other cars to reach the highway. When he drove into town, he spotted them in front of the restaurant. She was so attractive it took him a second to realize she wasn't holding any packages. That surprised him.

Ross slowed down and leaned across the seat to open the door for them. "Hey—" He smiled at Andy who slid in first. After Kit had shut the door he took off, heading for the main artery leading out of town. "Did you have a good day?"

"Yeah. Thanks for picking us up."

"I was glad to. What did you do?"

"All kinds of stuff." Which told him nothing.

"After the kids got home from school, they wondered where you were."

"How was their first day?" Kit asked.

"I couldn't tell. They're swimming right now."

"That's what I want to do." Andy looked at him. "What did you do today?"

"I had a meeting with my partners, and we made the decision to start the drilling for the well on Monday."

"That's wonderful news," she exclaimed.

Right now he couldn't appreciate it. Before long they were back at the ranch. Ross was coughing more than usual and needed his inhaler. He got out and walked upstairs with them.

"That doesn't sound good," Kit said in alarm.

"I'll be all right." Sometimes sleep deprivation made his condition worse. Last night was the worst he'd ever lived through since coming to the ranch.

Andy looked anxious, too. "Are you sure?"

"I just need my medicine. If you'll excuse me, I'll see you two downstairs later for a game of Ping-Pong."

"I'm not very good at it."

"Neither am I, but we'll still have fun."

"Yeah."

Ross entered his apartment and shut the door. Once he'd used his inhaler, he intended to lie down. Sleep was what he needed to find forgetfulness. But before the medicine kicked in, he heard a knock on the door.

"Andy?"

"No. It's Kit. He's gone down to the pool. May I come in, or is it a bad time?"

Those were the words he'd been waiting for last night after Charles had left, but they'd never come. He walked through the apartment and unlocked the door, still coughing. "Are you sure you want to?"

"Yes," she said with enough emotion that he knew she meant it.

He opened the door wider so she could enter. "You're not well."

"It'll pass in a minute."

"Does it help to lie down?"

"Not really, but I often do because the medication makes me sleepy."

"Then, please, do it."

"What's so important?"

"Our lives." Her voice shook. She followed him into the bedroom and sat down on a chair while he lay back against some pillows. "Last night Charles came with terms of surrender. He can't bear to lose Andy. There's a house near the mansion he'll buy for me. He'll give me an allowance and won't force Andy to attend that school."

Ross jackknifed into a sitting position. He didn't know Genghis had it in him. His thoughts reeled. "What did you tell him?"

"That he was ten years too late, that Andy and I had other plans. I told him that after Andy and I were settled, he and the family could visit us when they wanted. He got angry and left.

"Andy had been listening from his bedroom the whole time. He came out and we had a talk that lasted a long time. My son told me a lot of things. Above all, Andy has grown to love you and can't understand why I can't live in Jackson and work so we can all be friends.

"He loves it here. I believe it because I love it here, too. Neither of us has ever been to Galveston. It has no appeal for either of us except it's Nila's home and she was willing to help me relocate."

By this time Ross had gotten to his feet. "Does Nila know any of this?"

"Not yet, but she knows what a huge decision we have to make. As I told Andy, she's a mom as well and wants us to be happy. And so do I," she said as a tear slipped down her cheek.

"This morning I told Alex we had several things to do in town and wanted to be dropped off at the Teton Book Shop. I looked it up in the directory thinking I could find out if there was a job opening for a salesperson. I told Alex I'd call you to come and get us so she wouldn't wait."

Ross couldn't believe what he was hearing.

"After leaving the shop, I contacted a Realtor who showed us quite a few rental properties, and we discussed some business opportunities."

"And?" The medicine had started working, but her news had created a new breathing problem for him.

"We've seen one rental house we really like, and the manager at Carter's department store told me they were thinking of making their books area more reader friendly. He liked my ideas for the coffee bar and told me to come back next week and we'd talk about it."

Ross was afraid to trust what he was hearing. "What's really turned things around for you? Aren't you terrified I'll influence Andy and create another crisis for you? Last night I heard you tell Charles you don't need any man."

"I don't, but you're not any man." She moved closer. "You're my guardian angel. I love you so much that the thought of losing the love you say you have for me right now fills me with unbearable anguish." She lifted her eyes to him. "You're everything a woman could desire in a man. I don't even know where to start telling you all the things you mean to me. It scares me I won't be able to live up to you."

His hands cradled her face. "You want to know scared? I'm still learning how to be a rancher like Carson. I don't have a lot to offer yet, but it's the life I love. After I left you and Andy in the cabin that first afternoon, I knew you were the woman I wanted. I knew it in the way you know the sun's going to go down behind the Grand Teton every evening.

"You're the most beautiful woman inside and out I ever met. You talk about *me* being some kind of angel… when I saw the courage you had to run away from a horrific situation in order to free your son, when I felt and witnessed your great love for him, that was it. I had to have you for my own and hoped that one day you could love me half as much as you love him."

She threw her arms around his neck. "Oh, darling—" Kit kissed every inch of his striking features. "I'm so in love with you it hurts."

"Enough to marry me?"

"If you're sure. I come with so much baggage and don't want to be a disappointment to you."

"Oh, Kit—how can I explain what you mean to me? There aren't enough words."

"I feel the same way."

The tight bands squeezing his lungs relaxed, and he began kissing her in earnest. He needed this. She was life to him. He picked her up and carried her over to the bed. Following her down, they began to communicate what they'd been forced to hold back. Instead of being in a frenzy of need, Ross kissed her slowly, deliberately.

"Oh, sweetheart—" He sighed later against her neck as his lips roved over her scented skin. "I've been single for so long, waiting and wondering if I'd ever find fulfillment like my buddies. To be holding the woman of my dreams in my arms at last and know you're mine forever—" Instead of more words, he finished saying them with his mouth.

"This is heaven," she whispered much later. "With the right man I knew it could be found on earth. But I had to come to the ranch to discover my soul mate. On the campout, Andy wanted to know if I would marry you if you asked me."

"What did you answer him?"

"That you and I barely knew each other, but that didn't stop him. According to Johnny, Carson got married within five weeks. As for Buck, it only took ten days."

Deep, free-floating laughter rumbled out of Ross. "I want to marry you today, this very instant. I'm sure Buck told Alex the same thing. Unlike Tracy, she didn't have a big family to invite."

"But *you* have one, darling. If we wait six weeks, it will give you time to put in that well while I get settled in a job. Then we'll invite both our dysfunctional families out here for our wedding. Maybe they'll see we're truly happy and wish us well, if only for Andy's sake. What do you think?"

"I'd rather invite them for a visit next year when we've built a house and some of my plans to make the ranch operate in the black for a change come to fruition. But all of it can be negotiated because we're equal partners, Kit. I want you to know that."

"I do. I trust you with my life."

"Enough to live upstairs with me until our house is built? I don't want you to move to a rental."

"I don't want to either. I'll pay rent here."

Ross knew not to fight her. He'd learned his lesson. "Fine. Now let's stop talking. Right now there's only one thing I want to do."

He crushed her mouth quiet as desire took over, blotting out the world.

Suddenly they heard Andy's voice calling from the hallway. "Mom?"

Ross moved off her fast and got to his feet so she could sit up, but she was much slower to respond. "Come on in, sport."

When Andy walked in the bedroom, his eyes lit up.

"Hi, honey. I thought you were going to swim."

"We *did* until Buck closed the pool and sent me up here."

They'd been up here a long time. When she darted Ross a guilty look, he just laughed.

"I need to freshen up."

He grabbed her around the waist so she couldn't get away. "Before we go anywhere or do anything, there's something your mom and I want to tell you."

"I already know."

"What do you think you know?" Kit exclaimed.

"Johnny said the reason you and Ross never came down was because you're going to get married."

Both Ross and Kit roared with laughter. "One thing you're going to learn, sweetheart. That kid is psychic, and there are no secrets in this house." Then he sobered and put his hands on his shoulders. He stared at Andy. "I love you, son. It would be an honor to be your new dad."

"I love you so much," he cried and grabbed Ross around the waist.

Ross was moved almost without words. "If it's all right with you, we're thinking about getting married in about six weeks. Maybe by then your grandfather won't be so upset, and he and your grandmother will come." If Kit could forgive them, Ross certainly could.

No words came out of Andy. Only hugs and tears of pure joy.

* * *

Kit and Andy had just entered the dining room for breakfast the next morning when everyone yelled, "Surprise!"

Ross's partners and their families had assembled at one of the big tables. There were waffles and French toast and bacon and eggs. A real feast. The kids had made a banner fastened to the log wall that said, "Congratulations Kit and Ross," done in their own printing. No doubt Andy's work was in there somewhere.

Her throat swelled with emotion until she couldn't swallow. Ross squeezed her hip. "What a homecoming," he whispered.

The ranch *did* feel like home.

She wiped her eyes and sat down by Johnny. "I can't begin to tell you how much this means to us. Not just because of today, but because of every day since we first arrived. I'm overwhelmed with all the things you've done for us."

"We've enjoyed you, too," Carson murmured.

She stared at the three men. "You know the saying about if you want something done, ask a marine? It has taken on a whole new meaning for me since your letter came inviting us to the ranch. Just know we think the world of all of you and will be forever grateful."

"We're glad you're going to marry Ross." This from Johnny.

He always made her smile. "I feel the same and love that banner you made for us. It's fantastic! But aren't you guys supposed to be at school?"

"Yup. But we didn't want to go today because daddy said this is a red-letter day, and he made an e-excep-shun."

"Nana says we're going to celebrate." Jenny looked at Andy. "Do you want to go to Funorama?"

"What's that?"

"This real fun place with rides and stuff, and you get to eat pizza."

"Sure! That sounds cool."

Kit smiled at Jenny. "Do you like school, Jenny?"

"I love it."

"How about you, Johnny?"

"It's pretty fun."

"What's your favorite subject?"

"Recess."

More laughter broke out while everyone ate. Toward the end of the meal, Buck tapped his water glass with a fork. "It appears our experiment to honor our fallen soldiers has been a huge success, so we're planning to invite more widows and their children next summer. You children are going to be a big part of it, and we're always going to need your help."

He winked at Ross. "There's only one problem. We don't have any more single men to marry off."

"Yes, we do," Johnny interjected. "Willy!"

Chapter 11

Six Weeks Later

Ross was still in the shower. Kit waited feverishly for him to come to bed. When she saw his tall physique in the semidarkness of the master bedroom, it was a surreal moment with the silhouette of the Grand Teton framing him. She reached for her new husband, hungry to belong to him forever.

"My love," he said, his voice thick with emotion. "I didn't think our wedding night would ever come."

"I know. I love you," she cried as they began giving and receiving pleasure she hadn't thought possible. They clung to each other throughout the night, living to make each other happy.

Kit was shocked how late it was when she awakened the next morning tangled up with him, their bed covers askew. She couldn't describe this kind of fulfillment. You had to experience it.

You had to be married to Ross.

She lifted her hand where a gold wedding band with a diamond dazzled her eyes. Mrs. Ross Livingston. What joy!

All of a sudden he coughed. He did it in his sleep. It wounded her every time. She doubted she'd ever get used to it. Ross teased her, it was his badge of courage, but it was a lot more than that. It was an honor to be married to him. She knew that, and she was determined to be the best wife on earth.

She felt him stir, then he was kissing her again. "Good morning, sweetheart." He pulled her on top of him. "This is what life is all about."

She was too breathless to answer him.

An hour later he opened his eyes and stared into hers. He played with her hair. "Tell me what you're thinking."

"That the ranch house made a beautiful place for a wedding and I could lie here with you forever."

She was aware of time passing. They only had time for a two-day honeymoon. Kit had to be back to work at the department store on Monday. But in reality, since she'd first met Ross, she felt as if she'd been on a continual honeymoon.

Carson and Tracy had insisted the newlyweds stay at their house, and they'd moved in the upstairs of the ranch house for the weekend. Andy was sleeping with Johnny in Buck's old apartment. The guys had arranged for all the cabins to be available this weekend for the wedding guests that included Nila and her family.

"I loved your family, Ross, especially Georgianna."

"I knew you two would get along."

"The look of pride on your father's face when you told him the well was a big producer was priceless."

Ross grinned. "It was, wasn't it? But the big shock was seeing your in-laws show up at the last minute."

"That was a shock all right." Kit and Ross had sent out invitations, but she'd never received an answer from her in-laws and hadn't expected one. "The fact that they came proves to me no one is all bad. They came for Andy, and I know it made him happy."

"I'm sure it did. They should have come, not only to honor their son's boy, but the fabulous mother who raised him. This was the way to do it."

"Yes. I have to tell you I'm so glad I didn't have to sell the ring. One day I'll give it to Andy so he can give it to the woman he loves."

"It'll have great meaning knowing his father gave it to you. I've been waiting until now to give you something else. It's an envelope Charles handed Willy to give to you."

"Did you open it?'

"No, darling. It's for you. I'll get it." He slid out of bed and put on a robe. In a minute he came back in the bedroom with it and handed it to her.

She opened the envelope with her father-in-law's letterhead. Inside she saw a check made out to her for $2,000,000. He'd put in a note. *Winn would have wanted you and Andy to have this. C.*

It was hard to swallow. "My grandmother used to say, faith precedes the miracle."

He covered her face with kisses. "You've taught me that. Faith brought you here. I don't know what I ever did to deserve you, but I'm going to hold on to you for dear life. You and Andy *are* my life now, Kit."

She threw her arms around his neck. "You're *my* miracle. I'll love you till the day I die and beyond."

* * * * *

Rachel Lee was hooked on writing by the age of twelve and practiced her craft as she moved from place to place all over the United States. This *New York Times* bestselling author now resides in Florida and has the joy of writing full-time.

Books by Rachel Lee

Harlequin Special Edition

Conard County: The Next Generation

A Soldier in Conard County
A Conard County Courtship
A Conard County Homecoming
His Pregnant Courthouse Bride
An Unlikely Daddy
A Cowboy for Christmas
The Lawman Lassoes a Family
A Conard County Baby
Reuniting with the Rancher
Thanksgiving Daddy
The Widow of Conard County

Harlequin Romantic Suspense

Conard County: The Next Generation

Undercover in Conard County
Conard County Marine
A Conard County Spy
A Secret in Conard County
Conard County Witness

Visit the Author Profile page at Harlequin.com for more titles.

REUNITING WITH THE RANCHER

RACHEL LEE

Chapter 1

Holly Heflin walked into the lawyer's office in Conard City with more uncertainty than she had felt in a long time, and she was used to facing some pretty ugly situations. But this was different—the reading of her great-aunt's will. She was, as far as she knew, the only heir, so her concern didn't lie there.

But she had arrived in Denver after a red-eye flight, hopped into the cheapest rental car she could find and driven straight here to make this meeting. She felt tired, grungy and most of all overcome by memory. Facing this meeting seemed so *final*.

Returning to Conard County wasn't easy, but she had the fondest memories of visits to her aunt's from childhood and early adulthood. They had begun washing over her from the instant the surrounding country began to look familiar, and with them came the numbness she had been feeling since the news of Martha's death had begun to give way to a deep well of grief.

The last of her family had died with Martha, and a sense of her solitariness in the world had been striking her in an utterly new way.

But she shoved all that down as she spoke to Jackie, the young receptionist. *Get through this. Get to the funeral home to watch Martha's ashes placed in a mausoleum.* Martha had always used to say she wanted to sprinkle her ashes around the ranch, but apparently that wasn't allowed, because the attorney had been quite definite, and Martha had paid all the expenses in advance.

God, the ache was growing. The reality was beginning to settle in, tightening her chest.

The receptionist ushered her into a spacious but ancient-looking office. She supposed the balding man behind the desk was the attorney, but then she saw the cowboy in one of the chairs facing the desk.

Her heart immediately jammed into her throat. Cliff Martin? Here? Of all the people on earth she never wanted to see again, he topped the list. She'd been busily burying her memories of him for nearly a decade now, trying to forget, trying to forgive herself. Apparently she hadn't succeeded.

He had always been attractive, but at thirty-two, Cliff Martin had become attractive to the point of danger. Weather and those ten years had etched themselves a bit on his face. Age had taken away any softness and his face now looked hard and chiseled. Those eyes were the same, though, an incredible turquoise that would make him a standout anywhere.

An instant shaft of remembered passion pierced her

numbness, arrowing straight to her core and causing her insides to clench. She'd never wanted to see this man again, but apparently her body had other ideas. She glanced quickly away.

Both men rose immediately at her entrance, a courtesy that seemed quaint after the life she had been living. She tried not to look at Cliff, but couldn't help noticing that he seemed taller. Was that possible, or had her memory shrunk him? Broad shoulders, narrow hips… *Stop,* she ordered herself. *Just stop it now.* She didn't need this.

She immediately shook the lawyer's hand as he introduced himself. "John Carstairs," he said. "Good to see you, Ms. Heflin. And you remember Cliff Martin."

She turned to Cliff, wishing he didn't look as if he had just stepped out of a movie poster or ad. Darn, his dark hair didn't even show a thread of gray, unlike hers.

Cliff Martin. The man who had been helping her aunt keep the place up the past few years. The man who leased most of her aunt's grazing land. The man she had ditched. Her hand trembled a bit as she offered it.

He spoke. "So you finally got back here."

It sounded so much like a criticism that she had to bite back an angry retort. All she could do was drop her hand, turn away and take the empty chair. Working on the streets with troubled kids had taught her to be wary of how she responded to people. Problems could start in a flash.

She managed to keep her voice even. "I've been back."

The men sat. She avoided looking at Cliff Martin and focused on John Carstairs. "I traveled all night," she said. "I may be a little slow this morning."

He at once reached for his desk phone and punched a button. “Jackie? Could you bring some coffee for Ms. Heflin?” He arched a brow at her.

“Black, please.”

“Make it black. Thanks, Jackie.”

He released the button and sat back. Waiting. There was a strong sense of waiting, which made her even edgier after her race to get here. Then he said, “I’m sorry we had to meet under these circumstances. Your aunt was a wonderful woman.”

“Yes, she was,” Holly said honestly. “I’m going to miss her.”

“Really,” drawled Cliff.

At that she turned to stare at him. “How would you know? You know nothing.”

“You haven’t been around much.”

That wasn’t true, but again she bit back her retort. This man had no need to know anything, and she wasn’t going to dignify his criticisms with explanations he had no right to.

“Please,” said the lawyer, “let’s be pleasant, shall we?”

Holly was all for pleasant. She was too tired for the spat Cliff apparently wanted. Jackie entered, setting a cup and saucer on the edge of John’s desk in front of Holly. “Thank you.”

Jackie smiled, nodded and walked out, closing the door quietly behind her.

John leaned forward. “As I told you, Ms. Heflin, your great-aunt made all the arrangements. They’ll be waiting for you at the funeral home after we’re done here. But there are other things we need to discuss.”

“Yes,” she said. There was also one thing she knew

for sure, that a visit with a lawyer was supposed to be private. "But what is Mr. Martin doing here? You said I was Martha's sole heir."

"He," said John, "is the executor."

Holly's mind whirled. Maybe it was fatigue. Maybe it was burgeoning grief. All she knew was that she felt as if she had been sideswiped by a Mack truck. "Why not you?" she asked quietly.

"Conflict of interest. And it was your aunt's decision."

"Of course." She was still trying to take this in. She was going to have to deal with a man who had every reason to believe she was hateful? Well, it wouldn't be the first time. Still. She reached for the coffee and took a few sips, hoping to assemble her brain into a more orderly pattern than it seemed to be following right now. She noted that her hand trembled, and she quickly put the coffee down.

Deal. The word wafted up. She always dealt. Whatever life threw her way, she was good at it. She'd deal with all of this somehow, from grief to that nasty cowboy.

"I'm going to give you a copy of your aunt's will to read at your leisure. In the meantime, I'll just go over the broad aspects here."

"That's fine." She certainly didn't feel up to dealing with anything detailed.

"You've inherited the ranch. It's free and clear except for the leases. As the law makes clear, those leases to Mr. Martin remain in place, and your aunt's will states that he is allowed to continue leasing the land at his discretion for the next ten years."

Holly felt her heart began to sink. That meant she

would have to deal with this ghost from her past indefinitely.

"Your aunt was also a very careful woman, and left you a great deal of cash, a quite surprising amount, actually. Mr. Martin has the necessary papers giving him management of the estate, and he'll take you to the bank to transfer the accounts into your name."

Holly managed a jerky nod. Nothing seemed to be penetrating except that she was now locked into some kind of long-term relationship with a man she had been avoiding for a long time. A man she had never wanted to see again. Martha had known that. What had possessed her aunt?

"In addition, you're not allowed to sell the ranch for at least ten years. But your aunt added something to that."

Holly lifted her head. "Yes?"

"She said to find your dream. I'm not sure what she meant."

Holly's heart rose, just a bit. God bless Aunt Martha, even though she didn't know what her aunt meant. "I'm not sure, either."

Carstairs shrugged. "Well, that's what she said, and if it has anything to do with the ranch, she made sure it would be possible for you. So those are the essentials. The rest is mostly legal stuff that you can call me about if you have questions."

Sooner than she would have believed, she was out of the office and back on the street. Downtown Conard City hadn't changed in any way she could perceive. It seemed to be cast in amber, preserved and unchanging. It had always charmed her, coming as she did from larger towns and cities, and she paused for a moment to soak it all in. There was a peaceful air to this place that had never failed to draw her during her visits. But since Cliff, she had never wanted to make this her home.

That wasn't likely to change. She started to turn toward her rental when Cliff's voice yanked her up short. "The funeral home is the other way."

She turned. "I know. I'm driving." What did he care?

"It's not that far. I'll see you there then."

He was going to be there, too? Somehow she had imagined herself quietly putting her aunt to rest. But of course Martha must have had friends. She looked down at herself, at her overworn black sweater and slacks, and wished she had thought this through. Surely she could have dressed better for this?

God, all that had been on her mind was getting out here in time. To do her last act for her beloved great-aunt. She'd raced to find a plane ticket, fought to reserve a rental car that wouldn't completely impoverish her, put on something black and fled her dingy apartment.

Now she felt as dingy as the streets she had left behind.

She climbed into her car, found a brush in her purse and ran it swiftly through her wavy chestnut hair. A glance in the rearview mirror told her that her makeup was long gone, not that she cared. Instead of primping any more, she headed for the funeral home.

Inside she found her fears confirmed. Some forty or fifty people milled about the place, and while she couldn't remember any of them, they all seemed to know who she was. She was quickly swamped in condolences and a sea of names. Some offered a memory or two of her aunt.

And with each memory her throat grew tighter. Soon she could feel the sting of withheld tears in her eyes, and wished only that this would be over so she could get out to the ranch and cry in private.

God, she hadn't even had time to get some flowers.

None too quickly, the funeral director announced it was time. The crowd followed him at a somber pace as he carried Martha's urn through a door, across a covered walkway to a large concrete mausoleum. There, one door to a niche stood open and waiting.

Holly swallowed hard. She swallowed even harder when a man stepped forward and said, "I was Martha's minister for many years. I know she refused a memorial service, saying she only hoped that she would be well remembered. We remember Martha well indeed. A generous woman, with a kind heart. We are grateful she passed swiftly and without warning, and know that she rests now in God's love."

Then he insisted on reciting the Twenty-third Psalm. Before it was done, the unbidden tears were rolling hotly down Holly's cheeks. When the funeral director slid the urn into its niche, she stepped forward and laid her hand on it, not wanting to see it disappear, hanging on for one last moment.

"I love you," she whispered. Then she stepped back and watched the director close and lock the door. A brass plate on the outside listed Martha's name, her dates of birth and death. Nothing else.

When she turned she found all those people looking at her as if they expected her to speak. A moment of panic fluttered through her, memories surged, and then she remembered something her aunt had once said to her.

"Aunt Martha told me that she wanted to leave a small footprint in this world. That she wanted to leave the land as it was meant to be, and nearly everything as she had found it. Except for one thing. She hoped that she would leave small footprints in the hearts of her friends, and that they would bring smiles. Thank you all."

Then she pivoted to stare at that closed vault. Great-Aunt Martha was gone. The times between her visits had been punctuated by weekly phone calls with her aunt. Now there would be no more calls and it hit her: there was a huge difference between being separated by miles and being separated by death.

A huge, aching chasm of a difference.

Cliff Martin watched Holly Heflin with dislike. She was still a pretty sprite, with wavy auburn hair and bright blue eyes. He felt that all too familiar surge of desire for her and had to battle down memories of how her gentle curves had felt in his arms. But too much lay between them for him to like her. While Martha had defended Holly more than once, he had the wounds to show for how she had treated him. A long-ago summer affair, brief, fleeting, had left him an angry man for a long time and convinced him that Holly was as self-centered as a woman could be. Martha's talk of her youth hadn't helped one whit.

Regardless, now he was tied to this woman by Martha, who for reasons he couldn't begin to understand had made him executor of her will. Not that there was a lot to carry out. And there was Holly, a woman even more beautiful than at twenty, now part of his life again whether he liked it or not. He didn't like it.

What had Martha been thinking? He was grateful to her for protecting his leases. It would have killed his ranching operation to give up all that land. But what was with the ten years? And the stuff about Holly following her dream?

Not that he cared about Holly's dreams. Holly's dreams had nearly killed him once. To his way of thinking, she wasn't trustworthy. Maybe Martha felt the same, and had put the leases in her will to ensure Holly didn't kick him off the land. But damn, this was going to be miserable. He needed that woman like he needed a hole in his head.

But for all he had wanted to think Holly was an uncaring witch, nothing could make him believe those tears weren't real.

He didn't get any of this, but he supposed it didn't matter. Martha had gone her own way, quirky and delightful and always surprising. Why should she end her life any differently?

He watched Holly decline to go to the church for a covered-dish supper. Martha had wanted no memorial, but others were going to give it to her anyway. How that would have made her laugh.

But her niece seemed determined to follow her aunt's wishes. He watched her walk to her car, a slender woman with beautiful auburn hair and blue eyes, and thought how utterly alone she looked. And how very sexy. Since those thoughts had gotten him in trouble once before, he clamped down on them hard, and wished them to hell.

No way was he going to fall for that blue-eyed seductress again.

With any luck, Holly Heflin would blow back out

of town as fast as she had blown in, taking whatever funds Martha had left her and leaving the ranch to rot. She was a city girl, after all.

He wondered if she'd let the house and barn turn to dust. He certainly wasn't going to do all the maintenance for her as he had done for Martha. He didn't owe her that and she wouldn't even qualify as a neighbor.

Damn, he felt angry for no good reason that he could figure out. He'd had a low opinion about Holly for years, so no shock there. Absolutely no reason to be angry all over again.

Cussing under his breath anyway, he skipped the potluck and headed home. He had a ranch to take care of and only one task remaining as far as Martha went: to take her niece to the bank and see that the accounts got turned over to her.

And, he supposed, to ensure she didn't try to sell the ranch. It didn't look as if she would care, so what the hell.

Trying to get himself into a better mood, he turned on some music on the radio, discovered a sad country song and turned it off again.

Damn, he thought. "Martha, why do I get the feeling you left me a mess and I don't even know how bad it is yet?"

Of course there was no answer.

Holly arrived at the ranch with sand in her eyes and lead in her heart. She climbed out of the car and looked around, memories whispering to her on the breeze. As a child she had absolutely loved coming out here. As a young woman, after Cliff, the charm had rested entirely with her aunt's company.

Turning, she surveyed the changes. Cliff must have rented damn near all the land, to judge by how close the fences were now. But he'd also kept the place up for Martha, and sooner or later she was going to have to thank him for that no matter how the words stuck in her craw.

Memories wafted over her. She'd spent some summers here as a small child, then when she'd grown up her visits had been shorter because she had a job, but still she had come, for Martha. With one exception, every memory was good. Time and frequent visits, at least, had mostly cleared Cliff from her memories of this place. It almost seemed that only Martha remained here.

Great-Aunt Martha had been the kind of woman that Holly hoped she'd grow up to be: tough, independent, doing things pretty much her own way, but kind and loving to the core.

She made herself brush away her reaction to Cliff and climbed the steps of the porch to the front door. Her key still worked and she stepped into the past, into familiar smells that carried her back over the years, into familiar sights, into a place that had always been her second home.

In that instant, knowing she would never see Martha again, she burst into the tears she'd been trying to hold back.

She'd always felt close to Martha, despite the miles that had separated them for so long, and it hurt to realize she could never again pick up the phone and hear her aunt's voice.

Never again.

* * *

Keeping busy seemed to be the only answer. Holly was used to being busy all the time, and sitting around her aunt's house weeping and doing nothing went against her grain. Martha, thank goodness, hadn't been sick. She had died suddenly and unexpectedly of a stroke, a merciful way to go, for which Holly was grateful. But it also meant the house was in pretty good shape inside as well as out. Not a whole lot of housework to occupy her, other than putting away the groceries she had bought and changing bed linens.

That left going through things. Martha had been a minimalist most of her life, buying very little, keeping very little that she didn't use. But in going through drawers and looking at photos, Holly found plenty to carry her into memory. Pictures of her visits here, pictures of her parents, photos of Martha's own parents and grandparents. She wasn't awash in photos, as Martha hadn't been one for taking very many, but there were enough to be cherished.

The furnishings showed their age and use but were still serviceable. The house seemed to be ready for her, and she wondered if Martha had intended that. Maybe.

She certainly hadn't left any unfinished chores behind her.

Finally, unable to bear any more, she headed for the bedroom she had used during her visits. The big stuffed teddy bear Martha had given her as a child still occupied the rocker in the corner. Holly fell asleep hugging it and thinking of her aunt, the last of her family.

Morning brought no relief. Sleep had been disturbed, and she hardly felt any more rested than yesterday.

Then she remembered something Martha had been definite about. "You want to do something for me? Plant a tree."

So she decided, after choking down her breakfast, that today she would go find a tree to plant just for Martha. Its importance grew in her mind as she thought about it. Martha had wanted it, and Martha would get it.

After she finished washing her dishes, Holly gripped the edge of the counter, closed her eyes, and tried not to hear the empty silence of the house around her. She couldn't believe she wouldn't hear Martha's voice at any moment. Couldn't believe that Martha was really gone.

God, it was beginning to hit. Numbness had begun wearing off yesterday, but now it seemed to be deserting her completely.

Hot tears rolled down her cheeks, and her heart ached as if a vise gripped it. She had known it would hurt to lose her aunt, but she hadn't imagined this. It was every bit as bad as when her parents died in the car crash. Every bit, and that grief still haunted her.

Martha had been her anchor ever since, her family, the person who kept her from feeling like an orphan, and now Martha was gone.

Never had Holly felt so utterly alone.

She wept until she could weep no more, until fatigue weighed her down and her sides hurt from sobbing. But at last quiet returned to her mind and heart. Temporarily, anyway. She fixated on getting that tree, the one wish of her aunt's that she could still carry out.

She washed up, dressed in jeans and a hoodie, the clothes she wore when she was working with the children, and stared almost blindly at her reflection in the mirror.

Who was she? It almost seemed as if she had become a stranger to herself, as if grief were sweeping huge parts of her aside. Closing her eyes, she thought of the kids she worked with back home in Chicago, kids who were always hungry, often cold, flotsam in a sea beyond their control.

Thinking of them grounded her again, reminding her she had a purpose, and purpose was the most important thing of all.

When she finally stepped outside to face the day's duties, she paused in the drive, feeling the spring breeze of Conard County, Wyoming, whisper all around her. Here the air was almost never still, and it seemed to carry barely heard words on it, as if it were alive.

She opened herself to it, letting it wash over her like a tender touch, the kind of tenderness she wouldn't feel again, the tenderness of mother, father, aunt.

She took time to walk around the house taking in the small changes, having random thoughts about what she could do with this place. Her job as a social worker lay back in Chicago, but as she strolled around she realized that an ever-present tension had begun to evaporate. Today she didn't have to walk on those streets; she didn't have to visit tiny apartments in public housing where despair seemed to paint the walls. She didn't have to deal with the problems of too-skinny children who were having trouble in school or at home. She didn't have to wage a battle against desperation and hopelessness. Not today.

Then, squaring her shoulders, she strode to the car. A tree. She needed to get a tree.

She saw a vehicle coming up her driveway. A dusty but relatively recent pickup of some kind. Who could possibly be coming out here?

She didn't have to wait long for her answer. She quickly recognized Cliff's silhouette behind the wheel. A few seconds later he pulled up beside her.

"Going somewhere?" he asked.

She resisted the urge to tell him it was none of his business, because she might have to deal with him for a long time to come. "My aunt wanted me to plant a tree in her memory. I was about to go look for one."

He glanced at her rental. "Hard to carry in that. I was coming if to see if you wanted to take care of the bank account transfer. The sooner we clear the decks, the happier we'll both be."

Her teeth tightened. He *really* wasn't going to let her forget. "Fine," she said shortly.

He looked at her car again. "You planning to stay long?"

"I have a couple of weeks before I have to get back. If that's long, then yes."

"One rain and that car won't get anywhere. You'll bog down."

"It's a rental," she said defensively, feeling as if he was criticizing her somehow. "Do you *ever* say anything that's not critical?"

He paused. "I call things as I see them. So did your aunt. How about you?"

"What I see is a man I intended to thank for helping Aunt Martha, but right now I couldn't choke the words out to save my life. You're rude."

His lips tightened, but his response was mild. "I see a little of your aunt in you."

She didn't respond. Ordinarily she would have taken that as a compliment, but right now she wasn't in the mood. Besides, with this man, it must have been a sideways condemnation of some kind. He had plenty of reason to hate her, she knew, but after ten years, shouldn't he be over it? Stupid question, she thought immediately. Her own behavior still troubled her after all these years.

"Well, climb in my cab. I can carry a tree in my bed better than you can in that car, and we can take care of the bank."

She wanted to refuse. Oh, man, did she want to tell him to take a hike, and even more so because of the antipathy that radiated from him. She was starting to feel a whole lot of dislike for him, too. Before, she'd never disliked him, but now she wondered if she had been more wise than foolish all those years ago.

Damn this unwanted sexual attraction. Any woman would feel it, she assured herself. It was just normal. He was that kind of guy, a real-life hunk.

She didn't want it, though. Not one little bit. She'd tasted that apple a long time ago, and it hadn't been enough to keep her here. She'd grown up, but she was beginning to wonder if he had.

She had to give in to reality. He was right—carrying a tree would be easier in his truck.

Setting her chin, she marched around and climbed in the cab, prepared for a couple of unpleasant hours, not the least of which would be the way her body kept wanting to betray her mind and heart.

Chapter 2

As unneighborly as it felt, Cliff didn't say a word on the way to town. What were they going to talk about anyway? Discussing Martha didn't seem exactly safe right now, although maybe he was wrong.

On the other hand, he didn't want to renew his relationship with Holly. Not in the least. A summer-long torrid affair a decade ago had left him scarred and her…What had it done to her? She'd turned her back on him readily enough, giving him all the reasons why she couldn't stay in this county. She'd suffocate, she'd said. She had important things to do, she'd said. She was going to be a social worker and save the world, or at least part of the world.

He glanced at her from the corner of his eye and thought that social work didn't seem to be agreeing with her. She looked entirely too thin, for one thing.

He couldn't judge anything else because she was grieving for her aunt, after all, but if he'd been looking at a horse showing those signs, he'd have been thinking "worn to the bone."

Fatigue seemed to wrap around her. She didn't really have the spark he remembered. Much as he didn't want to, he wondered if social work had gutted her in some way.

But damned if he'd ask. She'd be leaving here in two weeks. By the grace of heaven, he hoped that wouldn't be long enough to open scars or get him all tangled up in her barbed wire again.

Because that was how he thought of it: barbed wire. Her departure had scored him deep, like a million sharp knives. No freaking way was he going through that again.

Of course, he thought, she might not be the same person any longer. He might not even really be drawn to the woman she had become. So far he hadn't seen much to like. It was almost as if he were the enemy, not the other way around.

Which got him to wondering how she had justified her cruelty. Ah, hell, leave that can of worms alone. Take her to the bank, help her buy and plant the damned tree, and then forget she was on the same part of the planet with him.

Listening to his own thoughts, however, yanked him up short. He was thinking like a kid again. She was causing him to revert. Well, to hell with that.

He was relieved the bank took only a few minutes. He showed the paper the lawyer had given him, Martha's account was moved into a new one in Holly's name and it was done.

Mercifully soon, they were climbing into his truck again. Holly, however, seemed to sag. Finally he couldn't keep quiet any longer.

"What's wrong?"

"Did you see how much money she left me? Cliff… I'm stunned."

"Well, you could take a decent vacation. Looks like you need one."

She bridled, but only a bit, not as she once had. What the hell had quenched her fire? "That's more than a vacation or even ten. And what do you mean I look like I need one?"

"You look too thin and exhausted," he said bluntly. "Whatever kind of work you're doing, it's not good for your health."

"You don't know what you're talking about."

"I never did." He waited for an explosion that didn't come. Oh, this was bad. This wasn't the Holly he remembered at all. Now, right alongside his annoyance at having her around for a while, he felt the first tendrils of worry. Was she sick?

None of his business anymore, he reminded himself. She'd made sure of that.

The town didn't have anything like a big nursery. Around here, most planting was reserved for hay, alfalfa and vegetable gardens. But there was a corner at the feed store where it was possible to buy houseplants and some ornamental trees. Not a huge selection, but no huge demand, either. They *would* order stuff in, though, if, say, someone wanted to plant a windbreak or something bigger.

"What were you thinking of planting for her?" he asked as they stood looking at the tiny selection.

"Well, she always said she wanted to leave a small footprint in the world, so it should be something native."

He hesitated a moment, wondering how far into this he wanted to get. "What are you looking for? Fast growing, flowering?"

"I want something pretty that will last. It doesn't have to grow fast."

He pointed. "That tulip poplar over there will give you fantastic autumn foliage. Almost like aspens, which are related. It's pretty hardy, though."

She looked at the tree, which right now was little more than a twig with a few leaves. "Will it get really big?"

"It'll grow into a great shade tree."

That decided her. Ten minutes later he was carrying it out to his truck for her.

Holly felt as if someone had let all the air out of her. Grief? Maybe. More likely it was the release of the constant tension she lived with in Chicago. Fatigue seemed to envelop her, demanding she go home and fall asleep for hours, if not days. But she still had to plant a tree. She doubted that could be safely put off for too long.

"You ever planted a tree before?" Cliff's voice broke the silence she would have liked to continue forever.

"No."

There was a notable pause before he said, "I'll help."

His reluctance couldn't have been any more obvious. Hers equaled it. But before her pride could erupt and get her into trouble, she faced the fact that she needed the help. If she did it all wrong, she'd kill the tree. And from the size of the root ball, she questioned whether she'd even have the physical strength to dig a hole so big.

She glanced at Cliff from the corner of her eye. He'd have the strength. Damn it. "Thank you," she said quietly.

Another mile passed, then he surprised her by speaking again. "Your aunt was a remarkably caring, giving woman," he said. "If anyone in this county hit hard times, she was there for them. I guess you take after her."

Reluctantly, she looked at him. "How would you know?"

"I'm assuming. You're a social worker, right? That means you help people, right?"

She heard the annoyance in his tone and realized her response to him hadn't been very gracious. In fact, it had been challenging. Sheesh, she needed to get a handle on this antipathy toward him. He at least was making some kind of effort, much as she really didn't want it.

"In theory," she said. "Yeah, in theory. Once in a while I feel like I've gotten something good done. Most of the time I'm not sure. It takes kids a long time to grow up."

"You work with kids?"

"Mostly. With their parents, too, depending on what the problems are."

"Do you get any short-term rewards?"

The question surprised her with its understanding. She hadn't expected that. "Sometimes. But I'm not in it for rewards."

"No, you're in it to help."

The echo of her words a decade ago was so strong

she winced. She distinctly remembered telling him that she had a bigger need to help people than she could meet around here as a rancher's wife. God, how full of herself she had been. She'd left wounds behind her as she'd set out like Don Quixote, with little idea of what she was getting into, or how many windmills would shatter her lance.

She didn't answer him, instead turning her attention to the countryside that rolled past. What was the point? They'd be better off having as little to do with each other as possible. It was just that simple. Hard to believe that a fleeting affair, however torrid, might have left scars that lingered this long.

She certainly hadn't expected it to.

One summer, a long, long time ago. She'd been visiting her aunt between semesters. He'd been gradually taking over the reins of his ranch from his father, just beginning to reach the fullness of manhood.

She had been sunning herself on a cheap, webbed chaise in the front yard, wearing a skimpy halter top and shorts, a book beside her on the grass. Martha had shooed her outdoors and was inside lining up a potluck dinner for her church. A potluck Holly had no intention of being dragged to. She was just a visitor, passing through, her sights set far away.

But then Cliff had come riding up. She hadn't seen his approach because he came from the rear of the house, but as he rounded the corner, she caught her breath. Against the brilliant blue clarity of the sky, he had looked iconic: astride a powerful horse, cowboy hat tipped low over a strong face, broad shouldered, powerful.

She should have run the instant she felt the irresistible pulse of desire within her. She should have headed for the hills. Instead, caught up in an instant spell, she had remained while his gaze swept over her, feeling almost like intimate fire, taking in her every curve and hollow. She'd felt desire before, but nothing like what this man had ignited within her.

Then the real folly had begun. She had to return to school in two months. She'd thought he understood that. When she talked about getting her master's and going into social work, she had thought her goals were clear. She had no intention of remaining in this out-of-the-way place as a rancher's wife, and just as she couldn't give up her dreams, he couldn't give up his ranch.

So who had been at fault, she wondered now, staring out the window. They had played with fire, they'd seized every opportunity to make love anywhere and everywhere, but then the idyll had come to an end. He had wanted her to stay.

She had snapped in some way. She had been living a fantasy of some kind, and he'd intruded on it with reality. She had thrown his declaration of love back in his face, then had called him stupid for thinking it could have ever been anything but a fling.

To this day she didn't know what had driven her cruelty. By nature she wasn't at all cruel, but that day… well, the memory of it still made her squirm. Maybe it had been a self-protective instinct, a way to end something that could move her life in a direction she didn't really want to go. Or maybe some part of her had been almost as desperate as he was, but in a different way.

She would probably never understand what she had done that day, but it had not only driven Cliff away, it had dashed the entire memory of that summer fling. She could not enjoy the memories of even the most beautiful or sexy moments of those weeks. All of it had to be consigned to some mental dustbin.

She had figured at the time that Martha must have known what was going on, but she'd never said a word. Now this? Maybe Martha hadn't guessed. If she had, then there was an unkindness here she wouldn't have believed her aunt capable of. And not just to her, but to Cliff, as well.

She sighed, pressing down memories that seemed to want to reignite right between her legs, reminding her of the dizzying pleasures she had shared with Cliff. That was gone, done for good. Over. Finished.

If only the words would settle it all in her body, which seemed inclined now to react as foolishly as it had all those years ago.

When he spoke, she felt so far away that his voice, deeper now than in the past, nearly startled her.

"I don't mean to sound like a rube," he said, then paused. "Hell, I *am* a rube. But I hear parts of Chicago can be pretty dangerous."

"They are," she said cautiously, wondering where he was headed.

"Did you work in those parts?"

"They're the parts where we're needed most, usually."

He fell silent, and she waited. Surely he wasn't going to leave it at that.

"You have guts," he said, and not one more word.

"No more than the people who have to live there."

"But you choose to be there, to help."

She couldn't imagine how to answer that. Yes, it

was her choice, but the need cried out to her. She only wished she could provide a safer environment for those children, but the problems were huge. No one person could solve them.

"It's partly drugs," she said. "They encourage gang wars."

"Like during Prohibition."

"Yes, like that. Turf wars. Other things. Poverty grinds people down and sometimes brings out the ugliest parts of them. I just try to help kids so that they don't get drawn into it. There's not much else I can do to protect them, unless there's abuse in the family."

"It must feel thankless at times."

She couldn't believe he was talking to her in this sympathetic fashion. Not after the dislike that had radiated from him on their first meeting. Was he trying to mend bridges? She squirmed a little, thinking that if anyone should be trying to rebuild bridges, it was her. "Seeing just one kid make it is enough."

"Is it?"

She had no answer for that, either. But the tension that seemed to have lifted from her just by being away for a short while was settling heavily on her. She had matters to take care of here, she reminded herself. She had to decide what to do with her aunt's possessions, whether to rent the house—a million ends to tidy up. She couldn't spend all her time worrying about her kids back in Chicago, not when she was too far away to do anything.

Mercifully, he dropped the subject, and little by little, she returned fully to Conard County. She wished her kids could come out here, taste life without gunshots up the street any hour of the day or night and know what it was like to live even briefly without the fear.

She sighed, twisted her hands together and reset her sights on all that lay ahead of her.

What *was* she going to do with the house? Her job lay over a thousand miles away. She couldn't sell it. But renting it might lead to its ruination if she wasn't here to keep an eye on it.

Too soon, she argued with herself. She had time. No decisions had to be made this moment. Just plant the tree for Martha and then try to find comfort in residing in Martha's house, with all the good memories she had of her aunt.

She felt her eyes sting as she thought about Martha. The world had lost a true character and a great soul.

Cliff watched her from the corner of his eye, glancing her way from time to time as the road permitted. On a weekday, on these back roads, there wasn't a lot of traffic. Ahead of him stretched an empty road, its only danger the potholes left behind by winter. Along either side ran fences, often hidden behind the tumbleweeds caught in them, creating a low tunnel. But in those grasses to either side of the road, he knew there were drainage ditches, invisible in the grass, but enough to cause a minor accident.

So he really should keep his attention on driving. But just as she had done all those years ago, Holly drew him. The windows were open, thank goodness, otherwise he'd be assailed by her scents, and if there was one thing he knew for certain, he hadn't forgotten them. She still used the same shampoo; she still had the same enticing scent of femininity. Not strong, as it had been after they made love, but enough to remind him.

So here he was, stupidly walking into hell again. She'd only be here two weeks, long enough to get him all knotted up again, but completely lacking any kind of future. He hoped he had the sense to help her plant the tree and then go his way. Oh, he'd be a good neighbor and offer to keep an eye on the house when she left, but keeping an eye on a house wasn't anywhere nearly as dangerous as keeping an eye on Holly.

He wished her thinness, her evident fatigue, would turn him off. Instead, all it was doing was turning his insides into protective mush. He couldn't have this.

Inwardly he cussed himself for a fool, and warned himself to raise his guard. Do the minimum, stay away and turn his fullest attention to his own ranch, which had been all that had saved him all those years ago. Hard work was the answer.

Then she surprised him. She hadn't made a single friendly gesture, but now she did. Damn it.

"How's the ranch and business?"

Well, that ought to seem like a safe, casual question. Coming from her it felt freighted. "Okay," he said. Then realizing how abrupt he sounded, he added, "Leasing the acreage from your aunt has been a great help. It allowed me to expand."

"I heard cattle were getting more expensive to raise."

"Out of sight. We're transitioning to sheep. The wool market is still good."

"Good."

Clearly she wasn't really interested in his life. If he was honest, she hadn't been all that interested years ago, either. He might have found it easier to excuse her self-interest as youth if she hadn't followed it up with the coup de grâce.

Then, "Are sheep more difficult to raise?"

"Troubles come in all sizes and all degrees of fuzziness."

She surprised him with a laugh. "What a description!"

"It's true." He hated himself for wanting to smile. This was a demilitarized zone, not a party. "I traded one set of problems for another not so very different. The thing is, the sheep do better grazing on my land, and the wool comes every spring without me having to reduce my flock to make some money. Renewable resource."

"I like that."

He volunteered some more, testing her interest. "I also have a small herd of angora goats. They're a bit more susceptible to parasites, but their wool brings a higher price, so naturally it's more expensive to get going. Of course. So I'm growing my herd nature's way."

"It sounds like you have a plan."

"I hope so. Independent ranchers are in danger of becoming an extinct species. But I'm actually doing pretty well."

"I'm so glad to hear that, Cliff. So the sheep and goats get along well?"

"Well enough. My main headache is that the goats are more independent and adventurous. Keeping track of them can be a pain sometimes, and they need dietary additives. But when all is said and done, I like their antics."

Oh, well, he thought. He was going to have to deal

with her at least some over the next couple of weeks. Greasing the skids with some superficial chitchat and courtesy ought to be safe enough. But no way was he going to fall into her honeyed web again.

Still, despite all the ugliness that had once happened, he couldn't help a twinge of concern. *Way too thin,* he thought as he glanced at her again. The bones in her face had become prominent, and her skin appeared stretched tightly across them. Not good.

But he didn't know how to ask without crossing into territory where she didn't want him to walk. Of that he was certain. He had begun to suspect that the past was no more buried for her than it was for him. Some things, it seemed, hurt forever.

He sought something else to say, and the question came out without thinking. "You married? Kids?"

"No and no."

It was a short answer, making it clear there were indeed limits to how personal she wanted to get with him. Hell, he thought, who was it who had taken out the scythe at their last meeting? Certainly not him.

"I tried it," he said finally, and waited.

Presently she asked, "And?"

"And it stank. Big-time. We couldn't shake the bottle hard enough to mix the oil and vinegar."

He waited, then heard a smothered laugh escape her. "I'm sorry, I shouldn't laugh, but your description…"

In spite of himself, he laughed, too. "Well, I can't think of a better one. Martha warned me."

"Really?"

He sensed her turn toward him for the first time. "Yeah. She said… Well, she was Martha. She asked me which head I was thinking with, and said that it would make more sense to ride my horse off a cliff than marry that woman. She was right."

"What happened?"

"Let's just say I went off the deep end for one woman and woke up to find myself married to a different one."

"Ouch."

"My ego needed some bandaging, but that was about it. Sometimes it just isn't meant to be."

She fell silent, and he let the subject go. It hadn't been right with Lisa, and chances were it wouldn't have been right with Holly, either. Not back then, for sure. Time to man up and admit it. He and Holly had been horses pulling in different directions, and if he'd been older and wiser he would have recognized it.

Well, he had learned his lessons. He hoped. All he needed to do was get that tree planted, see if Holly needed any other assistance and go back to his ranch, his sheep and his goats. It would take a special woman to want a life like that, and he couldn't afford to forget it.

They finally jolted up to Martha's house. "I need to get this road graded," he remarked. "It always goes to hell over the winter and spring, and that little car of yours is going to bounce like a Ping-Pong ball."

She didn't say anything, and he wondered if he'd trespassed by taking possession of the problem. He didn't know whether to sigh or roll his eyes. Oh, this was going to be fun. *Thank you very much, Martha.*

He braked without turning off the engine. "Where do you want to plant it?"

"I honestly don't know. I don't know how big it's

going to get, how much sun it needs." She screwed up her face in the way he had once loved. "City girl here."

How could he forget that?

"Southwest corner," he suggested. "It'll get enough sun, keep the house cooler in the summer and lose all its leaves so it won't keep you colder in the winter."

"Sounds good to me."

Slowly he rolled the truck around the house. "It's going to need a lot of water the first month. And that's going to be a drag. Martha doesn't have an outside tap, so no hose."

"Really? I never noticed that before."

Why would she? She'd never been here long enough to really learn anything, although she had been here long enough to cause him a peck of trouble.

"I'll have someone see to it after you go home." That's as far as he would go. Or so he told himself.

"Thank you."

Damn it, he could almost hear Martha laughing and asking, "When did you turn into a chicken, boy?"

Then Holly said, "Martha always had such a big vegetable garden. She had to water it somehow."

"That's where the hand pump comes in. Come on, you were here lots of times. Surely you saw."

She paused. "My God, I'd forgotten. Of course I remember. I used to love to do it for her."

"Right. She planted in rows and pumped until the water filled the space between them. Every couple of days. The last few years it got harder for her, so I put in a motorized pump for her. Maybe you missed it."

"I guess so. My job gives me only short vacations."

"Well, it won't help with the tree regardless. It's going to be buckets."

"I can do that," she said stoutly.

He had his doubts, but maybe she was stronger than she looked right now.

The truth was, and he readily admitted it, he couldn't imagine her life in Chicago, nor how she could want to go back to it. Gunshots on the streets? The crushing poverty? Gang culture? Like so many, he had only a vague idea of how some people had to live. She volunteered to face that every day. From his point of view, it had certainly taken a toll on her.

Even so, when she walked ahead of him to pick out the exact spot for the tree, he couldn't help noticing the way her hips swayed. Or that when she turned her breasts were still full. A beautiful woman. A desirable woman.

Too bad.

When she'd chosen a spot, he headed for Martha's shed to get a shovel. While he did that, Holly disappeared inside, then returned with two tall glasses of iced tea.

"I seem to remember you liked sugar," she said, handing him one.

"Still do," he admitted. "I know it's a vice, but I work it off."

The corners of her mouth edged up a bit. "I guess you do. I can help with this."

"I don't know if you've ever tried to dig this ground around here, but we're going to be lucky if we don't need a backhoe."

That drew another small laugh from her. Angling the spade, he stood on it with one foot and penetrated the ground by about six inches. Good, the spring rains hadn't completely dried up yet. Dirt instead of concrete.

"Being in the house is difficult," Holly said quietly.

He looked up after tossing another shovelful of dirt to the side. "It is?"

"I keep expecting to hear Martha. To see her come around a corner. Even when it was just her and me, it never, ever seemed so silent in there."

He hadn't thought about that. He paused and looked back at the two-story clapboard house. "Yeah," he said finally. "I guess it would be quiet."

His gaze returned to Holly and he saw a tear rolling down her cheek. Whatever else he thought of her, he'd never doubted that she loved her aunt.

But talk about putting a man in an impossible bind. The thing to do would have been to hug her and comfort her. With anyone else, that's exactly what he would have done. But Holly was so far off-limits he couldn't even offer the most common act of sympathy. Finally he asked, "Are you going to be okay?"

She dashed the tear away. "Eventually. I just miss her so much. Damn, Cliff, I can't even call her anymore. That keeps striking me over and over. I'll never hear her voice again."

He deepened and widened the hole with a few more spadefuls, then leaned on the handle and glanced at her.

"You can hear her voice," he said. "She's in your mind and heart now. Just give in to it and listen. If I know Martha, she's probably whispering something outrageous in your ear right this instant."

He finally got the hole big enough and put the tree in it. Kneeling, he tested the soil near the bottom and found it still held some moisture.

"Get a bucket of water," he told Holly. "Just flip the switch on the side of the pump and it'll start coming. There's a bucket in the shed."

She hopped to obey. It occurred to him he might have to prime the pump, so he was checking it out as she returned.

"Okay, it's ready. Put the bucket under the spout, hook it here." Like all good pumps, it had a nipple to hold a bucket handle. He showed her how to turn it on, then waited with her while it filled.

"There you go."

To his surprise, she lifted the five-gallon bucket and with both hands carried it over to the tree. Layer by layer, they watered lightly and refilled the hole. When he was done, he ridged the dirt in a ring around the tree. "Now fill this ring and just let it soak in. You'll probably need to do that every day."

He pulled off his work gloves, leaving her to it, and put the spade away. When he returned from the shed, he found her standing with an empty bucket, staring into space.

"Is something wrong?" he asked.

"It's just so peaceful out here. I wish some of my kids could experience life like this, even if only for a short time."

Then he said the stupidest, most idiotic words to ever cross his lips. "So why don't you bring some of them out here?"

She looked at him then. *Really* looked at him, her blue eyes wide and almost wondering. His groin throbbed a warning. Had he really just suggested she come back here?

Man, he needed to finish up and get out of here *now.*

Chapter 3

Cliff left shortly after the tree was properly planted and watered. He'd even staked the slender trunk with bands in three directions so the wind wouldn't tip it over, or make it grow crooked, at least for now.

But then he was gone, and empty prairie winds blew around her. She stood looking toward the mountains, still dark green and gray in the early-afternoon sunlight, but soon the sun would sink behind them and the light would paint them purple.

She couldn't remember ever having felt so alone. Well, except for one night in Chicago, on a dark street when she had been attacked. She had felt alone in the world then, and it had seemed like forever before the cops had arrived. Someone in the poverty-stricken area had taken a huge risk calling them. She never knew who, and she didn't want to because she feared for the caller.

She had mostly gotten used to the conditions she worked in. When she wasn't making home visits, she was working with various programs designed to keep youngsters busy and off the streets. She was used to hearing random gunfire, though, used to the screeching of tires as some gang blew by, showing off their disdain for traffic laws and any unfortunate person who might be trying to cross a street.

Never alone, whether surrounded by good people or troublemakers. Except that one night. And now.

After the attack, she'd been given a few weeks off and had come here to recover. The contrast had really struck her then, and it was striking her now.

Except this time Martha wasn't here to listen, to advise, to sympathize. Another thing struck her right then: for all the tea, sympathy and advice, Martha hadn't even hinted that she should find a safer job. Not once.

She lifted her eyes to the sky and asked, "What's it all mean?"

Of course there was no answer. She turned from the tree and stared at the house. She could stay here. Martha had left her more than enough money that if she was careful she needn't ever work again.

But that didn't seem like something Martha would want for her, a dead-end existence without purpose. Martha had always been doing something for someone. A giver by nature.

And a great example.

So why don't you bring some of them out here? Cliff's question came back to her. Why not? She could imagine the red tape. Taking kids across state lines to spend a few weeks with her here? Not likely.

It was all too easy to imagine the hoops, then the structure she'd have to build. She couldn't do it alone. She'd need help with the kids, trained help. She'd need things for them to do. Would they stay in the house or should she build a bunkhouse?

The next thing she knew, she was sitting in Martha's rocker on the front porch, rocking steadily, staring out over wide-open spaces, feeling an oddly healing touch in the emptiness of the world around here.

Those kids deserved a taste of this, she thought. An opportunity to live for a short while without the hunger and fear that filled their lives. To be able to fall asleep at night to quiet instead of gunshots.

She tried to dismiss the idea as utterly impractical. The amount of work in just getting it rolling, all the obstacles and roadblocks she'd run into. And while she was working on that, how could she keep up with her job?

Nor did she want to be so close to Cliff. He'd been pleasant enough today, she gave him credit for that, but her tension around him was almost as bad as her tension on a dark city street. It was an incautious, overwhelming desire for him, every bit as strong as it had been all those years ago when she'd given in to it and caused some serious pain.

And while she had never let Cliff know, leaving him behind hadn't been easy for her, either. No, she hadn't wanted the commitment he was offering. Hadn't been ready for it. Had been set on her goal to help kids to the point that she couldn't imagine any other life.

So she had gotten what she really wanted, and now life had brought her full circle to deal with all the unanswered questions.

How could she best help those kids? And why did she still want Cliff?

Why don't you just bring some of them out here?

Why had he asked that question? What had he been thinking? His face had revealed nothing, but he'd been quick to leave after that, as quick as he could.

Could she stand being this close to him for any length of time, which bringing kids out here would require? But as soon as she asked herself, she felt selfish. If there was some way to help kids with her legacy, then she needed to do it, Cliff or no Cliff.

But maybe bringing those kids out here for even a few weeks or months might not be kind at all. To give them a taste of a different life and then plop them back into their old messes? It would help only if she could make them see possibilities to work for when they got home. Dreams they could believe in.

Propping her chin in her hand, unaware that the afternoon was fading into twilight, she twisted the idea around in her head, half wishing Cliff had never mentioned it, half wishing she could find a useful way to do it.

The chill of the night penetrated finally, and she went inside to make herself a small supper. Once again the empty silence of the house hit her hard, making her eyes sting and her chest tighten.

Live here alone forever? No way. Somehow there had to be another way. A better way. A useful way.

Damn memory, Cliff thought. He'd given up all hope of sleeping. Again. Since he'd heard that he was going to have to see Holly again, he'd been an insomniac, and now the insomnia had grown to devour most of the night hours.

As for memory…there were all kinds of it, he was discovering. He wasn't remembering the way Holly had looked all those years ago. No. Mental pictures had nothing to do with it.

Instead his mind was plaguing him with the sounds she made during passionate sex. His hands, indeed his entire body, were resurrecting the way her skin had felt against him, the way she felt beneath him. His palms itched with the certain knowledge of how it felt to caress her, how her breasts felt in his hands, the hard way her nipples pebbled, the dewiness of her womanhood.

And scents. They filled his nostrils almost as if she were right there, sated and content.

He even remembered exactly, *exactly,* how it had felt to plunge into her warm depths.

Much as he tried to banish the thoughts, they planted themselves and stayed like unfinished business. He couldn't see Martha's house from his place, but it didn't matter. There weren't enough hundreds of square miles in this county to make him comfortable when she was in it.

His body ached with a need to take her again, to touch her again, to fill her again. Not even his wife had ever awakened such a craving in him.

Damn Holly, damn Martha and, God, he hoped that she didn't take that stupid thought of his seriously. Bring those kids here? He couldn't imagine the scope of the undertaking, but even less could he imagine life with Holly nearby. This county wasn't big enough for both of them.

He shoved out of his bed impatiently, aware that if he didn't watch it he was going to make love to Holly in his mind. Maybe that had been part of the problem in his marriage with Lisa. Maybe at some unconscious level he had considered Lisa second best.

He didn't know, but if so, he ought to despise himself. Staring out the window at a night as dark as pitch, he wrestled his internal demons.

Ten years later, even after the awful way she had treated him, he still wanted her as much as the very first time. Did that make him sick? He didn't know that, either.

He just knew that seeing her had fueled a fire that had never quite gone out. Now what the hell was he going to do about it?

He'd thought he'd finally learned to roll with life, the good and the bad, but now he wondered. That woman out there had the ability to turn him into a kid again. He was randier than a goat, and it didn't please him.

Sometimes, on rare, restless nights, he'd go saddle up Sy and take a ride. The gelding seemed to enjoy those nighttime rambles. He let Sy choose the course and the pace, and sometimes that gelding would open up his throttle wide and gallop hell-for-leather.

But it was a moonless, dark night, not safe for riding, and besides, he had a feeling that if he mounted up, he'd end up at Martha's place like a lovesick dog.

So he stood there aching, remembering, knowing it had been a dream that could never happen again. He needed to get a grip.

But the grip kept slipping away, lost in dizzying sensual memories.

* * *

A few miles away, Holly wasn't doing much better. She had fallen asleep only to wake twisted in her sheets and drenched in perspiration. She had dreamed of Cliff, which she hadn't done in years, but it had gotten all twisted up in her dream with the guys who had attacked her last year.

How could she want something that still frightened her? That overlayering of the attack ought to be a warning. She'd avoided dating since then, because she couldn't quite erase the memory of stinking breath and pawing, filthy hands. Any time a guy got too close, she headed for the door.

But she'd done the same to Cliff before then, and for the first time she wondered who she really was and what might be going on inside her.

All she knew was that Cliff still drew her as he had from the first. At least the years had made her considerably less self-centered. She'd hurt the man badly, and she wasn't going to risk doing it again, whether she craved him or not.

She just wished she knew what it was about him. Nobody had ever gotten to her the way he had.

She took the teddy bear from the chair and pulled it over to the window. Even with the curtains open, she couldn't see much, but she didn't care. She lifted the sash just a bit, letting some chilly air into the room, hoping it would cool her down. Then she hugged the bear and sat, watching the impenetrable night.

Thinking about Cliff was the ultimate waste of time, she told herself. She'd hurt him badly, and while he'd been civil and even pleasant today, that had been common courtesy. It had been obvious to her at their first meeting that he ranked her somewhere near rat poison on his list of things he liked. Nor could she blame him. She had burned that bridge herself.

She tried instead to think about the little kernels of an idea he had planted today, but her mind remained stubborn. Even as her body dried off and began to feel chilled, Cliff persisted in dominating her thoughts.

A decade had passed and she still wanted him. That was surely crazy.

Then she saw movement outside. She leaned toward the window and strained her eyes. Horse and rider? *What the—* Jumping up, she pulled off her damp nightgown, pulled on a dry and much more modest one, then headed downstairs.

She was sure of one thing: only one person would be riding up to this house in the middle of the night.

She reached the front door just as he came riding around the corner of the house. He wasn't even looking in her direction, just kind of ambling along. She grabbed a jacket off the coat tree, pulled it on and stepped out.

"What are you doing?" she asked.

He drew rein and turned his mount in her direction. "Curing insomnia," he said. "We shouldn't have disturbed you."

"You didn't. I was awake."

"Sorry I didn't bring a horse for you."

Oh, that was a mistake, she thought as memory slammed her again. They'd gone riding together so many times during that summer, laughing and carefree until passion would rise again. They'd made love on a bed of pine needles, once on a flat rock in the middle of a tumbling mountain stream, another time…

Clenching her hands, she forced memory back into its cage. "Does it help the insomnia? Riding?" It seemed like a safe question.

"I don't think anything's going to help tonight," he said bluntly.

Even though she could barely see him, she could feel his eyes boring into her. The quiet night settled between them, disturbed only by the jingle of the horse's bridle as it tossed its head a little.

"Well," he said, "we'll just move on."

She knew what she should have done, but before she could act sensibly, words popped out of her mouth. "Want some coffee? I know it won't help you sleep…"

"It's almost dawn. No point in sleeping now." For a few seconds it seemed he was going to continue his ride, but then he swung down from the saddle. "Coffee would be great."

She turned quickly and headed back inside, partly to avoid getting too close to him, and partly to warm up. Late spring? The nights still got chilly.

She wished she'd grabbed a robe, but the long flannel nightgown she had put on was probably almost as concealing. Which led her to another question as she made the coffee. Why had she been in such a rush to get down here when she had been certain it was Cliff riding by?

She shook her head at her own behavior. Maybe this house just felt too empty with Martha, but it was pretty sad that she was reaching out to Cliff.

So there she was, missing Martha even more because she ought to be here, hundreds of miles from home, troubled by a weird nightmare that had somehow combined Cliff with the attack on her when the two were totally unrelated. She wondered if she was losing it.

Or maybe grief had just scrambled her thinking. It was certainly possible.

She heard Cliff come through the house to the kitchen, and it seemed his steps were slow. Evidently he wasn't really looking forward to having coffee with her. Well, why should he? But he could have just refused.

"Have a seat," she said. She remained where she was, staring at a coffeemaker that seemed to be taking forever and a window that stared back at her blackly, showing her more of the kitchen behind her than the world outside.

It was a big country kitchen. Martha had once talked about the days when the family was big, when they had hired help and everyone would gather here for the main meal of the day. At home she had an efficiency, with barely enough room for a narrow stove, small sink and tiny refrigerator. If she wanted to cook, she had to do the prep on her dining table in the next tiny room.

Still, the house was awfully big for one person, but she couldn't sell it for ten years. She definitely needed to find a good way to put it to use.

Wandering thoughts again, but when the coffeemaker finished, so did the wandering.

"You still like it black?" she asked.

"Yes. Thanks."

So she carried two mugs to the table, and finally had to sit facing him. No way to avoid it any longer.

He looked tired, she thought. Well, lack of sleep would do that. But damn him, he remained every bit as sexy as he had all those years ago. Maybe even more so. That didn't seem fair.

"You've lost weight," he remarked. "Have you been sick?"

She shook her head. "Just busy. Sometimes I just feel too tired to eat."

"That's not good." When she didn't answer, he spoke again. "I take it your job is draining. Want to tell me about it?"

"What's to tell? I work with people most of society doesn't care about. People who never had a real chance in life. Most of my job is trying to get children to do the things that will give them a chance. To avoid the things that will take away their chances. We try to give them a safe environment after school, encourage them to finish homework, feed them, expand their horizons a bit. And then they go home to the same despair."

He gave a low whistle.

"Maybe that's not entirely fair," she said after a moment. "There are some bad parents. There are in any group. When I first started I was investigating abuse cases that occurred at very nice addresses. Then I moved over to work with underprivileged kids. A lot of people may not believe it, but some of my strongest supporters with these kids are their parents. They want their children to have a better life. But it's kind of hard to believe in when you come home to a run-down apartment where no one cares enough even to get rid of the roaches, and there's little food in the refrigerator."

"Colliding worlds?"

She nodded, closing her eyes. "You have to take it a step at a time," she said finally. "Right now I'm organizing a couple of communities to demand exterminators. You'd think management would at least provide that. Little kids shouldn't be living with roaches, rats and mice. It's not healthy. Sometimes they get bitten."

"God!"

"Anyway, sometimes I feel like I'm trying to hold back a flood with a broom. These people are so ground down. But then you see the spark of hope in them when they think you can help their kids. They really care about that."

"But you're just one person."

"But I'm not the only social worker. We do what we can. It's hard not to get impatient, though. I could use a magic wand."

"I imagine so."

She opened her eyes, but looked back toward the window. "What you said earlier about bringing some of them out here?"

She noticed his response was hesitant. "Yeah?"

"I wish I could. I was thinking about it, but the problems are huge. And while Martha might approve, I'd need to get through all kinds of red tape. And then I asked myself what I could do for them in a couple of weeks here. Or even a whole summer here. Would I just make it harder on them when they had to go home?"

"That's a tough question. I didn't think about that."

She shrugged and finally managed to look at him again. "It needs a lot of planning in a lot of ways. But I keep thinking how wonderful it might be for them to have a month or two when they just simply didn't have to be afraid or hungry."

"So they're afraid, too?"

"They're living in a damn war zone. Gangs. Drugs. Turf wars. They learn to be afraid very early."

He cursed. "That's no way for a kid to grow up."

"I agree. But as one of my friends often reminds me, a lot of kids in the world are growing up exactly that way."

"But it ought to be different in *this* country."

He spoke with so much vehemence that she blinked. She'd never had time before to find out if Cliff had a social conscience. Apparently he did.

She glanced away toward the window again. She didn't want to find any reasons to like this guy. None. She'd be leaving again in two weeks, whatever she decided to do with this ranch.

But then her thoughts wandered a different, faraway path. "You get used to it," she said presently. "You just get used to it."

"Have you?"

"I guess so. I didn't realize until I got here just how much tension I was carrying all the time. My first night here I could feel it letting go. Something inside me is uncoiling. But it never uncoils for those children. Even in a safe place, like their homes, or at the youth center, I'm sure it never has long enough to let go because in just a short while they're going to step outside again."

He didn't offer any bromides, but she heard him drum his fingers on the table. She needed to get away from this subject for a little while, she realized, because even just talking about it and thinking about it was ratcheting up her tension.

She fixed him with her gaze. "Do you have a lot of insomnia?"

"Sometimes. Usually not this bad."

"I'd think with how hard you work, you'd just conk out."

"You'd think." He gave her a crooked smile. "Maybe

I'm just one of those people who doesn't need a whole lot of sleep. I certainly don't walk around feeling sleep deprived."

"I can't imagine it. Sometimes I think I could sleep around the clock."

"Maybe I should let you get back to it."

The perfect out. She should have grabbed it, but she didn't. "No, I'm fine. I think I'm done with sleep tonight. I was sitting upstairs thinking about things when I saw you ride up. I'm wondering if this house is always going to feel so achingly empty without Martha."

"I don't know. I wish I could tell you. I miss her, too, and I didn't even live here, but you're right, I keep expecting to hear her voice."

"Yeah. And for some reason I'm focusing on that. That I'll never hear her voice again except inside my own head."

He hesitated visibly, then said, "Martha told me you were attacked once in Chicago."

At that instant she seriously wanted to throw him out. His company had at least distracted her from that mixed-up dream where one instant she was with Cliff in the throes of passion and in the next she was being grabbed and pawed by that slimeball. She still didn't understand why her mind had hooked those two things together, even in a dream, but she certainly didn't want to think about the attack.

He must have read her face. "Sorry. I shouldn't have brought that up, but I've worried about you ever since."

"Why should you worry at all about me after the way I treated you?" she demanded, angry but not at all sure whether she was mad at him or something else.

"And that was *my* business. Why would Martha tell you about that?"

He responded to her anger, his face darkening. "She worried about you. Constantly. Maybe she never told you, but she did. And after that, I worried, too. There's a lot of crap between us, Holly. I've got plenty of reason not to like you. But that doesn't mean I don't care what happens to you."

He pushed back from the table. His face had grown hard, and his voice chilly. "Call me if you need anything. Martha put me on autodial."

Then he walked out. Just like that. Not even a goodbye.

She sat alone at the table, cooling coffee in front of her, trying to sort through the tangled web of emotions inside her, but it proved impossible. All of it was impossible. She couldn't imagine how she would ever get herself straightened out.

Coming back here had been a mistake. Dealing with rough neighborhoods by and large wasn't nearly as dangerous as dealing with emotions. Things that could kill your body weren't half as scary as things that could kill your heart.

Then she put her head down on the table and let the tears roll. Martha. Cliff. The past. The present. The only thing she was certain of was that she missed Martha with a grinding ache.

And sometimes, like now, her brain would furtively sneak in a question she didn't want to hear: Had she made a mistake by not staying here and marrying Cliff?

Too late now, but apparently part of her would always wonder.

Damn, when she had raced to get out here, she had assumed that she wouldn't see Cliff. He'd steadfastly stayed away during her visits to Martha after their affair, and it hadn't crossed her mind that it would be different this time.

But here she was, and Cliff wasn't staying away. Not at all. Although if she was to judge by the way he had just left, he might not come back.

That would be for the best, she told herself. Much better if she never laid eyes on him again. Even after all these years, he could still roil her emotions and waken her passions, and she really didn't need that. Not now, not ever.

Cliff steamed as he rode home, but he reserved his anger for himself. He'd been stupid to accept Holly's offer of coffee. He knew that woman could sting him, but he'd put himself right in the line of fire. Nobody to blame but himself.

As for her being upset that he knew she had been attacked, what was that? It hardly amounted to a shameful secret, and both he and Martha had worried about her. Hell, Martha had often talked about Holly and her concerns. Who else was she going to talk to? Nobody else around here knew Holly.

At first he'd found it uncomfortable to talk about the woman who had torched his hopes, but time had made it easier. He wondered about Martha, though, and about this whole setup.

Martha was no fool. She must have guessed what was going on between him and Holly that long-ago summer. At their age, she'd probably guessed they weren't just two friends who liked to spend long hours alone with each other. No, she had to have known, even though she'd never said a word.

Of course, she couldn't have known why they broke up. Maybe she thought it had been reasonably friendly. That much was possible, and might explain the current insanity of his being executor of the estate.

But why tell Holly she couldn't sell the house for ten years? And while being executor didn't exactly burden him with things he *had* to do, it remained that he felt Martha had meant him to keep an eye on things. Keep an eye on Holly.

Hell.

He almost muttered under his breath. Sy was getting a little antsy, though, probably picking up on his mood. The light wasn't so great yet, although the first signs of dawn rode the eastern horizon. Regardless, he slackened the reins, trusting Sy to choose his own pace and safe ground. He'd long since learned it was the safest way to let a horse open up. They seemed to smell prairie-dog holes well in advance, and to see other obstacles quickly.

With the lack of tension, Sy cut loose. He hit a full gallop across the rangeland, maybe half a mile, then settled into a comfortable walk again. Cliff leaned forward, patting his neck.

"Better, boy?"

Sy tossed his head.

"I guess so." But it wasn't better for Cliff. He hadn't been the one galloping. The question remained: What had Martha expected of him? And if she'd expected something, why hadn't she given him a clue? Apparently, she hadn't given Holly any clues, either, except that stuff about finding her dream. That was certainly opaque.

He sighed, feeling the last of the night's chilly air, and tried to corral his thoughts. He had a lot to do today, and no energy to waste on thinking about Holly. He'd deal with whatever turned up as it became necessary.

In theory she was going back to Chicago in just under two weeks. Back to the job she had always wanted. A job that he thought might be slowly killing her. But what did he know?

He rode around to the barn and turned Sy over to one of his hired hands. He usually cared for the horse himself, but this morning he didn't feel like it.

Ruben took the reins from him. "You got company, Boss."

"What kind?"

"The kind that comes in a sports car."

"Out here?" Cliff's brows raised. He tried to think of anyone who might have business with him, because his neighbors and friends sure didn't drive those cars. Useless out here.

He walked in through the back door and mudroom. His housekeeper, Jean, was at the kitchen sink. She looked at him, and her expression held none of its usual welcome.

"She's in the living room."

"Who?"

"Go look."

He shook his head, wondering what the hell was going on. "Coffee?"

"Grab some."

So he did, then headed for whatever was awaiting

him. He reached the threshold of the living room and froze. "Lisa?" he asked with disbelief.

His former wife was stretched out on the sofa as if posed for a photo, showing her cleavage to best advantage, her long black hair draped perfectly as if to draw attention to her most notable feature.

The only good thing he could say about her arrival was that he felt no response whatever to her blatant sexuality. At least that part was dead for good. But his dislike of her lived on. He wanted to roar at her to get out of his house.

"Hi, Cliff," she said, her voice sultry. "I've been thinking a lot about you and missing you. You don't mind, do you?"

Did he mind? Hell, yeah. He was already trying to figure out ways to make her leave. But he needed a minute to put a lid on his temper, too. She couldn't have called to ask first? "I've gotta get some breakfast. You wait here."

In the kitchen, Jean simply frowned at him.

"You should have sent her away," he said.

"Not my place. But if she stays, I go."

Back to that. Lisa had almost cost him Jean six years ago, and Jean was part of the family—she'd been here his entire life. "She's not staying."

"Ha!"

"I mean it."

"She already brought in her suitcases."

"Then I'll take them out."

"Good luck."

He opened a cupboard. "Breakfast?"

"Find your own. I'm not cooking for that woman."

Cliff closed his eyes for a moment, wondering if

life could get any more complicated. Well, of course it could. Lisa was here.

He settled for a bowl of cold cereal and headed back to the living room. He took the chair farthest from Lisa.

"So what's going on?" he asked bluntly.

"I told you. I missed you."

"You haven't missed me in six years."

She pouted. "That's not true."

"Just spit it out, Lisa. Spare me the drama."

"Oh, all right then," she said, sitting up, but leaning forward so her cleavage remained on display. He wondered why he had ever found that attractive. Right now he felt repelled.

"I'm between jobs," she said.

"Really? Between marriages, too, I guess." He knew she had married some guy up near Gillette, because once she had he'd no longer owed her alimony.

"Well, yes."

"Sorry. What am I supposed to do about any of this?"

"Like I said, I'm between jobs. I just need a few weeks."

"A few weeks?" His entire household would fall apart, and even some of his hired hands might desert him in that time. Lisa was nothing if not imperious.

"Yes."

"And how are you going to find a job out here?"

She frowned. "I already have a job. Damn it, Cliff, don't be a jerk. I start my new job in two weeks. I just need a place to stay until then."

He was finding this hard to believe. Something about this smelled to high heaven. "What else aren't you telling me?"

"Nothing." Her dark eyes flashed. "You're still a jerk, aren't you."

"I don't like being lied to."

"Well, I'm not lying. I have a job in Glenwood Springs, but I have no way of getting a place to stay until then. If I spend money renting a place now, I won't make it until I get my first paycheck. That is all there is to it."

It was almost believable. Maybe it was even the truth. But he sat there wondering whether she really wanted to stay here for two weeks, or if she wanted him to front her some money. Either one looked impossible right now. It was late spring, he hadn't yet gotten the money for his wool, he had vet bills, especially for the new lambs and kids, he needed to… Well, he just wasn't flush at the moment.

He looked at his bowl of cereal and realized that while he might need to eat, he couldn't swallow a thing right now.

"I want you out of here," he said flatly. "Try your sob story on someone else. Jean is already threatening to leave."

"Jean always mattered more than I did," she pouted.

"Unfortunately, I made the mistake of letting you matter more once upon a time. I lost three good hands because of you, and barely kept Jean. You have no idea of the havoc you managed to wreak and how long it took me to put things back together. I'm not doing that again."

She stood up. "When did you become so cruel? I have nowhere to go!"

He felt a twinge of conscience, but tried to quash

it. If this woman weren't poison, he'd give her the two weeks. But he'd learned his lesson the hard way.

Without a word, he got up and went back to the kitchen. Jean was sitting at the table at a time of day when she would ordinarily have been working on something for the midday's big meal for him and his hands. He dumped the cereal, rinsed the bowl and sat facing Jean.

"She says she has nowhere to go."

Jean scowled.

"For two weeks."

Jean's frown deepened. "Do you really believe her?"

"Damned if I know. The thing is…"

"The thing is, you've always been too generous for your own good." Since Jean had helped raise him, he was used to her having her say. "You don't want her here. I don't want her here. She's a troublemaker."

"But if she's not lying…"

Jean sighed. "If she's not lying, then whose fault is it she has no one to turn to but you?"

Hard to argue with that. But despite his anger that she was here, he couldn't exactly kick her to the curb. "Can you handle it for a few days?"

Jean rolled her eyes. "I knew it. I knew it the minute she marched into this house right past me with a suitcase. As if she owns the place even now."

"I know what she's like. I'm asking *you*."

"I put up with her for two years for your sake. I suppose I can manage a few days. But I warn you, I'm not going to bite my tongue this time. Not like I did before."

"It's better for you if you don't. I'm going to figure out a way to get her out of here as quickly as possible."

Jean just shook her head. "When did you ever get that woman to do what *you* wanted?"

Good question, he thought as he marched back into the living room. Lisa had given up on the sultry pose, exchanging it for one that looked like avenging fury. As if she had a right. But Lisa had never needed anyone else to grant her a right. She took them all as she chose.

"You can stay here a couple of days until you find something else. That's it. And be forewarned, I don't want Jean or anyone else upset. Period."

He watched Lisa struggle to find a grateful smile. She almost made it. "Thank you."

He grabbed a couple of bananas and headed out to work. All of a sudden it seemed the world was determined to turn upside down.

Oh, to hell with it. They could endure anything for a couple of days, even Lisa.

Chapter 4

Holly had spent the day puttering around, getting used to the silent house, deciding which things she should keep and which should go. Martha's clothes needed to be donated, but beyond that she found decisions remarkably hard. She did find a small stack of bills in Martha's desk, unopened, so she pulled out her new checkbook and paid them. She supposed she needed to have the utilities and so on put in her name. She wondered if she would need Cliff for that.

She didn't especially feel like seeing him again, even if her thoughts kept wandering his way. She wished she could just understand why she felt so attracted to him. That should have faded, shouldn't it?

Apparently not.

On and off, though, she remembered his remark about bringing some of her kids out here. During the late afternoon, she went outside to water the tree and walked around, thinking of what she might be able to do on the land that hadn't been fenced. There was a surprising amount of space. Martha's big vegetable garden, now mostly a memory under a layer of grass and weeds, was still there. There was room to build some kind of bunkhouse, maybe two, where the kids could stay, either with their families or with counselors, depending. There was even enough room to make a pen for a few goats or sheep for them to work with.

She stood there for a long time, envisioning, still wondering if it would be good or bad to take these kids into a whole different world for a few weeks or months. She ought to call her friend who was a child psychologist and ask. Opening up possibilities seemed like a good idea overall. Sending them back home to a misery that might feel even worse once they knew it didn't have to be that way, not so good.

"Hello."

Startled by the voice, she pivoted to see a striking woman astride a horse at the fence line. She wondered if she had been so deeply lost in thought that she hadn't heard her approach or if the wind had whisked the sounds away.

Either way, it astonished her. Could she have relaxed so much here already that her situational awareness had dulled? She didn't like the way her stomach sank at the possibility that this was Cliff's current girlfriend. He hadn't mentioned one, but that didn't mean a damn thing.

"Hi," she said, managing a smile, trying to tell herself she didn't care. Her visitor was quite a beautiful woman, with inky hair and dark eyes. Exotic, even in jeans and a plaid shirt with rolled-up sleeves.

"I was looking for Martha," the woman said.

"I'm sorry, she passed away. I'm her niece, Holly. Did you know Martha well?"

"I used to. I've been away. I'm Lisa. Cliff's ex-wife."

Talk about a bombshell. Holly didn't quite know how to answer that. In fact she didn't know if she wanted to say anything at all. Even less when she suddenly realized that this woman had totally skipped the usual and conventional first response of "I'm sorry about Martha." She remained silent, waiting. Maybe she was being rude, but something about this woman raised her hackles. She hoped it wasn't jealousy, because she certainly had no reason to be jealous. The part she didn't want to think about was the way her stomach had sunk. She ignored it as best she could. She had no hopes here, no reason to feel kicked by this news.

"So do you own the place now?" Lisa asked.

"Yes." Every instinct warned Holly that this conversation wasn't headed somewhere casual. It had a direction.

Lisa smiled broadly. "I was coming to ask for Martha's help, but maybe you'll help me out instead."

Bingo, thought Holly. "How's that?"

"I need a place to stay for a few weeks. Cliff won't let me stay for more than a couple of days."

Good heavens. The chutzpah! Asking her ex to take her in, and then when he was reluctant she asked a total stranger? Without even a brief expression of sympathy for Martha's passing?

Holly felt as if she were looking at an alien. However, she wasn't prepared to be rude just yet. Maybe this woman was in need? If so, she had to help. That was a deeply ingrained part of her nature. "Are you talking about renting a room?" That would be impossible, given that Holly had to go back to Chicago. She didn't know that she wanted to turn this house over to a total stranger, certainly not when it was full of Martha's belongings.

Lisa looked woeful. "I wish I could. I'm between jobs and it's just awful that Cliff won't let me stay. I can't afford to rent a place. Am I supposed to live in my car?"

"A lot of people do," Holly couldn't help saying, and while those people didn't like it, almost none of them whined about it. They felt fortunate to have shelter better than a cardboard box. "I work with some of them."

"Then you know how awful it would be!"

Holly couldn't deny that. Especially for a woman alone. And, in spite of herself, she was getting interested. Regardless, she could either do the decent thing or feel guilty. It wouldn't be the first time she'd taken in a stranger, although when she did it in Chicago, it was usually a woman in much worse straits than this.

"I can offer you a room," she said finally. "But not for long. I'll be closing the place up in ten days because I have to get home."

"That would still be a great help! I'll get my things."

Holly watched her ride away, wondering what she had gotten herself into. But ten days? It was a short time and the company might be welcome. At least she wouldn't leave the woman to live in her car.

And at least she wouldn't be alone in the echoing silence.

* * *

"You did what?" Cliff demanded as he watched Lisa load her car. They stood outside in the driveway, near her red sports car as she put suitcases in her trunk. He didn't offer to help her.

"You didn't want me, but the woman who owns Martha's place now said I could stay with her until she has to go home." Lisa sniffed. "She's kinder to a stranger than you are to your ex-wife."

"There's a reason you're the ex." He swore.

"Well, you got what you wanted," Lisa said with a toss of her head. "I'll be out of your way, and your precious Jean won't be bothered."

He watched Lisa drive away, then hurried into the house to grab a phone. Holly answered on the second ring.

"You offered my ex a place to stay?"

"Well, why not? It's only a few days. Maybe I need the company."

"Not this company."

"Cliff, I understand she's your ex, but we're strangers. We don't have any problems between us."

"You will," he said grimly. "Jean nearly left me because of her. I had three hired hands quit because of her."

"Oh, she can't be that bad."

"Wanna bet? She's a princess in her own mind. I hope you're ready to take on cooking, cleaning and laundry for her."

"I just won't do it."

"Right. I'm coming over."

"You don't need to."

"Look, she's on her way. I'm coming over and you and I are going to have a talk about Lisa."

"Why?"

"Because I need to defend myself and maybe you." He hung up. Hell and damnation!

This was getting truly bizarre, Holly thought as she hung up the phone. If Lisa was homeless, even temporarily, then it was only right to help her out. Her conscience wouldn't allow otherwise. She could understand why Cliff wouldn't want his ex to stay with him. Regardless of what the woman was like, there was probably a lot of tension there. But what had he meant about his hired hands and Jean?

She guessed she was going to find out, just as she was going to find out why he needed to defend himself and possibly her.

Sheesh, she thought with amusement. He was making Lisa sound like the plague. Surely she couldn't be that bad. Insensitive, yes, that was already apparent, but short of thievery or murder, how bad could she be?

She went back inside to check Martha's room to make sure it was ready. Fresh sheets already graced the bed, but after a moment's hesitation she took Martha's jewelry box to her own room. Not that Martha had had any expensive jewelry, but Holly had liked some of it since childhood, like an enameled pin of a black cat with a rhinestone eye and gold collar. She didn't want to lose any of it until she'd had a chance to go through it.

Then she grabbed some bags and began to fill them with Martha's clothes. Sorting could wait, but for now she needed to make space for her guest. If guest she was.

She had just finished emptying the drawers and closet and dragging the bags to the top of the stairs when she heard a car pull in. That must be Lisa. Once more she wondered what she had gotten into, but decided yet again that it ought to be interesting, whatever it was. The distraction would be a good thing. Rattling around in this house, expecting Martha to come around a corner or out of a door, was just making her sadder. She needed to grieve, yes, but nothing said she had to do it in solitude and without interruption.

Besides, she was beginning to discover that time was hanging heavy on her hands. Deciding what to do about the house and its contents seemed almost beyond her right now, and she wasn't used to being alone all the time. She was used to having a job. Having friends. Needing solitude only after a truly trying day. Being alone too much was also allowing her mind to wander all kinds of paths, too many of which seemed to lead her right back to Cliff. Cliff, who should have just remained firmly in the past, but now was very much in the present.

Along with his ex-wife. She almost laughed at the total absurdity of all this.

She dragged the bags down the stairs, but before she reached bottom Lisa had opened the front door and walked in. No knock, no ring, no polite request to enter. Just Lisa and a suitcase.

Holly began to get an inkling of what this was going to be like. Maybe Cliff hadn't been exaggerating.

Nor did Lisa offer to help her with the bags of clothing. She just stepped to the side, set her suitcase down and said, "When you get done with that you can help me with my other things."

In a flash, Holly's dander rose. "I am not your maid. Get your own things. Top of the stairs, room on the right."

"That wasn't very courteous."

"Neither were you."

Wasting not another glance on the woman, Holly placed the bags by the back door. Just as she was considering what the heck she was going to do about dinner when all she had was one small chicken breast and some leftover salad, she heard another vehicle pull up. Cliff?

Leaving dinner for later consideration, she hurried to the front. It was indeed Cliff and he was standing with Lisa beside her car, looking very stubborn.

She opened the door and stepped out in time to hear him say, "You never asked anyone if you could come here, you just showed up. Now you're imposing on my friend, who is in the process of grieving and trying to sort out her aunt's affairs, and the only thing that concerns you is whether I'll carry your suitcases?"

"It seems like the polite thing to do."

"When you learn some politeness, we'll talk about mine."

He turned from Lisa and saw Holly. "Let's take a walk, Holly."

"Now that really is rude," Lisa snapped. Then she, too, turned toward Holly. "Don't believe a word he says about me. Exes never have anything nice to say."

Holly kept silent while she and Cliff walked toward the fence, far enough from Lisa that they wouldn't be heard if they kept their voices low. Then she said, "I guess I really stepped into the middle of it."

"It's not your fault. She put you in the middle. I just wish I knew what her game is."

"Why does there have to be a game? Maybe she really does just need a place to stay for two weeks."

He leaned against a fence post and faced her. "Maybe. Not likely. Regardless, I know I look like a total boor refusing to carry her bags for her, but I am absolutely not going to help her move in on you. Maybe she'll get mad enough to find another place. I'm certainly going to try to find her one."

Holly hesitated. "Was she always this demanding?"

"It got worse with time."

"And Jean was really prepared to leave?"

"When the woman who helped raise you says, 'It's her or me,' you listen. Which is not to say I divorced Lisa just over that. I'd been building up a head of steam in that direction for quite awhile." He paused, then gave a shake of his head. "I got so I couldn't stand her anymore. She was driving me and everyone else nuts in her own special way, but I'd taken a vow. Funny, but I take vows seriously. Even when keeping them is driving everyone away and nearly ruining my business."

"Wow! What in the world was she doing?"

"Like I said, driving people away. Spending as if money grew on trees." He shook his head again. "I finally got sick of getting to the bills, only to find that I needed my credit extended because there was nothing left. Or getting overdraft notices. So I gave her her own checking account and told her that was all she got for the month."

"How long did that work?"

"For about two weeks. Then the bank would be calling. Then she'd be whining or screaming. Honestly, Holly, if I'd had any inkling I'd never have married her."

Holly frowned, looking down at the ground and kicking at a tuft of wild grass. "Some of that is straight up abusive behavior. I've watched men cut their girlfriends and wives off from everyone until they hadn't a friend or family member left to turn to. I've seen men, and women, who'd spend all the money as soon as a spouse's paycheck arrived and leave nothing for food, nothing for the kids. It's common enough, sad to say."

"I guess. My friends started dropping away because Lisa was always there, then three of my hands quit because she treated them like her personal servants and was always asking them to do things they hadn't been hired to do, and Jean began to feel like a maid...." He sighed. "I've never seen anything like it. But I guess you have."

"Some of it anyway. It's never a happy situation."

"So anyway, my reputation began to suffer, my business began to suffer and by the time I figured out just how bad it was all really getting, Jean threatened to leave. So I made my choice."

Holly wanted to reach out and touch his arm in a gesture of sympathy, but resisted. Lisa might be watching, and there was no telling what that might precipitate.

"Well," she said after a moment, "I did offer her a room. I don't want anyone to sleep in a car if I can avoid it. Since I'm not in love with her, dealing with her ought to be easier for me. I've met the type, if not the exact version."

"You're kindhearted," he said. "You took her in so she wouldn't have to sleep in a car?"

"Anyone would."

"A stranger? But apart from that, don't be so kind-hearted that she takes advantage of you. And don't let her know Martha left you any money, or she'll find a way to wheedle something out of you."

Holly laughed. She couldn't help it. "News flash, Cliff. I've dealt with manipulative people before. The hardest part of being a social worker in the early days, aside from the horrors you see, is realizing that some of those cute, sweet kids you want to help are master manipulators. It's survival and they learn it early." She paused. "I take it Lisa didn't grow up here?"

"No. She came to town with her parents. Her dad was a lawyer and he was working for some big development company."

"The ones who have the sign outside town about the ski resort?"

"Yeah, the ski resort that's never going to happen. Anyway, he was here about three months trying to work things out with the county and forest service. Long enough for me to get in serious trouble."

"I wonder why she came to you instead of Daddy."

"I haven't a clue. Maybe he had enough of her, too."

"Did she give you any idea of why she came here now?"

"Apparently she's not only between jobs but between marriages." He sighed. "I swear I'll try to find another arrangement for her. I'd already told her she could stay for a few days with me. I figured that would give me time to sort something out."

Holly felt a grin split her face. "Did you have to beg Jean?"

"Practically. Which reminds me, she sent over dinner for the two of you. She figured Lisa wouldn't do anything about it and she thought it was a damn shame you should have to."

"That's really nice! I always thought Jean was a sweetheart."

"She is. She was also a good friend of Martha's."

They started walking back toward the house and Holly couldn't resist saying, "I guess Martha left out all the good gossip."

"Martha never gossiped," he said drily. "It's probably why she had so many friends all her life. Listen, call me if Lisa gets to be too much."

"What can you do?"

"Throw her over my shoulder and carry her out of here? Hell, I don't know. Just don't let her get around your kindness again. She's a taker, Holly. Not a giver like you."

Which, when she thought about it, was probably the nicest thing he'd said to her since she had returned. Maybe they'd get over the hump after all.

But as she watched him walk to his truck to pull out a cooler, she knew there was one hump she wasn't going to get over. She still wanted that man. She wanted him as much as she had from the first all those years ago. The sight of his narrow hips cased in denim as he walked away from her was enough to bring back memories of touching and holding him. Feeling him fill her, feeling…

"He's not worth mooning over," Lisa said. "He's not a very nice person."

Holly had to resist an urge to snap at her. "It hardly matters," she said quietly. "I'm going home in ten days. Like I told you."

The words were true, but a different truth seemed to impact her heart. She wasn't quite as eager to get away from Cliff as she had been even this morning.

That realization disturbed her more than Lisa's presence.

Then Cliff astonished her out of her thoughts. "I'm staying for dinner," he announced as he walked toward them with the cooler. "Jean sent plenty."

"Why?" Lisa demanded. "You think your friend here needs protection? Funny, I never saw you as a watchdog."

"No, just a lapdog," Cliff said as he passed her. Then, where Lisa couldn't see, he winked at Holly. "And by the way, my friend has a name. It's Holly."

Oh, man, Holly thought as she followed him into the house. This was going to be an interesting evening.

Lisa finally carried her own bags up the stairs. Holly was surprised at how small they were, not the kind of thing any healthy young woman should need help with. Clearly Lisa didn't need the help, because she didn't have the least struggle getting them upstairs all by herself.

Shrugging inwardly, she followed Cliff to the kitchen. He unloaded the contents of the ice chest. "There's enough in here for a few days. I'll take you to the grocery tomorrow if you like."

"I can find my way."

He paused and looked at her. "Do you ever let anyone help you?"

"You helped me with the tree."

"Because I didn't let you escape it. I want to help.

I could help with a whole lot around here. Including my ex."

Holly couldn't help an almost furtive giggle. "She's really got you on edge."

"I'm more on edge because she's here with you. Bad enough having Jean put up with her, but Jean has experience. You have no idea about Lisa."

"So what should I expect?"

"Lisa doesn't cook, doesn't clean, doesn't pick up after herself, doesn't do laundry… In fact, all she likes to do is ride horses. Crap, I guess that means I'll deal with her every day anyway."

"She'll come to borrow a horse?"

"Probably. It'd be nice if she would take care of them, too."

A short silence fell as they put food away. Fried chicken. Potato salad. A whole host of filling foods, almost enough for an army. From above they heard some banging around.

"I guess she *does* unpack," Holly remarked.

Cliff paused then broke into a hearty laugh. "Evidently. Although not cheerfully."

He surprised her by reaching for her hand and holding it. Holly almost jerked from the electric zap that ran straight to her core. Oh, damn, she didn't want this. Or maybe she wanted it, but she didn't need it.

Cliff spoke. "I wish she hadn't come here. Maybe she can behave reasonably well for a few days. She used to know how, but that all depends on what she thinks she can get out of it. Now that she's got a room, she might not care what you think of her. I don't know."

"I've dealt with worse," she assured him.

His turquoise eyes held hers. "I guess you have.

Did you give any more thought to having some of your kids out here?"

He dropped her hand, leaving her feeling bereft. Even that simple touch reminded her of how much she had given up when she left him to pursue her dream.

"Actually, I have." She had to clear her throat, as it felt oddly tight. "I'd just begun to consider it after what you said. Of course, there are a million hurdles, but I could see it in my mind's eye." She heard the growing excitement in her own voice. "It could be so great."

He put the lid back on the ice chest and set it near the door. "I hear a *but* in there."

"I think I need to talk to a friend of mine, Laurie. She's a child psychologist."

"Why? What worries you?"

She met his gaze, feeling her smile fade. "Taking those kids and showing them life out here, then throwing them back onto the same city streets? I'm not sure it would be good in every case."

"Don't some of these kids already go to camps of different kinds?"

"Some do. I just need to get advice on the right way to do it so that it's helpful, not harmful."

"Makes sense. It's something that never would have occurred to me. I guess that's why you're the social worker. I was just thinking how great it would be for kids in the city to spend some time on a minifarm."

"Oh, it would!" She felt her excitement return. "I could see having a vegetable garden, maybe a few sheep or goats, bunkhouses for them. But I'd have to come up with a whole raft of confidence-building ideas for them, maybe get some trained counselors to participate…but that's the end idea, the big idea. First I think I'd have to start pretty small."

She was bubbling again with the ideas that had been percolating before Lisa had showed up. "Maybe I'll have them stay for the entire summer break."

"That might be good. And don't give up on winter. We have Nordic skiing, sledding and ice-skating. Hell, I could make you a skating rink out back over the garden plot. And there's a new guy up north of here. He bought out the old Olmstead place and is running sled-dog trips over the winter. I bet you could get him interested, and he might even like some helping hands from time to time."

Her eagerness was growing by leaps. It always helped to find that someone else thought an idea was good. "Really? You'd help?"

"Of course I would."

Lisa's voice startled them both. "Of course he'll help," she said with acid in her voice. "He's quick to promise and quick to change his mind."

Whatever she might have thought of Cliff in the past, in that instant Holly's heart went out to him. She saw his face tighten, saw his brilliant eyes darken. He appeared all too much like a man taking another lash from a familiar whip.

Before he could respond, Holly turned to Lisa. "I don't remember including you in this discussion. How about we have some ground rules if you want to stay here? First, you look after yourself. Second, if you don't have something nice to say, don't say it."

"Or what?" Lisa demanded.

"Or I'll throw you out."

Lisa rolled her eyes. "Yeah, right."

"Listen," Holly said calmly, "I've dealt with a lot worse than you. This is *my* house, so it's *my* rules. Live by them or leave. And yes, I can throw you out. Easily."

Lisa glared, then flounced out the front door, slamming it behind her.

"Bravo," Cliff said quietly.

"She's actually quite breathtaking," Holly admitted. "She doesn't know me, but she's carrying on like this. And no, I'm not going to ask."

"Ask away. The answer is no, she wasn't this petulant when we were dating. So she *does* know how to behave."

"Only when she wants something, evidently. I guess she really does believe I won't throw her out, so she has all she wants from me."

"Damn, Holly. I don't want you to have to put up with this. I swear I'm going to find another solution."

"It's just ten days. I've dealt with worse, believe me. We'll either jolt along or she can clear out."

His frown darkened his whole face; he looked as if he wanted to say something, but chose not to. Finally he asked, "So is it all right if I stay for dinner? I can take some of the load off you."

"It's up to you." The truth was, she wanted him to stay. Funny how she'd changed her perspective so fast, at least when it came to Cliff. But even as she was trying to act casual about it, she wondered why. Was that any way to respond to a courteous offer? Or was she just so damned determined to be independent that she could be unintentionally rude? It was possible. Life had toughened her quite a bit out of necessity. She wrapped her heart up to keep the pain at a distance, to avoid being used.

"I'd like you to stay," she said quickly. "Really. But from what I've seen, that's a lot to ask."

He surprised her with a short laugh. "I've dealt with her before. I was prepared to deal with her for a few days. I can't imagine why she came hotfooting over here. She didn't need to."

Holly tilted her head. "You're right."

"So that leaves me wondering what she's really up to."

"Maybe it was spur of the moment when she saw me."

Cliff shrugged. "I guess anything's possible. I'll never understand her, that's for sure. I can often predict her, but I don't understand her."

That, thought Holly, was probably the most succinct description she'd ever heard of a problematic relationship, and a good measure of what Cliff had been through.

She actually felt sorry for him.

Chapter 5

Holly asked if they should wait for Lisa. Cliff rebelled immediately. He supposed he wasn't presenting himself in the best light, but too bad. Holly didn't care about him anyway. As for Lisa, his answer was simple: "Best to start the way you mean to continue. You've got plenty to do over the time you have left. I'll be glad to help as much as I can. But don't start treating Lisa like a guest or you'll regret it. If I'd had any idea, I wouldn't have been such a pushover in the early days."

He caught the twinkle in her eye. Was she warming to him? When he was acting like an ungentlemanly jerk? He had the worst urge to just sweep her into a hug and kiss her until she was breathless. The way he once had. But look where that had gotten him.

"You? A pushover?" She gave him a gentle shove on

the shoulder with her palm. "Okay, then. Let's just fill our own plates. It was so nice of Jean to think of this."

"I think Jean was feeling a great deal of sympathy for you."

"So she really did mutiny?"

"Believe it." He found the plates in the cupboard, still where Martha kept them, and pulled them out while Holly got silverware. "I've never seen her as furious as she was the day she decided she had had enough. She followed me into my office at the end of the day and let fly. Honestly, she'd been keeping so much to herself that I had no idea how bad it had gotten."

"But you'd already had some of your men leave, right?"

"Oh, yeah. They weren't paid to carry shopping bags, or plant flowers she bought, or… Well, it was a pretty long list, all of it full of things I hadn't hired them to do. So they left, one after another, as soon as they found other work. Meanwhile, I was going nuts with the bank, the money and all the rest. They didn't want to be personal servants and I didn't want to lose the ranch. Then Jean."

"What did she say?"

"That she couldn't stand watching me be treated this way. That was her major thing, I guess."

"I can understand that." They sat at the table with plates of fried chicken, potato salad and glasses of iced tea.

"But there was other stuff, too, little stuff that must have been chapping her for a while. Having to pick up wet towels and dirty clothes in the bathroom and bedroom. Dirty dishes and cups left all over the house. Cleaning up spills. Ironing whatever Lisa wanted to wear at that moment. The list went on. I don't even remember it all. The main thing that struck me was her insistence that she couldn't stand to watch Lisa take advantage of me, and that she'd have to leave if things didn't change."

Holly paused as she put her fork into the potato salad on her plate. "I'm sorry. It must have hurt to hear all that."

"I was past being hurt. I was mad most of the time. I knew something had to give, but I'd said those vows, you know."

Holly nodded. He thought she looked pained. For him? The idea shocked him. "I've watched plenty of people break up over less," she said slowly. "But I'll say again, her behavior was abusive."

"Maybe so. But now it's in your house. Damn it."

As they ate, he wondered how the hell this had happened. He had told Lisa she could stay for a few days until he figured something else. What had caused her to move in on Holly?

He had a thought that caused him to pause in midbite. "You," he said.

"Me what?"

"She said she came over here looking for Martha. But what if she'd heard something about the two of us?"

"I thought we were pretty secretive." She colored faintly. "I'd have sworn nobody knew but Martha, and maybe Jean."

"Martha never missed a thing. But what if somebody else had mentioned how close we were that summer?"

"It's possible. I mean, we did go out a few times with your friends."

"So she could have guessed."

Holly nodded. "Still..."

"What if she said something to Jean about staying with Martha? It'd be just like Jean to tell her to forget that, because Martha had passed and you owned the house now."

He watched Holly's eyes widen. "It would fit her pattern of trying to keep you away from your friends."

"Her pattern of trying to spread nastiness about me."

"Either way." Holly resumed eating. He realized that he was sitting there staring at her as if he was moonstruck. He'd better stop it. That time had come and gone.

He finished a few more mouthfuls of chicken, then asked, "What makes people act that way?"

"I can't be certain about Lisa because I just met her. But generally speaking, I think a lot of them must be control freaks. Extreme control freaks. She wanted you cut off so you had no support system. She wanted everyone else to do her bidding and if they left, so much the better for her, because then she'd have total control."

"I wasn't going to cook or clean for her."

"No, but if Jean left, she could hire someone and then she'd have control. She couldn't completely control Jean because she knew you'd never get rid of her. So she sought other ways of getting rid of her."

"Crap."

"I'm just guessing," Holly said. "I've had some psychology training, obviously, and this is also based on my observations of abusive relationships."

"I guess you've seen more than a few."

"I have. Trying to convince someone to get out of

a relationship like that can be difficult, because the victim is steadily trained to feel responsible for everything that displeases the abuser. I guess you were strong enough to withstand it for two years."

"I'd have been stronger if I'd gotten rid of her sooner."

She astonished him by putting her fork down and reaching across the table to clasp his hand. "Love is a dangerous thing," she said quietly. "All of us begin with a huge desire to please the one we love. If one of the parties is unscrupulous, the other one can wind up in trouble. I don't think you were weak. Far from it. You got mad and got out. Congratulations."

He turned his hand over to clasp hers and their eyes met. She had such beautiful blue eyes, he thought. The years had thinned her too much, but she was still every bit as gorgeous as she had been a decade ago when he had believed the only thing he wanted in life was a future with Holly.

Looking into her eyes, he had that impulse again. His entire body began to sizzle, and he felt his groin grow heavy with desire. Her eyes darkened and he recognized her response to him. She still wanted him, too.

Before he could remind himself there was no future in it, a sarcastic voice said from the kitchen doorway, "My, isn't this cozy."

Holly snapped her hand back as if she'd been scalded. Cliff felt the surge of an old, familiar anger. Right then he'd have loved nothing more than to carry that woman out to her car, throw her clothes in after her and tell her to get lost for good.

"I don't get invited to dinner?" Lisa asked. "What a rude way to treat a guest."

Cliff stood and faced her. “You’re not a guest here. You’re a stray that a kind lady offered to take in for a few days. She could change her mind and I wouldn’t blame her. So find your own food in the fridge and feed yourself. You can do at least that much on your own, can’t you?”

He turned back to Holly and was surprised to see a faint smile dancing around the corners of her mouth. “Would you like to take a walk and finish eating later when the company is more pleasant?”

Holly rose instantly. “I’d love to.” Her smile became visible.

Cliff held out his hand and to his amazement, she took it. They grabbed jackets from the mudroom, because spring evenings cooled down quite a bit, and stepped out back.

“I’m sorry,” he said when they’d left the house a few yards behind. “I probably just made it worse for you.”

She shook her head. “It’s okay. I’ve dealt with tougher nuts. Gang members. Street fighters. Men who were pummeling their wives or kids. She doesn’t scare me.”

He took her hand again, squeezing her fingers. “I can’t imagine what you’ve seen or been through.”

“Good. Not everyone needs to. So, if Lisa hadn’t turned up, it would have been nice to use you as a sounding board about this camp idea.”

“We can do that anyway. Maybe if we ignore her enough, she’ll leave. You know what occurred to me today as I was working? Before Lisa arrived, anyway.”

“What’s that?”

He drew a deep breath, preparing for any kind of

response, and said, "I'd have loved to take you riding, visit some of our old haunts."

He half expected her to get angry for bringing up that long-ago summer. Especially when he'd initially been so cold to her when she returned.

He heard her sigh. "Cliff, you can't go back in time."

"I know that. But we had a wonderful summer and sometimes I go to our places and just remember it. Good memories are rare enough in this life."

She stopped walking and faced him. "Really? You do that?"

"There's only one part of it that wasn't good. Why the hell would I want to forget?"

She looked down at her feet. "I try hard not to, but sometimes I think about it, too," she admitted quietly. "On nights when I start to feel worn-out or burned-out. I'm not complaining, mind you. I chose the life I needed, and I'm sorry my choice hurt you, but yeah, sometimes I remember. I was happier then than I've ever been."

He supposed he could be content knowing that. His memories weren't addled. "Me, too," he said quietly. "Me, too."

Another look passed between them, this one almost smoldering. It was a fire they couldn't douse with Lisa in the house nearby, and now he had a new reason to curse his ex. On the other hand, it was probably best that they couldn't. She intended to go back to her job. Neither of them needed a repeat of the summer long ago, and sex wasn't enough. It was never enough.

He was just getting to know this Holly. Best not to muddle things any more than they already were.

He dragged his gaze away, and they walked farther along the fence line. "These leases…" he said.

"Yours, you mean?"

"Yeah. If you need more room, you could use some of the land. I don't need every square inch of it. But I do need most of it. It's allowed me to expand my operation because of the added grazing. The ranch is actually turning a profit, not an easy thing to do these days. But you're talking about bunkhouses and things like that. You might need more room."

"That's a long way down the road," she answered. "But that's a generous offer. Thank you."

"It might not be as far down the road as you think. We could transform this place pretty fast. The main thing you need to do is figure out what you need."

"And figure out the red tape."

He was glad to see her brightening again. He wanted to know more about her life in Chicago, about the things that had brought her here looking so worn, but he didn't feel he had the right to get so personal. Not yet, maybe never.

Ten days, he reminded himself. She was leaving in ten days. She kept mentioning it, maybe as a warning. Evidently she didn't want to repeat the mistakes of their long-ago summer romance.

Except, much as it had hurt him in the end, he just couldn't think of it as a mistake. But maybe it had been for her. She hadn't accepted his offer to visit some of their old haunts, even though she'd admitted to treasuring at least some of the memories.

Maybe for her it hadn't meant what it had meant for him at the time. Maybe her heart hadn't been in it. Maybe for her it had been just a fling.

The thought soured his mouth and stomach. *Be smart,* he told himself. *Keep your guard up.* It was possible to be helpful without going any further.

Maybe for once in his life it was time not to throw his entire being into something. For sure, the only thing he gave his all to that had never betrayed him was his ranch.

It would be wise to remember that.

Cliff headed out an hour later with a handwritten thank-you note from Holly for Jean. She stood in the doorway watching him drive away, feeling as if something really important had happened, as if the ground beneath her feet had shifted in some way.

She had certainly seen a side of Cliff she'd never imagined. He had survived a poisonous relationship; he seemed firmer and steadier than she remembered him being. He had certainly grown up well. And he had evidently turned into a protector. Imagine him spending all this time here just to try to keep Lisa in line. That had to have been uncomfortable for him, even after all these years.

Her attraction to him hadn't faded one little bit, either. Maybe he was even more attractive now. It was pointless to give in to it, but considering she hadn't felt any attraction to a man since she was attacked last year, it was good to know she still could respond this way.

"How do I get wash done?"

Holly turned slowly, closing the door on the night and preparing to deal with Lisa. "Laundry?"

"That's what I said."

"Well," Holly said slowly, "there are machines at the back of the house. Help yourself. If you want someone to do it for you, I think there's a laundry in town where they charge by the load for washing, drying and folding. I'm not sure they also do ironing."

Lisa frowned.

Holly smiled politely, then headed for the living room. She needed to find something to read, a wall to put up between her and this woman. She had a feeling she was going to regret taking Lisa in more than she had ever regretted providing shelter to someone in trouble numerous times in the past.

Lisa wasn't really in trouble. She *was* trouble.

Unfortunately, the woman followed her into the living room. "I can't afford to pay someone to do my wash."

"Like I said, there are machines in the back of the house." Holly sat in her aunt's rocker and reached for a magazine. Something about embroidery. She'd never had time for that.

"I'll need help," Lisa said.

Holly looked up. "Really? You don't know how to do laundry? I've worked with *children* who do laundry for their entire families."

"You're mean."

"If I were mean, you wouldn't be staying here." Holly returned her attention to the magazine.

But Lisa wasn't ready to go away. "I saw how you looked at Cliff. You have the hots for him." She sat on the sofa facing Holly.

"Really?" Holly tried to sound disinterested.

"Well, he's a looker. I fell for it, too."

Holly arched her brow, but refused to take her attention from the magazine. Her heart had sped up, and she could feel her annoyance building. Was this woman trying to precipitate a fight? "Looks aren't everything."

"They certainly aren't. That man should have married his ranch instead of me. He's nailed to the place."

"Seems to be the usual thing for ranchers."

"When we first got married, he'd take me to Denver for the weekend sometimes, but then that stopped. He said it was too expensive. So I went by myself. Then he got mad because I bought clothes and got my hair and nails done. It wasn't like I was buying fancy jewelry or something."

"Hmm."

Silence for a blessed minute or two. Just as Holly dared to hope it would continue, Lisa spoke again. "So did you ever live here?"

"No. Just visited my aunt."

"She was a strange bird."

At that, Holly's head snapped up. She put the magazine aside. "Are you looking for a way to make me angry? Because you're close to succeeding, and if I can't have you around here without me getting angry, you're going to be leaving. I'm torn up enough about my aunt's passing. I don't need you to pile on. Find another way to entertain yourself."

"Out here in the middle of nowhere?"

"You have a car." With that Holly rose and headed upstairs. Enough was enough.

How the heck had Cliff survived this for two years? She couldn't stand it for one evening.

Upstairs, she pulled out a book, climbed into her pajamas, then forgot all about reading as she stared out the window into the night. Cliff wouldn't be riding this direction tonight, she thought.

She remembered what he had said about occasionally visiting their old haunts. Her cheeks heated a bit because she knew exactly what haunts he meant. Like young, healthy animals, they'd made love anywhere and everywhere they could find the privacy. Looking back at it, she was surprised at how voracious they'd both been. Oh, they'd had fun, and laughed a lot, but they'd also been insatiable.

She leaned her forehead against the cool glass, remembering, and wondering if that hadn't had something to do with her reluctance to stay with Cliff so long ago. Even at the age of twenty it had seemed to her that you needed more than sex for an enduring relationship.

But in all honesty, it wasn't just that. She had things she wanted to do, things she couldn't do as a ranch wife. Back then it had looked like a kind of dead end.

Right now, it looked like heaven on earth. She almost laughed aloud at herself. She was just tired. She'd been fighting burnout before she got here, before her aunt died. She had definitely needed a break, and right now this place was providing peace and relaxation. Well, except for Lisa, and that woman didn't come close to the stressors she faced on her job.

Hell, she felt guilty from being away from her kids for even two weeks. She tried to maintain a professional distance, had even gotten better at it, but she still cared. Deep in her being, she cared about those kids and their families.

But she also remembered something one of her colleagues had said a month or so ago: "Holly, you need a break. Take some desk time, rotate into another area. If you don't, you're going to be useless to everyone."

She had acknowledged the justice of what Carla had said, but hadn't taken any action to rotate into something less taxing. Stubbornness? Hubris? She didn't know. Certainly most of her other colleagues were capable of stepping in for her, capable of looking after her clients.

So what was it with her? Maybe she hadn't realized how close to the edge she was getting? Certainly, not until she got here and felt the weight lifting from her had she realized that she was tense in every fiber of her being.

Cliff's words floated back to her, about her reluctance to let anyone help her. Maybe that was at the rock bottom of it all. She put her mind to something and let nothing deter her. That had cost her Cliff, and now it might be harming her health.

She turned and caught sight of herself in the mirror over the dresser. She'd lost twenty pounds since the attack. Some of them she had needed to lose, but the woman who stared back at her right now looked almost hollow.

Quickly she turned back to the window, concealing her reflection there by pressing her forehead to the glass again.

Maybe she had a lot more to deal with than just her grief over Martha and closing this place up. Maybe she needed to deal with things deep inside her that drove her mercilessly.

There was really no reason for it. She'd had a normal, happy childhood. Well, as normal as the child of parents in the diplomatic corps could have. She'd bounced around the world, but had always thrived on the changes. It was during those travels that she had developed a deep ache in her soul for the world's suffering innocents. It was that experience that had driven her into social work.

But still, Carla was right. If she didn't take a break, she'd wind up being useless to the very people she most wanted to help.

Maybe her dedication was more than dedication. Maybe some of those starving children she had seen around the world had become a demon that drove her, yielding to no reason.

One thing for sure, she had never forgotten their faces. Their hunger. The rags they wore. Her parents had tried to shield her from the worst of it, but they hadn't always succeeded. While she'd never been in a war zone—her parents wouldn't have been allowed to take their daughter into one, even had they wanted to—she'd been in many countries that could easily be called famine, disease and neglect.

The same famine, disease and neglect that collected in pockets in this country like untreated sores. And always, always she felt the anger than she couldn't do more.

Her mental mirror was proving no more comfortable than the one above the dresser. How many times in training had she been warned that she needed to keep a distance, reserve time for herself and turn it all off when she went home at night? That she could lose her effectiveness if she didn't? That she could make herself seriously ill if she didn't care for herself.

Damn, she thought, closing her eyes. Maybe *she* needed a caretaker. Clearly she wasn't doing the job for herself.

Then another thought struck her. Her head snapped

up and she scrambled for the extension phone beside the bed. Thank God it had a list of numbers on autodial, even though her aunt had seldom used this room. Martha must have been getting worried that something could happen to her at any time.

"God, Martha," she said out loud. "Why didn't you call me?"

Because she would have come running at the drop of a hat if Martha had needed her.

She hit the button labeled *Cliff* and listened to it ring. At last he answered.

"Martin Ranch."

"Cliff? Cliff, it's Holly. I need you, please. Meet me out back by the fence."

"Want me to bring a horse for you or drive?"

"I don't care. I just need you."

"On my way."

There was a click and the line went dead.

It was too damn cold, and high clouds had moved in overhead, turning the night dark as pitch. It was not a night for riding hell-for-leather over open ground, so Cliff hopped into his truck.

Holly had sounded tense, but not in pain, so he assumed Lisa must have finally found a button to push. If so, that woman was going to be out of there on her butt before the sun rose if he had to call the sheriff to do it.

Damn, he should never have left the two of them alone. But what the hell was he supposed to do? He had no right to override Holly's decision to ask Lisa to stay. Not his house.

The drive seemed to take forever, although at the speed he was going he should have gotten a half dozen tickets. Still, it took him twenty minutes to arrive, and he hit the brakes so hard at the end of the gravel drive that he skidded.

Out by the back fence. So he set out at a dead run until he saw the ghostly figure of Holly standing out there alone.

"Holly?" he asked quietly, slowing his approach.

"I'm sorry," she said tautly. "I'm sorry. You didn't need to race. I should have told you, but…" Her voice broke.

That sound did him in. He didn't care about the past, about the future, about whether Lisa saw and found additional reasons to be nasty. He just stepped into her and wrapped her in a bear hug as tightly as he dared, his chin coming to rest on her sweet-smelling hair. "What?" he asked, trying to shift from the fury that had been building in him to the gentleness he needed now.

"I need…I need to talk," she said brokenly, then burst into wrenching sobs.

He didn't ask any questions. She couldn't have answered anyway, and for right now he felt deep inside that she just needed to be held and comforted, whatever was going on. He could do that much.

God, it felt so good to hold her again. He rubbed her back, feeling his own chest tighten in response to her pain. Gradually she began to quiet and he dared to speak.

"Want to go for a drive or over to my place?"

She drew a sharp, choked breath. "Yeah," she whispered. "Away."

So he took her away.

He drove more slowly this time and decided to take

her to his place. It'd be more comfortable and they'd have the privacy she seemed to want. Why else had she stood at the back fence alone?

He wanted to ask if Lisa had done something but kept quiet. Let her talk in her own time, when she was ready. She didn't need any pressure from him.

She remained hunched beside him, her arms wrapped tightly around herself as if she were holding something in. He doubted Lisa could have done anything to make her feel that bad. God, she had said she wanted to talk; he couldn't help in any way unless she talked and here they were, barreling through the night in silence.

He forced a lid on his impatience, reminding himself that she had called out to him and now the best thing he could do was give her space and time until she let him know what else she needed.

At least she'd called him. Turned to him as a friend. A week ago he would have said he never wanted to see her again. Now here he was all wrapped up in her with no idea whether he'd be left like roadkill again.

Okay, maybe that wasn't entirely fair, but it was how he had felt. He could look back now and see how egotistical he'd been. He'd ignored all her intentions to pursue a career, just so absolutely certain she wouldn't be able to say no to his proposal. Certain she loved him enough to spend the rest of her life here, with him. She hadn't misled him—he'd misled himself.

Not until the lights of his house appeared out of the darkness did she speak. "Your ranch?"

"I figured it was warmer and more comfortable than this truck. Plus, I can get you something hot to drink."

"Thanks."

Her voice sounded steadier to him now, and that was a huge relief. He brought them to a stop at the front door. Hardly had he turned off the ignition when Jean stepped out.

"Everything okay?" she called.

"Fine," Cliff answered. "I brought Holly over for a visit."

He walked around the truck to help Holly out. She didn't resist, and moments later Jean had enveloped her, leaving Cliff to stand there bemused, keys in hand. Well, maybe it was woman stuff. Maybe Holly would rather talk to Jean. Crazy, but he felt as if he'd just been cut off at the pass.

Chapter 6

Holly was beginning to feel stupid. She'd called Cliff out late at night because she was having an emotional crisis? She should have called Laurie or Carla or Sharon. And now elderly, gray-haired Jean was fussing over her like a mother hen, getting her settled in the living room, asking what she wanted to drink.

It was embarrassing. She had reached out because she needed not to be alone, and now she was surrounded by caretakers, with a man who was certainly going to want some kind of explanation, whether or not she felt like talking about it now.

She accepted the offer of tea with honey, thinking that she should have just handled her emotional storm by herself. The way she usually did. She could have walked it off. What had possessed her to call a man who had absolutely no reason to want to be her confidant?

But he had come racing to the rescue nonetheless, and that hug he had given her had meant the world. All by itself it had been healing. She wondered how she could possibly thank him.

"I'm going to bed," Jean announced. She bent to give Holly another quick hug. "Cliff knows where everything is if you need something. The guest room is ready, too, if you want to stay."

Not a word about Lisa. A coded message, perhaps? Maybe Jean thought she was here because of something Lisa had done. Boy, would she like to leave it that way.

She gave Cliff credit, though, for not pushing her in any way. Hell, he hadn't even asked a single question, which was kind of amazing considering the way she had called him and then sobbed in his arms. He must want to know what all this was about, but now that she was looking at him, she wasn't sure she could explain it.

She curled in one corner of a big leather couch. He'd settled in a matching chair facing her and sat forward with his elbows on his splayed knees and hands clasped. He ignored the tea Jean had put on the table at his elbow.

"Feeling a little better?" he asked finally.

"I'm sorry I called you." The words burst from her.

He lifted his brows, but didn't move. Those darn turquoise eyes of his kept right on looking at her. She wished she had a hole to crawl into.

"I hope," he said, "that you mean you're sorry for bothering me, not that you're sorry I came."

Ouch! She grabbed a throw pillow and hugged it, staring down at it because it was easier. "I'm sorry I bothered you."

"No need. It was no bother at all. Obviously you needed someone. Excuse me, but I just can't imagine you dumping those tears on Lisa."

In spite of herself, she saw the humor in the notion. "Uh, no," she said finally. "But I'm still sorry to have bothered you. Honestly, I should be able to deal with things myself, not call you out late at night."

"It's not that late. And the amazing thing is, well..." He paused. "My mother always used to say that a joy shared was a joy multiplied. I think it goes the other way, too—a burden shared is a burden lightened. That's what friends are for, right?"

"Are we friends?" That burst from her, too, and she began to wonder seriously about the state of her mind. What was she doing? What was she trying to get at with him?

"I think we're getting back to friendship," he said. "Admittedly, we avoided each other like the plague for the past ten years. Admittedly, when I saw you at the lawyer's office I was nasty. I think there was a buildup of things not said a long time ago."

"Then maybe you should say them."

"Why? That *was* a long time ago. Anyway, this isn't about me, it isn't about us. Is it?"

She shook her head, pulling on the fringe that rimmed the pillow.

"Was it Lisa?"

"That woman couldn't push me to that point. Ever."

"Then...?"

Holly sighed, darting a glance his way. Damn, he looked concerned and sympathetic. "I was just thinking generally about things. About myself."

"And?"

She picked at the pillow some more, then tossed it aside. "I was thinking about how driven I am. Some of my colleagues have been pushing me to take a rotation to an easier job for a while. It's not unusual. Casework, the kind that takes you on the streets and into homes, can get to you. They even warned us to leave the job at work and not bring it home."

"Why do I think you find that difficult?"

She gave him a humorless half smile. "I guess you know me."

"A little, anyway. So even your colleagues think you need a rotation?"

"Yeah. And I haven't been listening. And that got me to thinking about why social work was so important to me, and just what demons might be driving me."

"I gather the answer upset you."

"Very much." She was grateful that he didn't press her, just waited for whatever she wanted to say. At this point she didn't know. "It's quite a mess," she said finally. "Hard to explain. But then I made a link I hadn't made before and I kinda fell apart." That part embarrassed her. She was tougher than that, right? Well, maybe not, and it appalled her to be faced with her own weakness.

"There are," she said slowly, "a lot of good social workers. I could name a dozen right off the top of my head who could take care of my clients. They'd do a fine job. There's no *need* for me to feel like I can't turn it over to someone else for a little while."

"Are you worrying about your relationship with the children?"

"A little. You develop them, you know. No matter how hard you try to maintain a professional distance, a balance, with at least some of those kids you become a trusted person, someone they can rely on. To just shift myself out of the picture, even if only for a month or so, might not be good."

He hesitated. "You came out here for two weeks. You explained to them, right?"

She nodded.

"Are any of them too young to understand that you need to go away for a little while but that you'll be back?"

"Probably not. And that's when I looked hard at myself. Just by its very nature, social work results in kids and their families getting different caseworkers from time to time. We try to ease the transition, both of us showing up together at least once, but it happens all the time."

"So the kids get it. You're not a parent but a professional they work with."

"Yeah, and that's what makes what I'm doing so ridiculous. It's not like I'm the fairy godmother with the only magic wand in town. I started thinking that I'm getting too full of myself. Started feeling too important. The truth is, if I dropped off the earth tomorrow, plenty of competent people would step in to help my clients and they'd be just fine."

"Maybe so. Aren't you being a little hard on yourself? I mean, you care. That's not something to apologize for."

"Another thing they warn us about is that if we don't take care of ourselves, we won't be able to take care of anybody else. I've been pushing that line for the past year. Driven. Driven to the point that my colleagues are commenting. That's bad."

"Wouldn't a supervisor step in?"

"If we weren't always so shorthanded, maybe. Right now, if I rotate, I'll probably increase someone else's load."

He gave a low whistle. "That's a rock and a hard place all around."

"But it's not the whole story. I've been taking my work home with me. I think about nothing else anymore. So anyway, as I was standing in the bedroom, I caught sight of myself in the mirror. I've lost twenty pounds in the past year."

"I noticed. A little too much?"

"Too much. Five pounds needed to go. Maybe even ten. But not twenty."

He waited, and she got the feeling he wasn't going to accept her weight loss as an excuse for her tears. She sighed again and put her head down. When her voice emerged, it was muffled. "That's when I made the connection."

"To what?"

"To the attack a year ago. I've been avoiding dealing with it by working myself to death. By letting my job consume me. It was easier. Yes, easier. I got sick of people saying how strong I was because I came back to work two weeks later. Because it wasn't true. I was a scared, nervous wreck, and I think tonight I finally had the breakdown I should have had back then."

There, it was out. She'd admitted that she was a coward, that she couldn't deal with what had happened to her and that she was driven not as much by concern for her clients as by a need to escape her own mind and emotions.

From where she sat, that was a pretty ugly, cowardly thing.

Worse, she felt she had just revealed something sordid to Cliff. This wasn't a light she wanted him to see her in. Then another thought struck her. Why should she feel sordid about what had been done to her? God, she was losing it.

"Holly?"

His voice pulled her back from a dark cliff. She dared to look at him.

"I'm not asking for details here. I'm not an inquisitor or a prosecutor. Hell, I'm just an ordinary guy who probably knows more about sheep and goats than people. But can you give me an outline of what happened? Martha just said you were attacked but you were okay. I'd like to know generally what we're talking about here."

She closed her eyes.

"You don't have to tell me if it's too painful."

"I think," she said in a thin voice, "that facing this is exactly what my mind is trying to tell me to do. I can't bury it any longer."

He waited, giving her space and time to gather herself enough to look into that black pit she'd been avoiding for a year now.

"I stayed out way too late. Not that that area of town is exactly safe in broad daylight, but I stayed too long with a client. They were having some serious trouble in that house and I was worried about violence erupting. Nothing had happened that I could call the police for. I mean, nobody got hit, nobody threatened anybody, but it was building that way, and I was trying to mediate and calm it down, and wondering if I should get the children out, at least for the night. Anyhow, I lost track of time."

She opened her eyes in time to see him nod.

"So when I came out of the complex, the streets were fairly empty, although not completely. They seldom are. But at least in the daytime, there are plenty of people out and about. It helps. But I knew I was in trouble when I was halfway to my car and all of sudden there was nobody at all on the street. They just melted away, except for three guys. I knew I needed to get to a safe place or into my car fast. I didn't make it." She fell silent, fighting for control as her heart hammered and her fists clenched so tightly her nails bit into her palms.

Cliff rose swiftly and came to sit right beside her. His powerful arm wrapped around her shoulders. She turned into him as if he were a bastion of safety.

"I was lucky," she said. "Very lucky. As soon as they grabbed for me, I started screaming my head off. They just laughed. They thought they had me. Except…" Her voice broke. "Do you know how much courage it took for someone in the surrounding buildings to call the cops? I do. I didn't expect it. I thought I was done."

"Why so courageous for someone to call?"

"Retaliation. It's another world, Cliff. People there don't dare call the police about much. Between gang retaliation and the way the cops themselves can behave, it's all too often a lose-lose situation for them."

"God!"

"But somebody called. And for once the cops did it right."

"What do you mean?"

"They didn't come in with a dozen cars, sirens screaming. They didn't give away that they had been called. I barely remember, I was down on the ground by then, but I heard this engine purr, and then the spotlight came on, and some time later there were a half dozen patrol cars there. It's all confused. You'd think something like that would be etched so clearly in my brain I couldn't forget a bit of it."

"Maybe not remembering is better."

"Maybe. I don't know. I remember the terror, I remember fighting as best I could, I even remember the way one guy's breath smelled. He was so damn drunk. Anyway, I got off easy, with a few bruises and scrapes and some torn clothing."

"I don't know that I'd exactly call that getting off easy."

"Cliff, I was lucky. Very lucky because someone took a huge risk for me and called for help. I'll never know who it was. I'll never know who to thank."

He twisted a little and drew her closer, so that he could stroke her hair and cuddle her better. Liking it, she almost wanted to burrow into him.

"Maybe," he said slowly, "you need to think a little less about how lucky you were and face up to the fact that you suffered a horrible attack."

"That occurred to me tonight when I started thinking about how work obsessed I've become. I'm not leaving room for anything else."

"Not even eating, evidently."

She didn't answer for a few minutes. She was still trying to put pieces together in her mind. "I think I was putting myself in a prison of work because I was afraid of what was outside of it. Trying not to face what had happened to me. What could happen again. A lot of people were surprised I could go right back to work, that I didn't even ask for another neighborhood."

"You weren't going to let them defeat you, were you?"

"I guess not. Which is where my stubbornness comes in. I thought of it like getting back on the horse that threw you. Maybe I was afraid that if I gave in even a little bit, then the fear would grow and start encompassing more things."

"I suppose it might."

"But the end result is I never dealt with it, and to avoid thinking about it, I've been working myself to the ragged edge. As if I could beat those guys that way."

"You might just be too brave and stubborn for your own good."

She fell silent, not certain she wanted to say more, unsure of how much she wanted to share with this man who had returned to her life only a few short days ago. At first he'd seemed so determined to dislike her but now… What had happened? Had he forgiven her? Had she forgiven herself? She felt so messed up right now that she didn't know what was really going on inside herself.

He began to rub her back gently, soothingly. She tucked her head into his shoulder and risked winding her arms around his waist. His offered comfort started to fill her.

Then he asked the question, the one that gave her no quarter. "So what are you really afraid of here, Holly? Except for not being able to bury yourself in work, nothing changed by you coming out here."

"Yes, it did," she said, unable to silence the words, no matter how hard it was to speak them. "I don't want to go back."

* * *

Holy hell, Cliff thought. That was momentous. It left him speechless. He knew as well as anyone how much being a social worker meant to this woman. The scars of her determination still resided in his heart. Come to that, the scars of her determination probably resided in her heart and soul.

He couldn't think of a damn thing to say. All he could do was hold her close and let her go wherever she wanted or needed to go with this. He wasn't comfortable with feeling helpless, but he felt utterly helpless right now.

He vastly preferred to deal with matters, get them taken care of, pleasant or not, and move on. Not that he'd been great about the moving-on part with Holly. He remembered moping for a long time.

But now he certainly understood why she had needed someone to talk to. Just thinking that she shouldn't go back would have rocked her to her very core. The attack was bad enough, and the single detail of the guy's breath was enough to tell him what they'd been after. He had to admit he was surprised that she'd been able to return to her work in that same neighborhood. He couldn't imagine.

As he sat there holding her, he thought about the protected life he'd led. Not exactly sheltered. He'd dealt with other exigencies, like bad years, range fires, the deaths of animals, plenty of hard times. Holding things together with twine and a prayer, he sometimes thought.

But nothing like what she had been facing. He felt so damn inadequate right now. He didn't know how to comfort her; he didn't have any helpful words, nothing to offer. Nothing except that he could hold her, and that seemed a small enough thing to do.

Before long, however, it ceased to be a small thing. Memories of that long-ago summer began to burgeon in his brain even as his body responded to her closeness. There was an inevitability to it, as if she were the key to a lock that hadn't been opened in a long time. A key to feelings and sensations he had put away, only to discover that they hadn't even become dusty with time.

He was older now, though. He had learned some self-control, and some other basic truths, such as that anticipation had pleasures of its own.

The ache began to build in him, the need and the yearning, but he checked them. Now was certainly not the time. The time might never come again, but it certainly wasn't going to happen when she was in the middle of a crisis. Once he had been young enough to think that making love was an anodyne to everything. He was no longer that young.

Older and wiser, he might wish and want, but he could still maintain enough sense to know it wasn't right.

Although maintaining that sense was getting harder by the minute. His groin grew heavy and throbbed. His heart beat a little faster. His hands itched to reacquaint themselves with her every charm—charms he remembered as if they had been permanently etched on his brain and skin.

To him she had always been irresistible. When she had walked into the lawyer's office, he had realized in an instant that that hadn't changed, despite all the pain she had caused him. That's why he'd been so annoyed.

He'd long since learned a measure of forgiveness

for her. She had left because she had other things to do, things that didn't involve being buried on a ranch. She'd never made any secret of that, she'd never misled him. He'd misled himself, and finally he had become man enough to admit it.

He had thought he was in love with her. Maybe he had been. But he wasn't in love now. He didn't know her well enough, and probably never would. She might talk about not wanting to go back, but she would. It was her life.

And he was too smart now to put himself in that bind again.

But he sure wouldn't have minded making love with her again. Once, twice, a hundred times—the passion remained after all else was gone.

Kind of amazing, actually.

Right then he didn't dare move a muscle for fear he would make the wrong move. It would be so easy to kiss her, to fondle her, to pull her clothes away and bury himself in her welcoming depths. To reenact the folly of so long ago. A summer love, a time when he'd been high as a kite on her, and randy every single waking moment. They had frolicked endlessly and joyously.

And unrealistically. It had been a few months stolen from reality. He knew that now. Sooner or later, one way or another, reality would have intruded on their cocoon of laughter and passion.

It was intruding right now. The licking tongues of flame that devoured him and urged him to take her right this second couldn't have been more inappropriate.

He sighed and shifted cautiously, resigning himself to unsated need. Some things mattered more. He'd managed to grow up at least that much.

She stirred against him and for a second he froze as a rush of renewed hunger flooded him. He wished he knew what it was about her. Not even Lisa had ever managed to make him feel the kind of desire this woman kindled in him. Which was not to say he hadn't enjoyed Lisa, but Holly was in a whole different league.

He nearly voiced a protest when she eased out of his arms and sat back. Then she blew him away.

"I shouldn't do that," she said.

"Do what?"

"Let you hold me. All it does is make me crazy with wanting you again."

"Damn," he murmured. He clenched his fists and fought an urge to pounce on her right then.

"I guess I shouldn't have said that." She tried to jump up but he caught her wrist and stopped her.

"It's okay," he said. "I'm kind of feeling the same way." *Kind of?* He had fireworks going off in his head because of her admission.

"But we can't go back," she said.

"I know."

"I mean, how do I know what I'm feeling right now isn't just a memory?"

Memory? What he was feeling right now was no memory. Not by any stretch.

"Regardless," she said, giving him the sense that she was trying to be reasonable, "last time we let passion rule us, we got hurt. We'd be fools to open that door again."

She was probably right, but he was perilously close to not caring. He shut his eyes briefly, battering the caveman in him back to a darker corner, then looked at her again. He hadn't missed the fact that she had said, "*we* got hurt."

"Holly? Were you hurt, too, when you left?" This whole thing was beginning to take on some strange dimensions, and he had to figure it out.

"Of course I was."

"I wish I'd known that." He might have felt a little better to know her decision hadn't been easy, that it had cost her, too. It was a selfish feeling, and he despised it, but it was true anyway. He had felt cast aside, as if he didn't matter to her at all.

"I told you it hurt," she answered, her eyes widening. "I told you it wasn't an easy decision."

He remembered those words, all right, but he also remembered something else. "I didn't believe you. You made it look so easy to just get up and walk away from me that afternoon. Not a tear, not even one look back."

"You thought that was *easy?* Why do you think I had to say all those horrible things? I was taking a hatchet to the ties."

He couldn't tell if she was angry or surprised. Her face didn't give him a clue. After a moment, she just shook her head and murmured, "Wow."

There was no reply to that, so he just leaned forward, resting his elbows on his splayed knees so that she was behind him. Looking at her right now was difficult, between the desire that refused to completely quiet and the feeling that things were somehow going off the rails here. At the very least he had to adjust his memories a bit. At the worst… At the worst she was about to make a life-altering decision under circumstances that weren't the best.

"I'm sorry," Holly said. "I'm a mess and I'm making things messier."

He looked over his shoulder. "Stop apologizing. What mess?"

"I'm mixed-up," she said. "Everything's suddenly all mixed-up. My aunt, my job, what happened to me last year, you… It's all roiling together and I can't sort it out. It's not fair to dump all of this on you."

"I don't feel dumped on." He really didn't. Confused, yes. A little worried, definitely. Mostly for her. Come what may, he had this ranch and all that entailed. If she started doing things like quitting her job, she might wind up with nothing that mattered to her.

He wished he knew how best to help her out, but he suspected that in the end she was going to have to make her own decisions about everything. Well, she would. She'd been making her own decisions for a long time. There was only one thing he could think of to say.

"Just don't decide anything right now," he said. "Not with so much turmoil. If nothing else, there's plenty of time."

"Not really," she said quietly. "I fly back in less than two weeks."

"Why should that be a deadline? You'd have to go back to give notice regardless, so nothing about your job needs deciding this instant. If you're really thinking about a camp for kids, that's going to take a lot of time and planning. As for me…I shouldn't even be part of this. I'm here, planted like a tree, I'm not going anywhere and you have more important things to deal with, like your grief over Martha."

"God, I miss her. I could almost hate that house,

because it's so empty without her. Then I remember the good times."

"That's important."

"Yeah." She fell quiet.

He studied his hands as if they might have some answers when in truth all they wanted to do was reach for her. He folded them together and wondered how Holly managed to turn him into that young man who had spent an entire summer following her around like a buck in rut. He should be feeling stupid right now.

Instead he was feeling like a bull that had scented a cow in heat one pasture over, with a fence in the way. It should have been laughable.

"Cliff?"

"Yeah?"

"Remember how we'd ride out to that stream and sit on that flat rock?"

Boy, did he remember. He'd bring a blanket, she'd sit in his lap and there in the soft summer breeze, surrounded by running water, beneath the tree-dappled sunlight, he would open her like a treasure, touching, undressing, taking his time until he couldn't stand it anymore, which usually hadn't been very long. Desire had always seemed to overwhelm them almost between one breath and the next. Fast. Furious. He could still hear her cries and moans of pleasure echoing in his head.

"Yeah," he managed to say, his voice rough.

"I wish I could sit on your lap like that again."

"Why?" he asked, barely managing to get the word out.

"Because I felt so good there. I felt like I belonged there."

Right now she didn't feel as though she belonged anywhere, he thought. Not in her aunt's house, not in her job, not anywhere.

But hold her in his lap like that again? He'd suffer the tortures of the damned.

Still, her plea tore at him, and much as he'd been trying to be friendly without getting himself in a position to be wounded again, there was no escaping the fact that he wanted to help her in some way. She was going through a rough time and she was all alone out here. She'd never been here long enough to make friends with anyone except him and Martha. A stranger in a strange land, grieving and alone unless he was willing to put himself out there and take a bit of a risk.

Hell, he was no chicken.

So he slid onto the floor, sat cross-legged and reached back for her hand. She came willingly enough until she sat in the cradle of his legs, her back against him, her head resting beneath his chin.

"Those were good times," she whispered.

"The best." He'd never deny that. He wrapped his arms gently around her. "Close your eyes and remember how good you felt on those days."

She startled him by playfully slapping his arm. "If I start remembering how good that felt, we're going to be doing more than sitting here."

A surprised laugh escaped him, and he gave her a squeeze. "Okay, then think of something less inflammatory."

"With you?" She giggled then sighed. "It was a wonderful summer, Cliff. I wish it could have gone on forever. But it wouldn't have, even if I hadn't left."

"I know. Reality and all that. And while I was miserable for a while, I know that you would have been even more miserable if you hadn't pursued your own goals. Giving up something that big…well, it probably would have poisoned us. You'd have resented giving up your dreams, and I'd have resented your resentment. Not a good mix."

"Maybe so." She wiggled deeper into his lap, just as she had done so often all those years ago. He figured it was unconscious on her part, and he hoped like hell she couldn't feel how hard he was for her. She didn't say anything and didn't move, so he sat there suspended between heaven and hell with her warm rump against his groin.

In an instant he flashed back in time. They were on the rock, she lying on the blanket while he knelt at her feet. Her blouse was open, her bra riding up around her neck, revealing beautiful, full breasts with pink areolas and large puckered nipples. Nipples that had welcomed his mouth and drawn groans from her. Her narrow waist, her gently curved hips, the thatch of dark hair at the apex of her thighs…

He felt as if he were caught in a blacksmith's fire. He remembered joking that she had to stop wearing boots because they were a pain. The giggle that escaped her then died as he at last yanked them away along with her pants. Then he had slid up over her, his own jeans still twisted around his knees, and pressed his face to her honeyed womanhood. How she had groaned and arched into him, gripping his head…

He didn't want this moment, this memory, to end. Alarm bells sounded, because it was going to end, but he didn't heed them. "How about we go riding tomorrow?"

"I'd really love that. But don't you have to work?"

"The work is never done. But I can take a few hours for fun. Essential to sanity and all that."

"I should be working harder on Martha's house."

"Doing what?" He tensed, sensing another rejection in the offing. Probably a wise one, but it was awakening unhappy feelings.

"Whatever odds and ends there are. I haven't donated her clothes yet, for one thing. I just pulled everything out of the closets and drawers to make room for Lisa. I need to go through papers and see if there's any business that needs attending. Sort through things that I don't want to keep...."

"You know, a lot of it can wait. That house isn't going anywhere. I'll help you with the papers if you want. Martha was pretty open about her affairs, and I used to take her bills to town for her, so I've got a fairly good idea of where she stands there. Regardless, you can take a few hours."

Then he waited. He could almost hear her mental wheels spinning, and he wondered what concerned her most: Martha's affairs or spending a few hours riding together like they'd used to.

"I'd love to go riding," she finally said decisively. "When?"

"Tomorrow morning. About nine. I should have things under control for the day by then. All the lambing is done, so no worries there."

"Can I see the lambs sometime?"

"Absolutely."

Again she fell into a silence that left him wondering. He itched to turn her and take her down on the floor, to press his full length to her, to run his hands over every inch of her, the way he had once done. He gave himself a mental slap and corralled his thoughts yet again. Being with her, he thought with private amusement, was testing his willpower to the extreme. Ten years ago he hadn't needed any, but now he needed it all and then some.

"Cliff?"

"Hmm?"

"Why do you think Lisa came back? I know what she said, but do you really believe it?"

"Well, she's between marriages. That much I know. And with her that may be the whole story, just looking for a better marital bet."

"So you don't think she might have come back here for you?"

Everything inside him suddenly froze. Icicles seemed to drip through him. "The way we parted? She couldn't possibly think I'd be interested."

"It's been six years, didn't you say?"

"About that, but not even Lisa could be that dim. Her moving over to your place and making you miserable would hardly seem like the right move in that direction." But he vividly remembered the way she had tried to vamp him when she first arrived. Really? Did Lisa think he was that gullible?

"Moving over to my place and making me miserable might be her way of getting you to take her back, just to get her out of my hair. Then once she's here she could turn all sweet."

It wasn't beyond imagining. She'd been sweet as could be once...until she got the wedding ring. "No, that's too Machiavellian for her."

"Well, then, maybe she just decided I was a threat so

she moved in with me to control things. I don't know. The whole thing is just plain weird."

"I'll grant you that." But Holly had him thinking now. It *was* odd that Lisa would turn to him claiming homelessness for the next couple of weeks. And that she'd tried to vamp him at the outset. "I need to think about this. There's no question that she's manipulative. Maybe she's learned some new tricks."

"Or she isn't as good at manipulation as she thinks."

A laugh escaped him, even as his insides churned at the thought that that woman might be trying to find a way to get around his armor. God, the idea made his skin crawl.

"Why don't you stay in the guest room tonight?" he said. "I don't want to take you back over there, not with her there."

"I'll survive. But I don't want to give her any ammunition by staying here tonight. She's not a very pleasant person, and I may not remain pleasant for long if she starts implying things."

He could understand that. "You probably look at her and wonder how I could ever have married her."

"No, I've seen that kind of transformation before. You've got the person who is all sweet in order to get what they want, and then when they've got it they turn into monsters. Sometimes not right away. They're smart enough to build up slowly, hoping they don't lose anything in the process. But sooner or later they let it out."

"Yeah. Like I told you, I married one woman and woke up with another. It took a few months, but…" He shrugged. "It's done. Just let me know if she gets intolerable. I'll get her out of there."

"I should never have let her have a room," Holly admitted. "It's just that...well, I've done it before. Usually abused women with children who had no place to go for a night. I leap before I look sometimes."

"A kind heart is nothing to apologize for."

A few minutes later she asked him to take her home. He'd have felt a whole lot better if she'd been going back to a house occupied by nothing but the ghost of Martha.

Chapter 7

Mercifully, Lisa had not put in another appearance last night. Holly had still had trouble sleeping, wrestling with her own mixed-up desires, all of them complicated by the time she had spent with Cliff. Sitting on his lap had felt like a dream come true, a need so deep that she hadn't realized how much she had been missing it all this time.

It had brought back other memories, too, of what it had felt like to lie naked with him under the sky, surrounded by nature, free of inhibition. The way the breeze had felt on secret parts of her that hadn't ever been exposed that way. The slightly tickly sensation as it had ruffled the curls between her thighs. The huge aching sensation when his hot mouth had followed it, teaching her that pleasure could approach pain. The way she had spent most of the summer in a half-orgasmic state, constant anticipation of the next time, the next moment, the next touch. Riding a horse had transformed from a delight to a promise of pleasure. With every movement in the saddle the ache had deepened.

Damn, she had had it bad. And to judge by what she had felt tonight, she still had it bad.

Was that behind her urge to cut out on her job? Or was she just worn-out? And could she be truly serious about throwing away all she had worked for? Had she reached that point?

It was possible. She knew plenty of social workers who simply couldn't do the kind of work she was doing anymore. They moved to desk jobs. They moved to doing social work in other settings, where the emotional strain wasn't as overwhelming. Anywhere but the streets and the impoverished kids who grew up with the sounds of gunfire and the violence they could hear through paper-thin walls, even if it wasn't happening within their own homes.

It took a toll. Maybe eight years was enough. Maybe she had reached the point where she wasn't helping as much as a fresher person might. How would she know?

But morning came, dripping sunshine everywhere, with a sky as blue as an unflawed sapphire. She dressed eagerly, excited about riding with Cliff in an hour. It had been so long since she'd ridden a horse, not since her last time with Cliff, in fact. She loved riding, and that summer, with Cliff, it had become both magical and sensual.

She headed downstairs with some minor trepidation, wondering how Lisa would greet her and whether she'd be a little more pleasant this morning. Much to her relief, there was no Lisa in sight. She found a note on the table.

Gone to town for some shopping. Back in a few hours. Don't lock me out. L

Really? She couldn't afford a place to stay but had gone shopping? Well, maybe she needed some shampoo or feminine products. Something essential. As Holly remembered, there wasn't a whole lot to shop for in Conard City anyway. And hadn't Cliff mentioned that Lisa went on shopping trips to Denver? That would take more than a couple of hours.

Regardless, it was enough she could have her breakfast in peace, enjoy anticipating the ride with Cliff and maybe try to sort through some of her internal confusion.

It had occurred to her somewhere between waking and sleeping that building some kind of youth ranch or camp here might be the perfect compromise for her. If she really had grown reluctant to go back, then she needed to find another way to contribute, one that wouldn't feel like a cop-out. The idea energized her, and had from the moment Cliff had mentioned it, so that was a good thing. Whether she could bring it to fruition remained to be seen, but she doubted she would have time to work on getting a camp rolling once she was back at her job.

Excitement carried her outside once more, however. She had made a thermos of coffee for them to take along, but she knew from experience Cliff would arrive with saddlebags full of food and drink from Jean.

She needed to make a point of going over there just to spend some time visiting with Jean.

Standing there, looking around the space she still had, envisioning the bunkhouses, the kids, the garden, all of it, lifted her spirits the rest of the way. Martha would approve and she would enjoy it. So would the kids. It was time to stop thinking about it and talk to someone who could clarify the task so that she'd know where to begin. Somehow she suspected building the bunkhouses would be the very last thing on the list.

She turned around, taking in the vista, feeling the peace of the prairie and mountains settling over her. Something about these wide-open spaces suffused her with a calm it was impossible to feel at home in the city. She wasn't going to blame the city for that, though. No, it was something deep within her that seemed to be answered by the endless vista, the infinity of the blue sky, the gentle whisper of the morning breeze.

Martha could have deeded this place to Cliff, but she hadn't. Maybe her aunt had guessed how much she needed these spaces. She wouldn't put anything past her aunt. She'd learned over the years how canny Martha could be. She never pushed for anything, she never criticized anyone, but when she saw a need she found a way to do something about it.

Here at the base of the mountains, the prairie rolled gently. She saw Cliff appear at the top of one of those small slopes astride his mount and leading a horse for her. She lifted her hand and waved and suddenly felt twenty again.

He answered the way he always had, lifting the cowboy hat from his head and waving it in a wide arc.

Time rolled back ten years in an instant. She ran

toward him as she had done all those years ago, her heart lightening with sheer gladness. By the time she opened the gate for him, Cliff was only a few feet away and smiling broadly.

"It's a beautiful morning," he said.

"It most certainly is. I've got a thermos of coffee for us."

"Jean loaded me up as usual. Are you warm enough? Then grab the coffee and let's go. I feel like I'm on a prison break."

The laugh that escaped her was as carefree as any she'd given voice to in a long, long time. Everything seemed to have fallen away except Cliff, the horses and the beautiful day.

She mounted without help, although she realized certain muscles weren't quite what they used to be, and soon they were letting the horses pick their lazy way along.

"No Lisa?" he asked.

"She left a note that she'd gone shopping and I should leave the house unlocked for her if I went out."

"Did you?"

She glanced at him. "Heck, no."

He tipped back his head and laughed, and once again the years seemed to vanish. There had been so much laughter that summer. So much fun, so many tender moments. He was right; regardless of how it had ended, it was an experience to be treasured.

She urged her mount to a slightly faster pace. She wasn't ready yet to attempt a gallop, but she wanted to be moving, away from the house, away from everything. Seconds later Cliff caught up and rode beside her. He shifted his reins to his other hand and reached out to clasp hers. Now they rode so closely together that their knees brushed occasionally.

Just as they had back then. She felt a moment of resistance, fear of opening an old can of worms all over again, then ignored it. The time limit was set, and he knew it as well as she did. This was just a chance to have fun.

And she was so ready for fun. It wasn't long, though, before Cliff encouraged her to slow down. "I bet you haven't been riding recently. You don't want to get saddle sore."

He had a good point, but she still sighed as she reined in. "It's been ten years," she admitted. Since she had last seen him, but she didn't want to go there.

"All the more reason to take it easy. So do you want to go to the creek or somewhere else?"

The creek, of course. She didn't know why that flat rock had come to mean so much more than most of the other places they had visited. Hell, they'd made love everywhere, from a barn loft to the bed of his truck to an open field and a cave in the mountain. But somehow that place stuck with her—the sound of the water, the overarching trees that had made it feel as if they were in a room provided by nature. And the rock. She'd always loved big boulders and rocks.

"Did I ever tell you about my thing for big rocks?" she asked. "How much I love them?"

"I guess that tells me where we're going." He flashed a smile her way. "You mentioned it. How else would I know that you like them?"

"I think they're beautiful, but I could never put it in words as to why. They just grab my attention, maybe even my imagination. Sounds silly, I guess. It's not as if they do anything but sit there."

"Maybe that's what gets to us, their endurance."

He released her hand as the horses pulled farther apart, needing to pick their own way over the uneven ground. She tossed her head, drinking the beauty of the chilly morning and the bright greens that had begun to emerge from winter. Most of all she savored the sense of freedom that came over her, cutting her free of the detritus of the past, temporarily removing her from her grief for Martha. All of that would return soon enough. For now, just as she had ten years ago, she embraced an experience out of time, an experience so far removed from the burdens of reality that it felt like a sojourn in Eden.

"I've missed this!"

He glanced at her, his turquoise eyes smiling. "So have I."

The phrase seemed so weighted with the desires of the past that uneasiness touched her briefly. Was she making a mistake? But truthfully, she was past caring. So many things had begun to trouble her since Martha's passing that she couldn't deny herself this break. She needed it.

So she gave herself up to every relaxing and exhilarating moment. Going back to the rock could be a big mistake. It might also prove to be the answer to questions she had evaded for ten years. It might even help her, by its endurance and peace, to sort through the mess she seemed to have been falling into since Martha's death.

A half hour later, they arrived at the creek. Towering trees arched over it, leaves feathering out in stunning contrast to the deep green of pines farther up the slope. The creek itself rushed happily, filled with melt-water that had been steadily journeying down from the peaks as the seasons changed.

It was every bit as magical and beautiful as she had remembered it.

The last time she had been here, in early August, the stream had been shrunken, still lively but nothing like the rush and bubble she saw now. She wondered if they were going to be able to reach the flat rock in the middle when the stepping stones they had used before were under water.

Cliff had no such qualms. He just led her to a point where the bank was gentle and guided them down it on horseback. The horses didn't seem to mind at all. They picked their way carefully, but brought them to the huge flat rock that seemed to have patiently awaited their return for all these years.

"You dismount onto the rock," Cliff said. "I'll hand you the picnic things Jean sent, then take the horses back to dry ground."

"But you'll get wet," she protested, even as she swung down and found stable footing.

"I can dry out. The horses can't stand in this water for long. It can't be much above freezing."

She accepted the carefully wrapped bundles and a blanket from him and put them in the center of the rock, well away from the creek's splashing. When she turned, he had already tethered the horses within sight and was sitting on the bank, pulling off his boots and socks. Then he rolled up his jeans to his knees, probably a useless gesture, she thought with amusement.

Holding his boots and socks under one arm, he

stepped into the water and let out a yelp she could hear even over the rush of the creek.

She laughed.

"Yup, it's cold," he called. She watched him pick his way as carefully as the horses had, holding her breath once when he nearly lost his balance. Then he stepped onto the rock, spread his arms and said, "Voilà!"

She laughed again.

"Am I good or what?" he asked, a twinkle in his amazing eyes.

"You're good," she acknowledged.

"I knew you'd agree." He dropped his boots and reached for the blanket. Together they spread it out, then sat.

Propping herself on her hands, Holly leaned back and looked up at the fantastic canopy growing over their heads. "I think this is my favorite place in the world."

"Then stay."

He couldn't have said anything better calculated to dash the moment. She sat upright and looked at him. "Cliff…"

He held up a hand. "I get it. You're going back. You're doing important work. You'll be leaving and that's that. But I keep wondering."

"Wondering what?"

"Why the hell you can't just do good work here. I mentioned bringing your kids out here. I bet you've thrown up a million mental roadblocks. Hell, you were talking about how this might make it more difficult for them to go home. Maybe you're right. On the other hand…"

When he didn't complete the thought, her initial

stubbornness faded. And that had been the real basis of her reaction: stubbornness. Nobody told her what to do except at work. She made her own decisions, her own plans.

She tore her gaze from him and looked up at the trees again. On the other hand, there could be more than one road to the same end. She *was* getting burned-out. She was running from something so hard that she was in danger of making herself ill.

Maybe blaming it on that attack last year was just an easy excuse, a way to conceal something else in her that was dying.

Sighing, she closed her eyes and let her head fall to her chest.

"I'm sorry," he said. "I didn't mean to ruin this for you. It just seems to me that you're burning your candle at both ends, and the woman who came back here for a funeral has burned to a mere stub of what she used to be."

"Why should you care?" she asked wearily.

"Maybe for old times' sake. Maybe because I just care. I'm worried about you, Holly. I've been trying to ignore it, telling myself it's none of my business. You made that clear a long time ago. But seeing the way you were on our ride out here, and comparing it to the woman you've been since you got back here… Holly, you need *something* more than your job. I don't know what it is. I just know in my gut that you're killing yourself."

The old stubbornness tried to rear up, tried to tell her she could do anything she put her mind to, but since coming here she had begun to realize that wasn't true.

She had limits just like every other person in the world. Physical limits, emotional limits.

Her friends at work, Carla and Laurie and Sharon, had been trying to tell her that for the last few months. Rotate, they kept telling her. They could see what Cliff was seeing, too, and given how close they were to her, it was even more surprising that they'd noticed it. He, after all, was seeing her after an absence of ten years. They saw her every day, and the contrast shouldn't have been as obvious to them.

Unless it was so blatantly true that the whole world could see it.

She lowered her head again, listening to the voice of the rushing creek, seeking some kind of answer within herself. Did she just need a vacation? Did she need to take a break from the streets? Or did she need a major life change?

That latter idea scared her half to death. Yet wasn't that exactly what she was considering by thinking about a youth ranch here?

Maybe that scared her as much as anything. Not just the change, but the size of the task. She couldn't imagine where to even begin. She'd need advice from all kinds of professionals at the very start, and she wasn't even sure which ones. A lawyer? Probably. Psychologists, probably. And then what? What steps in which order?

"I don't know how to start," she mumbled.

"I'm sorry?"

She lifted her head, feeling the fear and hollowness that must be showing on her face. "I don't know how to start. Where to begin. I'd need so much help, there'd be so many hurdles. I'd need people who'd actually be willing to work with the kids when they come here. How can I afford that?"

"I don't know about affording, but you might find plenty of volunteers."

"Who?"

"Me, for starters. I could help you build what you need. I could teach kids about animal husbandry. Jean would probably love to teach gardening. Then we've got a whole slew of good teachers here, both at the community college and in the public schools. I bet they'd be willing to volunteer time to help. But that's not the immediate issue. Is it?"

No, it wasn't, she admitted to herself. There was the whole part about jumping off a cliff into the unknown. The possibility of having it all blow up in her face. "What if it doesn't work?"

"Then I'd be very surprised if you couldn't get another job just like the one you already have."

He had a point. What with budget cutbacks, jobs weren't as available as they once had been, but on the other hand a lot of people quit for the very same reason she was facing: burnout. So there were always new openings, and finding an experienced social worker wasn't easy. When most quit, they quit the streets for good.

"Do you think it would work?" she asked finally.

"Well, I'm not the biggest authority on youth ranches for inner-city kids, but I'd be surprised if there aren't enough needy kids in *this* state to keep you going."

She hadn't thought about that, either. It didn't just have to be inner-city kids.

"Do you know," she said slowly, "that one of the reasons poor kids don't do as well in school is because they don't enjoy enrichment opportunities over school breaks?"

"Really?"

She nodded. "It's like the spigot gets turned off during the breaks, and when they come back they have to make up lost ground, unlike the children of better-off families, who get to the library or visit museums or take trips. It's like their learning turns off every summer. But once they get back up to speed, they do every bit as well. And when there are summer enrichment programs, they never lose ground at all. We've been working on that, but funding is hard to come by."

"So you'd give them summer experiences that would help them keep up?"

"That would be part of it, along with taking them out of danger for a while."

"I think you'd find a lot of teachers around here who'd want to help with that. Want me to ask around?"

"Not yet," she said finally. "I haven't even figured out the first steps. I probably need a complete plan. And somewhere along the way I'll need licensing. But for now, I've got to figure it all out. Who it would serve and how."

She released the last of her resistance, and tried to envision the complete life change she'd only been playing with so far. Had this been what Martha had meant about finding her dream? It was possible.

Apparently he decided they had been serious long enough. He sat up straighter and said, "I don't know about you, but I'm starving. I had breakfast before sunup. If you haven't noticed, the sun is rising awfully early these days."

His change of subject came as such a relief that she giggled. "I didn't notice."

"Slugabed," he teased. "Jean filled me up before the crack of dawn."

"Then what happened?"

"I helped my hired men start the worming and the vitamin shots."

"You have to give vitamins?"

"You saw my range. Do you really think I'd have healthy, plump animals if I didn't supplement from time to time?"

"I wouldn't know," she admitted. "I feel kind of stupid."

"Why?"

"Because I never bothered to learn much about what you do."

He waggled his eyebrows at her. "I seem to remember we were busy with other stuff."

She felt her cheeks heat and hoped he couldn't see. Even though the trees weren't completely leafed out yet, they did cast the world in a greenish glow.

She accepted half a ham sandwich from him and bit into it, savoring it. "Great ham!"

She also noticed his bare feet. That long-ago summer she had told him he had beautiful feet for a man. He still did. They were masculine, for sure, but narrow and well formed with high arches. More than once she had made him moan with pleasure by giving him a foot massage. He had always reciprocated, too, teaching her that nothing could relax her as fast or deeply as having her feet massaged.

She missed that.

She squirmed as she realized there was a whole lot

more she missed, as well. Like being able to reach out and touch him at any time, in any way she chose. Like seeing that look come into his eyes that meant they were about to find a private place to make love.

She giggled unexpectedly as a memory returned.

"What?" he asked.

"The person who thought that making love in a hayloft would be romantic never tried it."

A laugh escaped him. "That wasn't one of our better ideas, even with a blanket."

"A horsehair blanket!" she reminded him. "That was almost as bad as the hay."

"Hey, it was the only one handy."

"I don't know what was worse, the stink or the itch."

The shared laughter filled her with warmth, relaxing her utterly. It was good.

And there was only one way it could be better. She quickly looked away as laughter faded and resumed nibbling at her sandwich. She'd had cereal for breakfast, but it seemed to have moved on, and despite the relatively early hour, she felt ravenous.

Crossing his legs, Cliff dove into the contents of the bags and came up with a leafy green salad to go with the sandwiches, some warming bottles of soda and a small plastic container of cupcakes. "A feast," he said. He held up a couple of sporks, making her laugh again. "I'm more in the mood for coffee than soda, though."

She passed him the vacuum bottle she'd carried. It had a double cup and he filled them both with steaming brew, passing her one.

A bridge had been crossed, she realized. They had moved beyond all the lingering tension left by that summer and were growing comfortable again. Only now did she understand how much she had missed that. Missed him.

Oh, yes, she had ached when she left him. Months had passed before she could stop thinking about him almost constantly.

But the weirdest thing was that now she was sitting here wondering why she had insisted on breaking it off with him. She'd been full of youthful idealism and determination, sure she couldn't be content being a ranch wife for the rest of her days, but in the process of making those decisions she had cut herself off from other possibilities and a number of wonderful things.

She put her sandwich down on the wax paper, wrapped her arms around her legs and rested her chin on her knees, staring up along the rushing, swollen creek, thinking about the way choices rushed by in much the same way, often with unintended consequences. Choices that couldn't be recalled.

Cliff, seeking to pursue his own life, had married the wrong woman. She had married no one. She'd dated a few times, but if she was honest with herself, no one had measured up to Cliff.

"It couldn't have been any different." She spoke the words aloud, musingly, then wished she hadn't. That was going to open up a whole bunch of questions she wasn't sure she could answer.

Seconds ticked by before he said, "Us breaking up, you mean?"

"Yeah. I guess."

He surprised her. "I don't think it could have."

She turned her head, resting her cheek on her knees. "Why?"

"You're asking me? And damn, I wish you'd eat more."

"I will." She waited, wondering if he was going to answer her.

He had started his second sandwich, but put it down and reached for coffee. "We were too young and we were pulling in different directions. You needed to go places, I needed to stay here. Hell, my family has been planted here since 1878, and how likely do you think I was to abandon the homestead? I couldn't."

"Certainly not with your mother ailing. How is she, by the way? I wish I could have met her."

"Nobody saw much of her back then. She couldn't get out of bed. She's doing okay. She and Dad have settled in New Mexico where the weather is warmer year-round and she cuts quite a swath in her motorized cart. Her multiple sclerosis hasn't worsened any. Maybe it's even improved."

"I'm glad they're okay."

"So am I. Anyway, I couldn't leave. You know that, even if I didn't tell you all the reasons. Primarily I needed to make this ranch run so that I could help them out, as well as support a family of my own. I couldn't just pack and leave, Holly."

"I understood that."

"Not saying you didn't. But you *had* to leave. Nothing of what you wanted was here."

"Except," she admitted quietly, "you."

He nodded. "I felt the same about you."

She hesitated, feeling her heart hammer with trepidation, but deciding it was high time she told him the truth. Hell, she should have had the guts to do it years ago, but back then she'd been too chicken to face up to herself. "I'm sorry I was so hard on you. God, I took an ax to you, to everything. I was horrid."

"No kidding."

She squeezed her eyes shut, feeling the rebirth of an old pain.

"You had to be cruel," he said after a moment.

With difficulty she forced her eyes open. "No, I didn't."

"Yes, you did. I was arguing with you, objecting to everything you said, fighting to keep you, which would have been about as good as caging you. You had to ax it. You made me so mad I started to hate you, which I needed. And you made sure you burned the bridge completely so you'd have no further contact with me. I get it. You deliberately left us with no way back."

She averted her face, looking up the stream again, thinking life was like that water, rushing by, here and then gone. Nothing to cling to. Her throat tightened, and her eyes burned. "I was still awful."

"I don't think there was another way to do it, so stop beating yourself up. At that time, there was no other way to go. You set us both free to do what we needed."

"It didn't feel a whole lot like freedom."

"No," he agreed. "It felt more like desperation. Anyway, I was furious with you for a long time. I'm not sure I ever really got over it until lately, but it eased, and eventually I could even see the justice in what you'd done."

"I'm not sure it was justice."

"It was at least right. Damn it." He threw out an arm. "We had an idyll. It wasn't reality, for the most part. Two crazy kids locked in a haunting and fantastic summer romance. But then like everyone else on the planet, we had to face reality. We were headed down different roads. End of story."

She nodded, unable to find her voice around the lump in her throat. He had described it perfectly, just the way she thought of it, as a summer idyll without a future.

But how often had she wished she could recapture those halcyon days, however briefly. They couldn't build an entire lifetime, but they could sure as hell make up a beautiful experience. Nor did she feel that she wanted this story to end again.

She watched him move the food out of the way. Then he reached out and gently unclasped her arms, easing her back on the rock. He leaned over her, his head framed by the trees and sky.

"It was perfect," he said, brushing her hair back behind her ear. "Absolutely perfect. Perfection is a rare and priceless thing. You don't find it often, and it seldom lasts. We were blessed."

She tried to swallow the lump, then asked, "Are you measuring everything else against it?"

He shook his head. "No."

"I think I have."

Despite the fact that his face was in shadow, she saw his eyes widen. "Oh, damn, Holly, no."

He scooped her into his arms and rolled over so that she lay on him, not the hard rock, then he caught her face between his hands and kissed her. Hard. The way he had once kissed her when the flame between them seared them with passion. She opened her mouth to him, wanting that kiss as much as anything she had ever wanted, well aware that this was dangerous, that they were still headed along their separate roads. If ever the universe had decreed that a relationship wasn't meant to be, this was it.

But she was helpless before the force of her longing and need. For some reason she needed him now, more than ever, but in different ways she could scarcely put a name to.

His hands began to wander, first stroking her back, then slipping between them until he held her breasts. It was so familiar, yet as new as the moment. The hunger within her strengthened, driving everything else away except awareness of him beneath her and the magic his hands worked. It was as if she had been made only for him. She deepened her kiss and lifted her arms until she dug her fingers into his shoulders, silently begging for more. Her entire body tingled and ached, and the throb between her thighs intensified, promising heaven. Her hips rocked against him, and she felt his hardness rise up to meet her.

It would be so easy, so right, and it would answer every craving she felt.

He startled her by tearing his mouth from hers. He pulled his hands from her breasts and cradled her face once again. "What's changed?" he asked.

She felt almost sideswiped by the sudden shift in mood. It took a few seconds for his question to reach her. The way he said it left her wondering what he meant: Was he speaking to her or to himself? "Changed?"

"Holly, I still want you every bit as much as I ever did."

She closed her eyes. "Me, too," she admitted, wondering if her heart might hammer its way right out of her chest. She was pressed to him so intimately now, her breasts against his chest, her legs splayed to either side of his, leaving her feeling at once open and eager. She had never, ever stopped wanting him.

"So what's changed?" he asked again. "We're lying here striking matches in a bed of pine needles, if you get my drift. Do we really want the forest fire? Has anything changed that much? You're leaving in less than two weeks."

She couldn't argue the truth of that. "One way or another, I have to go back. I still have a job."

"Exactly. So do we want to play with this kind of fire again if nothing has changed?"

"When did you get so sensible?"

She saw him smile faintly. "I grew up," he answered. "I think you have, too."

"Somewhat, anyway. I know we can't go back. I know we're playing with fire."

"So that leaves the question. What has changed?"

"This time," she said slowly, "I don't want to go back to my job."

"Ah, damn," he said quietly. He released her face and wrapped his arms around her, holding her close. "We can't go back in time. You said it yourself."

"I know."

"So it could be really stupid to set off this conflagration again. We're older now. We need something more. Right?"

"I don't know," she admitted. "I just don't know. I'm so confused about everything."

"Which is a good reason not to strike the matches." She felt him draw a deep breath, but at least he didn't let go of her. He lifted a hand and stroked her hair gently.

"I could make love to you right this minute," he said almost roughly. "I've never forgotten, not an instant of it. Sometimes, when I let my mind wander, I can feel your skin against mine, feel your curves in my palms, remember the way your nipples tasted, the way *you* tasted. I can remember your moans and sighs, and damn, I miss it all. I want it again. But I'm older now and I need more than a couple of weeks. And so do you."

"I can't promise that."

"Neither of us can right now. After ten years we're practically strangers. You're not sure which direction you want to take, and my direction is right here with sheep and goats and the land."

Her head lowered to his shoulder, and she inhaled his unforgettable scent as deeply as she could. He was right. She was more confused than she could ever remember feeling. It would be utterly stupid to light a fire that would burn them both, especially when they both remembered how badly it had burned them last time.

She had to get her head sorted out. She had to pick a path. She had to settle on something internally one way or another. Part of her wanted to stay here, but part of her also recognized her obligations at home. Nor would she be content with a life where she wasn't helping children.

So that left a choice between Chicago and trying to build that youth ranch here. The ranch would be a huge undertaking, and while the idea excited her, it daunted her, as well.

"I miss Martha," she said against his shoulder. "She had more common sense in one finger than I'll ever have."

"I'm not sure that's true. In a lot of ways, you're very much like her. She just had more years of experience. But if she were here, what would you ask her?"

"Which way to turn."

"You know what she'd say."

"To make up my own mind. I know." Holly sighed, then couldn't prevent herself from nuzzling him. She turned her head until her nose touched the skin of his neck, slightly stubbled just below his jawline. He smelled so good. Just taking that aroma into her lungs swept her back to that long-ago summer.

"Holly..." His tone was somewhere between a warning and a groan.

This wasn't good, she thought. It would be so easy to slip into the past, to feel so young again, so free, so heedless. But she wasn't that person any longer and neither was he. And that was the danger. To try to relive that summer, no matter how wonderful, would be folly, and whatever came from it wouldn't be based in the reality of now.

She lifted her head, propped herself on her elbows and looked down at him. His turquoise eyes looked almost smoky and were half-closed. He held very still, as if he feared a movement might push them over the edge. It might. That would not be wise.

But she rested as she was, savoring the close contact with him, realizing just how much she had missed lying with him this way, feeling his hard angles and planes against her softer curves. Not as soft as they had been back then, but still soft compared to him.

"I missed you," she admitted quietly. "Sometimes I missed you so much I ached and wondered if I'd been a fool."

He didn't answer, leaving her to wonder if he'd moved from love to hate in an instant. Even though he said that he now understood, she wondered how long that understanding had taken him. How long it had been before he could forgive her for the awful things she had said, deriding him and his choices in life as going nowhere and doing nothing important.

Cruel, hateful things that she still had trouble believing had emerged from her own mouth, things that remained etched in her brain as if with acid. She could hear herself and wanted to cringe.

It had been necessary? That was an awfully generous thing for him to say. Maybe it had been. But the person she hoped she was, the person she wanted to be, wouldn't have attacked him that way. She would have found a kinder way to sever the knot that had bound them over the summer, gentler words to explain that she had a different path to follow.

Except even now she wondered if it would have worked. She'd been open all summer about how she was going back to school and into social work. Never had she once wavered in her determination. Even that hadn't prevented him from falling in love with her.

Or her with him, if she was honest. What else could have caused her all those tears, all that pain, after returning to school?

For all these years, they had avoided each other. He'd never come over to see Martha when Holly was visiting, and she didn't think that was an accident. She hadn't dropped by to find out how he was doing, nor had she asked Martha, who had seemed to figure out quickly that all mention of Cliff was off-limits.

She had built a bubble, then a wall around that summer. She had even eventually shut down her memories of it as much as possible, refusing to entertain them at all.

So what had she given up, and what had she gained? Damned if she knew anymore, but she'd been utterly certain back then.

She pushed herself up a little, brushed a light kiss on that mouth she had once known so intimately, and rolled off him, staring up into tree boughs that seemed to brush the blue sky.

It was time to answer some questions. To make some decisions. To commit, one way or another, either to returning permanently to Chicago, or to trying to build her youth camp here. That decision could not be based on Cliff. It had to be her own. Otherwise she could make herself miserable, and possibly him. They both deserved better.

"It's odd," she remarked.

"What is?"

"How different things look now than they did back then. That summer with you, well, that was a time and place all its own. And all the times I came back to visit Martha, I came for her. I thought this was a peaceful place, but I couldn't see anything else here. I couldn't see how beautiful it is. I just saw emptiness. Nothing to do."

"Boredom?"

"Not exactly. Just…emptiness. I'm used to a pretty hectic kind of life, and there were times I thought I'd suffocate in the quiet out here."

"Some people do feel that way," he agreed. "We've got a movie theater the community had to buy to keep it open. One movie a month, sometimes two. We've got socials, if you're into that, barbecues, parades, and even roadhouses if you like country dancing and want a beer. A real hotbed of entertainment."

"I wasn't thinking of entertainment, exactly. I was thinking more off the wide-open space. Sometimes it felt so empty it seemed oppressive."

"Funny," he drawled, "I feel oppressed when I go to the city. Shut in."

She gave a little laugh and rolled over on her side to take a playful swipe at his shoulder. "You know what I mean."

His smile faded. "No, actually I don't. What are you trying to say?"

"I've changed," she said carefully. Some things were so hard to put into words. "I don't see emptiness here anymore. I see how beautiful it is. I even see possibilities. Like the youth-ranch idea. It seems overwhelming, but I think I could do it."

"I'm sure you could. What you've done already seems pretty impressive to me. You need to talk to your psychologist friend, and then to a lawyer to find out what's required at the minimum. Once you've got a clearer picture, you might feel less overwhelmed."

"You're probably right. At the moment, I feel like I don't even know where to begin." She reached out to rest her hand on his shoulder.

He sat up immediately, and she felt almost offended. But then he said, "Let's finish eating. And let's not strike any matches."

She had to remind herself that he had just told her he still wanted her as much as ever, and that he'd given her a passionate kiss, before she could settle down enough to eat.

He was protecting her, she realized. Protecting both of them. Remembering the young man she had once known, who had been far more impulsive, she was impressed by how he had grown. She wondered if she had matured as much herself.

Certainly she was not the same person she had been back then. Her ideals had taken a bit of battering, and her view of human nature wasn't quite as nice as before, but in what ways had she grown? She supposed that therein lay at least a part of the puzzle she was trying to solve.

She managed to finish the sandwich and some of the salad. By the time she stopped, she felt overly full, which gave her some idea of how little she had been eating. Twenty pounds in a year wasn't worrisome, but it had gotten to the point that even her doctor had told her she needed to put some weight back on. Imagine hearing that from a doctor. She was more used to hearing that she could do to shed five or ten pounds.

The stubborn five or ten that never wanted to go away no matter what. Well, they were gone now.

And maybe some other things were gone with them. A certain innocence had fled a long time ago. A sense of safety…well, her job had been chipping away at that pretty steadily, she guessed. Those guys on the street had just completed the change.

"Holly?"

She tilted her face toward him. "Hmm?"

"Why did you say you don't want to go back? Burnout? Fear? The attack?"

It was a fair question, so she gave him a fair answer. "I'm working on that. It's a bit of everything, I guess.

For some time now I've been wondering how effective I really am."

"Why?"

"Because most of the time I don't know. Cases come, cases go. People move. Other caseworkers take over if the situation changes to something they're better trained for. I spend a lot of time wondering how much difference I'm really making. You could say I'm operating on faith that what I do makes a real difference. Occasionally I get to see that difference, but that's rare. A lot of problems are intractable."

He nodded, encouraging her.

"So I don't get much of a sense of accomplishment. All these years are catching up with me, I guess. I'm starting to feel hopeless, and that's not helpful to anyone. Then since the attack..."

"Just don't tell me again how lucky you were."

"But I was. A lot of people live like that. I just dipped my toes into it during my workday. Until I was attacked. Then I was well and truly *in* what these people are dealing with. Anyway, I still don't feel safe on the streets. I went for a long time thinking that everybody in the neighborhood knew I was a social worker, and that put me in a kind of protective bubble. The worst the troublemakers ever did was make offensive comments when they saw me, but they left me alone. Then I discovered that bubble was of my own imagining."

She looked down and realized she was twisting her hands together. "I don't want to be a chicken. So it's all messed up. I despair sometimes, I feel overwhelmed sometimes, I'm not sure how much good I'm doing and I'm afraid now."

"Being afraid is sensible. Don't think you're a chicken. That attack was what, a year ago? You kept going on those streets. That's not a chicken."

"Maybe not. But it makes it all more difficult. I don't stay late as often as I used to, so I'm sure that's cut my effectiveness. It's just a whole mess I need to work through. But out here... Out here I see a different way to help. If I do it right, it could be so great."

"I'm sure it could. I need to take you over to see Cowboy."

"Cowboy?"

"It's what he goes by. Years ago he and his wife bought a ranch and they take in foster kids, lots of them. Some they've even adopted. It's working for them. Maybe they'll have some ideas."

"I'd like that."

"It may have to wait until your next trip out here. I'll check, but I think they just left on a big family camping trip. They do it every year when school lets out."

Man, that sounded good to her. Closing her eyes, she could easily imagine having some of her kids out here—heck, any kids—and showing them these kinds of joys. Tall grasses, big spaces, animals... Her eyes popped open. "What if I wanted my kids to ride horses? I'm not sure I could take care of them in addition to everything else."

He chuckled. "What are neighbors for? I'm sure we could arrange trail rides for the kids. If things really go well and you have lots of kids, we'll deal with the horse issue. One thing at a time."

"You're right. I'm jumping the gun. There's so much else I need to take care of first. It might take a few years to get to the point of worrying about horses."

"I don't think you're jumping the gun," he said quietly. "I think you're getting excited about the possibilities. You need that excitement, Holly, and you sure didn't have any of it when you got here."

No, she hadn't, and it wasn't just because she'd lost her aunt. Once she'd had excitement for her job. Then it had slowly seeped away. As difficult as it was to face, she had to be honest with herself. She no longer felt fulfilled by what she was doing. She no longer woke to each day raring to go. Far from it.

All of a sudden, Cliff stirred and looked at his watch. "Damn, we've got to go back. The vet's coming out today to vaccinate the lambs and kids. I need to be there."

She helped him pack up, then watched him go get the horses and bring them out to the rock. Taking care that she didn't have to get her toes wet. How many men did she know who were that solicitous?

As they were riding back, he asked, "Wanna take in a movie tonight with me? Given that we don't get the new releases here, it might be something you've already seen."

"I see so few movies that's highly unlikely. I'd love to go." Dating a man she had kissed off ten years ago. How likely was that?

"Great. I wonder how angry Lisa is at being locked out."

Holly couldn't restrain a laugh. "I guess I'll find out."

"I could come to the house with you. I don't have to leave you at the fence."

"Why borrow trouble? I'll deal with her."

At that moment she felt she could deal with anything. A great weight had seemed to lift from her as she faced her job dissatisfaction, almost as if she had made up her mind about what she was going to do. And she had a movie date with Cliff.

Lisa seemed like a small blip on a very big radar.

Chapter 8

At the fence, she dismounted and passed the reins to Cliff. "It's been wonderful."

"Yes, it has. Thanks." His smile was warm. A smile she had never thought to see from him again. "Call me if Lisa turns into a handful. I'll pick you up around five and we can have a bite at Maude's before the movie."

"I'd like that."

He tipped his hat and began to ride away with her mount in tow. Now all she had to do was head back and face the Lisa music. The woman's sports car was sitting in the drive, somehow managing to look ominous.

When she rounded the house, she found Lisa sitting on the porch swing looking majorly annoyed.

"Have fun?" Lisa asked acidly.

"Yes, thanks," Holly replied pleasantly. Reaching into her pocket, she pulled out the key and unlocked the front door.

"I told you to leave the house unlocked," Lisa said. "I've been sitting out here forever."

Holly let that pass. Even if Lisa had returned just after Cliff and Holly rode off, their entire trip hadn't quite taken three hours. "Sorry," Holly said. "I'm a city girl. I don't leave anything unlocked."

"Then you'll have to make me a key to use, if you're going to do this often."

"No, I won't make you a key. Sorry, but you'll only be here until I go back to Chicago. I guess we need to plan better."

Lisa followed her into the house and into the kitchen, where Holly started a pot of coffee. "You're not very nice."

For some reason those words clicked with Holly. She finished preparing the coffeepot, turned it on, then faced Lisa.

"You're right, I'm not being very nice. Have a seat and join me for some coffee." There was a gleam in Lisa's eyes, a smugness in her expression that Holly could read too well. She'd seen it countless times when a child tried to guilt-trip her or someone else. It occurred to her that Lisa was acting more like a child, and showing very little real skill at manipulation.

When the coffee was ready, she brought two mugs to the table, along with a growing curiosity. She sat facing Lisa. "So what's really going on, Lisa?"

"I don't know what you mean."

"I think you do. You came to your ex looking for a place to stay. Most women wouldn't do that. Then you came here hoping my aunt would put you up for a while because a few days with Cliff wasn't enough. Why not? Do you really have a job in Glenwood Springs?"

Lisa scowled. “Yes, I do. But it doesn’t start until the end of the month. And I really can’t afford to rent a place yet.”

“I believe you. But that’s not the whole picture.”

“What do you mean?”

“You come here looking for help but you’re nasty to everyone. I’m sure you’ve heard that you catch more flies with honey than vinegar. I know you can be nice enough, because Cliff wouldn’t have married you otherwise. So what’s eating you right now? Why are you treating me this way when I gave you a place to stay?”

Lisa glared at her. “What is this? Five-cent therapy? I don’t need that stuff.”

“Maybe not. I’m not a therapist anyway. I’m just wondering why you can’t even be nice to someone who is helping you. What are you afraid of?”

“What the hell makes you think I’m afraid of anything?”

“You,” Holly answered simply. “You remind me of barbed wire. That amount of fencing is designed to keep something in or keep something out.”

Then she rose with her coffee and went to sit on the porch. It was a beautiful afternoon, a great time to laze here and envision the life she would really like to have. Plus, she had a date tonight with Cliff. Only time would tell if that might be a mistake, but right now she didn’t care. Pieces inside her were shifting around, forming a new picture, and she was liking what she was seeing.

At some point she dozed off, into vague but happy dreams. She was wakened by the sound of steps on the porch. With effort, she opened her eyes, realized it was getting later, and then saw Lisa sitting on a nearby chair.

"I'm sorry," Lisa said. "You're right. I'm pretty angry."

"About what?" Holly stifled a yawn and tried to sit up straighter. Her coffee had long since grown cold, but she drank it anyway.

"A lot of stuff. Most recently it's the jerk I was married to until the divorce became final last month. He cheated on me, then blamed me for it."

Holly nodded. "Did he knock you around?"

"Some." Lisa fisted her hands. "Thing is, I hit back. So when I left you know what happened? I didn't get to take anything. Nothing at all. Didn't matter that I worked, too. No. A woman doesn't hit back, I guess."

"I'm sorry."

"I'm glad to be out of there. But that doesn't mean I have to be happy. So all I have is a little bit of my own money that he didn't spend because I made it on my own after I left, and a job waiting for me, and nothing in between."

"What about family?"

"There was just my dad. He's been gone for three years now. Funny, he told me not to marry the jerk in Gillette. One of the last things he said to me. I should have listened, because the creep spent my inheritance money, too." She shrugged. "Well, I spent some of it. I'm not good with money. Cliff probably told you that."

Holly kept mum. "We don't talk about you." *Much,* she amended silently.

"Anyway, I guess I was spoiled growing up. Jean sure seemed to think so. I caused Cliff problems, and I admit it. I was stupid enough not to get what he was trying to tell me. I'd never had to worry about money before, and sometimes I thought he was just being mean. Maybe he was, but he was no kind of mean like the guy I just divorced."

"You've had a rough time."

"My dad also used to say that we make our own beds." She sighed. "Anyway, don't get the idea I'm going to change or anything. I'm angry most of the time, and I don't see any reason to stop being angry until things get better, okay? But I'll try to be politer. I think I can do that."

"It would help," Holly agreed cautiously. She wondered how much of this was true, and how much of it was an excuse. In a way it sounded too damn pat. There was something missing here.

Two thoughts occurred to her, and neither of them was something she could ask Lisa: that her father had abused her in some way, and that he had used money as a means of control and punishment.

It would sure explain a lot, but she figured she would never know. It seemed like a good time to change the subject.

"I'm going out tonight for dinner and a movie," she announced, wondering what kind of trouble that might bring. "With Cliff."

"So you're the next victim?"

Victim? The word astonished Holly. "Why would I be a victim?"

"You know I was married to him. Big mistake."

"Why?"

"He was a whole lot of fun at first, when we were dating, and even for a while after we got married. Then it got so he was working all the time, and he claimed money was tight, so we couldn't go anywhere anymore. I started to feel like a prisoner, so I took off on my own. Then he said I was spending more than he could afford. He put me on an allowance and got upset when I overdrafted. It turned into hell."

Holly considered a cautious answer. "Ranchers have to work hard. And most are just scraping by."

"And Jean hated me. You know who Jean is? She nagged me about doing stuff. But she's the housekeeper, right? It's *her* job. I was hoping she'd get mad enough to quit, then we could get someone who'd do the job right. That was stupid, too, I guess. Cliff cared more about her than me."

This was certainly an interesting rendering, Holly thought. She'd have expected this kind of viewpoint from someone much younger and less experienced. Like maybe twelve or even fourteen. Certainly not a grown woman.

She looked out over the prairie, watching grasses blow in the warm afternoon breeze, and thought about it. "How old were you when you married Cliff?"

"Nineteen."

"What was the rush?"

"My dad was a control freak. I wanted to get away. I didn't know I was marrying another one."

"You've had a rough time," Holly remarked. The picture she was forming wasn't a happy one for Lisa. She felt the first inklings of real sympathy for the woman. And while she didn't know the exact pieces in play here, she was developing the definite impression that this woman-child had been arrested in her development in some ways. How or why she could only speculate. "So good things are waiting for you in Glenwood?"

"I hope so. I've got a job at a salon there. I'll be

doing hair and teaching courses in makeup. I'm good at it."

Holly nodded. Looking at Lisa, she could well believe it. "But they can't take you on right away?"

"Someone is leaving. I'll be taking over. But not until the end of the month."

"That really puts you in a bind."

"It sure does. Actually, I'm glad you said I could stay here. I don't know if I could have handled even a few days in the same house with Jean. She *really* doesn't like me. How well do you know Cliff?"

"I met him ten years ago," Holly said cautiously. "But this is the first time I've seen him since."

"Well, take it from me, all work and no play makes Cliff a very dull boy. Being stuck on that ranch was like being in prison. The only fun thing was riding. I miss riding."

But not Cliff, evidently. "Well, I'll only be here a little longer," Holly said briskly.

"Yeah, I guess you're safe. You have a life to go back to."

Which indicated that Lisa had not. She'd been fleeing her father and fell into exactly the wrong arms, at least for her.

Holly glanced at her watch. "I need to get ready. Cliff will be here soon. There's food in the fridge."

For once Lisa contented herself with a simple, "Thanks."

Cliff picked her up a few minutes after five. He'd spiffed up a bit, wearing new jeans and a carefully pressed white shirt. She almost felt grungy in comparison. Her jeans were well-worn and her lightweight sweater had come from the rack at a Goodwill store. It showed some wear.

But his smile was warm, and his eyes passed over her appreciatively, making her feel as if he'd drizzled hot honey over her. Her insides clenched in response.

"You look great," he said as he helped her into the truck.

Holly half expected Lisa to poke her head out and say something, but the woman kept out of sight. Interesting. Maybe they'd found a bit of peaceful ground on which to meet.

As they were driving away, Cliff asked, "How much hell did Lisa give you?"

"Not much, actually. I think we came to at least a minor meeting of minds."

"Congratulations. What happened?"

"Did she ever mention her father to you?"

"Not much. I gathered she had a tense relationship with him. She didn't like to talk to him."

"Well, from what she said, she married you to get away from him."

After a few seconds, he gave a low whistle. "That might explain a lot."

"It might. Anyway, she announced she's angry and doesn't intend to stop being angry until things get better, but she'll make an effort to be polite with me."

"I can applaud that." He flashed her a smile that quickly faded.

"What's wrong?" she finally asked when he remained silent.

"I was just thinking. I spent a whole lot of time wondering where I went wrong with Lisa. It takes two to make a mess."

"It's easier to make one when one person is in the relationship for all the wrong reasons. She picked you for an escape hatch. The problem was, it wasn't really the kind of escape she wanted. Anyway, I wasn't there, I'm not going to judge or even comment, except to say she still has some growing up to do. And you shouldn't be too hard on yourself. I think it was doomed from the start."

"Maybe so. The hole just kept getting deeper."

She looked out the window at the passing countryside. The days were getting longer as the solstice approached, and she liked the fact that the late afternoon was still bright. She supposed that her return, and now Lisa's, had given Cliff a lot to think about, and she suspected not all of it was good.

After all, he'd ultimately been rejected by two women, and basically for the same reason, whether he realized it or not. She'd had bigger things to do than be a ranch wife, and Lisa had seen the ranch as a prison. If he put that together, he was apt to give up all hope of marriage and family.

Yet here he was, only a few days after he'd initially greeted her with such dislike, taking her out for dinner and a movie. By any measure, that made him a truly big man.

"How'd it go with the vet today?" she asked. High time she showed some interest in his life.

"Pretty good. They all seem healthy. We have to do some eyedrops on some of the lambs and kids. We started vaccinations and should finish tomorrow, but all's good."

"Okay, how do you get eyedrops in those animals?"

He laughed. "With great difficulty. The mamas

don't like us handling the babies, and the babies don't like the eyedrops. We get a whole lot of caterwauling, I can tell you. And sometimes it takes three of us to get it done."

"Do the moms attack you?"

"They would if they could, but we separate them out. That's when the trouble begins. But overall, it's not too hard. Just sweaty. We get them into a holding pen one at a time and get it done as fast as we can."

"How do you tell who you've done?"

"That's why they invented washable spray paint. We just put a big X on them."

"Do you brand?"

"Ear tags."

"Oh, that must be fun, too."

He laughed. "Oh, yeah. Before you leave, you need to come over and meet my kids."

She joined his laughter. "That's a cute way to put it."

Holly had been to Maude's diner only a few times that long-ago summer, with Cliff. Aunt Martha had preferred to do her own cooking and viewed dining out as frivolous. After meeting Maude, as crusty a curmudgeon as ever walked the planet, Holly had privately wondered if the two women just couldn't get along, or if her aunt really was dead set against going to restaurants.

Maude was still there, hardly changed by a decade, and joined by one of her daughters, Mavis, who could have been a younger clone in both appearance and demeanor. Menus got slapped down like a dueling challenge, glares accompanied the taking of orders and it was a wonder coffee mugs didn't crack the way they got slammed down.

Holly had trouble keeping a straight face. If she hadn't known that this was typical service here, she could easily have been offended. Locals, however, were used to it, and Maude was a great cook.

Conversation lagged, though. Holly wondered what was bothering Cliff, as he was usually a chatty enough companion. Was he thinking about his marriage to Lisa? Linking it, perhaps, to the reasons she had left him? God, she hoped not. People changed, and the changes she was going through might lead her right back here.

But what made her think he would want her? Oh, she apparently still aroused his passions, just as he aroused hers. He'd made no secret of that. But what if he didn't want her in any other way? She couldn't blame him for that. They had a past, and in the end it hadn't been good. Especially for him. He hadn't spoken one cruel word to her, but she'd spat her share of them at him.

She had cut the cords that bound them all those years ago, and she'd been merciless. Ranching was a dead end. Yes, she'd said that. She needed to do *important* stuff with her life. Right.

She squirmed on the bench seat and wondered who that woman had been who had spoken such cruel things. She remembered feeling desperate, but that was still no excuse. A man had asked her to marry him, had told her he loved her, and that was how she'd responded?

God, she wished she could take an eraser to her brain and utterly wipe away all those harsh words. She was as guilty as Lisa of wounding him.

He certainly didn't deserve it. He'd been kind to her

back then, and was being kind now, except for his initial reaction to her. He worked hard, he was building a future, he was performing an important job. Where would the world be if everyone felt they were too good to raise sheep and goats?

She sighed and gave up on eating. The salad she had ordered was too big, too full of grilled chicken. She should have ordered the dressing on the side, because while it was delicious, Maude was as generous with it as she was with everything else she served. She could almost feel her arteries clogging.

"Something wrong?" Cliff asked.

"No. Yes. I don't know. I was just thinking that you've had rotten luck with women. First me, then Lisa. You didn't deserve any of it from either of us."

To her surprise, when she dared to raise her gaze, a smile hovered around his mouth. A devilish twinkle resided in his amazing eyes. "Who said I've been unlucky with all women?"

She felt her eyes widen, then she burst into a laugh. "Score."

He laughed with her. But as his laughter died, he said, "Just forget it, Holly. You did what you needed to, and while I felt scalded, I survived. We were a lot younger then. Who's to say you were wrong? What's more, if you'd been kinder, I might have been harder to shake. At that point in time, you needed to shake me. I seem to remember I didn't make it easy on you to say no."

"You're being awfully kind."

"I'm being awfully realistic. I've been through a marriage with an unhappy wife. I'm glad I didn't share one with you."

He had a point there, she admitted.

"Anyway," he went on, "we keep belaboring this. It was the wrong time, if nothing else. I wasn't going to stop you from finishing college, not even if you'd said yes. I should have been smart enough to realize that it couldn't work. Not then. You'd finish college, you'd take your master's and then what? Throw all that work away to come back here? Not likely. I wasn't using my brains and I know it. So let's just let go of it, okay? You've got a future you're trying to work out right now. That's what matters. And me, I'm still firmly rooted right here to the land. I'll help you if I can, whatever you decide, but I'm still going to be me, and you're still going to be you."

Her heart plummeted a bit as his words hit home. She supposed she ought to be glad he'd found such a kind way to essentially tell her it wasn't any more likely to work now than it had been a decade ago.

So that's what he'd been thinking about, she thought as they went to the movie. He'd been thinking about the fire they'd been so close to igniting that morning, and he had decided it probably wasn't a good thing for a lot of reasons. Nothing could grow between them, nothing permanent, anyway.

Amazing how bad that made her feel, especially when she remembered how unhappy and annoyed she'd been to see him when she arrived here. Worse to realize he was probably right. But that old tug was still there, the one that had drawn her to him in the first place and made it so hard to leave him.

Maybe the smart thing would be to light that fire, get it out of their systems. There was a darn good chance it wouldn't be as good as they remembered it, especially since they were older now and ruled less by hormones.

Just have the sex for old times' sake, clear the table of the constant yearning, get rid of the need for restraint, then see what happened. It might clear the air rather than making it murkier.

She was quite sure she had never had a stupider idea.

"Wanna go dancing?" Cliff asked after the movie.

Holly was tempted, but she also knew she was walking a fine line between giving in to her desire for Cliff and trying to keep them both unscathed. Have a fling? Look how well that had worked ten years ago.

"I don't think so," she answered, even though it would have been fun to do some line dancing, especially with him. "I've still got so much to do at Martha's."

"Yours now," he reminded her. "If you need any help, you'll let me know?"

"Sure. Thanks."

The closer they got to their houses, the darker and emptier the road grew, until several miles passed without sign of another vehicle. Of course, this was ranch country, full of early risers, most of whom were probably tucked into bed or about ready to land there.

The sky was full of stars, and Holly commented on them. "You don't see stars like this in town. In Chicago, I can only see a few. I've practically forgotten what the Milky Way looks like."

"Well, we can remedy that," he answered.

A short way down the road, he turned onto what looked like a wagon track, and jolted them down it a ways. When he stopped and parked, Holly suddenly felt very young again, much as she had the first time they had parked like this. Anticipation began to fill her, but she stepped down on it, trying to ignore the way her body wanted to wake up.

"Come on," he said.

They both climbed out and he spread a blanket in the bed of his truck. He opened the tailgate and gave her a quick boost. Soon they were lying side by side, looking up at a sky so full of stars that it was hard for her to believe it was the same sky she saw every night at home in the city.

"It's breathtaking," she said. "So many, many stars. And the Milky Way is so clear and obvious."

"When you see it out here, you can understand why so many ancients, and even some modern people, believe the dark spot is the womb of creation."

Indeed she could. It took little imagination to see that it resembled female genitalia. In fact, the resemblance was quite striking.

She sighed. "I've heard the legends and stories. But you have to see it like this to understand it. Didn't the Egyptians think the Nile was a reflection of it?"

"I've heard that, but don't ask me what an ancient Egyptian believed. You're the one with the education."

That stung her, and for a moment she forgot the stars. "Does that bother you?"

"I know enough to do what I do. I read a little more out of interest. But I sure as hell don't have any degrees."

"So?" At that she pushed up on her elbow. "Tell me that's not bothering you. Why should it? You're successful at what you do. What brought this on?"

"I don't know," he admitted. "I don't usually think about it."

"Well, stop it, then. I happen to think you're a pretty smart guy."

He laughed and just as she dropped onto her back to resume her study of the sky, he rolled up and leaned over her.

Everything inside her seemed to still in a hush of breathless expectation.

"Holly?"

She could barely make a questioning sound.

"I can't stand it. We either get you home now or I'm going to make love to you, consequences be damned. I'm going to light that match."

She caught her breath, then reached up and cupped his cheek, feeling as if her muscles had become spaghetti. "Is that why you've been so quiet?"

"It's getting to be all I'm thinking about. I want you and I want you every bit as much as I ever did."

"A one-night stand?"

"If that's what you want."

She wasn't sure that was what she wanted, but hadn't she been thinking that this might clear the table? Who the hell cared, anyway? There was nothing, absolutely nothing, she wanted as much as she wanted Cliff right then.

Seeing him leaning over her, a shadow framed by the infinity of sparkling stars, drove away all reason. She couldn't be sensible for another minute.

She slipped her hand from his cheek to his neck and pulled him toward her in an answer as ancient as the stars above.

* * *

Cliff had wanted to be sensible. Hell, he'd been trying since he'd gotten past his first irritation at seeing her again. In fact, he suspected that most of his irritation had arisen from realizing he was far from over her.

But his memories were memories, and the present was the present, and he knew how foolhardy it would be to believe that anything of the past still survived. They were different people now.

But the desire had survived. Oh, it had survived, and no rational argument or thought had been able to squash it. One-night stand? If that's what she wanted. Maybe it would set him free of her spell.

Because never, not once, in his life had he felt a desire as deep and wild as the one Holly awoke in him.

He'd known the instant that he'd pulled off the road that he was going to make love to her. He *had* to. It was either that or go insane. He was giving short shrift to everything at the ranch because he couldn't stop this pounding need from dominating his thoughts. Even Jean had finally said, "If you want the girl, go for her." How often did Jean offer comments on his love life? Once that he could remember, and that had been her threat to leave.

He must have been stomping around like a bull who smelled a cow in heat in the next pasture.

Then all attempt at thought vanished as his mouth met Holly's. As warm and sweet as ever, tasting slightly of the popcorn they'd eaten at the movie, but still recognizably the taste of Holly. He had never forgotten her taste, her scents, and now he knew he had never forgotten the way her lips moved beneath his, the little sigh that escaped her as she parted them and granted him entry.

Familiar, so familiar, yet as exhilarating as the first time. His heartbeat thundered in his ears, his body tensed and clenched in time with it, his groin grew heavy and ached.

He wanted to move slowly, to savor every single instant of what might well be the last time forever, but when her hands clawed at his back and she tore her mouth from his to groan his name, he lost his last restraint.

Rearing up, he tugged at her sweater. She ripped at his shirt.

The spring night was chilly and getting chillier. He felt the cold air raise goose bumps but he didn't care. All he could think was it was a damn shame the night was so dark. He could barely make her out, but memory recalled the size and shape of her breasts, the rosy pink of her nipples and areolas. When his hand cupped her, the feeling was at once so sensual and so familiar.

In an instant past and present slammed together and fused. That long-ago summer, they had been so eager in their lovemaking, impatient, filled with laughter, always in a hurry because later there would be another time. It was only after they were sated that they would linger over one another, lazily, gently, beginning to build the anticipation again.

He wanted to linger over her this time, but that thought was swiftly lost in need, and she was coming right along with him. He bent his head, sucking her nipple into his mouth, tormenting her with the lash of his tongue. She was already swollen for him, but his ministrations made her nipple grow larger and her groans grow deeper. Her nails dug into his back, urging him on. Her hips bucked up, her legs separating and winding around him.

It was going to be exactly like that long-ago summer. Except he couldn't remember reaching this peak of hunger with her before. It was as if ten years had merely built the desire to nuclear proportions.

The jeans had to go. He had just enough sanity left to pull a condom out of his pocket before he yanked the denim off both of them. Kneeling between her legs, he ripped open the packet. She grabbed it from him, pulled out the condom and rolled it on him. The shaft of hunger speared him so intensely he thought it might kill him. He ached in every cell for her, for completion.

She pulled him down. She didn't want to wait. So many things he wanted to do to her, all lost in a driving, overwhelming need. He lifted her knees, then dove into her. She twined her legs around his waist, opening herself fully.

They knew this path, one traveled many times before. But never before had it seemed so intense.

Almost before he knew it, they exploded together, soaring to the stars overhead and shattering into a million flaming pieces.

He wanted to never return.

Cold. It was the first sensation to penetrate Holly's awareness after a climax so intense everything inside her had seemed to freeze in the moment of satisfaction. She had hovered there, as never before, held on its rainbow and denied for so long the return to earth.

She could feel Cliff withdraw, too soon, but necessary. In the dark she couldn't see what he did with the condom, but suddenly his hands were there, trying to help pull her clothes back on.

She stopped him. "Not yet," she whispered, her voice barely louder than the rustling grasses that surrounded them. She ignored the night's chill, a minor inconvenience, and levered herself up on one elbow, pushing him onto his back.

He didn't argue. She wished she could see him better, but this was the darkest night she could ever remember. So her hands had to do all the work, drinking him in. She traced his contours, from his strong jaw down his neck, then lower.

It was like taking a well-remembered, well-loved journey, relearning his planes and hollows, the firmness of muscle over bone. She could feel the magic building again, the passion like a phoenix rising from hot ashes. Her touches were featherlight at first, but as she felt him quiver beneath each one, they grew firmer.

She rediscovered his small nipples, and bent to suck them and then give him a nip. The groan that escaped him filled her with a heady sense of power. He was all hers, for now, and that fueled her own desire, pumping it higher until she could barely hear anything but the drumbeat of her blood.

She trailed her mouth lower, caressing his hard belly with her lips, teasing him gently with her tongue, tracing patterns on him that she knew must feel cold as soon as her tongue passed.

He moaned again and his hand grabbed at her shoulder, as if he needed to feel that she was real. He didn't push her or direct her, just hung on to her.

Man, did she understand that feeling. Then she reached the nest of tight curls between his legs, smelled his musky aroma mingled with hers. Control was slipping away from her again, but she clung to it desperately.

His staff was hard again, already, and her first brush against it caused it to jump. The invitation was clear. She lowered her lips to it, running her tongue along its length, then at last taking him inside her mouth.

He called her name, his hand on her shoulder tightening until his grip was almost painful. She showed him no mercy, taunting and teasing him until he quivered from head to foot. Finally, with a sharp jerk, he erupted.

Then, astonishing her, almost before the ripples of completion had finished running through him, he shoved her back and settled himself between her thighs. Gentle fingers brushed at her most tender flesh. She gasped as she felt him part her petals, as the cold air touched her where it seldom did, and then the heat of his mouth settled over that tight knot of nerves, a sensation so good it hurt.

She wanted it to go on forever, but the intensity was shattering her, and there was no way to slow her climb to the pinnacle. Riding the lash of his tongue, she soared upward at dizzying speed until finally, inevitably, she tipped over the brink and drifted like embers back to earth.

This time she didn't stop him when he reached for their clothes. This time the cold penetrated the magic. Not a word passed between them until, at last, covered again, boots back on, they lay together in the bed of the truck with the glories of the heavens wheeling over them.

He wrapped her snugly in his arms, tucking her

head onto his shoulder, throwing his legs over hers. He even managed to pull part of the blanket over her.

"Too fast," he murmured finally.

"We were always fast." With her head pillowed comfortably, she looked up at the stars and wondered what it all meant.

"Yeah," he said. "Like rockets. Once the fuse was lit, there was no stopping the launch."

A soft laugh escaped her. "I guess that hasn't changed."

"I wish I could change it. I'd love to spend time lingering over you, but tonight is not going to be it. Too damn cold."

"Hey, I thought it was fantastic!"

"We were always fantastic."

In this way at least, she thought, but didn't say it. They'd lit the fire he'd warned about earlier, and she had discovered that it was all still there: the need, the nearly furious pace of their passion—none of it had declined. But there had been some other feeling there this time, and as she tried to tease it out, she worried about what it might be. She had thought casually about having a quick fling to settle this, but she felt nothing had been settled. Far from it. The entire past had risen up, reminding her what she had walked away from so long ago.

And part of her knew that walking away again was going to be even harder. Why? She couldn't say.

All she kept thinking, and feeling, was that the years hadn't quieted anything at all. Maybe they'd even fueled it more.

A shiver passed through her before she could prevent it.

"We need to get you home," he said. "Before you turn into an icicle."

"I'd forgotten how cold it gets at night."

"We're not really into summer yet. You can still almost smell snow on the breeze some nights."

A good description, she thought. Her body didn't want to move. She didn't want to leave his embrace. She wanted to stay just like this. But reality once again played the trump card as she shivered again.

"Let's go home," he repeated.

Home? That caused her to walk down another corridor of reflection as he helped her out of the truck bed and into the cab. Where was home now? She shivered a few more times until the engine warmed up enough to blast some heat at her. Silence had again fallen between them, and she wished she knew what he was thinking. That this had been a mistake?

Maybe it had been, but she wouldn't take it back. She had to make up her mind about some things, and quickly, she decided. No more playing around with a vague future. She had to nail it down. So where was home now? In Chicago? When she had arrived here, she'd been utterly certain she would return to her work there. Now she wasn't so sure.

Another door had opened, and she needed to decide if she would walk through it. Even if she did, however, there was no guarantee that she would ever have more from Cliff than episodes like the one they had just shared.

She could move here and they could become neighbors. He might even help her with her project. But he might not want one more thing from her.

Could she live with that? Could she live without it?

She had thought making love would clear the table. Instead it had left her more mixed-up than ever, feeling like a dandelion puff adrift on the breeze. Where would she land?

She honestly didn't know.

Chapter 9

The next days were busy and weird all at the same time. Far from being underfoot, Lisa drove out each morning and didn't come back until late afternoon. Holly couldn't imagine how she was occupying herself.

Clint didn't come by or even call. That troubled her, and while she realized he was probably seeking some necessary space after what had happened, she couldn't help but feel a little hurt. She understood it, it was probably wise, but to make love like that, then disappear off the face of the earth?

Then she remembered he had said something about needing to start vaccinations on his lambs and kids. Maybe that was keeping him busy. How the hell would she know?

She thought about calling him, but instead forced herself to attend other things. She spent a whole lot of time out walking the property, trying to envision what she would do with it. The walking stilled her thoughts and gave her some clarity, at least about that.

She laundered and organized her aunt's clothes for charity. She went through all the papers in her aunt's desk, trying to figure out what mattered and what didn't. She put the photos she found into an envelope to place in an album later. It was surprising, however, to realize that after all the generations that had lived in this house, after Martha had spent her entire life here, there was so little detritus. Martha had kept her footprint small, all right. There was really nothing to get rid of, nothing to throw out. The house approached sterility.

She wondered if Martha had planned that, or if that was just the way she had lived. She cried when she thought about it, cried a few times because she couldn't just sit down with her aunt and have one last chat about things. Anything.

Cliff.

He haunted her thoughts and she wished she had someone to talk to about him. Not that anyone was going to be able to untangle the mess inside her. No, she had created that mess, had been creating it steadily since she came back here. Now she had to deal with all the knots herself.

She told herself to stop thinking about him. She created a to-do list for her youth ranch idea and started with the lawyer, Carstairs, asking him to look into all the legal and liability angles. She couldn't take a single step without knowing that much.

Then she called her friend Sharon back in Chicago.

"You're thinking about doing what?" Sharon practically shrieked the words.

Holly repeated herself.

"I think that's a fabulous idea! How soon do you need me?"

Mixed-up as she was feeling, Holly still laughed. "Hold your horses there, girl. I haven't even found out what the legal aspects are yet. I'm mainly worried that if I don't do this right, I might not really help the kids."

"What in the world is wrong with you?"

"Well, taking them out of their environment and showing them something better and less frightening is great. But having to put them back…"

"Ah. You think it might be harder for them when they come home."

"It could be. I don't want to do that to them."

"Well, if you want my internationally recognized opinion, it all depends on what you do. A lot of places offer opportunities to disadvantaged kids. You wouldn't be the first or only, and it seems to work well. You broaden their horizons, keep them sharp for school and instill confidence." She paused. "These children need confidence, Holly. They get so little from life. You need to show them other opportunities, open new doors for them to walk through. And give them plenty of positive strokes. God knows, they get few enough of them. So when do you need me?"

"Are you serious?"

"As a heart attack. I love the idea. I want to help. I know I'm a city girl, but I used to visit my uncle's farm in Nebraska."

Holly laughed again. "You're on. But I've got to clear a lot of decks and hurdles first. And I'll have to come back to Chicago to clear out things there. I don't want to leave too abruptly. Make the transition smooth for my kids. At this point I don't even know how fast I can act here. It might be pointless to start anything but the legal stuff before next spring."

"Just as long as I'm on your staff. I'll work for my supper and a place to sleep."

The words touched Holly, making her throat tighten. "Thanks."

"I'll bone up on the psychological aspects for you. Now for the important question."

"What's that?"

"Did you meet your rancher again?"

Oh, man, she'd forgotten she had told Sharon about that a few years ago during an evening spent chatting with a bottle of wine nearby. Too much wine? Maybe. She didn't remember getting drunk, but she guessed she had gotten relaxed. "Yes," she said carefully.

Her rancher? She hated realizing that she wished that were true.

"So how was it? Tense? Has he forgiven you? Do you still feel the same?"

"He's nice, it was tense at first, but he's forgiven me and…we're moving on." Kind of a half truth, because she didn't know if anything was moving or where. He'd vanished.

"Is he still a hunk?"

Much as she didn't feel like laughing, she laughed anyway. Count on Sharon to cut straight to the chase. "Yes, he's still a hunk."

"Oh, yum. If you don't want him, maybe I can catch a flight out tomorrow."

Holly knew she was joking. Sharon couldn't afford

a plane ticket any more than she could. Buying one every year had stretched her budget to the snapping point. But apart from that, she felt a very uncharacteristic burst of annoyance at the remark.

She had no claim on Cliff, but that didn't keep her from resenting the idea that Sharon might set her cap for him. Damn! Talk about confused.

Sharon was no dummy, though. "I was just kidding," she said after a moment. "I wouldn't do that to you."

"I know," Holly admitted, swallowing her irritation. "Anyway, if there's anything between us, it doesn't seem to be going anywhere." Which was true, especially after the long silence from Cliff. Maybe he had discovered the magic was gone. Hard to believe, considering what she had felt, but he wasn't her, obviously. Or maybe he'd felt that connection between them awakening again and decided that distance was the safest course. "I don't know," she finally said to Sharon. "I poisoned that well a long time ago."

"People change. You said he's forgiven you. So you want my advice, girl? If you want him, go for it."

Easy to say, harder to do, Holly thought when she finally said goodbye.

She was just deciding what to do next when she saw a dusty delivery truck coming up her drive. She hadn't ordered anything. The driver must be lost, and she was probably the last person in this county who'd be good at helping him out.

She stepped on the porch, prepared to offer her phone if necessary, when the guy jumped out the passenger side, carrying a huge cardboard box. "Holly Heflin?" he asked as he mounted the porch steps.

"Yes."

He passed her a handheld computer and stylus. "Sign here."

Moments later he was driving away while she looked at an impossibly big box and wondered what it could contain. She'd have thought Martha had ordered something just before her death, except the box was clearly addressed to her. And she couldn't make hide nor hair of the sender's address.

Shrugging, she picked the box up and carried it inside, where she placed it on the kitchen table. Using a small knife from the drawer, she sliced the tape and opened it.

Foam peanuts in a variety of colors concealed the contents. She hated those peanuts and wished they'd go back to the old days of shredded newspaper. Not that anyone seemed to read a paper newspaper anymore.

Shoving her hand in, she felt another box. She pulled it out carefully without sending peanuts flying. Her heart almost stopped. She knew a florist's box when she saw one. Sympathy flowers? But part of her was hoping for something else.

She quickly cut the green ribbon around the box and the tape holding the lid on both sides. She pulled away the lid and gasped at the spray of long-stemmed red roses. A card peeked out from between the stems and she quickly lifted it.

I know a dozen is traditional, the typed note on the card said. *But this is one for each year. Cliff.*

Ten red roses.

Card in hand, she sat down at the table and let the tears come. She wasn't sure exactly how he'd meant that, but it somehow seemed to open up a part of her heart that she'd been keeping carefully closed. As the door on the past opened the last bit, agonizing pain filled her.

"Oh, God, Martha," she whispered to the empty house. "What did you get me into?"

When she was sure she no longer sounded as though she'd been crying, she called Cliff. Some corner of her mind noticed that the dial tone made a series of quick buzzes before steadying to the usual one, and she wondered vaguely if she was going to have to get someone out to look at it.

Cliff didn't answer his phone, so she left a message, thanking him for the flowers and asking him to drop by when he had time.

She just simply didn't know how to add up the flowers with his absence. He'd been there every day, and now that they had made love, he had disappeared?

She didn't know whether to be angry or hurt. She spent time talking on the phone again with Sharon and Laurie over the next few evenings, and she had one conversation with the lawyer, Carstairs, who told her he thought he could have the legal issues wound up by the end of the summer.

"You being a licensed social worker with a master's degree in Illinois is going to help you here. We can get you licensed, but to approve the ranch idea we're going to need some plans from you. Facilities, activities, the training of the people you'll have helping you. That's going to take longer, obviously, but I know some people around here. I'll check with them. They might know who can help staff your place."

He paused. "Liability might turn out to be the biggest issue. Taking care of other people's children, you know."

She didn't exactly know, but she got the picture. She'd dealt with various programs back home, and she remembered the kinds of inspections they had needed to pass and continue passing. But liability had been handled by the state and city.

"You know," Carstairs said, "you'd find it a lot easier if you opened a foster home. You might want to talk to Hugh and Anna Gallagher about that. The problem I see here is that you're just one person. It might take you several years to get through all of this. You'll certainly want to think about quitting your job and settling here. You're going to need to be on top of everything."

Well, she had several years. She was still young. As for quitting her job… Damn, she needed to settle one way or another, she supposed. Martha had made certain that she'd never have to work again, if that's what she had wanted and if she was reasonably careful, but this ranch idea…

She had another idea. "What if I bring kids out here with a parent or guardian?"

"Well, that would certainly be a whole lot easier. I could have you set up as a guest ranch in no time at all. Might be a better starting point while you build up."

It might indeed. After she disconnected, she sat staring at the roses in their vase. She'd tucked the card into her purse so Lisa wouldn't see it. The woman had all but disappeared from the landscape, but she still wasn't certain trouble couldn't appear in a flash.

Staring at the roses made her think of Cliff, of course. Was this his way of getting even? Had the note meant that she'd caused him ten years of hell?

It was possible, even if she found it hard to believe of him. Worse, as she sat there looking at the roses, as she wandered outside trying to envision what she wanted to build here, she was wondering more and more why she'd been so damn determined to leave this place behind.

Even now she knew she never would have been happy just being a rancher's wife. Needy kids had been tugging at her all her life. But had she been foolish in giving up what she had with Cliff? Why had she been so certain she couldn't be just as helpful here? There were needy children everywhere, with basically the same challenges. Kids out here might not be living with violent streets, but they could still be hungry, mistreated, abused, struggling to deal with poverty and broken homes. No place had a corner on that.

But for some damn reason, she had been convinced that staying here would be like staying in a cage. Ten years later, she wasn't at all sure about that. Maybe because her work had showed her that there were all kinds of cages.

She walked around the house, thinking that she had only a few more days here, Sharon's words still ringing in her head: "If you want him, go for it."

Apparently he didn't want her. The roses, which at first had touched her so much, were starting to feel like a goodbye. After all, he'd been spending every free moment with her, and now he couldn't even call? A roll in the bed of his pickup truck had evidently been enough to convince him that some things really *did* die. Unfortunately, she had discovered exactly the opposite. After years of ignoring her memories of that long-ago summer, now she couldn't seem to tamp them down.

It *had* always been fast and furious between them. A look, a touch and the explosion had become imminent. She remembered all the times they'd run giggling to find some privacy. Not too difficult out here. They'd made love under the stars, under the sun, under the trees and almost never indoors except that one memorable time in the hayloft. If the water hadn't been so cold in the streams, they'd probably have made love there, too.

Images of him, long forgotten, began to resurface. She sat on the porch swing and closed her eyes, giving them free rein. The way he had looked as he'd risen up out of icy water on a hot day, water sheeting off his gleaming, muscular body, his staff already hard for her. The way he had looked galloping toward her across the pasture after his day's work was done. Once, his hat had gone flying and she'd laughed so hard that she fell in the deep grasses, only to find him hovering over her a minute later, tugging at her clothes, trying to make a bed from their shirts, until the sun kissed every inch of their bodies.

How easy it had all been, from laughter to passion, as if they had been set free of all constraints to play in any manner they chose.

The other night had reminded her of how his hands had felt on her—slightly roughened from work, but always gentle no matter how strong. He knew exactly how to tease her with his mouth and fingers until her breasts swelled and ached for him, until she opened her legs as wide as she could just to feel those featherlight touches of his fingers. Then his mouth on her most private place, sampling and tasting until she lost her mind.

And it always happened so fast. For them foreplay

had become afterplay, when, lying in the glow of satiation, they had taken time to touch, look and learn. He had loved the mole on her rump, and never failed to kiss it, claiming it looked almost like a heart. She had retorted that only eyes blinded by passion could see it that way.

She had traced the jagged scar on his back from when he'd been thrown from a horse as a child and slid down a wooden fence post that had a nail sticking out of it. He had insisted that the tetanus shot had hurt worse than the nail.

She knew his body as well as she knew her own, maybe better. But there had to be more than that, didn't there?

Being like playful puppies for a summer was great, but it wasn't enough for permanence, right? So maybe she hadn't been wrong in her decision to pursue her long-held goals. If she had stayed here, she might have wrecked everything with resentment.

So why was she sitting here and wondering? It had become the road not taken, and there was no way to turn back and try it now. How many times did she need to remind herself? And why did she keep asking the same questions?

He had confused her. Last time she hadn't been confused at all, but now it was different. Older hadn't apparently made her wiser. Or maybe being older had opened her up to a broader range of possibilities.

Not that it mattered. The days were slipping away and he was avoiding her as if she had the plague. Maybe for good reason.

Swinging slowly back and forth, she watched the afternoon shadows lengthen. All she knew for certain was that she had to make up her mind about one thing: the direction she wanted to take her career now. Go back to Chicago, resume her duties and use this place as a vacation house? Rent it out? Or go for the guest ranch and possibly youth ranch?

Until she made up her mind and took action one way or another, nothing at all in her life was going to be settled.

Then everything got settled in one fell swoop. Lisa came back before dinnertime, waved and started to pass her.

"You've been gone a lot," Holly remarked with a smile. "Did you find a job or something?"

"I've been over at Cliff's." Lisa smiled back.

Holly froze as Lisa breezed by. For an instant the pain in her heart was so crushing she couldn't even move. Then anger rose in a tsunami.

Livid would have been a mild description of what Holly felt. She chopped vegetables for dinner as if she were killing them. The knife hit the cutting board with repeated, resounding thwacks.

Cliff hadn't wanted his ex around, but now she was spending all day, every day at his ranch? Feeling used and soiled, Holly tried to change her flight to an earlier day, but couldn't manage it. She was stuck here for another four days. So she took it out on the vegetables with the chef's knife.

Red roses, one for each year? She slammed the knife into a pepper. That was certainly an original way to kiss someone off: with roses. He should have sent dead ones.

Thwack!

Well, she had to give him marks for getting even. All that talk about forgiveness? Ha! If he had been plotting this all along he couldn't have done better. Then after all that stuff about Lisa, he had her over there every single day?

Thwack!

She supposed she deserved it. What she had said to him a decade ago could still make her cringe inside. But whether she'd deserved it or not, he shouldn't have had sex with her.

Because he had just turned something beautiful into something so sleazy she wanted to vomit. She felt more violated than she had after the attack in Chicago.

And *that* she did not deserve.

"I'm going out," Lisa called. "I'll be late coming back."

If she came back, Holly thought without answering. She whacked at an onion.

Well, if she knew one thing for certain now, it was that she was going to leave her job and move here. She was going to sit right under his nose, not give him the satisfaction of driving her off and do her thing with those children, come hell or high water.

He could live with his duplicity now, every single day.

She scraped the veggies into the heating oil to sauté them. She couldn't even remember what she had thought she was making, and she didn't care. As soon as the vegetables were cooked a little, she'd cool them down and shove them in the refrigerator.

She wondered if she would ever have an appetite again.

But she had to keep moving. She couldn't slow

down, couldn't sit around. Anger was driving her, and she had to let it out somehow.

After she cleaned up her abortive attempt at dinner, she pulled on her shorts, a T-shirt and her jogging shoes. She hadn't taken a good run in a while, but now she needed one.

She decided to run down the driveway toward the county road. It provided the safest surface and seeing how often her cell phone couldn't get a signal out here, it would be just her luck to step into a prairie-dog hole or something and need an ambulance when no one knew where she was. At least if she stayed on the drive and got into trouble, Lisa would find her eventually.

God, until just a short time ago, she would have thought it impossible for Cliff to be such a creep. She wasn't naive or anything. She'd met some real creeps in the course of her job, but still, she wouldn't have believed Cliff capable of this.

Well, what if he wasn't? a stubborn portion of her mind asked.

But how else could she interpret this? If he'd come over, if he'd even called, it might have removed some of the sting.

Well, maybe not, she admitted with brutal honesty. But at least she wouldn't feel quite so much like discarded trash.

She reached the county road, and by then began to feel a little better. She could handle this, all of this. She wasn't that invested in Cliff. She was more invested in her ideas to bring children out here to experience a whole different look at life. To receive the freedom to grow and explore new opportunities. She had enough money now. She could probably build a couple of small guest cabins and bring families out here for a few weeks at a time. She should probably start with older children, the ones at highest risk. She figured once she explained it back home to her bosses as a scholarship program, they'd probably do their best to make it possible, especially for moms who might lose their benefits if they took a few weeks off from looking for work.

Yeah, she'd find a way. A scholarship program all nicely tied up with a legal bow that would make it possible. She'd just need to get some established charity involved, and she knew more than one that might.

So it would work. She might have the basics ready to go next summer.

And to hell with Cliff anyway.

She heard tires crunching on gravel behind her and eased over to the side. *Probably Lisa coming home early,* she thought. *Must not have found what she wanted.*

But the thrum of the engine quickly told her it wasn't Lisa at all. Reluctantly, she glanced over and saw Cliff looking out the window of his truck.

"Get lost," she said sharply.

"What did I do?"

"You know."

"That's exactly the problem. I don't know. I sent you flowers. I got your message. I've called three times and you haven't called back. If I hadn't been so busy…"

"Busy with Lisa?" she demanded.

"Lisa? What—" He broke off. When he spoke again, his jaw was clenched. "Get in."

"Get lost." She kept running.

"Damn it, Holly."

"Just go away. I'm done with you."

"Really." He jammed on the accelerator then. Flying gravel missed her as he pulled away. When he reached the house, though, he didn't turn around and come back. No, he parked, and she saw him climb the porch steps and take a seat.

Damn it all to hell, she thought viciously, and picked up her pace. He'd messed with her ten years ago, even though he hadn't meant to, but he was messing with her again. This time he *had* to know what he was doing.

Apparently he'd even taken up lying. Called her three times? She hadn't heard the phone ring. When he didn't get an answer, he should have tried again later. Had he? Evidently not. Three attempts to reach her, even assuming that was true, was hardly enough for six whole days.

She reached the front yard, such as it was, and stood at the foot of the porch, stretching. "I told you to leave."

"Not until we straighten out a few things. Why didn't you call me back?"

"Because you didn't call."

"I sure as hell did. I left messages."

She paused in the process of stretching her hamstring. "Messages?" she said finally. The anger that had been boiling over suddenly turned down to a simmer.

"Messages," he repeated. "You *have* heard of voice mail? We even have it out here in the boonies."

She put her leg down and stretched the other hamstring. "How am I supposed to know I have voice mail?"

"Surely you've heard the beep on the phone." His tone was nearly acid.

She *had* heard a beep, she realized. "How would

I know what it is? I use a cell phone all the time at home."

"Oh, hell," he said.

She bent over to touch her toes a few times, then straightened, shaking her arms out. "It doesn't matter anyway. Apparently you've decided you want Lisa back."

"Like hell."

"She's spending all her time over there."

"I don't know what she's been telling you, but…"

"Oh, just give it up, Cliff. I know what's been going on. You got even with me and—"

"Even with you for what?" he demanded. "What the hell kind of person do you think I am?"

At last he stood up and marched to his truck. "Have a great life, Holly. I'm tired of getting blown up in your minefield."

Her minefield? Agape, she watched him gun his engine and tear out of there.

The dust cloud hung in the air for a while before the freshening evening breeze started to carry it away.

She felt like that dust cloud and didn't even know why.

Chapter 10

Holly couldn't sleep. When Lisa came home in the wee hours, she was still sitting on her bed, with a few folded shirts beside her and an open suitcase. She didn't have to stay here. She could get a room in Denver until it was time to catch her flight to Chicago. She could lock up the house and go, and to hell with Lisa. Let her stay with Cliff.

As she listened to Lisa come up the stairs, though, her chest tightened until she almost couldn't breathe. How many nights that long-ago summer had she come in terribly late from time spent with Cliff? The creaks of the stairs were still familiar and they mocked her.

But Lisa wasn't even trying to be quiet, unlike when Holly had made the same journey. In fact, from the unsteadiness of the steps, she suspected Lisa was drunk.

Drunk and driving. *My God!*

But not even that could shake her out of the painful despair that filled her, nor erase Cliff's final words.

Your minefield. What minefield? He was the one who'd made love to her and then immediately started seeing Lisa again.

God, that hurt. Her sense of rejection had no bottom to it. She had to leave as soon as possible, get away to clear her head and…

And what? In her heart of hearts she knew she wanted to do the youth ranch. It was as if Cliff's passing remark had unlocked a dream she hadn't realized she had. Her soul craved this whole idea, much more than it craved going back to the streets and constantly trying to hold back a flood with a broom.

Because that's how it felt. She often had no way to know how much she had helped, or if her efforts had an enduring effect. People vanishing from her caseload was the only indicator she got. It might mean things had improved. Sometimes it did. Once in a while she saw a child again and heard good news. Equally, it might mean that some child was gone.

Once they moved out of the system or into a different part of the system, she fell out of the loop. She had gotten used to seeing small strides and then picking up a new case without ever seeing the ending. A lot of times, the family court held that everything was okay now, no more visits were needed, and that was the end.

But her commitment remained to do as much as she could with the time and tools she had. And she felt she could do so much more out here. See more of the kids, get to know them better, share their successes as well as their problems. Much more personal attention to each child than her job allowed. She needed a more positive environment herself, and she needed to provide a positive environment.

So yes, she was coming back. The question was about right now, and a shaft of anguish that seemed to hold her paralyzed with its force.

Her minefield?

With just those few words, he had skewed her entire self-perception. Her thoughts crawled around, trying to understand what he was talking about and what it meant about her.

God, this was bad. She had to do something. Anything.

Finally she moved, surprised at how much she had stiffened. Hours of sitting caused her body to whimper a minor protest as she stood. Somewhere inside she had been deadened to the passage of time, lost in a maelstrom of emotions and careening thoughts.

She had come out here expecting to say farewell to her aunt and close up the house. She had expected nothing of what had followed, from considering a career change to a major move…and Cliff. She had thought that avenue closed a long time ago. Now it had opened again, just long enough to pierce her.

Downstairs, she made a pot of coffee, certain that she would see the sun rise. Sleep hadn't brushed her with the merest wing in all these hours. Her stomach growled, reminding her that she hadn't eaten, either, but she ignored it.

Martha, never far from her thoughts, returned. Holly could have sworn she felt her aunt sit at the table with her. Could almost smell the lavender sachets she kept in her drawers, a custom Holly had always found quaint and pleasant, but something she had never done herself. A child of the modern age, she used dryer sheets and went around the world with her clothes smelling like nearly everyone else's. But Martha had always smelled of lavender.

God, she wished her aunt were there. That they could have just one more conversation. Their last phone call had been just four days before Martha's stroke. They had laughed. They had talked about Holly's job. Martha had expressed her concern that Holly was sounding awfully tired and needed a break. Holly had promised a visit that summer.

Instead she had come early, to bury Martha. And what had she done with this time, time when she surely should have been grieving and recalling every memory she could about her aunt? Oh, she'd spent some time going through things, but mostly she had hidden from her grief, instead allowing herself to be distracted by planning for a future…and by Cliff.

Had she been hiding in his company to avoid the grief? Maybe. But if so, she'd gotten herself into a fine kettle of fresh pain.

God, she felt filthier than she had after that manhandling by those three guys in Chicago. Never, ever, would she have believed Cliff capable of such cruelty, to make love to her while resuming his relationship with his ex. She might have deserved it, but she had believed it was out of character for him.

She looked at the phone, thinking about calling one of her friends. It might help to talk, but God, it was a conversation she didn't want to have with any one of them. They'd get righteously indignant for her, and that wouldn't help. Or worse, they'd try to make kind excuses, whether for him or her. None of it would mend this pain.

But once she had looked at the phone, she couldn't stop remembering what Cliff had said about leaving messages. She wasn't sure she wanted to hear them. Her mind was capable of writing the kiss-off. *Thanks for a great lay, but...* Or, *now that Lisa's back....*

Bitterness filled her mouth. But the phone wouldn't leave her alone. The more she tried not to look at it, the more it seemed to pull her gaze. She could almost hear Martha saying one of her favorite phrases, always funny coming out of Martha's mouth: *Man up.*

Boy, how she used to laugh at that, and Martha's brown eyes would sparkle with humor. She could almost see them sparkling at her right now, even though there wasn't one bit of humor in this situation.

So man up, she thought. She probably wouldn't be able to get the messages anyway. That beeping wouldn't tell her how to dial.

But Martha had been meticulous in a lot of ways, and when Holly leaned toward the phone, she saw a list of names, neatly printed, and down near the bottom, next to a button, was *voice mail.*

It couldn't be that easy. Clenching her teeth but deciding to face the music and put an end to at least some of the questions that gnawed at her mind and heart like starving mice, she picked up the receiver and punched the button.

Immediately, she heard a voice say, "Please enter your pass code."

She didn't know the pass code. How would she? Useless. She started to pull the receiver from her ear when she heard a series of five tones. Was it automatically dialing the code?

Apparently so. After another second, the recorded woman's voice spoke again. "Please press one to hear your messages…"

She pressed one and listened. They came to her in reverse order, newest first.

"Holly?" Cliff's voice said. "I'm beginning to worry. Are you okay? You haven't called me back. Did I do something? I hope I can get over there soon. Call me, please."

The second: "I'm sorry I haven't been over. Maybe you can run over here if you want to see the downside of ranching. The lambs are still sick and we're running a twenty-four-hour hospital. Miss you."

And the earliest: "I'm glad you liked the roses. I wish I could get over there, but something's wrong with some of my lambs. It's pretty bad, and we're nursing them. Waiting for the vet. I hope like hell he can figure it out before we start losing them. Call or come over when you can. I miss you."

When she hung up the phone, she felt about two inches tall.

But Lisa said she'd been over there. What the hell had Lisa been doing over there? Not even in her worst imaginings could she believe Cliff would have called her three times, talking about sick lambs, if he was getting back into a relationship with his ex.

Now she had some idea what he had meant by a minefield. Her insides wrenched, nerves made her jump up and she wondered how in the hell she could fix this mess.

* * *

Cliff stood by the fold as the sun came up, watching the lambs. They were on their feet again, if a little unsteady, and nursing again. Whatever had hit so many of his lambs hadn't spread any farther. Mike Windwalker, the vet, wasn't sure what had happened, and had sent blood and tissue samples off to a lab somewhere, along with vaccine and wormer samples. Cliff didn't care if the cause had a name, although he supposed it would be good to know whether they'd had a bad reaction to the worming or vaccinations or if they'd had a bug of some kind.

Right now he was just glad they were recovering. Whether that recovery was due to time or the broad-spectrum antibiotics the vet had given them, he hadn't a clue.

He was just glad that nightmare was over. Everyone on the ranch, including Jean, had taken a turn at milking the ewes and trying to bottle-feed the lambs. For a while they'd been too weak to suckle, but when he and his helpers had squeezed the milk into their mouths, at least they had swallowed whatever didn't just run right out.

He should have been shouting hallelujahs. Hell, he'd wanted to share his joy when he'd gone over to see Holly last night. Instead, he'd been treated like a cow patty she wanted to scrape from her boot. Nice.

She'd done that to him once before, but at least he'd understood her reasons last time. This time he didn't care what her reasons might be. He had had enough.

Satisfied that the lambs were continuing to mend, he couldn't squash his anger anymore. Damn woman was a walking honey trap. He'd been the one who had warned her they shouldn't play with fire, then he'd gone right ahead and played with it. Idiot!

Maybe he'd let all that talk about a youth ranch go to his head, thinking she'd actually stay around. Or maybe she'd gotten to his little head. Again. Either way, he was a double-damned idiot.

It was possible that she hadn't recognized that beep on the phone as meaning she had voice mail. He could believe that. Cell phones were different. But not to have called him in all this time, except the once to thank him for the roses? Not to have wondered why he'd just disappeared?

Then to accuse him of getting back together with Lisa? He wasn't capable of two-timing like that, and it infuriated him to know that she thought he could do such a thing.

Damn! He turned from the fold, kicked at a clod of dirt and stomped toward the house. He should have just stuck with his initial impulse to stay away from her, to get the executor stuff done and then drop out of sight. He shouldn't have felt concern for her, shouldn't have worried about how thin and exhausted she looked. None of his business. Her problem, not his. But oh, no, he had to try to help. He had to walk right back into the trap, knowing damn well his attraction to her hadn't faded one teeny little bit. He needed a shrink. Even a native instinct for self-preservation had failed him.

Holly, Holly, Holly. She'd filled his thoughts and made his blood pound when she wasn't even around. Some invisible elastic had kept snapping him back to her side.

He'd thought she had changed. Ha! People didn't change—their faults just became amplified by time, evidently. She couldn't be trusted. And clearly she didn't trust him.

The last thing he needed or wanted to see was Holly coming toward him. She rounded the front of the house and walked toward the fold, catching him between her and the lambs. He almost deviated to the corral to grab a horse and get the hell out of here. He didn't need this. He'd been up all night for too many nights now, and his eyes felt gritty from lack of sleep. Now this?

He passed one of his hired hands. "Keep an eye on the lambs, will you? And if Lisa shows up looking for a horse, tell her to saddle her own."

The guy's eyes widened. He wasn't used to seeing Cliff angry. "Sure, Boss."

Every damn day he'd had a man pulled away from something more important, namely the sick lambs and herding, to saddle a horse for Lisa. That hadn't changed, either.

Damn all women to hell.

Well, at least Holly didn't look as if she were loaded for bear. Instead what he saw was a tired woman approaching him tentatively. Great, now he was an ogre. He stopped, making her come to him. *Deal with it,* he thought. Just deal with whatever hell she wanted to rain on him and then hit the sack. He could probably sleep for a week.

She halted six feet from him. Much as he wanted to ignore it, he noticed that her eyes looked sunken, her face pale and her mouth unsteady. What now?

"Cliff?"

"My name hasn't changed," he said shortly.

She closed her eyes briefly. "Can we talk?"

"About what? There's nothing left to discuss. You pretty much took care of that last night."

Her mouth quivered. God, not tears. "I got your messages this morning. I'm sorry."

"It's a little late for that."

"Probably. But I owe you an apology. If I had known the lambs were sick I'd have come over to help somehow. I didn't know."

That much he believed. "Okay. Apology accepted." He took a step to walk around her, but she stopped him.

"Cliff, please. We have to talk."

About what? He was tired, he was frustrated, he was still angry and when he should have been celebrating the recovery of his lambs, all he wanted to do was kill something. "You really don't want to talk to me now."

Her shoulders sagged. Seeing that, something else tried to poke its way through his anger. Concern? No, he wasn't going to step into that mess again.

"Okay," she said quietly. Her head dropped and she started to turn away. He should have let her go. Really he should have. His bed had been calling to him for days now, he was in an awful mood and what good was some talk going to do?

But as always happened with her, he couldn't do it. He couldn't be needlessly cruel, and she had curled in on herself as if he'd just struck her.

"Look," he said, causing her to still, "I'm exhausted, I'm in a hellacious mood and I can't guarantee I can follow a conversation. But okay."

She faced him again, squaring her shoulders as if drawing on every bit of her inner strength. "I messed up. Until last night I hadn't heard from you since the roses. I couldn't imagine why. I must have been out when the phone rang, because I never heard it, and I didn't know about the voice mail. Then when Lisa came back yesterday—she's hardly been there—I asked if she'd found a job. She told me she'd been spending her time with you."

Understanding began to dawn through his anger. "She was spending her time riding my horses." He wouldn't have believed he still had the energy to sound that sarcastic, but sarcasm dripped like hot tar from every word.

"She omitted that part."

"Why am I not surprised." He pulled off his hat, scratched at his head, then clapped it back on. "You believed I would treat you that way?"

She lowered her head, then gave a little nod. "I hadn't heard from you." As if that explained everything.

Not quite, but he guessed if she felt insecure… "Ah, hell," he said finally.

She peeked up at him.

"Quit looking like a whipped dog," he said. "Damn, I've never given you cause to look like this."

"I gave myself cause. I'm embarrassed. Kinda sick, too."

He cussed again, quietly this time, letting go of most of his anger. Okay, they needed to talk. "Remember that old oak by the river?"

She flushed as she nodded, telling him she did indeed remember.

"Let's drive out there."

"Will the lambs be okay?"

"They seem to be getting better faster. I've got enough people to look after them for a few hours. Let's just go where nobody can find us, because I'm getting damn sick of Lisa turning up any time she feels like it. Although I warn you, once we get there I'll probably fall asleep."

There was a wagon track part of the way. Usually they had ridden here, but he didn't have the energy to spare. Driving was his max, and he was grateful the only obstacles were the bumpy ground. At last he pulled up beside the tree.

It was a restful place, although they had seldom been restful for long here that summer. How many times had he tried to tell himself that whole summer had been some kind of aberration? Well, it hadn't been, to judge by the way he'd been reacting to her since she came back.

He grabbed the blanket out of the back and spread it in the shade. Then he sat, leaning against the trunk and waited for whatever was next, whether it was sleep, a discussion or an argument.

She didn't sit immediately, but stood looking up at the tree with her mouth open. "What happened to the tree?"

He twisted and look up at it. The trunk was split now, but amazingly enough both remaining sides still grew. "Lightning. A week or so after you left last time."

"But it's still alive."

"Incredible, isn't it." Some things never died, he guessed. Maybe they were too strong. Or too stubborn. His head was swimming with fatigue and he didn't even attempt to sort through that thought.

At last she sat on the blanket at the far edge from him. "Sleep if you need to," she said quietly. "I've never seen you so tired."

"Hang around," he tried to joke. "Ranching has this effect sometimes." He wasn't sure all the words emerged, because the tree seemed as comfortable as a pillow and sleep snatched him between one breath and the next.

When he awoke, the shadows had grown shorter and Holly had moved closer to stay in the shade. She was braiding some tall grasses into a long rope, and the sight carried him back a decade in time. She had often liked to do that when they lazed around talking.

But it wasn't ten years ago. It was around noon today, and he still didn't know what he was doing out here with her except that she had wanted to talk. About what, he had no idea. He thought she'd pretty well covered it all already.

He lay still, watching her, thinking about that long-ago summer, thinking about right now. He still felt her pull. In his groin, yes, but other parts of him still wanted her. He might have been the only one of them in love so long ago, but youth notwithstanding, he had loved her.

Some part of his heart and soul wanted to pick up as if a decade had never passed. Well, that wasn't going to happen. They'd been little more than kids then, but they were adults now, and evidently they still had a lot of detritus floating around.

"Thanks for letting me sleep," he said.

She started and twisted toward him. "I'm glad you did. You look better. I needed the time to think, anyway."

He had slipped down while he slept. Now he pushed himself up until he leaned against the tree once more.

"There's water in the cooler in the back of my truck. It's probably warm, but you must be thirsty by now."

She dropped her braiding and jumped up, returning quickly with a bottle of water for each of them. Then she sat cross-legged, facing him. Leaves tossed in a gentle breeze, causing sun and shadow to dance across her face.

"I hope you got some sleep," he said. Because she still looked hollow.

"A little. Thanks. What was wrong with the lambs?"

"We're still not sure. Waiting for test results."

"But they're okay now?"

"A whole lot better. For a couple of days, I thought I was going to lose a whole bunch of them."

"That must have been scary."

"It was," he admitted. "For a while they were even too weak to suckle, so we milked the ewes and used bottles to squeeze some nourishment into them. But it's better. They started standing again yesterday, and by late afternoon they were suckling again. So they made it."

"I'm so glad." She picked up the braid and fiddled with the end of it. "I would have helped if I had known. Really."

"I admit I was kind of surprised you never popped over."

She bit her lip. "I hate to imagine what you were thinking of me."

"Nothing near as bad as what you evidently thought of me."

Her cheeks reddened and her head dipped. "When you didn't call…well, when I didn't know you'd been calling, I kind of thought the roses were a kiss-off. A way of getting even for how I hurt you that summer."

"God!" He sat up a little straighter. "And then Lisa."

"Yeah. And then Lisa."

He mulled that around. "Have people been treating you that badly?"

"As a rule, no." She raised her head, met his gaze, then looked away again. "You have no idea what I see on a regular basis. I know what people are capable of, Cliff. A lot of it isn't pretty."

"So it's affected your expectations?"

"I think it's made me more defensive, yes. And apparently more suspicious."

"Damn, woman, you need a new job."

"Yes, I think I do."

Fully awake now, he leaned forward until his elbows rested on his folded knees. "You've made up your mind?"

"Well, when I wasn't busy imagining the worst, I started making some phone calls. A friend from Chicago wants to help me. She's a family psychologist and says she'll work for room and board. And I talked to the lawyer, Mr. Carstairs. He's looking into all the legal aspects, but he seems to think that I should start as a guest ranch. I can invite families out here. It'll get me up and running while we deal with all the stuff having just the kids here would require. So I think I'll do that. I can afford to bring some families out here, thanks to Aunt Martha."

"That sounds like a good plan."

She nodded. "I need to go back for maybe a month to close up everything. My cases, my apartment, giving notice, all that. But then I'm coming back here for good."

"In spite of me."

"In spite of you," she agreed. "My mind is made up."

"Good." He honestly meant it. The last thing he wanted was for her to move here because of him. He couldn't think of a worse reason.

He could see that wasn't the answer she had hoped for, but it was the only honest one he could give her. She had to decide to live here for her own reasons. Anything else could be poisonous, and she had herself to thank for teaching him that lesson. It had taken awhile after she left, but he'd finally gotten it.

She picked at the braided grass she held, then slowly started weaving again. "I bet this stuff with the lambs put a hole in your budget."

The change of direction surprised him. "Temporarily. We'll catch up soon. We'll be selling wool and lambs before long."

"Good."

Man, this was getting awkward. She clearly needed to say something more and couldn't find her way to it. Or couldn't find the words. But he couldn't stay out here all day waiting. He needed to get back, spell his guys so they could catch some sleep and check on those lambs again. Ten years ago, his parents had pretty much let him have huge chunks of time over the summer to go running around with Holly, but he was the one in charge now. He couldn't afford to be so careless.

At last Holly broke the silence. "I'm leaving tomorrow."

His stomach took a plunge. He swilled some water

before trying to reply. “I thought you had a few more days.”

“I do. But I’m trying to change my flight. If I can’t, well, a few days in Denver won’t hurt. There’s a lot I need to think about.”

“I thought you’d made up your mind?”

Her brows lifted. “I have. I’m coming back. But for some reason being in Martha’s house isn’t helping, being around you isn’t helping and I need to clear out some cobwebs. This is a huge leap I’m about to make, and I need some space to be perfectly clear in my own head.” Then she smiled. “I also need to talk to some people. I’m getting impatient to get rolling.”

That smile was heartbreakingly beautiful, he thought. Then she jumped up, wiped her hands on her jeans and said, “I imagine you need to get back. I’ll leave Lisa the house keys, and tell her to give them back to you when she’s ready to move on.”

Just like that. He drove her back to her car, she paused just long enough to squeeze his hand, then she drove away.

He felt as if he’d just been hit by a truck, though he wasn’t sure why. She’d said she was coming back. But why the hell was she leaving so early?

To get away from him?

Damn, he was feeling angry all over again.

Chapter 11

A month later when Holly walked up the Jetway in Denver, she could feel a spring in her step. A month had done wonders. She'd handed off her cases, easing the transition for her families. She'd found lots of interest and support inside the department and outside among charities in her idea for the ranch and she even had some commitments for donations once the place opened.

She'd put on five pounds while she was at it. And this time she wasn't coming to bury her aunt. No, she'd spent plenty of time in the past month saying farewell in a way she hadn't seemed able to do while staying at Martha's house: she had remembered. Somehow the indulgence of endless hours of remembering her aunt had brought her to a sense of peace. She still missed Martha, missed her deeply, but now it was a quieter, more comfortable grief, one she didn't keep trying to hide from by distracting herself the way she had during the time she had spent in Wyoming. She had faced it, and accepted it.

Maybe most importantly, she had felt an opening inside herself, a welcoming for whatever the future might hold. Yes, she'd been excited by the idea of all this before, but there'd been plenty of trepidation and uncertainty, even once she made up her mind. There would always be uncertainty of some kind, but she had emerged from her internal mental crouch and felt ready to open her arms to all the experiences life might bring.

So she was already smiling when she saw Cliff waiting for her once she left the security area behind. The cobwebs of the past no longer seemed to cloud her vision.

He returned her smile and held up a single long-stemmed rose.

For another year, she thought, and her throat tightened even as happiness bubbled up in her. She didn't know what was going to happen between them. The years had changed them, and the little time they'd had together had probably only shown her part of the man he'd become. One thing for certain, she knew she was a different person from just one month ago.

When she reached him, he caught her in a bear hug and kissed her soundly. "Welcome home," he said as he released her. Then he handed her the rose. "You look wonderful."

"So do you," she said frankly. "Thank you for the rose. It's beautiful. Now let's blow this joint. I hate airports."

He laughed and grabbed her carry-on. "You must have checked bags."

"I shipped some boxes yesterday. I decided Martha had the right idea—go minimalist."

"So what's all the news?" he asked as they worked their way through passengers and courtesy carts. Even though they had talked weekly on the phone during the past month, they'd avoided heavy emotional ground. She had talked about her job and her plans, he had talked about ranching. The only thing he had left her really sure about was that he wasn't angry anymore. They had become friends at last.

"Well, I got myself squared away, I think."

"Meaning?"

She glanced at him from the corner of her eye, wishing it was possible to just stare at him. He was certainly stareworthy. "I cleaned the cobwebs out of the attic. Let's just get out of here. There must be some place less hectic to have coffee and talk."

"I had bigger plans," he admitted. "How do you feel about staying in town overnight before we head back?"

How did she feel? Like a rocket being launched. Capable of dancing on air. *My God,* she thought, it had been a long time since she had felt this happy just to be alive. And to be with Cliff?

She cautioned herself to hold her horses. She had no idea whether he wanted anything from her beyond neighborly friendship. "I'd love it," she responded, hoping she sounded like it without letting her elation seep out with every word.

He took them into town, locating a coffee shop that didn't seem too busy. He ordered espresso, and she ordered a gloriously sinful mocha frappé. They sat outside, enjoying the early-summer warmth and a pleasant breeze.

"First you," she said. "How are the lambs and how is business?"

"Everything's doing great. Thank God the vet is attentive to detail. He marked down the vaccine lots he gave the sheep, and the fifteen who got sick all got the same lot, a different one from the other lambs. Apparently the bacteria in the vaccine was live and kicking, instead of being properly weakened. It's probably going to cause a major recall."

"So you made your lambs sick by trying to help them? That must burn."

"I'm just glad it didn't spread past them. It could have, and I wouldn't have been able to nurse hundreds of lambs. Anyway, we're doing great, we got some pretty decent prices on the wool and on the lambs we sold. We're set for another year, and we should have some more angora wool to sell this fall. You could say things are looking up."

"I'm glad." She meant it from the bottom of her heart, and found herself wishing they weren't in such a public place. She might have cleared out the cobwebs in her brain, but not her attraction to Cliff. Just sitting across from him like this made her insides clench with need.

"Now you," he said.

"Well, I got a lot of positive feedback on my ranch idea, and some charities have promised to donate once I get it started."

"Super." He smiled. "That must make you feel good."

"It does. Things are looking up." She hesitated, aware that her heart was beating nervously. The other things were harder to discuss. A lot harder. "I took time to grieve for Martha. I wasn't doing that when I was here. I was finding every excuse to avoid it. Somehow it was easier to do back in Chicago. I don't know why."

"Maybe because you weren't surrounded by constant reminders. I don't know, but it seems to me being in her house was like being caught between two realities."

"That's a good way to describe it, I think. Some part of me just didn't seem capable of accepting that she was gone." Sighing, she looked down. "It was a helluva month, Cliff. It was a week before I decided to turn in my resignation. It was like giving up a huge chunk of who I was. But once I did it, I felt light enough to float. So I guess I'd reached my limit. Everyone was very understanding, and reminded me that caseworkers have a limited life expectancy. We see too much sadness, pain and ugliness. As onc of them said to me, I'd have had to kill my emotions not to care that much, and when you care that much…well, finally things inside you start to shut down because you can't handle any more. That wouldn't have been good, and I was getting there."

He nodded encouragingly.

"Some things you said also helped."

"Me?" He appeared surprised.

"Yeah, just little things, but they made me step back and take a look at myself. I was living in what I think of as a mental crouch. I had gotten to the point of expecting the worst of everyone, Cliff. I don't want to live that way, but that's what I was doing. So I hammered away at that some, and managed to mostly shake it off.

There are lots of good people in the world. I need to spend more time with them."

"I'm so glad."

She met his turquoise gaze and saw real pleasure there. And the sparkle of something hotter, something that had never died between them. Her body responded instantly. That, she thought, would probably never change. But where would it take them?

All of a sudden she wanted to blow this joint, too.

"I only reserved one room," he said as they approached the hotel.

"That's fine," she managed. Her heart had begun to hammer with anticipation and even some anxiety, and it had risen to clog her throat. Her core began to throb as if climax was only moments away. She would never understand this chemistry between them.

"I can get another..."

She interrupted. "Oh, cut it out. No more games."

He laughed, but the sound was husky. "I know. Somehow we need to slow down. Maybe talk, fool around, that thing they call foreplay."

"I always like it better after."

At that a loud crack of laughter escaped him and despite her anticipation and nerves, a grin stretched her own cheeks until they nearly hurt.

She'd expected a relatively cheap motel, but instead he took her to a real hotel, a nice one, the kind where a bellman took their bags. The part of her that had been scraping by for so long made her wonder if he could afford this. On the other hand, he had chosen it, and as she had already learned, he was no spendthrift.

She expressed her amazement and appreciation

when they reached their room, which was not only lovely but had a great view of the Denver skyline. "I feel like a princess!" she exclaimed.

"I hope you always do."

Her breath caught and she turned to him. "Cliff?"

"That's still my name." But there was no smile as he closed the space between them and took her into his arms. Feeling him snugly against her reminded her how much she had been missing him. And for how long? Ten years. Ever since she had left him the first time. She'd had a mission, but in giving him up, she'd given up something very important.

Only now could she truly face that. Maybe she had done the right thing. She had certainly done what she was determined to do. Maybe everything had happened the way it was supposed to, but it remained that she had never stopped missing him.

"I could jump you right now," he said quietly. "But you know what? We both need more than that. We know that part is great. This time, damn it, I want us to share other things."

She remembered those lazy conversations that had always followed their sex. It wasn't as though they hadn't talked. They'd talked volumes during the afterglow. She remembered a summer of laughter, love and talk. Everything had clicked in its own time and way.

But that was ten years ago, so maybe he was right. Maybe they needed a different approach.

She sat at the table near the window while he called room service and ordered some food. "I'm sure the peanuts on the airplane weren't enough," he said as he joined her at the table.

"I've been eating more," she admitted.

"I can tell and it looks great. I was worried about you when you arrived last month."

"I didn't exactly realize it, but I guess I was worried about me, too."

He reached across the table and took both her hands. "I've been thinking."

"Yes?" She wondered if that was a good thing or a bad thing. All of a sudden she didn't feel like jumping for joy.

"I want to help you realize your youth ranch. I may not be able to help much financially, but I'm sure my men and I can help with construction and that kind of thing. Is that okay with you?"

"Of course." But the lump remained in her throat.

He smiled faintly. "Good. But there's more. If there's one thing I figured out when you were here, it's that I'm not over you. I thought I was, but I'm sure as hell not. The thing is, we can't pick up where we left off ten years ago. We're not the same people. So unless you object, I want to pick up here and now. I want to date you, I want to spend time with you. I want us to learn who we are now."

"I'd like that."

"I can learn all about what you do and want to do. You can get an understanding of what I do and why there might be long stretches when you hardly see me. We can find out if we mesh. I think we probably will, though."

"Why?"

"Because we're going to both be ranchers, even if different kinds."

Despite her nervousness, she had to laugh. It was true in its own way.

"The thing is, Holly, I'm pretty sure I'm still in love with you. So I don't want you to go forward on this with me unless you're pretty sure you might fall in love with me. I don't need a rerun of what happened before. So I guess what I'm asking is, blow me off now, because you might not be able to blow me off later. And we're going to be neighbors for a long, long time. There are limits to my masochism."

That was fair, she thought as he went to answer the door for room service, even though her heart wanted to sing at his declaration of love. Soon enough a tray of hors d'oeuvres occupied the table along with tall icy glasses of tea. Cliff rejoined her and encouraged her to eat.

But eating was the last thing she seemed capable of doing just then. "I think," she said slowly, "that I'm still in love with you, too. I didn't want to face it. I never wanted to face it. I was too driven, and then I had to believe I made the right decision."

"I think you did," he said, surprising her. "We were just kids. Honestly, if you hadn't dumped me, but had stayed, you'd probably have resented me. I get it. It was the wrong time, if nothing else. Maybe this won't turn out to be the right time, either."

"I'm not so sure about that." *Screw the food,* she thought. She rose and went around the table. He instinctively pulled back and she perched on his lap.

"You're striking matches again," he warned her.

"We always strike matches. Get used to it. It's who we are, at least together. What else do you want from me?"

"I'd like to have kids eventually."

"I love kids." She smiled. She wasn't sure who was

moving, but their mouths were getting closer together, then his hand ran up her back.

"Not yet, though," he said quickly. "We need to date for a while."

"I already agreed to that. A year?"

He blinked. "A year?"

"Sure. I want a June wedding. And neither of us will be able to say we didn't know what we were getting into after a year."

He laughed, then scooped her up and carried her straight to the bed. "You drive me out of my mind."

"I have no mind when it comes to you."

It happened as it always happened, fast and furious. Some people might consider their lovemaking to be backward, but not them. In the afterglow they shared the caresses and gentle explorations, the absolute knowledge of one another's bodies. And the passion built again.

"A year?" he said dubiously.

"A year," she repeated, sounding more certain than she felt.

"Damn," he muttered, just before he buried his head between her thighs and lashed her with his tongue to the highest pinnacle.

A year, she thought before all reason fled. It was going to be a great year.

Epilogue

Holly stood on the porch and looked out over the huge crowd that filled Cliff's ranch. She was happy, truly happy, and hugged herself.

Cliff had joked that they should get married on their flat rock. She had pointed out that it would be impossible to invite guests to attend there, and anyway, she wanted that rock to be their secret. Then he'd suggested their favorite tree. She'd simply looked at him until he laughed.

So here they were, married in his pasture, throwing a barbecue-cum-potluck for everyone who wanted to attend. It seemed most of the county had turned out.

She had also invited the three families who were now staying at her ranch in the three cabins Cliff had helped her build. They'd completed the structures last fall and spent the winter fixing them up inside.

Despite her fears that her families might be ignored, lots of people had welcomed them warmly, and their kids were enjoying horseback rides under the care of Cliff's hired hands and a few volunteers.

Children ran everywhere, screeching, laughing and having a great time. It was the happiest day ever. Her soul felt good and her heart filled to the brim with joy.

Strong arms closed around her from behind, probably crushing the back of her wedding dress, but she didn't care.

He pushed her short veil aside and nuzzled her neck. "How are you doing, Mrs. Martin?"

"I've never been happier, Mr. Martin."

He chuckled. "You never answered on the name thing."

"Right now I'll enjoy being Mrs."

He gave a pretend sigh. "Then comes Ms. I knew it."

She giggled.

"How's Junior?"

"Cliff! We don't know yet." She had just found out she was pregnant.

"I know, and I'm going to love it, girl or boy. But dang, it's hard to call it *it*."

She laughed again. "*Baby* will do."

He squeezed her gently. "You've made me the happiest man on earth. And look at your families. Folks are being nice."

"I was a little nervous about it."

"I know you were. But we're a hospitable people for the most part. And asking for volunteers instead of wedding gifts was genius on my part."

She turned within the circle of his arms. His eyes

were bright and happier than she had ever seen them, except possibly when she had told him they were pregnant. “What?”

He reached in the back pocket of his slacks and pulled out an envelope. “Jean’s been collecting them. Take a look.”

She opened the envelope eagerly and pulled out a stack of neatly folded typed pages.

Gene Winters—construction
Marybelle Jasper—gardening
Susan Peabody—sewing
Ransom Laird—livestock
Gideon Ironheart—trail rides/horse training

She stopped reading and looked up as tears sparkled in her eyes. “Oh, Cliff…”

“I know. I think you’ll find all bases covered. There are some teachers in there, people from the college, promises to provide feed for the animals, free vet care.… You’re off and running, Holly. A whole lot of people are behind you on this.”

“Wow,” she whispered. “Just wow.” She lifted her arms and threw them around his neck. “It’s a dream come true!”

Applause started somewhere out in the pasture and swiftly swelled.

“I think they want us to kiss,” Cliff said, his eyes sparkling.

“I don’t think we can light a match right now.”

“Obviously not. Can’t even escape because we postponed our honeymoon. But dang, we can give them a kiss to remember."

Which is exactly what they did.

* * * * *